ISOLDE

QUEEN OF
THE WESTERN ISLE

ALSO BY ROSALIND MILES

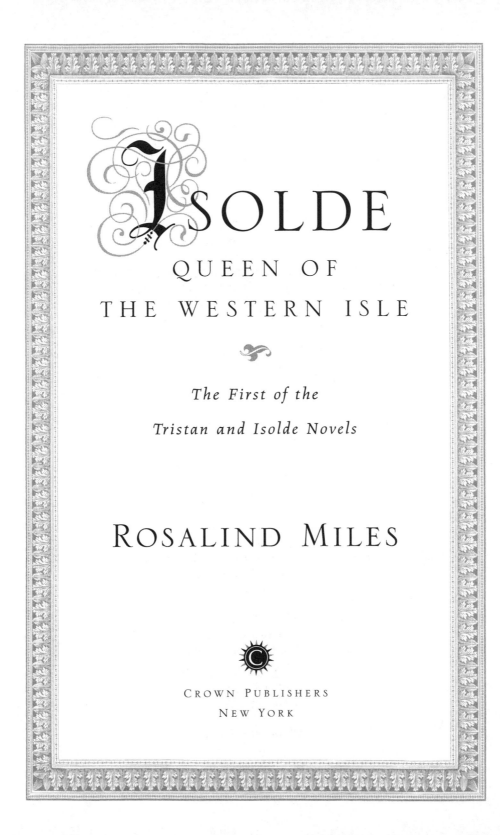

ISOLDE

QUEEN OF
THE WESTERN ISLE

*The First of the
Tristan and Isolde Novels*

ROSALIND MILES

CROWN PUBLISHERS
NEW YORK

Published by Crown Publishers, New York, New York.
Member of the Crown Publishing Group, a division of Random House, Inc.

www.randomhouse.com

CROWN is a trademark and the Crown colophon is a registered trademark of
Random House, Inc.

Printed in the United States of America

Design by Lauren Dong

Library of Congress Cataloging-in-Publication Data
Miles, Rosalind.
Isolde, queen of the Western Isle : the first of the Tristan and Isolde novels /
Rosalind Miles.
p. cm.
1. Iseult (Legendary character)—Fiction. 2. Tristan (Legendary character)—
Fiction. 3. Cornwall (England : County)—Fiction. 4. Knights and
knighthood—Fiction. 5. Arthurian romances—Fiction. 6. Adultery—Fiction.
7. Ireland—Fiction. 8. Queens—Fiction. I. Title.

PR6063.I319 I86 2002
823'.914—dc21
2002019435

ISBN 0-609-60960-2

10   9   8   7   6   5   4   3   2   1

First Edition

For the One before the One

Unforgotten

A true Irish Queen

the family trees of cornwall, lyonesse and pendragon

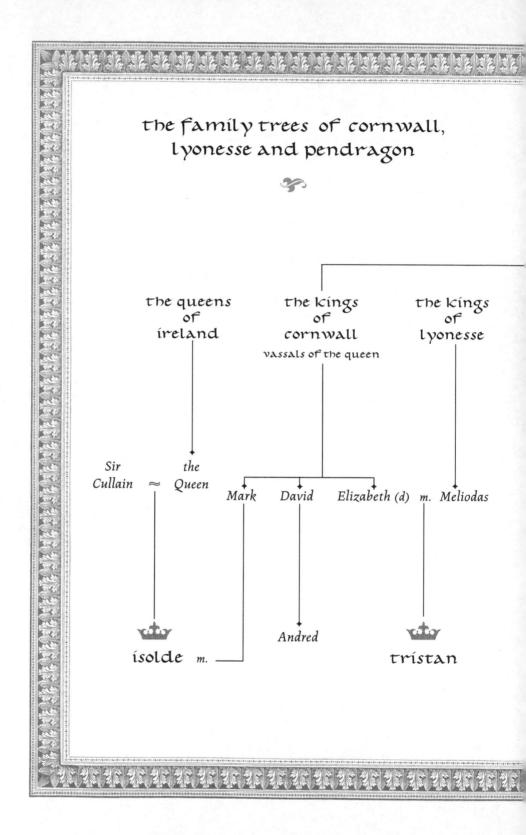

the queens
of
ireland

the kings
of
cornwall

vassals of the queen

the kings
of
lyonesse

Sir
Cullain ≈ the
Queen

Mark   David   Elizabeth (d) m. Meliodas

Andred

isolde m. ──────

tristan

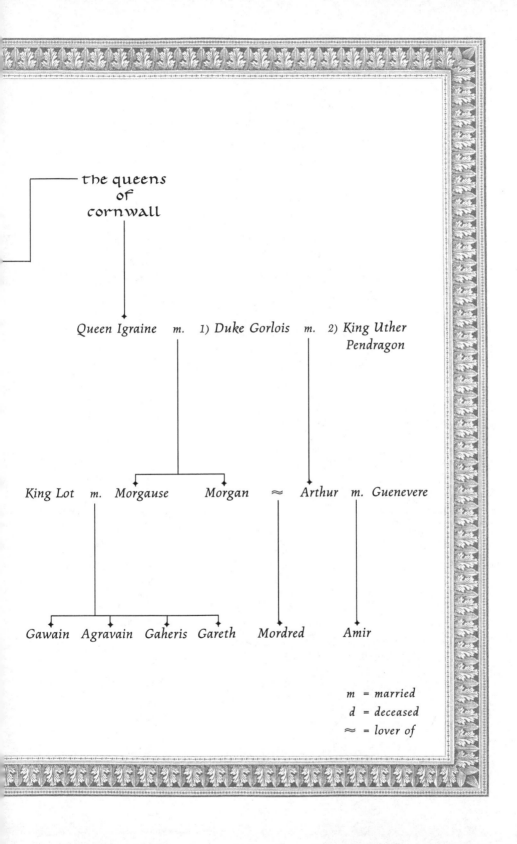

the queens
of
cornwall

Queen Igraine   m.   1) Duke Gorlois   m.   2) King Uther
Pendragon

King Lot   m.   Morgause   Morgan   ≈   Arthur   m.   Guenevere

Gawain   Agravain   Gaheris   Gareth   Mordred   Amir

m = married
d = deceased
≈ = lover of

ISOLDE

QUEEN OF
THE WESTERN ISLE

At the time of King Arthur and Queen Guenevere, there was a king called Meliodas, lord of the country of Lyonesse. By fortune he wedded the sister of King Mark of Cornwall, a lady both good and fair. Then he was unjustly cast into prison when his wife was great with child, and her travail came on betimes. She was delivered of a son after many grimly throes, and she called the boy's name Tristan for her sorrows, and so she died.

Then Merlin brought Meliodas out of his prison, and the King married another queen, who hated the young Tristan with all her heart.

So she ordained to poison him, but it happened that the Queen's own son drank the poison, and fell down dead. Then the King took her by the hand, and drew his sword and said, "Tell me what drink this is, or I shall slay thee." And she fell to her knees, and told him why she would have slain Tristan, so that her children should enjoy the land.

"Well then," said the King, "you shall have the law."

And so she was damned by the assent of the barons to be burned. And as she was brought to the fire, young Tristan knelt to his father and begged a boon.

"You shall have it," said the King.

"Give me the life of my stepmother," said Tristan.

"Take her, then," said the King, "and may God forgive her, if you can."

So Tristan went to the fire and saved her from her death. Then the King sent the young Tristan into France to learn deeds of arms, and Tristan became a knight great in all chivalry for his bigness and grace.

Then the Queen of Ireland sent her champion to King Mark of Cornwall to demand tribute, and King Mark could not withstand him, so the cry went out for a knight to do battle against him. Then some of his knights counselled King Mark to send to King Arthur for Sir Lancelot of the Lake, that was at that time named the most marvellous knight of all the world. But others said, "Have ye forgot your sister that married King Meliodas of Lyonesse, that hath a son that is become a fair bold knight?"

So Sir Tristan rode to his uncle King Mark, and took the battle on. And the Queen of Ireland who made that war had a daughter who was known for her beauty through all the world as La Belle Isolde. . . .

—Morte D'Arthur

chapter 1

*N*ight fell across the forest, tree by tree. A rising moon shone through the tangled branches, and one by one the creatures of the day slipped to their silent beds. In the shadows, the mounted figure waited, brooding on what was to come. His cloudy robes and long gray hair blended with the night, and his hooded eyes never left the road ahead. Any rider coming from Ireland had to pass this way. And the messenger was coming, he knew it. There was nothing to do but wait.

Leaning forward, he stroked the neck of his patient mule, and a crooked smile played over his ancient face. All his life, Merlin mused, he had known how to wait. Through all his lives, as Druid, seer, and magic child, he had watched and endured as the world went by. He drew in the rich smell of the woodland, sensing the pulse of the living earth. Beneath the moldering leaves of winter, he could feel the approach of spring. This, too, he had long awaited, through a hard season racked with storms and snow. All winters in the end gave way to spring.

But now—

Merlin's heart groaned in his breast. "Gods, give us peace!" he prayed. "Or if not peace, grant me a little time!"

Peaccce—tiiime—a mocking night wind whisked his words away. The old enchanter ground his yellow teeth. "I know, I know!" he moaned to the empty air. "You warned me, and I did not hear!"

For the signs had come, there was no doubt of that. Even in Camelot, joyfully ensconced with Arthur and Guenevere, he was always Merlin, and Merlin never slept. First of all, a month and more ago, wandering in the wilds, he had been enveloped by a soft wind from the west, full of sad murmurs and foreboding cries. Then a week or so afterward, alone in his chamber when all the court slept, he had heard the sound of women's voices raised in grief, keening over a battleground as women did in the distant isles. With it came a seeing such as only a Druid can bear. The same trembling in the wind had brought him the sight of women washing their warriors' bloodstained garments at a ford, and the stark glimpse of a green hillside darkened by gaping graves.

After that had come the saddest sign of all. On the first day of spring, all the court had turned out to greet the newborn sun, reveling in the pale beams warming the earth. Merlin had lagged behind as the short day ended and the crowd turned back to Camelot. On the outskirts of the forest, before the approach to the great palace with its white towers and golden roofs, he saw a windblown sea bird, miles from any shore. Bravely she battled over the darkling plain, and came to rest at last in his open arms.

She held a bright green trefoil in her beak. With infinite gentleness he took it from her and wrapped the small spent body in his cloak, cradling her in the bosom of his gown. She raised her long white neck and fixed him with an angry, tender eye. D'you hear, Merlin? she asked him without words.

"I hear," he replied softly in the Old Tongue, and blessed her head. Then she tucked her head under her wing, and breathed her last.

He touched the shamrock then, and knowledge came. The word was coming from the Western Isle—the plant with three leaves had no other home. Ireland, the Island of the West—he closed his eyes and memories sharp as knives stabbed him to the quick. Suddenly he was a love-crazed youth again, studying on the Druids' own sacred island, pursuing the Goddess in the place She called home, the land so beloved by the Old Ones that they had made it the sweetest spot on earth.

Gods above, how he had loved Her then! And any woman in Her shape or form. And in return, many women had loved him. At the height of his love for the Great One, he had found his power. Afterward he returned to Ireland whenever his spirit failed, and always found there the succor that he sought. Indeed, on one such visit, many lives later, the Queen of the Western Isle herself had come to him, and taken him for her own.

"The Queen," he breathed in delight, "ah, yes, the Queen." Gods, what a woman, born to have her way with any man! A warmth pulsed through him and he brought his crabbed hand to his lips in a phantom kiss. Fine days, they were, and even rarer nights. He would not forget.

But for days now he had felt the coming of another messenger. All day at court he had heard the Great Ones whispering in his ear, and at the end of the dinner hour, he had slipped away. His white mule had come at once to his call, and as soon as he was out of the palace, his spirit had soared. Whatever was coming, he would meet it here in the forest under the stars, and wherever it led him, he was ready for the task.

The mists of night were rising from the ground. All around him the creatures that loved darkness were venturing from their holes. A hunting vixen slipped past him through the grass, and soon he heard her victim's dying cries. A life had ended, but her young would live: life and death were all one in the end. Whatever came, it was only a new beginning to that age-old dance, a dance he had been treading since time began.

The old man eased his skinny haunches in the saddle and waited on. At last the mule pricked up its ears and raised its heavy head.

The old man cackled. "You hear it too, my dear?"

Soon the earth throbbed with the distant drumming of a horse's hooves. Merlin eased forward to greet the rider as he came.

And here he was, a cloaked figure flying furiously through the dark. Merlin broke his progress with a hail. "Ho there, traveler!"

"Lord Merlin?"

In the pale moonlight Merlin saw a youth, thin-faced and tense with purpose, his dark hair standing on end. He wore a rich woollen wrap of deep sea-green, fine breeches, and a pair of well-made boots. Gold jangled at his wrists and round his neck, and a band of gold held back his long black hair. He had the look of a young priest, a holy dreamer who had given his life to a Great One he worshipped and adored. Now he was fighting to hold down his panting horse as recognition spread across his face.

"Sir, it is you I seek!" he cried with relief. "I am sent to tell you that there will be war within the month!"

"I knew it!" Merlin gnashed his teeth. "Where, boy, where?"

"Cornwall will be attacked, the Druids say."

"Cornwall?" Merlin gasped. "But the Queen of Cornwall has no enemies. She rules for King Arthur, and she will protect the kingdom with her life."

"All the more reason for an enemy to strike at the King through her."

"Arthur installed King Mark there as her vassal," the old man cried, "to keep the old Queen safe."

The boy shook his head. "The danger now is more than King Mark can withstand."

Merlin gripped the reins in a trembling hand. "Danger—from where?"

"From the Island of the West."

"Ireland!" Merlin struck his head. "As the seabird warned me!"

Black thoughts rained down like thunderbolts on his head. A long-suffering land, ruled by an unruly queen. A people who relished warfare as much as they cherished love and laughter and the joy the Goddess gives. And Cornwall, a fine prize for any invader—a rich and fertile land, as green as Ireland and as beautiful, a mere step across the water for the skillful sailors of the Western Isle.

So—Ireland striking at Cornwall.

There was no time to lose. He turned to the messenger. "You have done good service, boy. What is your name?"

The young man's head went up with unconscious pride. "My name is nothing. I serve the Lady, and the Great One who made us all."

"But yourself—?" Merlin probed.

A rare smile made the boy's face beautiful. "Set me down as one who loves Ireland and her Queen."

Merlin frowned, his thoughts darkened by memories of a face ravaged by the misery of beauty, a body racked by passions beyond her control. "The Queen of the Western Isle?"

"Herself." The boy let out an ecstatic breath. "And her daughter, the Queen who is to be."

"Isolde, yes," Merlin agreed fervently. "Well, boy, to Cornwall it is!" He raised a hand in farewell. "First I must speak to the King. After that I shall follow you down the Great West Way."

He stood and watched the messenger gallop off. Then a gentle laugh behind him warmed his soul.

"No need to tell Arthur, Merlin, he is here." There was another chuckle. "But you knew that." Merlin turned. The cloaked figure in the shadows made a courteous bow, steadying his horse in firm but quiet hands. "I did not mean to intrude on your meeting here. But Guenevere saw you leave the hall and urged me after you."

"You are welcome, Arthur." Merlin's gaze roved over the newcomer's lofty frame and strong-featured face, clear gaze, and thick fair hair, and he sighed with delight. Not even his old lord and master, Uther Pendragon, had gripped his heart like this. Hastily he recollected himself and arranged his features into a forbidding scowl. "You have not come too soon."

Arthur's gray eyes were troubled. "War in Cornwall, then? When we still face the invaders on the Saxon shore?"

"And trouble within Ireland, too," Merlin said grimly. "But not as we think."

Arthur stared. "How so?"

Merlin closed his eyes and allowed his thoughts to gather around his head like moths. "Ireland is at peace. Her people have no reason to seek war. But if her Queen is nursing some dream—some desire—"

As she always did, he added to himself. Half woman, half goddess, the Queen's dreams were her desires. Especially when she was under the sway of a man. And when was she ever without one man in the shadow of another, treading hungrily on his rival's heels?

"She must want to extend her kingdom," he mused on. "And she has many good knights who adore her, men who would fulfill her every desire—" He broke off, his eyes opaque.

"But why attack Cornwall? What does the Irish Queen want?" Arthur wondered, his eyes never leaving the hawk-like face.

Merlin gave a sharp bark of laughter. "If only she knew! She is a creature of the lightest whim. Her passions rule her life."

"Then they must rule her country, too, since the Western Isle still keeps the Mother-right."

Merlin grinned savagely. "With a vengeance, boy! Queens have ruled there from the time before time. In her own eyes, the present Queen is as good as the Goddess Herself. She takes the best of her knights as her lovers, not caring that they get younger every year, and changes her consort whenever she likes."

"But she has a daughter, the maid they call La Belle Isolde?" Arthur demanded.

"True." Merlin paused. "And there's hope in that. Isolde will never support her mother's scheme. Young as she is, she has the best interests of her country at heart."

"But can she convince her mother not to make war?"

Merlin looked past Arthur with an impenetrable stare. "We shall see. I must ride to King Mark in Cornwall, and bid him prepare."

Arthur leaned forward urgently. "Tell him to make all speed to Tintagel to defend my mother. Guenevere and I will follow you with a force of men."

Merlin cackled to himself. "Oh, sir," he said softly, "think how often the Queen your mother has defended herself."

A hunter's moon broke through the watery cloud. The woodland track lay before him, as bright as day. Merlin lifted his eyes, and reached for the mule's silken reins. He felt the open road calling him like a lover, and itched to be gone. The Queen of the Western Isle, eh? he pondered with an inward smile. Out of the darkness of time, a vivid figure came striding toward him across the astral plane, her flame-colored silks hissing around her heels. Then the bright vision faded and he saw a broken bird beating her wings in pain, turning on the male beside her with the fury of the damned.

"Merlin?"

Arthur's voice came to him through a mist. "What ails you, sir?" the young King asked in concern.

Merlin's sight cleared and he straightened up. "Nothing," he said brusquely. "A secret lost in a dark forest, long ago." The gaze he turned on Arthur was full of pain. "Let me go now. And may the Gods grant that I get there in time!"

chapter
2

Storm clouds raced over the island like maddened sheep. The sea beat on the shore and the old stronghold of Dubh Lein bowed its head to the wind and rain as it had done for a thousand years. High above the bay, its lofty towers and battlements sheltered a sturdy keep, eternally defending the approach to the Western Isle. Now the last of the winter sleet lashed the sea-washed stones, and a troubled twilight hovered, ready to fall.

In the center of the fortress, the Queen's House rose from the living rock, a curious, ancient dwelling of shining white quartz. Many secrets lay hidden within its glittering walls, and a spring of sweet water fed a deep pool below. The Dark Pool, as the people called it, was no more than a wise thought by the ancients, to build their citadel where fresh water would not fail. Why then did they all fear it and take it as one of the Queen's enchantments, her secret way down to the world below?

The soberly dressed woman moving through the Queen's private apartments allowed herself to smile. Perhaps because they feared the Queen herself?

Not without reason. The lean figure shivered and drew a breath. In all the years she had waited on the Queen, no one could ever say what her mistress would do. And Queen or no, she had grown to her middle years without ever losing the urgent desires of a child. When would she learn to use her power for the good of all?

"Brangwain?"

"Here, madam!"

Startled, the woman turned toward the door as a shapely figure in fluttering silks burst into the room. She was brightly clad in shades of gold and red, but her strong, lovely face was dark with distress. Great clusters of black jet swung from her neck and ears and clattered round her waist as she moved.

"Dismiss the maids!" she gasped. "And send for Sir Marhaus!"

"Your Majesty—"

Brangwain hastened forward and drew her mistress through the ornate double doors, shooing away the maids following on her heels. "Later, my dears," she said softly, watching their young faces droop at being shut out. "Never fear, the Queen will send for you." She closed the door.

"Brangwain, where are you?"

The voice from inside the chamber was raw and harsh. The Queen threw herself down on a couch, tore off her headdress, and cast it to the floor. "Where is he, Brangwain?" she demanded wildly, shaking out her hair.

The rich henna-colored mop tumbled down to the flagstones, staining the gleaming surface with the color of blood. Racking sobs shook the long body with the passion of a child.

Brangwain was caught between pity and despair. "Sir Marhaus is here," she said steadily, "waiting for you."

The Queen leapt to her feet and paced frenziedly to and fro. "He must not go to Cornwall!"

"To Cornwall, madam?" Brangwain paused, all her senses suddenly alert. The lilt of the Welshlands she had carried from her birth grew stronger. "Why should he go there?"

The lithe figure turned on her, wild-eyed. "No reason!—it's nothing—where is he?"

"In your private quarters, madam."

Feverishly the Queen crossed the chamber, throwing open the doors to the room within. Outside the window the storm had reached its peak, and streams of rain pelted the greenish glass. As her eyes searched the shadows, she caught the strong, compact form standing in the far casement, outlined by the misty light. She knew every inch of the well-knit, battle-hardened body and had wept and marveled over its every scar. Though he was ten years or more her junior, he had lived and fought hard all his life, and every one of his wounds had been taken for her. Goddess, Mother, how she loved him! If she lost him now—

She shuddered with yearning and dread. Her fingers ached to touch the brown skin beneath his red leather tunic, his linen shirt, the great gold pendant on his breast set with her emblem, a pair of fighting swans. His strong musky scent rose to meet her, and she could bear it no longer.

"Marhaus!" she cried, and hurled herself into his arms.

"Lady, hush."

The knight stepped forward and gathered her to his chest. With a practiced hand, he stroked her neck and throat, supporting her with a sinewy brown arm.

"What is this, madam?" he asked lazily, his mind already turning toward the great bed with its billowing hangings, anchored like a ship at the far end of the room. He loved her in her passions, when she came to him quivering with rage or grief, and she loved him for releasing her from the storms and impulses she could not control. Afterward she would lie quietly in his arms, sated and appeased, remembering nothing but the bliss they shared.

So she would be now, he decided, feeling her trembling from head to foot. "Come, lady," he said roughly. "Let's to bed."

She stiffened against him.

"No!" she said shrilly, her black eyes alight with flames of fear. "I have seen it, Marhaus! You must not go!"

"Not go to Cornwall?"

He froze like a wolf in the forest, ready to leap. "My ship stands in the harbor," he said menacingly. "My knights and men have boarded, and you shame me now by saying I must not go?"

"You must not go to Cornwall," she babbled, already afraid of his anger, but more afraid of silencing her fears. "I know you said that the whole country would drop into your hand—"

"And so it will." His calm was more dangerous than any threat. "Think, madam—there's none to defend it but an ancient queen in Tintagel, and a coward king who knows not how to fight. You agreed I could challenge him for the throne. One little joust, and I win this land for you!" His voice hardened. "Do not deny me now!"

"I must!" she cried. "Queen Igraine had Cornwall from her mother in a line stretching back to the Mother Herself. It is against the will of the Great One, to make war against those who rightly rule."

Marhaus flushed. "This is your daughter talking, this is Isolde! Now you see the folly of sending her to Avalon to learn their weak, womanish faith of love, not war!" He stared at the Queen. "Your lovely daughter, La Belle Isolde," he added hurtfully, sounding each word like a slap in the face. "The beauty of the Western Isle."

Her hands flew to her face, to the tiny lines and creases her mirror knew so well. "Don't torture me!" She clutched at her head, crying out with pain. "Isolde's young, that's all. Any girl of twenty is still beautiful. The people only call her that because she heals their sicknesses and cares for them."

"She's a dreamer." Marhaus paused to weigh his words. "And a fool."

She flew at him, ready to scratch out his eyes. "She is my daughter! Show her some respect."

He caught her wrists in a savage grip. "Madam, respect yourself! Who is Queen here, Isolde or you?"

Her face suffused with blood. "I am! And I say you will not make this war!"

"Give me a reason!"

"We need no more kingdoms. Ireland is enough."

He looked at her with contempt. "Only yesterday you were hungry for Cornwall's safe harbors and green fields. Tell me the truth."

"If you challenge Mark, I fear for your life!"

"My life?" His disbelieving laughter filled the room. "The King of Cornwall could not kill a headless snake!"

"He might not be your opponent." She clutched at him. "One of his knights might take up the challenge and fight you in his stead."

He threw her off in disgust. "King Mark has no knights worth fearing! What decent man would serve a wretch like him? I know them all, and I can beat them all." He showed his white teeth in a savage grin as he thought of a secret he would never tell.

"You cannot go!" She was trembling so violently now that she could hardly stand. "I had a seeing—just now, as the storm came on...."

He was suddenly still. He knew her Otherworldly skills too well to ignore this. "A seeing? What?"

She closed her eyes, crooning in misery. "I saw a battlefield through a mist of blood—two knights fighting to the death—and one man down, facedown in the mud—"

"One man down?" He let out a cry of triumph. "Why, then, you saw my enemy, not me. No man in Cornwall could have me down!"

Her eyes dilated and he read the question in their midnight depths. Could this be true? Dear Gods, could it be?

"Enough of this," he said forcefully, taking her in his arms. "Send me to Cornwall, and I swear I'll lay the kingdom beneath your feet. I'll make King Mark your vassal, not Igraine's, and if he refuses, I'll send you his head in a box. Believe me, lady, the silly toad will scramble to kiss your hand!"

"Marhaus, no," she moaned.

He seized her face in one cruel hand. "Then you choose to keep me here as your lapdog? You allow all men to say, 'There goes the Queen's bed-slave'?"

"No!" She struggled to be free. "You are my champion and my chosen one. Is it not enough that I took you to my bed? All the world knows you are the companion of the throne."

"But not King." Swiftly he tightened his grip.

She gasped with pain. "Oh, I know you, Marhaus! Your heart believes that you should be King!"

"Only if you are my Queen. And only if you give me leave to carry your name and glory through all the world." His fingers found the silken hollow of her throat and moved down to brush her breast. "I shall blazon your beauty in countries yet unknown, and force their occupants to eat my sword." He buried his hand in her hair and drew her head back for a lingering kiss. She quickened like lightning at his touch, and his flesh stirred.

"Come, lady," he said thickly, turning toward the bed. The storm had passed and great shafts of evening light were bathing the crimson hangings in pools of gold. She would stretch out in the sun as sensual as a cat, he knew, awaiting her pleasure and taking it fully too.

He stroked her face, then opened the front of her gown, taking her heavy, full breasts in both his hands. "First let me love you as a queen deserves. Then afterward—" He paused. "I shall sail for Cornwall and bring a new world under your command!"

chapter
3

ere, Princess—up here!"

Moving with care across the rain-washed roof, the old courtier leaned over the battlements and waved down to the courtyard below. Among the busy throng going to and fro, there was no mistaking the slim figure darting across the cobbles who responded at once with a merry wave.

"Mind your footing," he called, "after all this rain."

The tiny form acknowledged his concern and hastened on. Watching the young woman skim past the keep and dart into the tower, the old man saw again the child she used to be, a young sprite as playful as a fountain, with a laugh of endless joy. Goddess, Mother, he prayed, praise and thanks for this girl! If there is any hope for Ireland, it lies with her.

And there she was, surging through the turret door onto the battlements, her face glowing, her smiling eyes alight. Up here she looked small no longer but lissom and well-formed, her body as slim and supple as a reed, her whole being reaching out for what was to come. Her tumbling hair shone like the sunset against her woollen wrap, and the gleam of her skin was the glow of the white trefoil. She wore a cloak of green and a gown of gold and within it she bloomed like the first flower of spring.

Gods above!

The old man shook his head, with a rueful smile. She always had the power to stop his heart. Would he ever harden himself against that trusting tilt of the head, that ardent air?

"Princess Isolde!" he cried with a flourishing bow.

"Good day to you, Sir Gilhan," she replied with a merry laugh, turning her face up to the watery sun. "And a grand day it is now the rain has stopped."

Sir Gilhan smiled. "Lady, I'm at your command. What can I do for you?"

The bright face became serious. "Sir, I need your help. You're the leader of my mother's council and before that you were her champion for many years. May the Mother grant me such knights when my time comes! But I have no one to advise me now." She shivered. "And if anything happened, I'm so ignorant!"

"Not quite, Princess," he said gently. "You learned a great deal on Avalon when your mother sent you to study with the Lady of the Lake. The Lady found you could already read the writing in the wind, and see the Great One's purpose in the stars."

Isolde's fair skin colored like a rose. "I was not the only one. Guenevere was there too. She was more gifted, she has the Sight."

Sir Gilhan studied her. Did the dear girl not know she had her mother's Otherworldly air? That she had the same spirit of enchantment and a brightness like the sea?

"Queen Guenevere is older than you are," he said. "You may well have the Sight, too, when your time comes. And don't forget the healing gift you have. Women in childbirth, sick babies, and knights half dead from the joust, you help them all." He chuckled. "I tell you, Princess, there's many a lord of the Queen's council who would gladly suffer some ailment for the pleasure of your cure."

Goddess, Mother, the loyalty of these men!

Isolde felt a sudden spring of love, and blessed him in her heart. "But until the Old Ones gift me with the Sight," she said impishly, "and the Little People whisper in my ear—will you tell me what I need to know?"

He could not hold back a laugh. "Gladly!"

"Then teach me, sir, what we have to fear. I've watched Guenevere and Arthur struggling to bring peace and justice to their land, and I want to do the same. We've had peace in Ireland all my life, but we must have enemies. Where are they now?"

"Beaten back to their own lands, lady." Sir Gilhan felt a grim satisfaction warm his bones. "We fought many hard battles when your mother was young, and she fought hardest of all, leading us to victory time and time again. And Cullain, your father . . ." He pointed to the thick band of gold glinting on the middle finger of her right hand. It was all she had left of the man who had given her life, he knew. "Gods above, what a man! He was her first champion and chosen one, and he swore she'd never regret making him her choice. He fought beside her in every battle but the last when she sent him on alone, and together they were unbeatable. Once, when the Picts invaded, we drove them back to sea before they could leave their ships!" He chuckled. "Wait till you see them! They're battle mad, and a hideous sight with their wild tattoos. But your mother, the Queen, why, she . . ."

Isolde listened entranced, seeing again her mother as she first remembered her. She'd seemed like a spirit from the Otherworld then, the tall, powerful figure at the helm of her battle chariot, racing round the training field in merciless mock-combat with her knights, her handsome face flaming, her silver sword flashing around her head. Isolde remembered her childhood delight and felt again the chill of betrayal as it slowly gave way to the endless sense of regret.

She heaved an involuntary sigh. *Why, Mother, did you never play war games with me, never train me for battle, never let me join in your councils debating peace or war?* Was it the urge to protect her, as the Queen said, that had made her mother always hold her back? Or was it an aging woman's jealous fear of being supplanted by someone younger, by a girl already loved by the people and called La Belle Isolde?

She dared not let her thoughts go that way.

"—keep the peace here, as long as we command the head of the bay."

Sir Gilhan was ending his tale. From the battlements they could see Dubh Lein's wide harbor and its strong defenses commanding the sea routes to the Western Isle. The castle itself was protected by deep ditches and stout walls, with towers and lookouts at each corner, and room for an army of men.

Isolde nodded, satisfied. "If our enemies come again, then Dubh Lein is well defended from the sea."

Sir Gilhan waved a hand toward the rear, where a massive gatehouse glowered out at the world beyond. "An attack by land would find us equally well prepared."

Isolde paused. "But out in the country, where the people dwell in crannogs . . . ?"

Sir Gilhan nodded. "It's true, the lake villagers have no defense."

"And all over the island there are places where an enemy could land?"

"There are indeed."

She turned to face him. "Who would invade us?"

Her question drew a wry smile from Sir Gilhan. "The same as always—our age-old enemies, the Picts." His smile faded. "Their lands are barren, ours are plenteous, and our nearness has often tempted them in the past. Their King is old, and the fire has left his sword, but his young son's already a fierce fighter, and they say he'll make his mark."

"But not in Ireland," said Isolde crisply, "if we watch them as we should."

The courtier gave her an approving grin. "Oh, we do, lady, we do. But there is more than one kind of enemy."

Isolde felt again the shadow of her concern. "Say on."

"Sometimes," the old knight said carefully, watching her face, "those who love a country can betray it for another, greater love."

She stared at him. "What could be greater than loving our country? The land is our Mother, it's the Great One herself—it gives us birth, and at death it calls us home."

Sir Gilhan looked away. His gaze was as gray and somber as the sea. "Sometimes a lesser passion may seem greater to one in love."

She knew he meant her mother. "What are you saying?" she cried, flushing with shame.

She felt him watching her again as he chose his words. "A knight may not speak against his lady, nor a lord against his queen."

He is treating me like a child. Anger flooded her, and she looked him in the eye. "He may when a greater evil threatens us all," she said levelly. "Sir Gilhan, if you honor me, speak out."

He bowed his head. "My fear is for the Queen. You know your mother has the spirit of incantation, and her passions are her gods."

She braced herself. "Go on."

"There are rumors that she means to advance Sir Marhaus—"

"Sir Marhaus?"—*Goddess, Mother, I knew it!*—"How?"

"He has been boasting that he will conquer new lands for the Queen—that she has given him her blessing to carry war over the sea."

"You mean invade another country? Where?"

Sir Gilhan shrugged. "Who knows? But any attack will invite attack in return. We destroy our own peace when we go to war."

And all for nothing.

For my mother's love, and Sir Marhaus's pride.

Suddenly she felt a thousand years old, no longer the girl who had stepped out so blithely onto the battlements before. She turned back to Sir Gilhan. "Well, sir, you have not trusted me in vain. I shall speak to the Queen and learn the truth from her."

He nodded toward the door. "We may know it sooner than we think."

Isolde turned. The dark shape of a woman appeared at the top of the steps. The neatly clad figure had a thoughtful, dignified air, and her calm movements showed an assurance far above her rank. Her face had lost the bloom of youth, but her dark-toned skin, bright eyes, and black hair coiled up in glossy braids still caught the eye.

"It's Brangwain!" cried Isolde, mystified.

Sir Gilhan craned his head. "The lady from the Welshlands who waits upon the Queen?"

"Yes, and my nurse, too, when I was younger—though she was only a girl herself when she came to us."

Brangwain approached with a curtsey. "Madam, a word?"

Isolde spread her hands. "Always, Brangwain." She gestured to the knight. "You may trust Sir Gilhan. He knows my mind."

Brangwain frowned. "Lady, forgive me if I speak out of turn. But the Queen said something strange about Sir Marhaus that I thought you ought to know—"

"Sir Marhaus?"

Isolde felt Sir Gilhan's troubled gaze. "Speak, Brangwain," she said steadily. "Tell us what you heard."

chapter
4

Panting, the white mule climbed to the top of the cliff. Merlin slid down from the saddle and stared out at the setting sun. Below him the sea prowled around the rocky shore, and a flock of seagulls squabbled overhead. The old man threw wide his arms and eased his aching back. Cornwall at last! Ye Gods, it was good to be here.

From the headland he could see the length of Cornwall and the country beyond, as far as the glittering point where the land disappeared into the sea. A grimace of satisfaction crossed Merlin's face. At least he did not have to fear for Lyonesse. Unlike the wretched Mark of Cornwall, the King of Lyonesse was both loyal and brave.

Lyonesse, land of silver sun and golden rain, land of dreams—

The scent of rosemary came drifting down the wind. Merlin closed his eyes. How long ago was it that he had hurried down there to free the young King out of prison at the prayers of his frantic Queen?

Long, long ago.

"But not fast enough, old fool!" he chided himself, feeling again the young Queen's despair and death. Not fast enough to save her, nor the child of sorrow she had called Tristan. Sadness enwrapped him like the rising mist. Such a fragile thing she had been, the little Queen, bird-boned, white-skinned, yet as dark-haired as one of the Old Ones, with the air of a frightened fawn. Even without the great child in her belly, a baby far too big for a wraith like her, her delicate frame would not have been long for this world. But to die in such sorrow, and leave such sorrow behind—

"Grief upon me!" Merlin mourned. "Grief upon all of us!"

Ahead of him the clifftop stretched away, a patchwork of tumbling thrift, blushing pinks, and daisies silver-white in the fading light.

Around them, clusters of yellow cowslips nodded down the slope, and great drifts of moonflowers flirted round Merlin's feet.

Far out at sea, a lone ship was sailing down the pathway of the sun. Merlin's sight faded, and he saw the harbor of the Western Isle, with the evening tide tugging at its shores. He watched with bated breath as a champion knight and his entourage boarded a handsome bark, its pennants, spars, and masts bathed in the last rays of the sun. The boat sailed into the sunset till every rope in its rigging was alight with golden fire. But as the boat neared the dying ball of flame, the white sails darkened to pink and turned to red and the ship was drowned in blood.

"Gods and Great Ones!" Merlin cried, fighting to be free. Shuddering, he came to himself again, drained and spent. Only wisps of memory lingered in his mind. But he knew that he had seen a ship of death. Arthur was due to follow him to Cornwall soon. Could it be Arthur's death that he foresaw?

Or worse . . .

Merlin screamed and tore his hair. Twice already he had failed the house of Lyonesse, when the King lay in prison and when the Queen died in the dark forest in terror and alone. Yet her child had lived. Could the boy born of sorrow be in danger now?

"On, on!" he shouted to the mule, trembling in his frantic efforts to mount. "Onward to Castle Dore!"

He caught at the pommel and heaved himself into the saddle as the well-trained beast moved off. "Gods, speed my path," he cried to the empty air. "Let me not come too late!"

❦

BUT IT WAS another day before he made Castle Dore, and later still before he could see King Mark. His Majesty was closeted with his advisers, Merlin was told, and all the attendants knew better than to disturb the King.

The sun was high in the sky when the call came. While he waited, Merlin patrolled every inch of Castle Dore, and was forced to concede that Mark had done well. The new palace he had built on the foundations of his forefathers' ancient fort was bright with fresh limewash and gleaming stone. Below the castle, a snug town with fair houses and clean streets clung to the skirts of the castle and served its needs. From its hilltop site, Castle Dore commanded the land all around, and its wide halls and chambers were fit for a king.

Even this King. Merlin groaned aloud. Mark's father had been one of the best, no man more serviceable in peace or war. All his life the old King had tried to make his unpromising son first into a man, then into a king like him.

But both roles had been too hard for Mark to play. His father's rough training had left the son all too short of manhood, a feeble fighter and a blustering knight. Nor had his father's kingliness descended on Mark when Merlin last passed this way.

The piping voice of a page broke into his thoughts. "Lord Merlin? King Mark will see you now."

"Thank you."

Merlin followed the boy with a sulfurous glare. The Gods only knew what it was for a High Druid and a Lord of Light to be kept waiting to see a vassal king like this!

But at least he knew what was expected of an audience with a king. His long velvet robe of woodland green was heavy with fur and its long, full sleeves whispered to the ground as he walked. His fingers groaned with rings like serpents' eyes, and the same topaz and amber stared out from the chains round his neck. A deep band of gold encircled his long curled locks, and a wand of golden yew gleamed in his hand.

"Lead on, fool," he growled at the page. "I am ready to meet your King."

And now here were a pair of imposing double doors, and behind the doors, what? Merlin stepped forward, stiffening his bony spine.

Ahead of him stretched a large audience chamber, its roof and walls bright with shields and banners from forgotten wars. The court was full, and the throng of courtiers met his appearance with buzzing whispers and a forest of curious eyes. The lofty windows made the most of the noonday sun, and a royal dais graced the end of the room. Fresh green rushes mingled with wild thyme and lavender on the floor, and an apple-wood fire roared on the wide hearth. Sweet savors all, Merlin noted as he strode down the room. Why then did the place stink of horses and dogs?

The dogs answered for themselves, a rough pack of hairy wolfhounds scratching and growling from their places round the throne. And horses, too, were clearly close friends of the figure seated on the dais, whose garments still bore the slubbered traces of his morning ride. Ye Gods!

Merlin fought down a surge of anger and contempt. Mark's four-footed attendants must be the only creatures in Cornwall who did not look down on their King.

For could that long, slack thing on the throne be a leader of men, a man of kingly height but without royal grace? True, the King's scarlet tunic and dark breeches were woven of fine wool, and the ancient crown of his fathers encircled his head. The sword at his side and the crossed lances above the throne were likewise both good and rare, their gleaming gold and bronze shaped with Otherworldly skill. But the lank forelock of pale sandy hair, the short-sighted gaze, and the oddly forlorn air betrayed the lost boy inside the would-be king. Gods above, Merlin thought with disbelief, how old is he? Thirty-five, forty at least. His heart sank. Too old to grow up now.

"Lord Merlin, welcome, after all these years!"

The ungainly figure rose to its feet, beckoning Merlin to approach the throne. To Mark's right stood a knight, to his left a short, misshapen older man in the garb of a monk. As Merlin drew near, the knight claimed his attention with a graceful bow. From his sleek black curls to the cut of his leather boots, the young man was formed to make women love him, while his strong fighting frame would endear him to men. But Merlin read the hidden pride in the poise of the handsome head and saw that it had only increased in the time he had been away. He saw something else, too, so slight it was visible only to a Druid's eye. Handsome as he was, from the faint, unmistakable marking on his upper lip, Merlin knew the young man had been elf-shotten in the womb.

But any hint of the harelip vanished with the young knight's flashing smile. "Lord Merlin, I am Sir Andred, at your service, as you may recall."

Merlin glimmered at him. "Sir, who could forget the King's nephew and chosen heir?"

The crowd round the dais was pressing forward to hear. Prominent in their midst were three or four watchful figures, the King's barons, Merlin guessed, who had served Mark's father and now tried with far less success to keep the son on course. In the front Merlin saw a well-dressed couple, the man elderly, plump, and complacent in rich velvets and furs, the woman dark and lean, with an angry, burning gaze. Her long face with its thin, sensual mouth was too strong to be beautiful, but her studied poise would draw any eyes her way. Her long white neck was offset by her livid green gown, and her glittering cloak coiled round her feet like a snake.

"And the Lady Elva," cried Mark eagerly, beckoning the woman forward while her husband grinned in the rear.

"Lord Merlin."

The woman dropped a curtsy, and Merlin glimmered again as he greeted her in return. All Cornwall had been amazed when the slow Mark had taken himself a mistress, and even more taken aback that Elva was the woman of choice. With eyes as hard and black as chips of jet, she flashed with Otherworldly fire, and the gossips joked that she had seduced the young Mark, not the other way round. The boy in him could not think what else to do, and the man in him could not make a better choice. But years later, here she was, still close to the throne, with her dull husband, who was too vain to wonder why King Mark showered him with gifts. Well, it was the way of the world. Merlin grinned to himself.

"Father Dominian is new to you, I think," came Mark's voice. "But we have many holy men in Cornwall now." There was an undisguised self-satisfaction in his tone. "The father has been revealing God's word to me."

Merlin turned toward the monk at Mark's left hand, standing with a young novice at his side. With growing revulsion he took in the harsh black woollen habit with its girdle of rope, the raw, sandaled feet, the savagely tonsured head. Merlin's gaze flickered on over the pitiful body with its twisted spine, the priest's hunched back emphasized by his monkish hood. Dominian's skin was unnaturally dark, and he met Merlin's eyes with a sloe-black stare. The old enchanter's hand flew to his own careful locks, each curled and perfumed, and he shuddered inwardly. When the Gods had made a man so ugly by nature, why did he have to make himself look worse?

"Greetings, Brother Dominian," he ventured haughtily.

The holy man stared, his glittering eyes intent. "Lord Merlin, you are a man of high concerns. What brings you here to us?"

"I was just about to ask him that myself!" cried Mark importantly. "What is it, Merlin? Speak."

Merlin drew a breath. "We have had word that an attack threatens Cornwall from the Island of the West."

Mark's jaw dropped. "It can't be true!"

Andred tensed. "Uncle, it can." He nodded at Merlin, tight-lipped. "Tell us what you know."

"I can tell you what I guess. The Queen of the Western Isle will not make open war. She will send her champion here to challenge you."

"Sir Marhaus?" Mark gagged. "God in heaven, he's the most ferocious fighter in the West!"

"And I have seen his ship," Merlin pressed on. "He is already on the way. He will say Cornwall should be the vassal of Ireland, not of Queen Igraine. He will call you to single combat, and by the laws of chivalry you may not refuse."

Mark gathered his scattered wits. "Queen Igraine!" he exclaimed. "We must march on Tintagel, to defend the Queen!"

Merlin frowned. "That is Arthur's concern. He is hastening here now with Queen Guenevere and a force of men. But Igraine is not in danger!" He struck the floor with his wand. "No knight will challenge an aged queen, and besides, Igraine is well accustomed to defending herself. No, your enemy will come here to Castle Dore. He plans to kill you, and take your throne!"

Mark tried to speak but could not. With a glance at his uncle, Andred leaned forward to take charge. Merlin could hear the young knight's mind darting like a fish. "Is there no way out?"

Dominian pursed his lips and filled the silence that ensued. "You may offer the invaders blood gelt for the life of the King. In the past, Cornwall has paid tribute to the Irish to keep them at bay."

"Yes, yes!" cried Mark. "Tribute—we can pay it! Cornwall is fertile and our lands are rich—"

"Sire"—Andred shook his head impatiently—"they would be back for more with every spring tide. That would only enslave us for years to come."

Mark's voice rattled in his throat. "Then in God's name, what can we do?"

Merlin waved a hand. "You may offer a proxy—a knight who will take on the battle in your stead."

"My knights, yes!" cried Mark. "Andred, who is there?"

There was a deep pause as the same thought went through every mind: no knight of ours could go against Marhaus.

Dominian raised a hand. "But ours are not the only knights in the land. Sire, you hold Cornwall from King Arthur himself. Send to him for help."

"Thank you, Father!" Mark straightened up in the grip of this happy thought. "Well, there's Sir Gawain, Kay, and Bedivere—who shall it be?"

Andred turned on him, scarcely masking his irritation. "Uncle, with Sir Marhaus on the way, we have no time!"

Merlin turned on Andred with a killing smile. "Well then," he said silkily, "it must be you."

Andred's eyes bulged. "I—"

"Never, Merlin!" cried Mark. "For God's sake, man, Andred's my nephew, my heir. Whoever has to die, it must not be him."

Never fear, Merlin chuckled to himself, your loving nephew has no wish to die. He drew a breath. "Sire, you say blood is blood. Sir Andred is your nephew on your brother's side. But had you not a sister who married the King of Lyonesse?"

Mark's soft eyes filled with tears. "My poor Elizabeth, yes. But you know she lost her life in childbirth long ago."

"Bringing forth a son?" prompted Merlin. "A son she called Tristan for the sorrow in which she died?"

Mark covered his eyes with his hand. "Gods above, Merlin, d'you think I could forget? But there was trouble at court and the boy went away. Tristan has been lost to me for years."

Merlin preened himself. "Tristan lost?" he cooed, relishing every word. "Not to me."

He was gratified to see Andred give a violent start. "Tristan lives?"

"And thrives," Merlin added with delight, "as a great warrior, and a man of might. Young as he is, he's famous for his skill."

"Tristan lives?" echoed Mark, stupefied.

Merlin's eyes glowed. "He handles a horse as if he were born in the saddle, and on foot he's at one with the woodland, where he hunts at will. And though he's as gentle as a child, he's a big man, and bold enough in combat to match Marhaus."

Mark leaned forward urgently. "Where is he, Merlin? Can you get him here?"

Merlin gave a lingering, yellow smile. "I can."

Andred stepped forward, a look of noble regret on his face. "God knows I wanted to take on this battle myself. But I am ready to yield the combat to him." With tears in his eyes, he knelt before Mark and reached for his uncle's hand. "All that matters is the life of my kinsman and King."

In tears himself, Mark leapt from the throne and crushed Andred to his chest.

"Why, there's a lad!" he wept. Over Andred's shoulder he threw Merlin a watery grin. "God has smiled on me, Merlin, no? With a nephew like this and young Tristan to come, Sir Marhaus will rue the day he ever came here."

Marhaus would rue the day . . . ?

Merlin stood in silence, gazing down the corridor of time. So might we all.

Mark's voice came caroling into his ear. "Get him here, Merlin, will you, no matter what?"

chapter 5

*I*reland *must not attack Cornwall.*

Goddess, Mother, make me strong now—

Isolde took a last breath of the crisp spring air and stepped out of the courtyard into the Queen's House. Ahead of her beckoned a bright space warmed by the evening sun, the oak floor gleaming with beeswax and a cheerful fruitwood fire burning on the hearth.

Brangwain came forward, shooing the maids away. "This way, my lady. I'll tell the Queen you are here."

Isolde nodded. "Thank you, Brangwain."

She moved into the chamber, scarcely noticing the lofty ceiling with its massive beams, the warm loam-washed walls, and the clusters of little swan lamps, sheltering their flames between upreared wings. But as Brangwain put her finger to her lips, ushered her into the inner room, and closed the door, she saw that all the windows were covered with heavy drapes, and her heart plunged. She knew what it meant when the Queen shut out the sun.

Oh, Mother, Mother, why do you suffer so?

When was it she first knew that the warrior queen, racing joyfully in her chariot round the field, or pitting her horse against the fleetest of her knights, was only one of the many souls that lived in her mother's fine frame? That the Queen's spirit could change as swiftly as a bird in flight, leaving those around her trailing in her wake?

And the lovers—how often had Isolde seen her radiant with love, rejuvenated with desire, hanging on the neck of a new companion of the throne? Then there would be music and dancing, with the haunting pipes wailing of grief and joy and the candles burning down to their sockets as long as the wine went around. Isolde sighed. How she had wished for that love herself when her time came!

Yet always there was the loss and the terror of loss, when the chosen one failed. Sir Nevin had betrayed the Queen with one of her own maids, brutally philandering under her very nose; Sir Fortis had rashly challenged the best of Arthur's knights and broken his neck in a joust, trailing the Queen's bright favor in the dust; Sir Turath had married another and fled the land; Sir Eilan . . .

From childhood she had wept with her mother, shared her fears, and shrunk from her public shame. And always she had known that this way of living and loving was not for her. The Queen had been eager to welcome her to the ranks of womanhood, pressing her to take a lover as soon as she could, but always Isolde resisted, though she hardly knew why. Now she thought of the procession of men trailing through her mother's bed chamber, and writhed with disgust. Not one of those knights had been worth the time of day.

And now Marhaus, Mother—

What has Marhaus done?

The room was as dark as a midnight cave. A lone torch sulked and sputtered against the wall. Slowly Isolde made out the tall figure facedown on the bed, abandoned to her grief. The Queen's chamber robes were as dusky as the shadows all around, and her hair lay tumbled in a cloud of amber and plum.

Isolde moved forward to take her mother's hand. Instantly she was a child again, betrayed by the familiar scent of bergamot, her mother's musky fragrance from the East.

Mother, you love all these men, why don't you love me?

I always love you, little one.

Why do you always leave me, then, to be with them?

There had been no answer then, and there would be none now. She forced herself to go on.

"Madam, come," she said strongly. "You are the Queen, the lady of the land. We all depend on you."

The Queen turned, anguished afresh to see her daughter's clear blue-green gaze and skin like a wild rose.

"Isolde, you don't know..." She fell back, clutching at her heart. "Goddess, Mother," she cried, "I can't bear this! Oh—oh, my love—"

Isolde took in the haggard, tearstained face and drew a breath. *This is the moment. Speak!* "Madam, it's said you will advance Sir Marhaus—send him to Cornwall—"

"Curses on Brangwain for betraying me!" the Queen cried, rearing up. "They warned me that all those from the Welshlands are Merlin's kin. Take her, then, let her serve you, I want her no more!"

"I shall be glad to take Brangwain as my maid," Isolde said firmly. "But Sir Marhaus—"

"What?"

"Why should he go to Cornwall? If you send him to make war, we offend the Old Ones, the Otherworldly keepers of the land."

"Wrong, Isolde!" The Queen threw her long legs to the floor and paced away furiously into the gloom. "We offend them far more if we keep our men idle here at home."

Isolde followed. "But why should we make new enemies, when we have old ones across the sea?"

"The wretched Picts?" The Queen gave a dismissive laugh. "Marhaus says their King is failing, and their Prince is a boy. We have nothing to fear from them."

"Mother, even the Romans feared the Painted Ones!"

"Listen to the child!" The Queen turned on her with alarming suddenness, then her snapping black eyes softened and she brought a tender hand to Isolde's cheek. "Little one," she said intently, "you must leave this to me." A pageant of emotions played over her long, mobile face. "One day you will be Queen here, the spirit of sovereignty and the mother of the land. Then you will know when to strike." Her voice hardened as her mood swung again. "And then you'll know that it's better to instill fear in others than to suffer it ourselves!"

Oh, Mother, Mother—"You sent me to Avalon to learn the faith of love, not fear."

The Queen wheeled around on her again. "Isolde, do you talk to me of love?" she cried furiously. "A miserable virgin—a girl who denies all the joy the Goddess gives?"

Isolde flushed with anger. "Mother, have a care—"

But the Queen raged on. "Gods above, every girl of your age on the island has seen her first Beltain by now! Every one has danced at the feast and lain down among the fires, watching and waiting for the stranger she can love."

Isolde's temper flared. "You call it love? Creeping to a bed on the bare hillside to lie with a man she has never seen before?" Her voice deepened. "You rule your body, Mother—I rule mine!"

The Queen's eyes glowed with an unearthly fire. "But, Isolde, to wake in the bracken with the man of the dream—a man from another country, tall and unsmiling in the dark. Maybe not even a mortal, but one of the Fair Ones themselves, hungry for mortal love. At Beltain, the doors of the Otherworld stand open, and the Fair Ones long to enter the circle of the Goddess as we do. And we creatures of earth add our vigor to Her struggles, as the Mother strives with the sun to be born anew."

Isolde stood transfixed. Suddenly she saw a mist rising, a ring around the moon, and a tall stranger shining in the night. *Goddess, Mother, bring me to my love—*

"And that's not all!" The Queen's voice came from very far away. "You refuse to take a lover here at court! How long has Sir Palomides courted you now? Any other girl would thrill to a Saracen knight, a king in his own land and a hero in ours. And still you rebuff him with your girlish ways and little frozen smiles." She strode around the chamber in increasing agitation, plucking at her gown. "I know what I must do! I shall hold a tournament and the prize shall be your hand. All the knights of chivalry will compete, and the worthiest will be yours."

"Madam, no!" Isolde cried. A strange sensation passed over her and she seemed to hear slow hoofbeats approaching down the avenue of time. Was that a mounted figure, the shape of a man? She brushed the sight away. "I will know my knight when he comes."

"Your knight is here!" The Queen seized Isolde's arm in a ferocious grip. "And you'll forget all about Marhaus when you mate with Palomides! You need a lover, since you're jealous of mine!"

Isolde met her mother's wild black eyes and did not flinch. "Hear me, madam!" she said passionately. "I wish you joy of Sir Marhaus, as I wished all your companions before. I know you must maintain your vigor, when your vital life is the life of all the land. A queen changes her consort for the good of all."

"So?" The Queen widened her eyes, then gave a tremulous smile. "Then you know more than I thought, Isolde."

"Champions fall, men grow older, flesh decays," Isolde pressed on furiously. "So we hold new championships, to let younger men triumph in their turn. As the Mother at Beltain renews herself with the young sun, the God Bel, so the Queen may restore herself at will."

The Queen's eyes were huge and luminous. "For the life of the people," she murmured dreamily.

She had to break into the dream. "But, Mother—a queen does not choose for herself. It may be her duty to renew the marriage of the sovereignty with the land by taking a new consort every year—"

Her mother stiffened. "Yes?" she said dangerously.

"—but a queen is married to her country, not to one man." She paused for emphasis. "She must choose for her country, not for the man she loves. If you send Sir Marhaus to Cornwall, that will not help us here in the Western Isle!"

"Isolde, enough!" the Queen raged. "Who is Queen here, madam, myself or you?"

Isolde shook her head. "We hold this island in a line of queens. Our foremothers had it from the Great One Herself. In Her name, we should not make this war." She raised her voice. "Sir Marhaus must not go!"

"Too late!" A peal of mocking laughter echoed around the room. "Marhaus has gone! He sailed on the evening tide!"

chapter 6

The high road lay open and shining in the morning sun. Ahead was a granite coast of soaring cliffs and ragged inlets, and the moist air was sharp with the tang of the surge below. A young knight was dreaming his way down the hill, singing along with the sea. Sometimes he heard sweet tunes on a fairy wind and wove them into fleeting melodies. But more often he sang his own songs of delight, especially on golden days like this.

Other days the sounds in his head were harsher and the music still and sad. The knight frowned, and a flurry of bleak thoughts chased one another across his well-made face. The life he had been living was hard, seeking gain and glory at foreign tournaments, living in camps or on the road, eating and sleeping with the worst and the best. But from his birth he had stood too near the sorrow at the heart of things.

At the foot of the hill the road dipped, then rose again to another mighty crag. His horse, a powerful gray, twitched his ears and fell into the rhythm of the song. To the right of them now the cliff dropped away to a sheltered cove, where the waves sighed and sobbed on the rocky shore. The knight saw the salmon leaping and the plump gray seals basking in the sun and his spirits rose again. "Tirra-lirra," he sang, "lirra-li."

The noonday sun shone on his silver helmet and the gold torque of knighthood round his neck. Across his back he carried a silver bow, with a silver quiver of arrows ready to his hand. Next to it hung a shapely silver harp just large enough to sit to the curve of his body when he played. His battle sword swung from his saddlebag beside a gold and silver shield, and he wore a slender ring of emeralds on the little finger of his left hand. His thick cloak was woven of summer green and gold, and his tunic was the color of ivy in winter when its black berries bloom.

Near the shore the road divided into two, one track leading inland toward the great bluff ahead, the other winding along the cliff above the rocks. At the fork in the road he saw a poor aged man in a ragged tunic and a cloak of flea-bitten fur, leaning on a staff of knotted yew. His legs were clad in bindings of rough cloth, and a beggar's bowl dangled from the cord around his waist. A tangle of wild gray hair spilled from his battered hood, and even in the spring sunlight, his withered arms were blue with cold.

The knight had traveled too far to take any stranger on trust, and his sword was never far from his right hand. But on closer acquaintance the old man seemed harmless enough.

"Greetings, old sir," he called, drawing up his horse. "Would you care to ride? If so, mount up, you need walk no further today."

The beggar turned, and from beneath the tangled mat of hair, the knight felt the shock of a glinting, golden gaze. With one bony hand the old man waved the offer away. "You come from Lyonesse?" he demanded brusquely.

The knight's fair face clouded. "Not recently," he said with pained reserve.

The old man craned forward, leaning on his stick. "So you have no news of the King's son—they called him Tristan, I believe?"

The knight stared. "I am Tristan, sir. Why do you ask?"

"No reason," returned the old man imperturbably. "But, meeting you, it came into my mind. Once I knew Lyonesse well, but I have not been there since the boy was born." He gave a courteous bow. "And boy no longer, I see, but a fine young prince. You have been traveling, my lord?"

Tristan nodded. "Across Gaul and down through France, following jousts and tournaments and deeds of arms." He gave a sardonic laugh. "I had a lot to learn."

"But you proved a great hero—success came to you?"

"Success?" Tristan thought of the days in the ring and the nights on the hard ground, the stink and the crowds in the camps and the screams of wounded men. "Perhaps. I cracked a few heads and won my share of the spoils."

"But you did not find a lady!" The old man cackled. "And a knight is nothing without a lady, just as a man is lost till he meets the woman of the dream?"

"Wherever she lies."

Suddenly Tristan had had enough of this. He straightened himself in the saddle and took up the reins. "Can you tell me, old sir, where this road leads?"

"Why, this is Tintagel, boy," the beggar cried. "Over that bluff lies the castle of Queen Igraine. The high road will take you there, but it's not for you." He pointed to the track along the cliff. "There lies your way."

With an effort, Tristan kept his irritation in check. "Sir, I go to Tintagel to pay my respects to Queen Igraine. Then I'm going on to find tournaments and feats of arms."

"You will, boy, you will. But before that—"

The old man raised his curious yew wand. There was a soundless stirring in the air and Tristan grew cold. "What do you mean?"

The beggar fixed him with a glittering eye. "There is a lady craves a word with you," he said abruptly. "And by your oath of chivalry, you may not refuse."

Gods above, would he never be free of the old man? Tristan drew a breath. "Refuse a lady? Never. But what does she want with me?"

The old man cackled. "She will show you where your pathway lies."

A woman who would show him where his future lay?

Tristan laughed aloud. Of course! She must be a fortune-teller, and this old man directed her trade! He'd seen these women at the tournaments, dark-faced Gypsy queens with dancing girls and music and all manner of good things. Well, why not? He might as well see her. He wouldn't get rid of the old beggar any other way.

He vaulted from his horse. "Show me."

The old man drew near, seizing Tristan's arm. "Leave your horse here," he commanded. "He will not stray. Then make your way down the face of the cliff. When you reach the sea, circle three times among the Maiden rocks and the way will open to you."

They had reached the edge of the cliff. The sea was pounding on the rocks below. Tristan felt the rushing, roaring wind, and looked up the high road to the world he knew. Beyond the great bluff lay a broad smiling plain, while dread and desire alike drew him down to the sea.

"Go, boy, go!" cried the old man tetchily. "The Lady of the Sea waits for no man."

"So be it." Tristan turned and, lowering himself over the edge, began to climb down the cliff face.

Shaking his head sorrowfully, the old man watched him go till the spread-eagled figure looked no bigger than a fly on a wall. Then the air shivered and changed shape as the ragged beggar became Merlin again, his golden eyes glowing, clad in his robes of power. Extending his arms, the old enchanter made the sign of grace in the air over Tristan's head.

"May all your Gods go with you, boy," he breathed.

Carefully Tristan picked his way down the trackless cliff. Halfway down, a small hawthorn tree clung to the furzy turf, blooming its heart out in blossoms of foaming white, and he rested there, braced against its knobbly trunk. As he went on, bright tufts of lichen, orange, black, and green, offered themselves to his grasp and he came across toeholds carved in the face of the rock. Nearer to the ground the cliff sloped and the climb became easier, till at last it felt like going backward down a rough flight of stairs. But still he was trembling in every limb by the time he reached the shore.

The tide was out, and a half-moon of wet sand was densely crowded with jagged, sea-washed rocks. A dozen or twenty, all higher than himself, clustered around a taller rock leaning back against the wall of the cliff, like maidens dancing attendance on the lady they served. Tristan smiled. So—three times among the Maiden rocks . . .

He began to circle, making his mind a blank. Around he went and around, till it seemed to him that the rock he had called the Lady was beckoning to him, leaning away from the cliff. Behind it he glimpsed a shadow, like the mouth of a cave. Moving forward, he threw a last glance around. A mighty sea eagle hovered overhead, and the air throbbed with the force of his clamorous wings.

Tristan stood for a moment, then saluted him with a solemn wave. Near the shore, a great salmon leapt in a shining arc to inspect him, and Tristan met his yellow eye and greeted him, too. Where the sea met the shore, he thought he saw female forms riding the white crests of the waves, laughing girls like mermaids slipping in and out of the foam, but he could not be sure. Yet still he felt bright eyes all around him and knew that whoever the Lady was, her sea courtiers guarded her well. With a swift prayer for their blessing, he slipped into the crack in the rock.

At once a dark tangle of boulders barred his way. Threading his way through, cursing his size and bulk, he found himself in a low tunnel leading into the side of the cliff, surrounded by a darkness like that of a tomb. Now he was wading through water, and the pebbly base of the stream was slipping beneath his feet. Losing his balance, he threw out a hand and his fingers met a slimy mass of seaweed on the wall. Cursing, he forced himself on.

He did not know how far he went into the dark, only that the crashing of the waves outside became a distant roar. Each time he thought he was there, the low passage turned and led him on again. But then he came to the end of the tunnel and could no longer doubt. Brightness surrounded him, and he found himself looking into places he had never dreamed of. He took a long breath of the warm, sweet air and his mind filled with the simple, joyful thought, *I have come to the place where the Fair Ones live.*

A great peace invaded his soul. He thought of the mother he had never known and it seemed to him that all his life had been tending toward this point.

Whatever it was, he was not afraid. "I am ready, Mother," he murmured, and stepped forward into the light.

chapter
7

The mounted troop rode slowly through the trees. The long procession, bright with lances and flags, had left the broad highway behind, and now followed a path through the heart of the wood. Overhead the dark pines had knotted themselves into a thick roof of spiny green, and the air beneath was stale and moldering after the fresh spring outside. A dank morning dew on the branches dripped onto horses and men, and through all the vast forest, not a bird sang.

At the head of the column, riding behind the King, Gawain shuddered and looked round. The eldest of the Orkney princes, Arthur's closest kin, Gawain proved his courage every time he took up arms. As well built as Arthur, and born with a rougher streak, he was the only knight who, in jousts and tournaments, could bring his great kinsman down. So he knew his fellow knights would not mistake his reluctance for fear as he pointed ahead. "Ye Gods, Kay," he growled, "what are we doing here?"

Kay sighed. He knew Arthur loved Gawain as the first of the knights who had rallied to his side when he pulled the sword from the stone, but that did not make Kay care for the big Orkneyman any more. As Arthur's foster brother, brought up with him from boyhood, Kay was quite sure who Arthur's first knight had been.

"You know as well as I do, Gawain," he snapped, his sallow face flushing with mild ire. "We're heading for Cornwall to relieve King Mark. And on the way, we're calling on Earl Sweyn."

Gawain shook his head. "But why?" he persisted. "He lives harmlessly here and we hardly know he's alive. Why turn aside from our road to flush him out?" His broad face brightened. "We should be in Cornwall for the battle there."

Gods, these beef-witted, blood-crazed Orkneyans! Kay held back a groan. "A king must know his lords if he's to keep the peace. Remember what happened as soon as King Uther died? All his lands were lost, and we had to fight to get them back."

"So!" Gawain nodded owlishly. "Earl Sweyn could be an enemy?"

"Who knows? But the King must take note of a large estate like this, midway between Cornwall and Camelot." He shrugged. "The Earl has a lot of tenants, Arthur says, so it's not clear who owns much of the land." He gave a sardonic laugh. "And that's as good a way as any for a landowner to get out of parting with the men and money that the King needs."

"To fight the Saxons," Gawain put in importantly, with the air of one who understands the game.

"Not only the Saxons." Kay suppressed the weary urge to turn over the conversation to the good-natured Bedivere riding at his side. "All the petty kings who still resist Arthur's rule, the rogue lords and knights, outlaws and masterless men—there's much to be done to restore peace in the land."

"So Earl Sweyn . . . ?" Gawain puzzled on. "He lives alone here in the depths of the forest with his daughter, they say—did he never bring her to court or to a tournament?" A misty look passed over the bright blue eyes. "I think I remember the name, once, long ago—Kay, you were there too, d'you remember it?"

Kay was saved by a sudden shout from the head of the line. "Castle Sweyn up ahead, sir, still a good way off. But the scout says we'll be there before noon."

Kay smiled sourly. "There you are, Gawain. The castle, the Earl, and doubtless the daughter, too—you can ask them yourself."

THE SUN HIGH in the sky, not a breath of rain, all the pathways clear now that spring had come—any man would be glad to ride out on a day like this. And any horse would be dancing about on its toes, snuffling the sweet air with delight at the chance of a gallop through the woods. Any except this sorry bunch of nags, dull-eyed and stark in the coat, hanging their miserable heads over their stable doors as if it were their last day on earth.

Yet what could he do? Cursing, the stable master patted the last hairy rump, and stepped out of the stable with a sense of defeat. This one had been the last hope and now it was gone. Bad enough to have no horse in the stable for any master, but worst of all for Earl Sweyn.

Trembling outside in the yard was the groom, a runt of a youth already too friendly with the Earl's heavy hand. Meeting the huge, fearful eyes in the pale, starved face, the stable master jerked his head toward the barn.

"Hop it, lad," he said not unkindly. "Make yourself scarce till the Earl's gone. The mare's lame, all right. No sense in letting him take it out on you."

Twitching like a rabbit, the boy bolted for cover and the stable master watched him go. Even the grooms here were the worst to be had. Oh, the place was fine enough for a king, with its handsome cobbled courts and an array of towers and battlements any lord would be proud to call his own. Only a man like Sweyn would think of trying to run a nobleman's castle like a tightfisted churl.

"Wake up, man!" came a harsh, cawing voice behind. "Where's my horse?"

"My lord?" The stable master turned as slowly as he dared. "Cast a shoe, sir, and torn her sole. She can't be ridden today."

"Cast a shoe?" The lean, choleric figure in front of him slapped his whip balefully against his boot. "She was shod only last week."

The stable master kept his gaze steady and made no response. Every lad in the yard knew that the Earl used the worst farrier for miles around, in his eternal quest to pinch a few pence. Only the best of everything for himself, of course—the finest leather for his boots, even for his whip, and burnt velvet for his habit with a rich cloak to match—not bad for a man who couldn't spare a farthing to keep a good horse on its feet.

The Earl read his silence and glowered, hunching his short body like a crow about to strike. "What about the gray?" he said menacingly.

"Spavined, sir. Like I told you, he shouldn't have been sent out in the fields."

"Well, the big bay then, that great useless brute!"

The stable master stared stolidly ahead. "Got the bots." He lifted his hand and began to count on the fingers of one hand. "The chestnut's shoulder-shotten and the gelding—"

"Shoulder-shotten, spavined, they'll have the staggers next! Keep your horse cant to yourself, dolt, and hold your tongue. Are you telling me there's no horse to ride today?"

"Yes, sir."

And that'll mean old Tom gets another night in the hovel where he's lived for the last forty years, thought the stable master with satisfaction, watching the same realization pass over the thin face with its beak of a nose, clenched mouth, jutting cheekbones, and cold black eyes. All the castle knew that the Earl was going to cast out the old herdsman and his wife and not a soul dared defend them for fear of sharing their fate. But the Gods had given them a reprieve today.

"My lord! My lord!"

It was one of the guard, running from the lookout tower. "There's a troop of men coming, sir," he cried, "a hundred knights and more, with a great lord at their head and a lady in white and gold."

The Earl stood thunderstruck. "What banner?"

"A red dragon rampant on a white ground—it's the King, sir, with Queen Guenevere!"

"King Arthur? Gods above, no!"

The Earl bunched his hands and bit back a scream. The King and a hundred knights, coming here? Blanching, he saw a month's provisions gone, every living thing slaughtered to fill a hundred hungry mouths. God's blood and bones, he might as well have a flock of gannets in the place.

His mind reeled. Desperately he tried to master his sense of doom. Think, man, think—

"Father!"

Raising his eyes, he shuddered and groaned again. Hurrying out of the main door of the castle was a figure in rose silk and velvet, her gown and veil streaming in the wind. "Father," she called, "is it true? The King and Queen coming here?"

"Lienore, not now!" he bellowed furiously. "Get back to your quarters, and stay there till they've gone!" If the King meets a family welcome, he groaned inwardly, we'll never get rid of him. "Go back, I tell you!" he screeched. "I want you out of the way!"

But the shapely figure did not check her stride. Shaking with rage, the Earl watched her coming on. How was it that he could make boys faint and soldiers weep, and have no control over this bitch of a girl?

Look at her now, he screamed silently, knowing that the stable master and the men-at-arms were watching her raptly, too, taking in the wide eyes, the moist lips and open mouth, the gown straining across the bobbing breasts—

"Get about your business, fools!" He scattered them with a snarl, fighting the urge to take after them with his whip.

Behind Lienore now he could see a waiting woman following her out of the doorway, with a child in tow. God's blood and bones! A fresh burst of rage battered at his heart. "Take the bastard away," he howled, "and lock him in his room!"

"Your grandson, Father!" Lienore returned with sublime indifference. "Your own flesh and blood."

She came to a halt before him, stroking down her rosy skirts. In repose her pink cheeks, delicate skin, and round, girlish eyes looked soft and cherubic, tempting to any man. But Earl Sweyn knew how deceptive her softness could be. His gaze turned to the boy, a tall, sturdy child of seven or thereabouts. "So it's not enough to bring a bastard home? You want to shame us now in front of the King?"

"I only did what every woman does," said Lienore. She raised her lovely eyes in an innocent look. "What your mother did to give birth to you."

Oh, the impudent slut! Earl Sweyn's fingers itched. If he hadn't known his departed wife so well, he'd have doubted this trollop could ever be his child. But he'd married Lienore's mother for her Christian piety, and got more than he expected, a wife unhappy from the first to come to his bed. Their struggles between the sheets had convinced her that sex with him was an unrepeatable sin, and as soon as Lienore was born she had withdrawn to a nunnery, where she lived to this day. Nothing he could say had been able to change her mind. And the girl gets that stubbornness from her, he thought venomously. But at least his wife knew who had fathered her child!

"My mother," he said with cruel emphasis, "had a ring on her finger when she lost her maidenhead. She didn't get so befuddled with drink she lay down with a stranger in a Gypsy's tent!"

"It wasn't drink," said Lienore, with what he would have sworn was a sly relish. "It was the fumes the fortune-teller raised." She closed her eyes. "Fumes," she repeated. "The rarest scent you ever smelled—"

"Fumes, you harlot?" He was yelping with rage. "I took you to that tournament to make a good match! I thought you'd come back with a husband for our house, not a babe in your belly and a cuckoo for our nest!"

Lienore reached out a velvet-covered arm and coolly plucked the child away from his nurse.

"He's not a cuckoo," she said carelessly, "he's a big fine boy." She tousled the child's thick, fair hair and treated the Earl to a smile every bit as cruel as his own. "Whoever his father was, he was a lusty lad. He could keep any woman happy all her life." Unlike you, Father, her innocent blue eyes said.

The Earl felt the child's bright gaze on him and suddenly did not care that his wife had left him and his daughter had proved a strumpet. His grandson was indeed a big, handsome boy, fair and open-faced, one any grandfather would be proud to call his own. The Earl secretly rejoiced that the lad had long, strong limbs, a clear gaze, and a fearless air, and nothing of his own dark, crow-like features and unimpressive build. When the time came—and now he was seven, it would come soon—the boy would leave the house of women to become a squire, a knight, and his grandfather's heir. And at that same time his dear mother, Lienore, to her great surprise, the Earl promised himself with a silent vengeful smirk, would find herself singing Hail Marys in the same nunnery as her mother, dispatched with an endowment large enough to make sure the good sisters kept her there all her life. He sighed with anticipation. Oh, it would be sweet, so sweet.

But until then ... He turned back to Lienore and composed his features into a contemptuous sneer. "You call him a fine lad, when the shame he's brought on us keeps us at home? When the King has to track us down here, because we can't go and pay our respects at court?"

She played with her veil, teasing out a small curl at her temple and smoothing it down beside her full, pink cheek. "You're not shamed, Father," she said with an easy shrug. "I know you. You're just too mean to take us all to court." She pointed a sly white finger over his shoulder to the yard behind. "Which is why they have come to you."

"What—?"

The Earl whirled round. At the foot of the courtyard, a great gatehouse gave onto the forest beyond. Coming through the trees was a troop of knights on horseback, escorting a finely dressed couple in royal red, white, and gold. Behind them came another body of knights and a war band of fighting men.

"Find the chamberlain!" he shouted at the dumbstruck nursemaid. "Tell him to scare up all the servants and get ready for the King!"

The procession was emerging from the forest and making its way up the castle mount with the King in the lead. The Earl stared like a man at the stake. Arthur's tall, broad-shouldered physique was finely displayed in a scarlet tunic and a gold cloak. His Queen was a perfect foil to the great bear-like shape, a womanly figure radiant in white and gold.

Now the glittering entourage swept into the courtyard, with Guenevere riding beside Arthur, a warm smile on her lips.

"My lord Sweyn," called Arthur, "forgive our unheralded descent. A war alarm calls us to Cornwall to relieve King Mark, and we would not pass by your lands without greeting you."

"You are most welcome, sire," the Earl cried with desperate gaiety. "You and your knights."

He nodded to the King's four companions and a new danger seized his unquiet mind. The sallow, sardonic Kay and the mild Bedivere did not trouble him, but the smiling Lucan was too handsome by far, and that brute Gawain was already eyeing Lienore with open interest on his beefy face. So! Earl Sweyn's gut tightened. Not only the boy but his loose-loined mother, too, would have to be put under lock and key till the visitors had gone—

"Father—"

He felt an urgent tugging at his sleeve. "Your Majesties," he pressed on, ignoring her, "will you feast with us tonight?"

"You and your daughter, I hope," returned Arthur courteously, bowing to Lienore.

Guenevere gave a kindly smile. "And is this your grandson?"

She signaled to the maid to bring the boy forward, and both the King and Queen leaned down from their saddles to make much of him.

"Father—" came Lienore's voice again, with a raw edge of excitement this time.

"Peace, will you?" Earl Sweyn hissed. "Sire," he called, "my poor house is yours."

Arthur bowed. "For this night only, my lord, then we must be on our way." He glanced round the castle, following Guenevere's gaze. "I look forward to hearing about your estate."

The courtyard was slowly filling with excited servants, the chamberlain at their head. The Earl watched Arthur and his knights and felt the first dawnings of pride. The King and Queen here, under his roof—it was the greatest honor to the house. The cost would be terrible, of course, but was not their family motto *Noblesse oblige*?

"Father—" came Lienore's tense whisper again.

Death and damnation, would the girl never cease? He turned, twitching with the urge to knock her down. But a cunning joy was written in her eyes and wide, knowing mouth. She pointed to Arthur as he lifted Guenevere down from her horse, and her head was nodding like a flower loose on its stem.

"It's him, Father," she said.

"What?" The Earl caught his breath. "Who?"

Lienore stared at him, excitement leaking from her like sweat. "The man at the tournament. The one who fathered my child."

chapter
8

Tristan stood in the mouth of the tunnel, hardly daring to breathe. Stretching before him was a great hall of gleaming rock with many chambers, each bigger than the last. A swift rush of water ran through the center of the cavern, finding an unseen passage to the sea. Torches of sea fire flickered round the walls in tongues of green and blue, and pillars of crystal rock held up the roof. Wreaths of white spindrift blossomed round the pillars, and an Otherworldly light shone everywhere.

He looked around in awe. As his eyes softened to the mystic light, he saw alcoves in the rock piled high with all the riches of the sea. Seaweed-hung chests spilled over with silver and gold, and gold chains and jewels lay in tumbling piles. His gaze roved over emeralds and sapphires alight with hidden fire, and rubies glowing with their own heart's blood. Scattered among them were branches of white and red coral, hoards of dusky jet, and pearls like angels' eyes.

Amazed, he ran his fingers over some of the stones. Here, a rainbow of glittering quartzes in yellow, mauve, and green; there, heaps of ambergris, filling the chamber with its distinctive scent. Who lives here? he marveled. Then he heard a sudden cascade of sound, a tinkling fall of notes above the torrent rushing through the hall, and there she was.

At the far end of the chamber, where the stream emerged from the cave wall, was a figure muffled in sea-like draperies from head to foot. Outlined against the black and gleaming rock, she seemed to float above the water around her feet. Her gauzy veil rippled with the rushing torrent, and her foaming robes ebbed and flowed with the roar of the sea. A moon-shaped diadem crowned her head, set with great pearls shading from midnight to dawn, and the mother of all pearls adorned the Goddess ring on her hand. She bore a wand of coral as red as a sunset at sea, an he knew then he was seeing the Lady herself.

The lofty shape raised her arms. "Sir Tristan, approach!"

As she spoke, it came to him that he had heard the low music of her voice long ago, at the dawn of time. As his sight cleared, he could see that the tall, still form was not floating on the water, but enthroned on a foam-flecked rocky platform in the midst of the stream. The air was full of the zestful tang of breaking water, and a slender shape rose like a fountain from its midst. The spray bejeweled her cloudy robes, and tiny drops of sea dew hung on her like diamonds on a queen.

Tristan found his voice. "Are you the Lady? She who sent for me?"

A tender chuckle took him by surprise. The mellow voice had seen all the seasons of life, and was rich with love. "Ah, Tristan, your fate brought you here. And that was written when the stars were young."

"But are you the Lady?" Tristan persisted, unafraid.

The veiled form inclined her head. "I answer to that name, but not alone. The Lady of the Lake holds Avalon, and the Lady of Broceliande keeps the lake in Little Britain, where Sir Lancelot was reared." He could hear the deep voice softening as she spoke. "They are my younger sisters on this plane of earth. The sea was here before the lakes were born."

It was more than Tristan could grasp. He looked around. "Where are we?" he demanded.

The gauzy figure held out her long, sinuous arms, embracing the teeming waters and the rocky cave. "In the womb of life—in the place where our race began. All our people once came out of the sea, and beneath its surging main lie the lands of youth."

"You are the Mother." A strange delight pierced him, bringing a warmth and sweetness he had never known.

"I serve the Mother," the Lady corrected gently. "But the Great One Herself is above us all. It was She who girded our world with the sea, and the great ocean is the circle of life itself. You entered the circle when She brought you here. She wishes you to go to Castle Dore."

Tristan tensed. "The castle of my uncle King Mark?"

The Lady nodded. "And your cousin Andred, your mother's brother's son. You have not seen King Mark for many years, but he has never forgotten his sister's son. If you choose, you may do him a dear service now.

He is under a challenge he cannot win, while your deeds of arms are known far and wide."

"So I may take this battle on—defeat his opponent and restore peace to the King?" Tristan's eyes glowed like moons, and he felt an animal power surging through his veins. "Lady, thank you," he said abruptly. "When I went away from Lyonesse, I never meant to lose my only kin. I must go to King Mark now!"

"Then go with this."

The Lady gestured toward the stream flowing around her feet. Tristan saw a long shining shape borne along on the torrent, a great sword in a scabbard of gold, richly engraved and emblazoned with the signs of power.

The deep autumnal tones rang around the cave. "Take it, Tristan. It was sent for you."

He plunged into the stream. He did not feel the shock of the ice-cold water, only the strange warmth as the scabbard came to his grasp. Seizing it with both hands, he hauled himself back onto the rocks and, trembling with joy, drew the sword from its sheath.

In his hand lay a weapon such as warriors only dream of. It was a massive broadsword, worked to perfection by Otherworldly hands, with a deadly sheen and an edge keening for blood. The hilt was set with all the stones of the sea, cabochons as pale as pearls and jasper and agate gleaming like salmons' eyes. A skein of crooked marks ran down the blade. *My name is Glaeve,* he saw written in runic script. *She who was and will be sent me to you.*

"Glaeve!" he murmured, entranced. Reverently he passed it through the air, and could hear the sword humming in a high, etherial tone. He brought the blade to his lips in a cold kiss. "Welcome, brother. You are mine till death."

The Lady's voice now was like the roaring of the sea. "The Goddess has sent you a sign. Take it, and do good."

"Lady, I shall!" Tristan cried. "Give me your blessing and I'll be gone!"

His pulse was racing, and he was on fire to leave. But a deep sigh drew him back.

"Hear me, Tristan. Ahead for you now lie the two great trials of a man, the fear of loss in battle, and the death of the heart. You must fight a great champion, and only one of you will see the sun rise again. You will find a great love that leaves you dead to all else, and will have to face every day love's killing hurts."

She paused, and he felt her spirit grow till all the cavern resounded with her words. "To face a man in combat is challenge enough. To find the Goddess in a woman is the life work of a man. Hard though the first may be, the second is the harder, longer road. But every man seeks the woman of the dream, and only the best of men finds what he seeks."

Tristan drew a deep breath. "I shall not fail," he said.

There was a sigh like the moaning of the sea. "Ah, Tristan, only the Mother never fails. All of us leave this world on the evening tide. Then we come again when the tide is full and free."

Tristan's heart quailed. "Lady," he cried in anguish, "how shall I be worthy of the task?"

"Do not fear." Her voice was blending now with the surge of the sea, and the lights in the cavern were dimming with every word. "You will come to the place of terror and find miracles."

"Lady!" He tried to speak and could not. The thought of leaving filled him with nameless pain. Would he ever return to this sacred place again?

"Take heart, Tristan."

The cavern was darkening, and the great figure was fading before his eyes. "Remember the Mother is with you wherever you go."

Her spirit surrounded him as the stream boiled and bubbled around her, and he felt the cold kiss of the spray. "Go then in grace and strength. But hurry—hurry! For the last wave is coming that will bear us all away!"

chapter
9

*A*lmighty God, bless the work I do this day. . . .

Father Dominian stepped out of his narrow cell and crossed the walled enclosure at a rapid pace. Dawn already, and a tender summer sun, as pink and perfect as the inside of a rabbit's ear—where had the night gone? He rubbed his aching eyes and quested on. After thirty years, he no longer saw the other small stone cells clustered around, the long refectory that served the brothers' needs, and the proud new church at the center of it all. This was his world. The community was all.

Across the grassy enclosure a fine stone gateway led to the world outside. His pupil was waiting for him by the gate, a young monk who bowed when he saw Dominian, then fell in beside him without a word. Dominian nodded, pleased. Simeon's gentle manner hid a fiery soul, burning with devotion to the Lord. When his time came, he would spread the word of God like a row of flaming crosses on every hill.

Together they passed through the gates and plunged into the woodland, thickets of ancient oak, holly, and dark yew so dense that they often had to force their way through. At last Dominian saw ahead of them the low stone housing of a sacred well. Behind it was a moldering clump of stones, a lonely hermitage, encrusted like the well with bright green moss.

"Wait here," Dominian said and ducked into the cell.

The small domed chamber was too low to stand. Dominian eased his misshapen frame down onto his haunches and squatted with his back against the wall. Slowly his eyes grew accustomed to the gloom. One slit window admitted a little light, and a rambling sunbeam picked out a low pallet in the corner of the hard-packed earthen floor. Beside it stood a beaker of water, and a wooden cross hung over the door.

Dominian breathed deeply and allowed the damp peace of the place to seep into his soul. *Quam delecta, Domine, domus tuas.* . . . How amiable are Thy dwellings, Lord God of Hosts. . . .

Ahead of him, a frail ancient sat cross-legged on the ground, his sightless gaze turned toward the door.

"God bless you, Father," Dominian said fervently.

"And you, my son."

The old man's voice had the dry rustle of a cricket's song, and the hands he clasped in prayer were skin and bone. His monkish robe was worn and green with age, and his face was washed with cold. But a radiant joy shone from his milky eyes, and he smiled like one who has seen the kingdom of God.

The very sight of him soothed Dominian's soul. "I am going to King Mark," he ventured after a while.

The old man nodded, "May God advance your work."

"He does." Dominian allowed himself a grim smile. "Cornwall is ours—we have won the King's soul." A soul hardly worth having, he reflected, but where a king leads, his subjects must follow too.

"You have brought him to God?" the old man asked, excitement lending a tremor to his voice. "After a lifetime of following the Mother?"

The Mother . . .

Dominian felt the age-old fury convulse his bones. How could these pagan fools believe in a Creator called the Mother, when She spawned monsters like him? When he was born, his mother was sure she had lain with a demon, to throw such a black and wizened, ugly, misshapen child. She had reared him with kicks and curses and kept him like a dog, forced to feed on scraps and sleep with the strays by the fire. The Mother? When he was seven, his own mother had driven him from the house and left him weeping in the woods, praying to die.

But then the old holy man had found him and told him that there was a Father in heaven who loved little ones like him. He had fought like a cur, biting and kicking till he had no more strength, and still the old holy man held him lovingly in his arms.

"My name is Jerome," he had said gently. "We shall call you Dominian, for your first task is to achieve dominion over yourself. And then perhaps over others in the name of the Lord." The old man had reverently made the sign of the cross on his forehead, and at his touch, Dominian had grown quiet and fallen still.

Later, old Jerome taught him that his hunchback and his never-ending pain marked him out as one of God's chosen, destined for a special place around His throne. Jesus Himself meant abandoned boys like him when he said, "Suffer little children to come unto me, for of such is the Kingdom of God." From then on, the lost child had become old Jerome's pupil and later the first priest of his church, on fire to build the kingdom of God in this land. And now their community was known in Rome itself as a center for pilgrims and all men of faith.

Dominian reached for Jerome's hand, and brought it to his lips. "Guide me, Father," he said urgently, "for great things are stirring in the kingdom, and I must guide the King. The champion of Ireland is coming to demand the throne, and Merlin has promised us a knight who is nowhere to be seen."

"Ireland," the old man pondered, "where they keep the Old Faith. Where their queens listen to their Druids and they follow the Mother-right. Where we have made little headway." The same thought hung in the air between them both: If the champion wins, we shall be swept into the sea.

"Ireland, yes!" Dominian snorted. "Where even their Christianity is tainted by pagan thought and rotten to the core. We must root them out and impose the rule of Rome."

The old man raised his head. "In my Father's house," he said gently, "there are many mansions. These are the words of the Lord."

Dominian shook his head. "The faith of the Celts," he said with heavy emphasis, "is too close to the old power of women and the rule of queens." He gave a mirthless laugh. "Not a man among them can dictate to a woman, or expect her to follow God's law. They are all daughters of Eve, born to sin."

The old man inclined his head. "Yet Our Lord was born of woman."

"Yes indeed." Suddenly Dominian had an overwhelming urge to be gone. He struggled to his feet. "Farewell, Father."

He stooped for the old man's blessing, placed a kiss on the wrinkled forehead, and came out into the light, beckoning to the young monk waiting patiently there.

"Hurry, hurry," he snapped irritably, striking off down the path.

"Yes, Father." Simeon knew better than to take offense.

Doggedly Dominian led the way through the wood, making for the high road to Castle Dore, immersed in his own thoughts. "Could he be one of us?" he burst out.

"Sir?" Simeon was used to questions such as this.

"If this knight Merlin promised us comes," Dominian brooded on, "the King's nephew—if he exists." He gave one of his savage laughs. "But Druids have no conception of the truth. Merlin probably dreamed him up from some moldy tale."

"Sir Tristan?" Simeon ventured. "But even if he does, will he defend the King? Coming from Lyonesse, surely he'll follow the Goddess?"

Dominian showed his teeth in a nasty laugh. "The Great Mother, yes. The old whore we are driving from the land."

"As soon as we have taken Her ways for our own?"

Dominian frowned. "What d'you mean?"

An earnest student of both history and the modern world, Simeon had been waiting for the moment to bring this up. "Did not the first Christians take over the apparatus of the Mother?" he began importantly. "Her threefold incarnation of Maiden, Mother, and Wise Woman, is that not what people in those days called the Holy Trinity?"

Dominian paused. "This is not something to share with the common folk," he said carefully. "We teach them that God the Father was here before all things."

"But our Communion, too," Simeon pressed on. "At the feasts of the Mother, the Lady is the loaf giver to all who come and pours wine from her loving cup with her own hand. When we offer bread and wine, haven't we taken this from the first power of the Lady, to feed and to provide?"

"The Lady, yes." Dominian's face set. "The great priestess of the Great Whore."

Simeon stared at him ardently. "Father, has any man seen the Lady of the Sea?"

Dominian saw the boy's longing in his eyes. "Never!" he breathed. "Nor do we want to see the wretched hag." He drew a breath. "But we hear much of the riches in her secret hoard. Now if only we could get hold of these for the Church..." His dark face lit up, and for a moment the eyes of coal caught fire. "Think of the jewels, the rings, the gifts we could present to Rome—if that did not buy us the Pope's favor, nothing would!"

Simeon stifled a gasp. God in Heaven, what a leader Dominian was! No man on earth knew where the Lady was to be found. Some said she lived beneath Castle Dore, others swore she ruled in Tintagel from a great cave. But Dominion meant to work on the weak King Mark and through him on Queen Igraine till he tracked down the Lady to her lair. And when he found her, there would her treasure be, too.

Simeon's soul took flight. And I can be God's humble instrument in this great work, ordained to serve a man of vision, a true father of the Church.

Dominian's harsh voice thundered in his ear. "Do you hear me, boy? We must take from them all they have. Not only their wealth, but their feasts and festivals, too."

The young monk started. "What, all of them, Imbolc, Samhain, and Beltain?"

Dominian tensed. His mother had gone to the fires of Beltain every year, taking the way of the Goddess to ensure she had no sons. Whoever had fathered him had broken the spell, and his mother had cursed him as the runt of a litter of fine girls.

"Beltain above all!" he spat. "D'you think we can tolerate the feast of the Great Whore, when the people warm the hills with fire and flowers? When every woman has the right of thigh-freedom to lie with any stranger of her choice?" Venomously he resumed. "No, in God's name we must root out the Beltain feast. Our Lord teaches that we must bring women under the control of men. Remember that all women would be whores if they could."

His master's voice was shaking, Simeon noticed, and he wondered why. But could it be true that all women were whores? "Sir, Father Jerome says that Jesus loved the Magdalen, and found room for both Martha and Mary in His heart."

Dominian heaved a black sigh. Saint though Jerome was, the old man had only a primitive vision of what the Church might do. He believed in love and comfort, when the task was to seek mastery over all benighted souls and dominion over all the world.

Dominion...

The monk's spirits lifted. This was what he had been named for, and what he would achieve. He had willing instruments like young Simeon here, and a lifetime ahead to teach the lad all he needed to know. He cocked an eye at the sun. They had a long walk ahead to Castle Dore, and time was on their side. He cleared his throat. "Regarding women, St. Paul teaches us ..."

chapter
10

The woodland lay before them like a dream. Through the thickets ahead, clusters of golden sunbeams dappled the path. Delicately the two mares picked their way under the trees, careful to avoid the low branches now in full midsummer leaf. Hearing the white doves calling in alarm, Isolde turned to give Brangwain a smile. The forest was giving warning of their approach.

Along the path, ivy and honeysuckle brightened each mossy trunk, and clusters of white trefoil spangled the grass like stars. Tiny insects danced and sang under the trees, and all around them the warm air pulsed with drowsy life. Isolde loosened her reins to give her horse its head. *All may yet be well.*

The woodland path wound onward through the trees. The soft loamy scent of the forest floor rose to meet them with every pace of their horses' hooves, and the peace of the place began to work on Isolde's soul. Already her mother's revelation seemed less terrible than before. And nothing would shake the strength of her belief. *A queen is married to her country. She does not choose for herself.*

True, true, cooed the white doves overhead.

You are right, said the bright eyes of the hare at the side of the path.

Courage, little mother, hold fast, whispered the old oak tree overhead as the silver birches giggled and tossed their heads. Isolde nodded, and thanked them from her heart.

With a tremor she felt her horse pick up its pace. And there it was at the end of the path ahead, the clearing of the Goddess, a pure circle of sunlight amid the dark oaks. Here the Druids came at midwinter with their silver sickles to cut the golden bough. And here in the sacred grove was the man she sought.

Softly the horses padded forward into the glowing pool of gold. The whole forest fell silent as the sacred glade welcomed them in. Isolde looked around, dazzled by the noonday sun. Slowly she made out a lofty figure standing motionless beneath the trees, his dark-dyed robes blending with the shadows around.

She dismounted, passed the reins to Brangwain, and crossed the sunlit clearing to the darkness beyond. In this sacred place, Isolde knew, the Chief Druid spent his days in fasting and prayer, seeing visions when the Shining Ones came. Here he led the worship of the Great One, and taught the young Druids to follow in his steps. Here he lived alone, and for the hundredth time Isolde wondered why.

Many of the girls of Dubh Lein cast eyes at the handsome Cormac, and there was no reason why he could not take a wife. Christian priests were forced to live celibate for their God, but Druids lived to celebrate the joys the Goddess gives. With his long, lean frame and his deep-set dark blue eyes, Cormac could have had the heart of any woman alive. But the Great One of the Western Isle was his only love.

He stepped forward to greet her with a searching look, and his beauty filled her eyes. A Druid band held back his thick black hair and his pale face glowed like a flower in the forest when nothing else is by.

"Welcome, Princess. You have brought a great trouble, I see."

She knew he could read minds with the same skill as he divined the secrets of the stars. She nodded.

"The Queen has sent Sir Marhaus to claim Cornwall as her own. Can you advise her? Make her change her mind?"

A smile of terrible sadness crossed his face. "Ah, lady, only Sir Marhaus can do that."

"But a queen may not choose for herself," Isolde said stubbornly. "You are her Druid. You can tell her so, she honors the old ways."

Cormac threw back his head. "Princess Isolde, the old ways are changing faster than you know," he said tensely, his midnight eyes fixed on hers. "In ancient times, when a queen took a new consort, the man she discarded was given to the Gods. The old priests hung him on a tree for three days and nights, then took his manhood with their golden knives. Afterward his blood and his flesh, his seed and his sex were given together to enrich the earth."

Isolde turned her face away. She had heard such things.

"They did this every year." Cormac pressed on, ignoring her. "Then it became three years, and then seven, before the King must die. Now the chosen one lives on as part of the warrior band, and all the world knows that a queen must have her knights." He paused. "That is all your mother knows."

"But surely you can make her understand!"

"Your mother understands one thing only, her own will and desire," the Druid said passionately. "Think of yourself now, Princess. When a star falls, those who hold on may go down to the darkness too."

Isolde felt a breath of fear and with it a strange wind from the Otherworld. *If I had a knight to defend me, a true love of my own—*

"Ah, Princess..."

A white dove was singing in a distant glade. She looked up to see Cormac's slate-blue eyes burning like sea fire. "Already you know what it is to be a queen. Soon you must learn what it is to be a woman, too."

Feverishly she turned her father's ring on her hand. "When I find love, you mean?"

There were tears in his eyes, and his face glistened with pain. "True lovers may never know what love means. A man may love a woman out of his reach. She does not know he loves her, and he will never speak of it."

A woman out of his reach?

A dull shock exploded in Isolde's brain. *He loves my mother!* came to her with the force of a sudden blow. *And she does not know!*

But surely, if he told her— She laughed aloud. *Gods above, my mother and Cormac—how wonderful that would be!*

A wild hope invaded her heart. "Lord Cormac, it lies in your power to save us!" she cried out. "If you love the Queen, you must marry her. You could stop Sir Marhaus from attacking Cornwall, and keep our country from making war—"

"Lady, lady—" Cormac shook his head and turned away. "I beg you—no more—"

He was weeping, she saw with a sudden shock. What had she said? A random breeze chilled the summer air and understanding came to her in a great wave. *He does not love my mother. He loves me—and I do not love him....*

She could hardly speak. "Cormac, I—"

"No words."

He held up his hands, palms outward, in a gesture of defeat. The Druid mark was pulsing between his brows. "Some men are fated to dwell forever outside love's house, and never know the enchanted place within. My love is always broken torchlight, shining where it is not felt. Farewell, Princess. Think of me in your prayers."

Step by step he withdrew under the trees. His parting words reached her from far away.

"Have faith, lady. Trust to your knight."

A strange agony seized her and she shuddered from head to foot. "I have no knight!" she cried.

There was no reply. The evening birds were calling through the trees, and the earth was softly breathing out the dews of night. Cormac was lost to sight, part of the woodland again, no more than a deeper shadow in the forest shades. She turned away.

A last farewell whispered through the trees. *Trust to your knight. He will come to you.*

chapter 11

In the King's private chamber, the air was dank with fear. The side tables were loaded with food, but no one could touch it, though noon had come and gone. Shuffling on his throne, throwing glances of desperation around, King Mark eyed his advisers resentfully.

"In the name of God," he moaned, "Merlin promised us a champion! Why doesn't he come?"

Father Dominian hunched his black shape forward, like a spider preparing to strike. "Druids are dream weavers, sire. Merlin must have lied."

"Or the knight he promised us may be dead," Andred put in, furrowing his brows with concern.

"Where's Merlin himself, then?" lamented Mark, nervously shifting his ungainly legs around. "There's Marhaus at our gates, Merlin nowhere to be found, and no hope of a knight to take Marhaus on!"

There was a silence as all three men relived the horror of recent days. First the dark sail in the channel, then the great ship looming larger as it neared Castle Dore. Next a grim war band of Irish knights marching up from the quay, and at last the appearance of the Queen's champion himself.

Mark's gut twisted with shame. Why was it that the very sight of the knight from the Western Isle had robbed him of what little courage he had? Was it the champion's powerful, threatening frame, his dead eyes, his hideous array of weapons or his slow, predatory stride? None of these, Mark decided in the misery of fear, but his white, wolfish smile. Here was a man who would kill because that was his nature, and his pleasure, too.

The champion came to a halt at the foot of the throne. He threw Mark a glance of pure contempt, then his scornful cry went ringing around the court.

"Vassals, today a new ruler claims you for her own. The Queen of the Western Isle offers Cornwall her full protection and a mother's love. You will pay tribute to her from now on, and take her as your new sovereign and Queen."

Mark bit his knuckles as he remembered it, stifling a low moan. The champion had challenged in a loud, manly voice, and he could answer only in the accents of a fool.

"We have a sovereign lady," he had blustered in a voice not his own, "our Queen Igraine. She holds the land for her son, King Arthur himself. And he'll be on his way here now, I promise you that!"

"The High King himself!" cried Marhaus mockingly, rolling his eyes. "Then pray to your Gods, sir, that he gets here in time. I shall renew this challenge for three days. If no man answers me, your land is mine by the rules of war."

Three days—and this was the third. What hope was there now? Already his barons had left him in disgust and taken to their estates, vowing to defend their own lands if the King could do no better than this. Their leader, Sir Nabon, had talked angrily of Mark's father, openly wishing the old king were still alive. With a groan, Mark recollected himself and struggled to cut a more regal figure on the throne.

"So, lords," he ventured as boldly as he could.

Outside the window the harsh clatter of a raven sounded through the air. A raw panic leaped up and gripped Mark by the throat. "What time is it? The champion must be here!"

Andred started. "Not yet, uncle, I swear!"

But he will come.

Standing with Simeon beside the throne, Dominian folded his hands inside the sleeves of his gown and began a silent prayer. *Saepe expugnaverunt, Domine . . .* Many a time, O Lord, have they fought against us, all Your enemies. . . .

He bowed his head. Dear God, Lord of Hosts, he went on humbly, You did not choose to make me a fighting man. But spare us from this swordsman of the pagan Queen. Send us a miracle, Lord, large or small.

"Sire!" There was a flurry at the door.

"Marhaus!" howled Mark, covering his eyes with his hand.

"No, sire," came the voice of the chamberlain. "But a stranger knight begs to see you—shall we let him in?"

THE HEAVY OAK doors rolled back on their iron tracks. Tristan looked in, his hope rising with every beat of his heart. Within the chamber the sun was pouring through the windows, bathing the occupants in rays of light. Slowly he made out a king, a knight, and a priest on the dais at the far end, and the gilded shapes dazzled his eyes. *Blood of my blood,* throbbed joyfully through his veins, *my mother's brother the King and my cousin the knight, both my own kin. And a man of God, to share faith with us all.*

Now he saw the rosy fire on the hearth, the rich furnishings, the side tables laden with welcoming food and wine, and his heart soared. *Goddess, Mother, praise and thanks for this.*

How had he come here? He hardly knew. He had scrambled back up the cliff and mounted his horse, his body moving without volition while his mind raced with all that he had seen. At Castle Dore he hardly saw the fine white walls and thriving little town, so busy was his soul on the astral plane. Only when he entered the King's chamber and saw its three occupants waiting for him did his roaming mind and body come together as one.

He fixed his eyes on the King and stepped forward with a bow. "I hear you face a mortal challenge, sire," he said boldly. "Grant me to answer it, and I shall redeem your land!"

"Sir?" Gaping, Mark looked the newcomer up and down. With a wild surge of relief he took in the towering height and exceptional physique, and knew that this knight could hold his own with any man. A moment later he saw that the knight's broad shoulders and strong frame made him look older than he was. The young man carried himself like a seasoned warrior, but a powerful innocence lit his bright brown eyes and the same sweetness shaped his full, wide mouth.

The eyes—the mouth—

"Who are you?" he gasped, though he already knew.

"I am the son of your sister, who died in the forest giving birth to me."

"Young Tristan?"

Weeping, Mark heaved himself out of his throne and folded Tristan to his chest. "God in Heaven, Nephew, but you are welcome to me!" He held Tristan at arm's length and looked him up and down. "Oh, poor Elizabeth, how you remind me of her!" His lips trembled, and his eyes filled again with tears. "Did you know she was my twin? The best part of me died with her. Now God has sent her back to me in you!"

Awkwardly Tristan drew back. He could see the dark-haired knight beside the throne eyeing him with an impenetrable stare. He had hoped for a warmer welcome from his cousin than this.

"My lord—" he began.

"And I thought I'd lost you," Mark rushed on, "after that terrible business in Lyonesse. God Almighty," he burst out in sudden rage, "when your father married again, why did he make such a dreadful choice?"

Tristan looked away. "My stepmother was a princess of the blood."

"From Little Britain, wasn't she? Well, they're all false, the French!" cried Mark. "He should have married one of our own. No woman of Lyonesse would have tried to poison you so her own son could be king." He gave an angry laugh. "But you were the one who had to go away."

"I could not stay at court when they were reconciled," Tristan said with an unmistakable note of reserve and pain. "I was too much of a reminder of all they had to forget."

"But you saved her life!" Mark swung a clumsy punch at Tristan's arm. "Quite a hero—after what she did to you."

Tristan's head went back in unconscious dignity. "Any man would have done the same."

Mark bared his teeth in an unpleasant grin. "Not I."

Tristan stared. "But surely, sire, a woman—a queen—should never be killed?"

Mark returned his stare. "Even when she tried to kill her husband's son?"

Tristan shook his head. "Woman is life and the source of life," he said decisively. "And under the Great One, every woman is a Goddess and a queen."

Oh, you young fool! Fastidiously adjusting his gown, Dominian observed Tristan with pitiless contempt. Every woman is a witch, my son, as you will find out.

Mark slapped Tristan's shoulder approvingly. "You have a good heart, nephew, I'll say that." His slack face hardened. "But if I'd been your father, I'd never have pardoned her." Something dark and cruel played at the back of his eyes. "Death by fire would have been a merciful end. A queen of mine who betrayed me would fare far worse."

Tristan stood still. For a long moment he felt the earth falter in its course and a shadow of the future darkened his path. What is this? he chided himself. Mark had no queen. And any queen of Mark's could be nothing to him.

"My Lord—" he began.

But Mark had launched onto another tack. "Your mother loved you," he said mournfully, clutching at Tristan again, "and God knows how your father loved her!"

Tristan felt an ancient pain tighten round his heart. "My nurse told me that when she died he laid her to rest in her wedding gown."

"With a garland of May blossom round her head." Mark nodded owlishly, like a great boy. "She looked..." His mouth twisted and the words tailed away, before a fresh idea set him off again. "You should have been called after me, did you know that?"

Tristan started. "No, sire."

Mark puffed out his hollow chest. "But Elizabeth called you Tristan before she died. And your father was true to that last wish of hers."

Dominian gave young Simeon an almost imperceptible nudge. "Mark will favor Tristan over Andred now," he murmured without moving his lips. "To those of the Old Faith, a sister's son is a man's closest kin, since in the old world, women always took precedence over men." A thin smile curved the edges of his mouth. "God has corrected that gross error now, of course."

"Nephew!" Mark took a step back and seized Tristan by the shoulders. "You are here in our hour of need. The Queen of the Western Isle has challenged us for the throne."

Tristan threw back his head. "I will take the challenge on."

A pang of conscience plucked at Mark's heart. God forgive him, was even his kingdom worth his nephew's life? "He is a fearsome fighter," he said in sudden dread.

Tristan smiled grimly. "Never fear, sire, I have met many such."

"God Almighty Himself has brought you back to me!" Mark blurted out. "And I'll treasure you as the son I never had. You'll save me, Tristan—I know you won't fail!"

A strange sensation knocked at Tristan's heart. "Uncle," he forced out. "Every man fails—"

"Sire! Sire!"

A trembling servant flew through the door. "The Irish knights are here, in a great band. They say the champion awaits you on the meadow beside his ship. If no man answers his challenge, then your throne is forfeit and our kingdom falls into his hands!"

Mark raised his head. "We are ready." He stepped forward with awkward dignity and took Tristan by the arm. "Nephew, come. Your enemy is here."

chapter
12

The meadow was sweet with tender buds of May, daisies and butter-cups blinking in the sun. Beyond the level green they could see the river winding inland from the sea, and the ship from the Western Isle moored at the dock. In happier times, Tristan knew, this field must be home to the town market and its busy, crowded stalls, peddlers of all kinds, and Gypsy travelers who beguiled the townsfolk with their dark faces and exotic ways, then disappeared as mysteriously as they had come.

Already the townsfolk were streaming out of Castle Dore, as word of the challenge ran through the narrow streets. A troop of Irish knights were waiting at the far side of the grassy space, all armed for war. With the flag of the Western Isle flying overhead and every man glittering in silver from head to foot, they were a fearful sight, and the champion in their midst looked the fiercest of all.

So! Tristan paused for a moment to return the knights' war-like stares, then with King Mark at his side and a bevy of pages and squires in attendance behind, took up his stand at the side of the field. Already, he noted grimly, his opponent had staked out the place of advantage with his back to the sun. He felt the blood coursing through his veins. So be it, then! It was time to take arms.

The leading squire helped Tristan into a gleaming ox-hide tunic, its blood-dark surface inlaid with gold wire. Next to it a squire held up a great shield of golden-brown bronze, while a page brought forward a helmet shaped like a hawk about to strike.

Mark reached out to touch the bronze feathers of the bird, shudder-ing at its fierce emerald eyes. "Your father equipped you well," he said admiringly.

Tristan smiled. "These are my own arms, sire," he said. "Won by knighthood and the rules of war."

Mark's eyes widened. Only a great warrior would have arms as fine as these. To win such treasures, Tristan must have beaten the very best. So young, and already a fighter of such grace . . .

A primal jealousy stirred in Mark's deepest heart, and he could have cried out with pain. The next moment he forced himself to stumble out a blessing as Tristan picked up his weapons for the fray. "God speed you, nephew! May a thousand angels ride on the point of your sword."

"Sire."

Bowing, Tristan turned to face his enemy advancing down the field. Marhaus's shield bore the Queen of Ireland's crest, a pair of fighting swans with a trefoil above. The champion's silver helmet was adorned with great swan's wings, and his body was protected by plated armor of silver and gold. In his right hand he carried a massive broadsword, and two short stabbing daggers swung from his belt. From his silver-tagged boots to the thick gold torque round his neck, it was clear that the Queen of the Western Isle had equipped her knight like a king.

Marhaus swaggered to a halt.

"King Mark!" he cried, his eyes bright with scorn. "Is this your champion, the lad that rode in with the harp on his back?" He swiveled his gaze toward Tristan, and grinned through his open visor like a shark. "What are you doing here, boy?" He gave a jeering laugh. "Get back to your country, while you still can."

"Sir Marhaus!" Tristan grinned back, and felt an almost sexual stirring in his loins. He knew the very accents of this boast and would enjoy taking his loudmouthed opponent down. "On behalf of the King of Cornwall, I accept your challenge," he cried out. "And if I win the day, I shall spare your life."

"No quarter!" came Marhaus's harsh reply. "I fight to the death."

Tristan paused. He had not expected this. "Sir, this challenge of yours is not worth your life."

Marhaus's eyes widened in disbelief. "You will not kill!" he cried, crowing with delight.

Tristan raised his voice. "My vow of chivalry means I choose life, not death!"

"The man who has never killed is a virgin!" Marhaus taunted. "Well, boy, prepare to die."

Marhaus's mocking laughter filled the field. Behind him all his knights were chortling, too. Anger flooded Tristan's veins. "The Great Ones, sir, will be the judge of that." He gripped his sword. "Lay on!"

There was a sinister chuckle. "Have at you, then!"

Laughing, Marhaus slammed his visor down. Then he moved toward Tristan with a slow sideways gait, swinging his hissing broadsword around his head. "Come on, boy!" he called.

Already Glaeve was keening in response. Tristan brought the cold blade to his lips: Patience, brother, not yet. The next second he felt Glaeve leap in his hand as the great sword rose to meet an unforeseen attack. With a swift prayer of thanks, Tristan blocked Marhaus's vicious thrust, and furiously set himself to match the sword strokes as they came.

For Marhaus was fighting now like a wild boar, thrashing venomously to and fro. Feinting to the right, attacking from the left, he slipped his sword under Tristan's defense and pierced his side. Tristan felt the blood running down inside his armor and cursed his opponent's speed. Before long he had had his revenge, and knew that he had wounded the champion in return. But Marhaus gave no sign that he had been hurt. Doggedly Tristan struck out and renewed the assault.

On they fought, and on. Step by step the sun climbed up the sky, and began its slow descent.

Goddess, Mother, help me. . . .

Tristan lifted his eyes to the horizon, cursed Marhaus in his heart, and prayed for the time when his youth and strength must wear his enemy down.

The day wore on. Now the trampled grass was a sea of mud and blood, and the evening shadows were lengthening over the land. Above their heads the sky was loud with ravens, and great flocks of birds were making for their roosts. Tristan's soul sickened at the iron smell of blood and he longed to lay Marhaus out on the broken earth.

Suddenly Marhaus let loose his battle cry, and leapt forward, whirling his massive sword around his head. Dazzled by the great blade flashing through the air, Tristan did not feel the dagger in Marhaus's left hand find the chink in his leg guard and bite into his thigh. Parrying

Marhaus's sword stroke, he rallied his forces for a counterattack, assailing Marhaus's head and shoulders with a rain of blows. But the fire had gone out of Marhaus's attack, and he ducked away from every stroke.

Baffled, Tristan noted the change in tactics and felt a sudden fear. Why was Marhaus retreating from the battle now? Breathing deeply, he called on the woodcraft of his youth, and steadily tracked his prey all over the field. As he went, he was aware of a stinging in his thigh and he felt his body take fire. Then the heat left him and he was weak in every limb. A creeping numbness stole over him, and Glaeve's hilt felt loose in his hand. With a surge of despair, he knew he was losing his grip.

Come—

Tristan, come—

A thin singing reached his ears, and he knew that Glaeve was trying to rally his master's forces, calling Tristan to himself. But the wound in his thigh was a throbbing point of pain and his legs would not move. Muttering, Tristan heaved the weapon high above his head: I hear you, brother, come, be my good friend now. Struggling to hold the sword aloft, he knew this was his last blow; he would not be able to lift its weight again. As he angled the blade to strike, he felt it slipping from his nerveless grip.

In despair, he heard Marhaus laugh, and he knew that his enemy thought he was done. Triumphing, the champion made no move to finish him off, but dropped his guard and stood waiting for Tristan to fall. Like a man in a dream, Tristan lifted his eyes to see Glaeve split Marhaus's silver helmet along its seam and cleave the champion's skull.

"Darkness and devils!"

With a scream, Marhaus threw his own sword to the ground and gripped Tristan's blade in both hands to tear it out of his head. He threw it down, then stood swaying like a tree about to fall as the sun sank behind him in a pool of blood.

"Let me die standing," Tristan heard him cry. "Let me see my death!"

Tristan threw back his head and howled. "Gods above, if I could have avoided this—!"

Stumbling forward, he pushed up Marhaus's visor, and looked into the champion's empty eyes. "You need help, sir," he cried hoarsely. "Let me call your knights."

Marhaus's face was running with blood from the wound in his head.

Suddenly a raven appeared out of the darkening sky, and alighted on his shoulder with a fierce grip.

"So! The last enemy!" Marhaus gave a savage laugh. "I did not think that I would see him yet."

The champion's gaze was fixed and Tristan knew that Marhaus foresaw his death. Now he could see the hero light growing stronger around Marhaus's head as his enemy's bright eyes faded and grew dull.

"Bear me to my ship, get me back to the Western Isle," Marhaus commanded hoarsely. "The Queen's daughter will heal me, if anyone can."

"At once, sir."

Tristan turned and waved up Marhaus's knights, standing frozen in grief at the edge of the field. In silence they hurried forward and carried the champion away.

King Mark came striding up with Andred and Father Dominian. "God bless you, nephew, for this victory!"

Together they watched as the stranger knights took Marhaus on board ship, and began frantic preparations to cast off.

"So perish all our enemies," exulted King Mark. "Now I can send to King Arthur and tell him of our success. We shall not need his help, or that of his knights." He threw his arms around Tristan. "Thanks to you!"

"Sire . . ." Tristan felt a great deadness from head to foot. What was wrong with him?

Andred stepped forward with a broad, manly smile. "Well fought, sir."

"Now I may truly claim you as my own," cried King Mark. "Kneel, nephew, for your knighthood oath to me!"

Tristan fell to his knees. Dimly he reached for the King's proffered hand.

"Father Dominian?" Mark called.

The priest came forward, making the sign of the cross. "Sir Tristan," he intoned, "do you take the King as your liege lord? Will you honor and defend him, keep all evil from him, and treat his enemies as if they were your own?"

Tristan bowed his head. "I will."

He gripped Mark's hand and brought it to his lips. A wave of sickness broke over him, and he struggled to remain upright.

"Do you swear fealty to the King above all others, never to betray him to your dying day?"

Tristan felt a cold wind brush his cheek. "I do."

"Arise, Sir Tristan!" cried Mark in a voice full of tears. "Now you are mine till death!"

Tristan struggled to his feet, and found himself folded in the King's embrace. Taken off balance, he swayed and clutched at Mark for support.

Mark recoiled. "What is it?" he said fearfully. "Are you ill?"

"No, sire." Tristan felt a red shaft of pain shooting up his thigh. "I am overbattled, nothing more."

"It was a hard-fought fight," Andred said wonderingly, watching Tristan rocking to and fro.

Dominian eyed Tristan's pale and sweating face. "And it seems to have cost Sir Tristan more than he knows."

A dull mist swirled through Tristan's aching head. Have no fear, sire, I am well enough, he wanted to say. But something else altogether came out of his mouth.

"I pray you, lay me beside my mother," he said, and fell to the ground.

chapter
13

The meat was stringy and the wine was bad. Sour smoke from the smoldering fires filled the caverns of the roof, and the sweating servants were too few for the guests. On the high table, even the good-natured Arthur was inwardly rejoicing that they would stay here for only one night. But Earl Sweyn sat at Arthur's right hand, lost in delight. His grandchild, young Sweyn, was the son of a king!

And Arthur had no sons, there was no other heir. Gods above! The Earl felt like hooting and yelping with glee. Deliriously he blessed the ancestors who had dignified the name of their line, dropping the "herd" from "swineherd" and turning "swine" into "sweyn." The race of Sweyns, who had started out keeping pigs, would end as kings, and father a line of kings.

And none of this Arthur knew! The Earl hugged himself with glee. He was longing to see the King's face when the story came out. But the whole thing needed exquisite handling. It would take time, and care, and cunning to succeed.

And of course, Arthur could always have children with Guenevere, he cautioned himself, almost unnerved by the giddy visions in his head. They were still young, and many couples were slow to bring forth. But as the only child of another only child, Queen Guenevere came of poor breeding stock. And even if she had twenty sons, young Sweyn would still be the first.

Young Sweyn—soon to be royal Sweyn, for surely Arthur must make his bastard a prince, once the truth was known—the Earl laughed aloud. And the lost boy, the child without a name, would have a father at last. What a blessing Lienore had disobeyed his orders to stay out of sight!

Lienore—

He looked toward his daughter, sitting next to the Queen, nodding demurely at Guenevere's every word. Clad in a modest, well-cut gown of cornflower blue, she was the picture of innocence, and with her son at her side, of maternal devotion, too. The Earl snickered to himself. With her flawless skin and round-eyed stare, she could have sat for the Christians as an image of their Virgin and Child.

Joyfully he recalled the moment it had all changed, when he had followed her pointing finger, gasping with shock. "The King got you with child? He's the man who ravished you?"

"Not ravished, no," she said with a lascivious glint. "But he's Sweyn's father. He was the man in the tent."

"You're sure?" he had grilled her, reeling with half-formed hopes. "There were hundreds of men at the tournament."

She pointed again at Arthur's broad shoulders and massive frame. "Not as big as he was." Something indescribable fleeted across her face. "That's something I'll never forget."

What did she mean? If only he knew what had happened that dreadful day! But he'd been far too busy wooing fat knights with even fatter estates and foolish, rich old lords, and he'd been only too happy to let the girl run and play. What harm could she come to in a Gypsy tent?

Knowing his daughter, he had escorted her to the very door, well aware of all the knights and squires sniffing around. But Lienore had sharp wits as well as twitching desires, and the fortune-teller's tent had more entrances than one. All this he had learned six months later and more, when the bulge in Lienore's belly could no longer be concealed. A bastard for the Sweyns! The Earl ground his teeth, feeling again the torment of that shame. And Lienore had been locked up for the rest of her term, when she had barely redeemed herself by bringing forth a boy.

And Gods above, what a boy, big and fair, bringing a warmth, a joy never known—

To his horror, the Earl felt his eyes misting with tears and hastily redirected his attention toward his guests. At the head of the table sat the King himself, handsomely clad in royal red and blue, the great dragon of the Pendragons rampaging across his magnificent chest. On his left, Guenevere smiled round the table, radiant in a gown of white and gold. Her cloak was the misty blue of Avalon, her gold diadem trembled with crystals and pearls, and the candlelight bloomed on the moonstones at her neck and wrists.

"So, sir," Arthur asked, his clear gray eyes on Sweyn. "What is your holding here?"

He wants money, the Earl thought. Or men. "Indeed, my lord"—he gave a hopeless smile—"a few poor acres of sandy soil, fit only for goats."

Arthur searched his face. "But your lands are extensive, are they not?"

Sorrowfully the Earl shook his head. "Serfs and petty farmers who never pay their rent—alas, these wretches hold most of it, not I."

"But if you have tenants"—Arthur reached for his goblet and drained the thin red wine—"how many men can you summon to the horn?"

"The horn?" the Earl repeated, as if he had never heard the word.

"The trysting horn, my lord," said Arthur patiently. "When you call your men to war."

The Earl gave a feeble shudder. "The Sweyns have avoided war for many years."

Arthur laughed grimly. "Do you hear nothing of the world beyond Castle Sweyn? Ireland is attacking Cornwall even as we speak, and God alone knows how they are faring there. And year after year, the men from the North break like waves on our eastern shore. They ravish our women and kill all the children and men, they burn down the houses and carry off all the grain. We need men and money to keep these sea wolves at bay."

Guenevere leaned forward, a thousand lights from the candles shining in her eyes. "And that's not all," she said earnestly. "We want to make the land safe from rogue knights and outlaws here at home. But the lords who should help us are often selfish and cruel themselves."

With this remark came a look that Earl Sweyn chose to ignore. "We have suffered, too," he said loudly, working himself up into a state of complaint. "Three bad harvests in a row, then the plague last spring carried off half my men. All I have left are cripples and ancients who can barely lift a hoe—"

"Not quite, my lord."

The Earl paused. He did not like the amusement in Guenevere's tone. "Madam, I—"

"Your grandson, sir, is more than all of this," Guenevere said joyfully, putting her arm round young Sweyn.

The child gazed up at her with a sturdy self-regard, and the Earl showed his teeth in a smile. "True, madam, he is the hope of our house. As you say, we have been blessed in him."

The boy put a trusting hand in Guenevere's and leaned into her to speak. "You are the Queen, they say."

Guenevere beamed at him. "They say true. And what do they say of you?"

The boy regarded her with a child's age-old eyes. "I am called like my grandsire, Sweyn. He is a great lord, you know."

A great lord . . .

The Earl glanced from the boy to Arthur, and a glow warmed his shrunken soul. The same fair hair with its promise of red-gold, the same wide, blue-gray eyes, sturdy body and lofty frame, all marked the child as Arthur's from head to toe. Lovingly he traced the resemblance and his thin lips twitched. Young Sweyn was a true heir of Pendragon and would follow the same destiny. With the help of his grandsire . . . The Earl's inner vision bloomed.

Farther down the table, Gawain looked at the Earl and dug his elbow into Kay's ribs. "If the King thinks he'll get men or money here, he's come to the wrong place!"

For once Gawain's right, thought Kay with unease. Sourly he took in the worm-eaten table and the meager feast. Below the salt, the viands had run out, and the lowest diners were feeding on bread and herbs. Kay's lip curled and he nodded to Gawain. "Who would have thought a wretch like that could be grandsire to such a fine boy?"

Gawain peered up the table with feigned interest, and laughed approvingly. In truth he had had eyes only for Lienore, and could not shake the conviction that she was watching him.

"Truly he looks more like our kin than like the Sweyns," he said to Kay. Then his eyes returned to the mother, a woman with the face of a cherub but, he would swear, the instincts of a polecat below. Gawain's broad face creased in a sensual grin and he flexed his massive shoulders contentedly. He could always tell a woman who relished the game. And this one reminded him of something—he'd remember it soon. They were here for only one night, but a man never knew. . . . Gawain felt his flesh thicken and laughed to himself.

Kay read Gawain's expression and gave him an angry nudge. "We're guests here, man," he hissed in Gawain's ear. "Can't you behave your-self?"

Gawain gave a guilty grin. "Listen, Kay," he began. "I've seen the Earl's daughter before somewhere—no, don't laugh. . . ."

Laugh all you like, thought the Earl viciously, watching the two knights. With a secret like this, the King was in his power. First he'd take Lienore and the boy to court and let Arthur get to know his son. Then he'd surreptitiously track down others who had been at the tournament and establish proofs of paternity that the King could not shrug off. If the price was right, someone would surely recall the great King Arthur rut-ting like a hog in a tent. . . .

Earl Sweyn sighed with content, and reviewed his plan. As time went by, he'd find or make other allies, too. Arthur's barons must want an heir, so he'd surely have their support. The main thing was to play his cards close to his chest. Not a word of this must come out till the time was ripe.

Suddenly he felt a buzzing in his head and knew there was danger, though he could not say where. Arthur was playing tenderly with young Sweyn, and Lienore was staring at him with an unfathomable look in her wide, pale eyes.

Arthur smiled at Lienore and ruffled young Sweyn's hair. "You are blessed in your son, my lady. Any man would be proud to call this boy his own."

Lienore paused, her fair head to one side. Suddenly Earl Sweyn knew where her silence was leading and opened his mouth to cry out. But he knew in the same moment that he was too late.

Lienore gave a sublime, malicious grin. "Well, sir, you can."

"Can what?" Now it was Arthur's turn to hesitate.

"What I say, sir," Lienore said blithely, fluttering her shoulders in a glorious shrug. "You fathered this child. You can call him your son."

chapter
14

by the light of the candles, the figure on the table looked like a slumbering giant from a former age, a monster, not a man. But the blood, the quivering flesh and the stink of decay, these were all too human and meant only one thing. Isolde straightened her aching back and worked on. Whatever could be done to save Sir Marhaus, she would do.

Behind her the Queen prowled the chamber like a wild beast, whimpering in her throat. *Goddess, Mother, how will she live if he dies?* Firmly Isolde put the bleak thought away. Time enough to deal with her mother when this was done.

On the high wooden bench before her, Marhaus lay deeply unconscious, his handsome face in repose, his muscular frame relaxed. When his weeping knights had carried him from the ship, he had been alert enough to mock them as a gaggle of silly girls, and to check the Queen sharply when she wept too. Then he had pressed her hand to his lips and closed his eyes. Sir Houzen, the leader of his knights, fell to his knees and offered the fallen champion's sword to the Queen.

She snatched up the weapon. "Marhaus, what have you done?" she howled. Then she whirled it round her head and, keening like a banshee, sent it spinning into the sea. "Save him, Isolde!" she cried.

Isolde's heart was burning with words she could not say: *Mother, his soul is leaving us on this tide. Let us not clog its flight to the astral plane.* She took Marhaus's hand and its clamminess made her fear he had already begun his journey between the worlds. But when she felt his pulse, something whispered back. She gave a decisive nod to Marhaus's knights.

"The infirmary, sirs—and hurry! This way, if you please."

She strode ahead to the castle, making for the low, whitewashed hospice where all came to her with their ailments and woes. Fumbling into a clean apron with Brangwain's help, she ran a practiced eye over the shelves of lotions and compounds in the spare, well-scrubbed healing place. As a girl she had seen such chambers hung with foul-smelling roots, and pieces of hare's foot, newt, and dried frog. Her own place, she promised herself, would have no noxious tubs of tallow fat and dung, jars of bats' eyes, or the shrunken remains of infants who died in the womb. All her herbs and salves stood in well-ordered rows, clear aromatic liquids and fiery lotions the color of amber and gold.

Brangwain followed her gaze. "Woundwort, feverfew, all-heal, my lady," she said quietly. "They're all there."

"Yes." Isolde nodded. "Everything we'll need for his injuries." The Queen strode in and began feverishly pacing the floor. *And heartsease for my mother,* she thought sorrowfully, *at the end of this.*

Swiftly she laid out her instruments, blessing the old Druid who had taught her all he knew. Before he died, Gwydion of the Welshlands had traveled as far as the land where bodies were kept sweet for their spirit's return with rich spices and unguents and yards of linen wraps. He had taught her the way to relieve pressure on a damaged skull, how to set bones, to cure an ague, to deliver a child. But here in Ireland, in a land at peace, she had never learned how to treat the wounds of war.

"In here, my lady?"

The knights bearing Marhaus were at the door. As they brought him in, a mighty storm darkened the sky. Soon the casements were washed with rivulets of rain, and bright streaks of lightning split the summer clouds.

"More light!" Isolde ordered as Marhaus was placed on the table under Brangwain's care.

Goddess, Mother, help me. . . .

Isolde tensed as Brangwain slit open Marhaus's tunic to reveal the bloodied mess beneath. The raw gashes on Marhaus's chest were too numerous to count, some weeping pus, some gaping like open mouths. But as she took up her instruments, feeling the cold clean metal in her hand, her calm returned. *Wherever your spirit walks, Lord Gwydion, be with me now.*

In the silence that followed, the old man's voice dropped quietly through the air. *First deal with the lesser wounds to the chest and neck, then move to the cleft in the head. . . .*

Steadily she set to work with Brangwain at her side, probing and salving the cuts great and small. As she worked, she felt herself rising above her work and drifting away. Suddenly she was walking the astral plane and old Gwydion was coming toward her, wreathed in stars. His eyes had the kindly gleam she remembered so well, and the light from a thousand moons shone around his head. *You have done well, brave heart,* he said fondly to her without words, *and there is more to come. But do not judge yourself by the fate of this man.*

She worked on. Marhaus's knights huddled silently by the door, and she shut her ears to the pacing of the Queen. Then she heard a noise that could not be ignored. At the back of the room, two old women of the household were struggling in with a smoldering fire in a thick clay pot. A third carried a bundle in her arms, which she handed to the Queen.

Isolde had seen them before, but never like this. In place of the plain gowns and head coverings they wore in the Queen's household, they were garbed in dark draperies, with their hair unbound. Three grizzled manes floated wildly down their backs, and three pairs of glittering eyes peered out through the tangled locks. The Queen rushed forward with shrill cries and welcomed them in. Isolde drew a breath and tried to hold her temper down. *Have pity, try not to blame her, think what she must feel. . . .*

The crones set the firepot down on the floor and strewed herbs and crystals over the glowing coals. A rich, thick odor began to seep through the room as the Queen opened the bundle and shook the contents out. With a lurch, Isolde saw a pair of round, dead, painted eyes and the stunted body of a man-doll crudely carved out of wood. Its oversized member jutted like a thumb, and its stare would have mocked the undead. But the Queen clasped it raptly to her breast and rocked it to and fro.

"Hush, hush, my love, don't grieve," she crooned, her eyes very bright. "Isolde will save you, we shall love again."

Behind her the three old women began to chant, spinning harsh melodies as they fed the flames again. The billowing fumes blew green and blue and white, and the scent in the chamber made Isolde's pulses race.

"Now!" hissed the elder wildly, rolling her eyes. The Queen crushed the Marhaus doll fiercely to her breast, then gave it to the crone. Swooping like a bird, she passed it through the smoke, once, twice, and then again, before handing it back to the Queen.

With a cry of triumph the Queen cradled it furiously in her arms, dropping a flurry of kisses on its hard, cold head.

"You will live, my love!" she rejoiced with a high, mad laugh. "You won't go before me to the Otherworld."

The chanting rose to a shriek. "Live, Marhaus, live!"

"Madam . . ." Isolde laid down her probe and turned to the Queen. "Sir Marhaus must have quiet if he is to get well! All this may make him worse."

The Queen rounded on her like a beaten mare. "You're lying!" she cried. "The old ways can save him just as well as yours!"

The leader of the women raised her gray head. "Hail to the Queen," she howled, "the Mother of the Land! And blessed be the Gods of blood and bone!"

Isolde's stomach heaved. Fuming, she returned to the figure on the bench. Marhaus lay like a statue, his flesh white and cold. But his breath was regular, and her hopes revived. All the lesser wounds had been cleaned and dressed. It was time to face the great cleft in his skull.

Brangwain stood ready with a bowl of fresh rosemary water and a handful of clean cloths. With infinite care Isolde swabbed out the terrible wound. As she went to dress it, a sudden sharp glint caught her eye. Something was buried in the depths of the quivering cleft. Steadying herself, she reached for her pincers and took a fine grip. A bright sliver of metal shone in the candlelight as she drew it out and dropped it into the bowl.

"Aaiihhh!"

The Queen threw down the doll and pounced on the metal shard, and her hollow scream rang through Dubh Lein and beyond. Washed clean of Marhaus's blood, the silver splinter glinted with malign power. The Queen gazed at it in horror, then clutched it to her breast. "This is his death warrant! He cannot live."

"Madam," Isolde began, "he may—"

Through the window she could see the sea and the clouds above forming a great womanly shape, its head bent in welcome, its loving arms spread wide. Between the sobbing of the wind and the cry of the ebbing tide, she heard the withdrawing murmur of life itself. *Come to me, come. All men enter the circle of the Goddess when they leave this world. Come in peace, Marhaus, to the plains of joy.*

She took Marhaus's hand. *The Mother greets you, Marhaus, go to Her.* The sick man's breathing eased, and a great quietness settled on his face. A moment later his spirit slipped its mortal shell, his features relaxed, and the embattled warrior was a handsome youth again.

"The Dark Lord!"

The three crones set up a high, toneless wail. "The Dark Lord, Penn Annwyn, has come from the Otherworld to take him home!"

The Queen was stroking Marhaus's face like a crazed child. "Has the Dark Lord taken you, my love?" She picked up his cold hand, and raised the metal sliver to her lips. "Never fear. We'll have revenge for your precious soul!"

"Revenge!" intoned the chorus of crones in the rear.

The Queen closed her eyes and stretched out her arms. "May the man who killed you die a fearful death!" she howled. "May all those he loves and all who love him suffer till the sea kisses the sky, and the trees bow down their heads at his cursed feet!" She paused, panting, then gathered her forces to go on. "May the woman who loves him never know peace or joy! May she sorrow for him till her heart turns black, as mine must do now for the loss of my lord!"

"Mother!" cried Isolde in terror, watching the Queen growing taller with every word she spoke. A wind from the Otherworld roared through the chamber, and she shook with dread.

The door flew open, and Sir Houzen came thrusting in. "Is he gone?"

Isolde nodded. She could not speak.

Houzen glared at her with eyes of fire. Then he laid a hand on Marhaus's shoulder and bowed his head. "Have no fear, my lord," he cried bitterly. "The wretch who murdered you won't be far behind."

The look in Sir Houzen's eyes chilled Isolde's soul. "How so?"

The knight gave a malevolent glimmer. "Marhaus thought it was a secret he would never tell, but we all knew. He poisoned his dagger when he went into battle, in case he couldn't win outright with the sword. That's why he was champion for so many years. One touch of it, and his enemies were dead."

"For sure?" Isolde heard a roaring in her ears.

Houzen nodded, and his face set in a vengeful grin. "As this last one will be now, big as he is."

"The knight from Cornwall?" The roaring increased. Isolde shook her head. What did it matter to her? Why should she care?

"Yes! Marhaus struck him in the thigh, and even you, Princess, can't cure him of that!" Houzen's laugh of triumph rang round the room. "He's a dead man now, Tristan of Lyonesse!"

chapter
15

*S*et on, old fool, get on!"

Muttering sharply to himself in the Old Tongue, Merlin pushed his way through the tangled undergrowth. Twilight was blooming in shades of purple and gold and soon all the stars would be doing their dance of fire. But here in the depths of the forest, dusk had turned to darkness long ago. He tugged on the leading rein.

"Mend your pace, damn you!" he grumbled to the mule plodding behind.

Briars tore at his legs, and studded his gown with thorns.

"Let an old man through, brothers," he chided irritably, and he heard them sniggering like schoolboys as they obeyed. Ahead of him, one oak tree towered over others nearby. Merlin set his course for it with a prayer of thanks.

The oak tree had come from an older world than this. Time had worn away the earth round its base, and now its roots writhed above the ground in fantastic shapes. Through a split in the bark, its hollow trunk led down to a warm, sandy den below. Merlin gave a weary grin. Tonight he would rest here and call the place his home.

Rest...

He could feel every one of his ancient bones creaking, craving to lie down.

"Yes, yes," he told them tetchily, "soon, soon."

His thin lips curled. Tomorrow he would make for Arthur's side again and hurry to the castle of Earl Sweyn. But tonight... A crazy tune took shape and flew round his head like a bee. Soon he would be safe and snug in the underground cave.

At the foot of the tree, he unbridled the mule and turned it loose to graze. Then, slipping through the hollow in the trunk, he dropped down into the space beneath. With practiced hands he felt in his saddlebag for his flints and soon raised a light. Contentedly he set his back against the wall, and looked around.

Above him the roots of the tree made a strong, domed roof, curving down to a dry sandy floor. Along the walls were cushions of fragrant bracken and dried leaves for his aching limbs. The air was rich with the sweet, loamy scent of the earth, and he feasted on the savor for his evening repast. Then, wrapping himself up in his cloak, he lay down and drifted away.

Sleep came soon, great waves of fatigue breaking over his head. Smiling, he sailed the dreamless depths of night, and set his course for the mountains of the moon. How long he wandered there he did not know. Then the voice of the sea rushed softly through his mind.

Merlin, Merlin—

He stirred. "Who calls?" His sleeping eyes looked out beyond his den and he saw the wide ocean with a great shape above.

The figure bowed and leaned down to him, rippling across the sky. *Hear me, Merlin. Your path tomorrow does not lead to Castle Sweyn.*

He sat up urgently. "Not to Arthur—why?"

The veiled shape nodded. *You must take the road to Cornwall, to Castle Dore.*

Now he was bright awake, and scrambling to his feet. "Tristan?"

Tristan.

"Defeated by Marhaus?" He groaned in dread. "Surely not! What then? I saved his father—must I save him, too?"

Save Tristan, too.

So! Merlin could not speak. Fumbling around in the dark, he seized his bag and forced his skinny body back up through the hollow tree. Above him in the moonlight, the pale figure floated in the void, her soft voice now the wind rushing through the trees. *Hurry—hurry—*

He stumbled forward and bridled up the mule. Then, sobbing with tension, he set off back down the track.

Hurry, hurry—

"I go! I go!" he screamed to the careless sky. The vision was fading from his waking eyes, and the forest lay dark all around. But still the mellow voice pursued him like the incoming tide: *Hurry, Merlin, hurry, or you will come too late!*

GODS ABOVE, HOW vile to be lying half dead, waiting for the dregs of life to drain away! With a hearty shudder, Andred stepped out of the sickroom, glad to be alive. It was bad to see any man suffer, and sickening to watch his uncle at Tristan's bedside, weeping like a girl. But how lucky that the gallant young champion should defeat the invader then die, leaving him sole heir to Cornwall as before!

Strolling down through the courtyard with the sun on his back, Andred tried not to smile. With the whole of Castle Dore watching and King Mark wild with grief, he must not seem to be enjoying himself. Still, he could not pretend to be sorry for Tristan's death. Only now did he realize what a shock it had been, the sudden appearance of a rival for the throne.

"Thanks be to God," he breathed piously. This turn of fate would be worth many candles in church when Tristan had breathed his last.

And it could not be long. Turning into the Knights' Hall, Andred permitted himself a grin that split his face. When Tristan collapsed on the battlefield, they had felt the fever raging through his limbs. And then they had found the poisoned wound that had set him on fire.

After that, there was little they could do. When the fever died, Tristan had taken a mortal cold, his limbs set like stone and his jaw locked in a grin like death. Then the great heat returned and his body filled with blood, till his arms and legs jerked wildly and could not be still. Mark had had him bled many times, and still the deathly cold came back worse than before.

Well, God was good. Tristan could hardly last another day. Andred sighed. By sunset, the shadow on his future would be gone.

"King Andred!" he whispered, and his eyes grew bright. To the tiltyard then, while the sun shone. And how could it be otherwise, now that his own sun was rising once again?

THE SICKROOM STANK of rotting flesh, and worse. But the figure on the bed was beyond care. Tristan lay like a marble knight on his tomb, and his breath was so shallow that each could have been his last.

Unconscious as he was, he could still hear all the doctors' low pronouncements, each one sounding unhappier than the last. In the heat of his fever, he had raged with distress at Marhaus's treachery, then the fire left him and he knew his life was done. He would never sit his horse again, never see another May morning or glory in the lovelight in a lady's eyes. Yet the Lady had promised him a true love—where was she now? Cold—all cold. He shivered uncontrollably, and began to weep. Then soft arms lifted him to another place, and he drifted away.

Pacing the chamber or sitting by the bed, Mark watched Tristan sinking and was in agony.

"God help me," he groaned, tears pouring down his cheeks. "I'd rather lose my kingdom than see him die!"

Dominian raised his head. What? Of course Tristan must die. Far better that the young knight should pass away swiftly than that a Goddess worshiper should come so near the throne.

"Compose yourself, sire," he said sternly. "We may not rail against the will of God."

But Mark was not listening. "We need more healers!" he cried feverishly.

"Sire, you have called for healers from far and wide." Dominian ground his teeth as he reviewed the false pretenders of recent weeks. First was the fever surgeon, a bright-eyed loon who brewed up his cures from the slime on the castle pond. Next came the leech woman, so greasy, fat, and sluggish that she looked like a leech herself. She brought hundreds of her hateful creatures on her back in a leather sling and covered Tristan with the black, blood-eating things.

Dominian felt his anger curdle in his throat. God preserve us from these pagan slaves, there was no end to their vile mummery. One old witch even wanted to lay cobwebs in Tristan's wound, swearing that they cured infections and had saved the great Alexander of Greece. He had seen to it that the old crone received a sound lashing for her lies, and told

Simeon that the rule of God would mean witches like this hanging from every tree.

Well, he had done all he could. And Tristan would soon be with God—never had a soul so sick returned from the borders of the Otherworld. Dominian raised his hands and resumed his prayers.

There was a knock at the door. "Sire, your barons crave a word with you."

"Oh, God, no!" groaned Mark.

Reluctantly he followed the servant to the anteroom. Waiting for him were a dozen or so older knights and lords, with their leader, Sir Nabon, at their head. A tough, compact man of middle age, Nabon had given his youth and three fingers of his right hand to defending his country, and had headed its council for most of his adult life.

Nabon stared unsympathetically at Mark's tearstained face. "Sire, we need your presence at our councils of state. You neglect your kingdom by grieving here."

Mark tensed. "Don't talk to me, I forbid it!" he shrilled.

But Sir Nabon had served Mark's father, and had no fear of the son. And with Mark as weak as this, there could hardly be a better time to drive a point home. "We were debating the succession again today, sire," he said trenchantly. "And our concern is all the stronger now Tristan is so sick."

"Indeed, yes," came the stern voice of Sir Wisbeck at Nabon's side. Wisbeck was so old, Mark brooded resentfully, that by rights he should be dead. But the soldierly frame was straighter than his own, and the white thatch covered one of Cornwall's best brains.

"A king's first duty, sire, is to his land," Wisbeck said gravely. "And if Sir Tristan dies—"

"Don't say that!" Mark cried superstitiously. "Tristan will live, he must! And don't forget there's my nephew Andred, too."

Nabon drew a breath. Mark would never know that his barons deeply distrusted Andred and would never accept him as their king. Tristan's appearance had seemed like a gift from the Gods, but that hope had hardly been born before it was gone. No, Mark must marry. Nabon returned to the attack. "Even with a hundred nephews," he growled, "a king needs a son."

Behind Nabon, a short figure thrust forward to be heard. Despite his strutting gait and unimpressive frame, Sir Quirian prided himself on his lineage and was much given to ideas of dynasty. "Without a son, my lord," he said loftily, "the throne is not protected when you die."

"Why should I die?" Mark blustered.

Sir Nabon clenched his fists. "For the same reason that we all do, sire!"

Mark eyed him fearfully and longed to knock him to the ground. "Well, then?" he muttered.

Nabon looked him in the eye. "You must take a bride. A fine young princess or, better still, a queen. One who will grace your throne and increase your lands."

Sir Wisbeck smiled encouragingly. "And give you many sons as time goes by."

Mark clutched his head. "Tell me who!" he shrilled.

There was a sudden commotion outside the room.

"Hold there, sir, you can't go in!"

"Out of my way, fools!"

The door burst open and Merlin came surging in. His green garments fluttered round him like leaves in a storm, and his yellow wand was groaning in his hand. One ring-encrusted finger was pointing at Mark, but his stinging curses fell freely on every head.

"Blindworms!" cried the old enchanter bitterly. "Asses, mules, and dolts!" His yellow eyes were flaming like winter suns, and his gaze found Mark and stabbed him where he stood. "What have you done to Tristan?"

Mark goggled at him. "He's had the best care that money could buy! Why, the astrologers alone—"

"Mountebanks, quacks, and frauds!" Merlin screamed. "You're killing him with this foolery, don't you see? You should have sent him to Ireland on the first tide!"

"To *Ireland*?" Mark's eyes bulged. "Why?"

Merlin threw up his hands. "Every poison has its antidote, but it's only found in the place where the poison grew. Surely you knew that?"

Mark stared at him in horror. "But Tristan can't go to Ireland," he gasped. "They'd murder him there!"

Merlin gave a furious laugh. "Your crooks and horse-leeches are killing him here!"

Sir Nabon stepped forward, to nods from the barons all round. "It must be Ireland then. But we'll have to conceal who he is, to protect him from their revenge."

"I saved the father." Merlin's eyes glowed like moons. "I can save the son."

"No!" Mark shed a few round, childish tears. "I don't want him to go."

Sir Wisbeck gestured toward the sickroom and shook his head. "Sire, we have no choice."

"He's too ill to be moved." Mark cast a desperate eye at the great figure lying motionless on the bed. "He won't live through the voyage."

Merlin snorted with contempt. "He'll die for sure if he stays!" He turned to the barons. "Sirs, will you give me your help? I have a ship lying ready at the dock."

VENUS, THE LOVE star, was blossoming over the sea. The solemn group stood in the twilight on the misty quay, watching the dark-sailed ship as it drew away. Tristan's unconscious form had been installed belowdecks, and the boat was sailing on the evening tide.

At Mark's right hand, Dominian was silently praying for Tristan to pass into the arms of death. With his uncle's loud weeping in his ears, Andred, too, put on a sorrowful face and doomed Tristan in his heart. Let the tide take him, he prayed fervently, let the sea demons eat his bones.

Salt spray fell round them like a weeping cloud. Merlin stood on the prow of the ship, arms raised, cloak flapping, chanting above the roaring of the tide. With his wand in his hand, he wove a string of spells, charming the sea to speed the boat on its way. But still he could hear the soft sigh in every wave, *Hurry, Merlin, hurry, or you will come too late!*

chapter 16

In the inner chamber, the talking had gone on for hours. Things had gone quiet in the small hours, then the tears and anger had started up again. Arthur was accounting to his wife for the sudden appearance of a bastard son, and none of those listening envied him at all.

The four companion knights had been in attendance all night, sprawled in the antechamber, snatching a little broken sleep. Lienore's casual claim that Arthur had fathered her son had scattered the royal banquet to the winds. Arthur and Guenevere had withdrawn in frozen shock, promising to meet Earl Sweyn and Lienore the next day. Since then, they had not left the inner room.

Now the sun was up, its golden fingers warming the dusty room. Gawain yawned, heaving himself out of his chair, and crossed to a window to greet the day.

"How much longer do we have to wait?" he mourned. Outside the June dew was pearling the grass and he hungered for the hot thrill of the chase, thundering through the woods or charging at the thickets to flush out the wild boar. He turned to Kay. "How long will the Queen keep him dangling like this?"

"As long as it takes," snapped Kay. The air was stale with the bodies of four men and the dapper little knight was longing to escape.

"Well, I still don't believe it!" Lucan jumped to his feet and raked a hand through his hair. "Not Arthur—he's too pure!"

"You're right about that," growled Gawain, who had felt Arthur's displeasure at his own amorous exploits often enough. He grinned at Lucan. "Now if it had been you, you wretch..."

"More likely to be you!" Lucan retorted. "But there were so many knights there, how can we know what happened so long ago?"

"It's true." Kay shook his head. "But Guenevere's not the woman to forgive him, all the same."

"It's a lot to forgive." Bedivere's quiet voice surprised them all.

Lucan stared. "What, a moment of madness eight years ago, before they were married, before they even met?"

Bedivere shook his head. His mild brown eyes were full of foreboding and pain. "A moment that's brought him a child, when the Queen herself has no offspring of her own? And a son besides, who might inherit the kingdom, when she must want to keep the Summer Country in the rule of queens?"

Lucan shrugged. "At least we have an heir, and a likely one, too."

Gawain scratched his head. "He's a fine boy," he agreed, stroking down his rough fair hair, "and he favors our kin. Why don't we bring him to court, teach him everything he should know?" His big chest swelled. "I could take an interest in the lad myself. If he's Arthur's son, he's my kinsman too."

"Gawain, hold your tongue!" Kay could have howled with rage. "Don't you see that bringing young Sweyn to court would mean having the mother and grandfather there too? A pair of scheming crooks who'd give Arthur no peace. . . ."

There was a thunderous knocking at the outer door. The guards threw it open and a travel-stained rider was shown in, carrying a scroll. "Message for the King!"

The inner doors opened to the sound of weeping within, and Arthur came out. "Yes?"

The rider knelt and delivered his missive with a broad smile. "From the King of Cornwall, sire. He has defeated the Irish challenge for the throne. Your mother, Queen Igraine, is safe in Tintagel and the champion of the Western Isles is no more."

Arthur's face cleared. "Thank you, sir." He set down the scroll and bowed, surveying the signs of the messenger's long, hard ride. "We shall attend to this later. You will be well rewarded for your pains."

He watched the man go, then met the waiting eyes with a pallid smile. "That's some good news at least. No need to press on to Cornwall till we've dealt with things here." He paused and gave a hollow sigh. "It could be true, you know, what they're telling us." His anxious eyes sought Kay. "We were at that tournament. You must remember it?"

Kay nodded. They had spent hours talking of nothing else. "We went for the jousting," he said stiffly. "To try our skill."

Gawain laughed self-consciously. "And don't forget the fair. We knew there'd be jugglers and acrobats and all strange things. And we wanted to meet some girls. . . ."

Arthur paced to and fro, avoiding their gaze. "You remember the fortune-teller?" he asked in a low voice.

The fortune-teller? A hot flood of memory rushed over Kay. Flashing black eyes, two heaving mounds of olive-skinned flesh, a fearsome set of white teeth, and a wildcat grin—she had frightened him then, and she terrified him now. He forced himself to laugh. "She stopped you in front of her tent."

"Then she dragged us in," Arthur muttered, looking at the floor.

"It was packed with people waiting to have their fortunes told," Bedivere put in quietly, "and more Gypsy women, dancing and selling ale."

"What else?" demanded Arthur hoarsely.

Kay could still see the rich and glittering gloom, the dark silken hangings, the odd pinpoints of light. "It was very dark."

Arthur rounded on them. "But the brazier, d'you remember that?" he demanded. "They threw herbs and crystals on it, and made sweet fumes?"

Sweet fumes, oh yes—

Tears started to Kay's eyes. Breathing their rich savor had made the little knight as tall as Arthur and as wise as Merlin himself. Like a slow-worm in spring, he had shed his dark hair and skin and had been reborn in all the fair splendor of Arthur's comely kin. In this fume-filled sleep all women had loved him as much as they loved Arthur, and one above all had loved him and claimed him for her own.

Bedivere sat very still, remembering, too. "Sire, we saw wondrous things in the fumes that day."

Things beyond speech—almost beyond recall. Bedivere sighed with wonder. His own seeing had been of the Welsh Marches, the magical hinterland of his childhood home. There as a boy he had seen the Fair Ones walk, for they loved the misty borderlands between one world and the next. With the fumes, they had come to him again, and this time he had seen the Shining Ones wrapped in their veils of light. One above all, a great womanly veiled shape, brooding above the waters of the sea . . .

"Great things we saw, sire . . . as you must have done, too," he trailed off lamely.

Arthur drew himself up. "In truth, I can't quite remember what I saw. But I swooned in the fumes and slept, as we all did. So a woman could have taken advantage of me, Guenevere says." He tried a manly laugh. "That's the only way this thing could have come about."

Yes and no, Arthur, Kay wanted to say, but would not. "What now, my lord?" he forced out.

Arthur's face cleared. "Well, at least I have a fine son. If Earl Sweyn can convince me that the boy is mine, then he must be acknowledged, and I've told Guenevere so." He smiled. "Of course his mother will have to come to court as well, and his grandsire besides, if the Earl can leave his lands."

Kay gasped. Already he could smell the sweet stink of disaster ahead. "But, sire—"

Arthur held up his hand. "No buts, Kay," he said reprovingly. "A knight will always honor his own son." He gave a rueful smile. "I may have done wrong, but I will turn it to good. I shall honor my oath of chivalry while I live."

Wrong, Arthur, wrong! Kay's inner voice screamed in his ear. We need no dubious bastards, cunning whores, and crooked kingmakers around the throne.

"My lord—"

It was Guenevere, translucent with sadness, standing in the door. The gold at her neck and waist caught the rising sun as she shook out her white silk gown. "Sir, if we are to welcome your newfound son to court, there is one above all who should be there."

Kay's heart leaped in his chest. Clever woman, clever Guenevere! If any man could tell true Pendragon from false and reject a false pretender without delay—

Arthur's brow relaxed. "Merlin!" he cried joyously. "He's the man. We must send for him." He smiled fondly. "He'll be so proud that I have a son!"

Maybe—maybe not, thought Kay thankfully. But Merlin will know.

He could tell from his fellow knights' faces that they felt the same. "We'll get him here, sire," he said.

If it is not too late.

Kay shivered as he heard a cry from another world: *Hurry, Merlin, hurry, or you will come too late!*

chapter
17

Sorrow behind, and nothing but trials to come—
Goddess, Mother, help me and strengthen me now.

"Take care of the Queen, Brangwain. She will sleep soon, when the all-heal starts to work."

Straightening her back, Isolde stepped out of the Queen's House and crossed the damp cobblestones of the courtyard to the Great Hall. High over the castle great blue and black clouds labored with unshed tears and a weeping mist was rolling in from the sea. She nodded. *Yesterday we laid the champion to rest. Today the whole world is grieving for his death.*

In the Great Hall the Queen's lords were waiting around the green baize council table with Sir Gilhan at their head. She saw their open surprise as she approached and moved calmly to the place of honor to take the Queen's seat.

The bronze arms of the throne were cool to her fevered palms. *Will they accept me?*

"Welcome, my lords," she said.

The nods and muttered courtesies as they sat down did nothing to answer the question *Who is with me now?* Of the dozen or so men round the table, some grizzled, others still in their prime, she could count on Sir Gilhan, she knew. And Sir Houzen, red-eyed and deathly pale: he would be mourning the loss of Sir Marhaus for a long time to come.

But the well-groomed knight opposite, appraising her with an oblique, dark-eyed stare—Sir Vaindor had been the Queen's champion and chosen one before Marhaus had defeated him and replaced him in her bed. Would he be scheming to get back into the Queen's favor now that his rival was gone?

And old Sir Doneal farther down the table, lighting up the gloom with his white hair and blazing eyes—he'd always been loyal to the Queen—what would he do now? Next to him she caught another cool survey, then another, and knew with a shock that the handsome Sir Vaindor was not the only man weighing up his chances after Marhaus's death. *Goddess, Mother, are they all hoping to get into my mother's bed?* Her stomach lurched as a worse thought was born. *Or—Goddess, no—surely not mine?*

No, she was dreaming, this was too gross to be borne. Briskly Isolde took herself in hand. "The Queen has asked me to attend your meeting today."

Seated at Isolde's side, Sir Gilhan narrowly suppressed a snort of glee. From what he'd heard, the mourning Queen had no thought of her council, locked away in her own world of pain. But thank the Gods for this girl! She at least knew that a kingdom had to be governed, and was ready to try. She'd dressed for it too in a regal gown of rust-red velvet bright with gold beading on the bodice and sleeves. Tall and intent, her clustering hair held back by a woven gold fillet, she looked every inch a queen. Gilhan's subtle mind leaped eagerly ahead. Now, if she could rule for her mother, with their help—

"How is the Queen?" he asked carefully.

Isolde did not want to think of the deranged thing on the bed, tearing her hair and crying out for revenge. "She is not well."

Sir Gilhan assumed a sympathetic air. "The loss of Sir Marhaus is a grievous blow."

Isolde looked at Sir Houzen. "How did he die?"

Sir Houzen's head snapped back. "Like a knight of Ireland," he said defiantly, "valiant to the end! But the coward King of Cornwall brought in the greatest champion of Christendom against him, a knight who'd fought in France and Gaul, even the Holy Land."

Sir Gilhan leaned forward with interest. "Who's that?"

"Sir Tristan, they called him." Houzen's ravaged face composed itself in a sneer. "Tristan of Lyonesse. They said he was the King's nephew, but he was twice the size of the King."

"A giant, then?" queried Sir Vaindor, stroking his thick glossy hair and uneasily calculating his chances against such a man.

Houzen's eyes flamed. "A monster!" he affirmed. "Like a wild man of the woods."

Isolde shook her head. "So Sir Marhaus was overwhelmed?"

"And he must be avenged!" Houzen fixed Isolde with a bloodshot stare. "I beg you, lady, when the war band strikes back against Cornwall, grant me the command. I was his chief companion—it is my right."

War band?

Isolde leaned forward. "Sir—"

"Their champion's finished, Marhaus saw to that," Houzen raced madly on. "Their knights are cowards, they can't defend their King. One swift strike at his stronghold is all it'll take. I could do it with thirty—no, twenty-odd good men."

Around the table, Isolde saw, no man would speak. Every eye was on her, waiting for her response.

"And then?" she inquired in measured tones.

"Kill the King!" Houzen's swollen eyes lit up. "Pillage the town and put it to the sword—make every one of them pay for Marhaus's death. Then we'd lay the whole kingdom at our Queen's feet. And that would honour Marhaus as he deserves!"

They call this honor?

Yes, and my mother would, too!

She strengthened her voice. "My lords?"

An unhappy silence hung about the room. Sir Gilhan was the first to speak. "Marhaus is gone. Is this the best way to remember him?"

Sir Vaindor regretfully stroked his luxuriant mustache. "We'll miss Marhaus enough as it is. We can hardly spare the lives of more knights as well."

Isolde nodded, bleak visions of burned-out houses and ruined crops filling her eyes. "And the cost is not only in lives."

Sir Doneal gave a harsh, rusty laugh. Gods, what it was to get old! Once he would have relished such a fight, but not now. "Especially if the King of Cornwall strikes first!"

"Will he do that?" Isolde took a thoughtful breath. "Cornwall has never threatened us before."

Sir Gilhan sighed. "We invaded his land, and would have taken his throne. Now that our champion's dead, we're wide open to attack."

Isolde sat up. "But King Mark does not act alone. He's Queen Igraine's vassal and he has to answer to her. Would she let him invade?" All her life Igraine had suffered at the hands of warring men. But never had she sought war herself. Isolde shook her head. "I strongly suspect that Queen Igraine will want peace."

Sir Vaindor laughed unpleasantly. "But the King of Cornwall will still want his revenge."

Houzen rose swaying to his feet. "And so do I!"

Blood rushed to Isolde's head. Her mother's cries were ringing in her ears. *My mother, now Marhaus and King Mark—revenge, revenge, revenge!—can they think of nothing else?*

She struck the table with her fist and a warm and healing anger filled her bones. "Enough of this!" she cried in ringing tones. "You talk of death when we should honor life! How can we end it? That's our duty now!"

Sir Gilhan's eyes widened with a new respect. "To end it, madam, with the least loss of life?" He paused for thought. "If the King invades, one of our knights must challenge him to the death."

One of our knights?

Gilhan himself, or Vaindor, of course. Isolde nodded angrily. Older knights as they were, they were the island's strongest fighters now. One of them would die a hero, and the land would be bereft. What answer was that? Her silent fury grew.

"No more deaths!" she pronounced. "We must look for ways to make peace, not seek war. There is nothing to do now but keep a steady watch and wait for the danger to recede with time."

She looked around, assessing the response. Agreement was written on every face except one.

"Sir Houzen." She leaned toward him and spoke as gently as she could. "I do not see support for a war party here. Sir Marhaus was a brave leader and a loyal knight. I hope time will ease your loss now that he is gone."

Gone—

Houzen's grief leaped up and savaged him anew. With bleak certainty it came to him that he would never be whole till he saw his lord again—till he met Marhaus in the Otherworld. Tears poured down his face and he stumbled to his feet.

"Lady, lady," he wept, "give me leave to go. I have lost my lord. The moon shines on a world where he is gone, and I must wander till I find him again."

Goddess, Mother, help him—

Isolde rose to meet Houzen and took his hand. "Go with our blessing, sir," she said steadily. "And may you find your lord."

Tears stood in her own eyes as she watched him go. They would not see Houzen again. Wanderer, seafarer, he was fated to search by land and sea till he joined his lord in the world beyond the worlds. Isolde shook her head. *Goddess, Great One,* she swore to herself, *if men are ready to die for each other like this, grant me a man who will love me and want to live!*

Sir Doneal's rusty old voice broke into her reverie. "Forgive an old man, my lady," he said abruptly, "if I say—"

Isolde favored the old man with a kindly smile. "What, sir?"

Sir Doneal looked out through the walls of the chamber and she saw with him the emerald-green rolling pastures, low black hills, and pearly sky of the island they so loved.

"Peace, lady, will bring other challenges. The Queen is sick with grief for Marhaus's death." He paused. "If she follows him, all our hopes lie with you." He paused again. "Only you, lady. You are all we have."

She felt the sudden weight of countless eyes. There was a fragile silence as all their unspoken thoughts clamored in the hollow hall, beating like wings.

We need an heir for the throne of the Western Isle.

Or at least a champion—one to fight for the kingdom by day, and lie by the ruler at night.

Breathing heavily, Isolde sat back in her chair. To her horror she saw Sir Vaindor toss back his chestnut curls and smile unmistakably into her eyes. He raised his eyes to the roof, and stroked his chin. There was no need for words.

Goddess, Mother—

She could scarcely contain herself. *If they think, any of these lords—*

But another voice was sounding in her head.

Yes, Isolde! Every girl of your age has seen her first Beltain by now. Every one has danced at the feast and lain down among the fires, watching and waiting for the stranger she can love. And you're still a miserable virgin—a girl who denies all the joy the Goddess gives—

Mother, Mother, spare me—

And you know all the hopes of our line lie with you! I've made powerful earth magic with countless men, but only your father could ever put a child in my womb. The seed of the rest was too weak to mingle with my blood. You must give us the child who will save our house.

Mother, women are not cattle made to breed—

But you scorn all men! You even refuse a lover here at court. Any other girl would thrill to a Saracen knight—

Sir Palomides, yes, it's true—he's courted me faithfully since he saw me at his first tournament and stayed on here in the hope of winning my love.

—a king in his own land and a hero in ours—

I know—and a man of honor and a valiant knight—

—yet you still rebuff him with your maidenly ways and little frozen smiles.

Yes, Mother, yes—I should have given him a chance.

She was dimly aware of the silence in the room. Looking around at the solemn faces, she collected herself.

"Thank you, Sir Doneal," she said. "I shall bear this in mind." She raised her head. "So, lords, may I carry your deliberations to the Queen?"

The council was over. Patiently she endured the lengthy farewells, then recrossed the courtyard in a sombre mood. Sir Palomides—indeed, she had given him no thought. Now she saw again the Saracen knight's keen gaze and courteous bow, felt the strength of his arm as he handed her down from her horse, and recalled all the times he had appeared at her side, seemingly with no other desire than to please.

Trust to your knight. He will come to you.

Cormac's Druid blessing floated softly down through the air.

My knight?

Palomides? The prince from the East with his warm brown eyes, his gleaming golden skin, his gentle ways? Palomides, who walked every evening in the garden, watching the tower window where she slept, keeping a nightly vigil of hopeless love?

Could it be?

The Queen's House lay ahead in the setting sun, its white crystal facade glittering with shafts of light, red, pink, and gold like a million broken hearts. The doors opened to greet her and Brangwain was there.

"The Queen's at peace, lady," the maid called. "Fast asleep."

Palomides?

Could it be? came drifting down the air.

Isolde gained the threshold and stepped into the hall. "I'll go to her now. Then get me out of this wretched gown, it's too heavy to bear! After that . . ." She paused, and the answer came. "After that we'll take a walk in the garden—it will be lovely at this time of day."

"The garden?" Brangwain's blackbird eyes were suddenly alert. "As you wish." Then the narrow face softened into an understanding smile. "But first let me help you change. You'll want to look your best."

Isolde paused and shook her head. "No, not at all," she said crisply.

Look her best? Why would the maid think that? She turned away. "Not at all," she repeated. "We're only going out to take the air."

chapter
18

the evening lay before them, cool and sweet. White wisps of cloud rode in a pink and blue sky, and all the land was bathed in an opal light. Isolde came out of the lower courtyard with Brangwain at her side and felt her spirits lifting step by step. All around them the gardens of the castle ran down to the sea below, and their feet trod softly on the green trefoil. The trees were in the fullness of late-summer leaf and trailing red roses hung down their heavy heads, breathing out their fragrant souls before they died.

Could it be?

She knew she would come before him like a cascade of sweet peas, pink, white, and violet fluttering as she moved. She would not admit that she had dressed for him, but still she was glad he would see her in her lightest silks, floating through the dusk with a veil of creamy lawn over her hair.

And there he was, attended by his knights, a group of unsmiling, dark-faced men in silken robes. He was standing apart from them in the place where he stood every night, on the edge of the terrace giving out over the sea. From there he had a clear view of the tower where she slept and could watch till her last candle went out.

Seeing her, he started like a boy. "Lady?"

"Sir Palomides."

She gave him her hand as his knights bowed low and respectfully backed away.

"Princess, you honor me," he said, pressing her fingers to his lips. His voice was heavy with the accent of his birth and the guttural tones rang strangely in her ear. "How is the Queen?"

"She is not well."

"I am sorry she is so sick," he said earnestly. "I waited on her today to condole with her in her loss."

Or to press your suit with me? came to Isolde, but she shook it off. In Palomides's country, even a king had to court a sultana if he wished to win her daughter, as a mark of respect. And a Saracen knight always honored his wife's mother.

His wife's mother?

Gods above, was she thinking of marriage now? Hastily she turned her attention back to the knight. He had the largest, darkest eyes she had ever seen, and his well-trimmed beard and mustache were the same lustrous black. He wore a tunic of amber silk shot through with gold, and a long flowing overgown with sleeves like the wings of a bat. His damask train swept the ground, and a length of crushed silk was wound turban-style round his head, holding back his gorgeous pomaded hair.

His stare unnerved her. *Why did he look like that?*

"Ah, lady!"

He seemed to sense the fluttering of her pulse, moving a step nearer and lowering his tone. "The Queen your mother suffers now for love," he said, watching her closely. "But love should bring joy, not grief. When a man and a woman come together as one, they honor the Creator who has made them flesh. Your faith and mine are alike in this. Our God bids us rejoice in our bodies as much as your Goddess does."

He reached gently for her hand. The pearl in his ear trembled like a teardrop ready to fall, and his great liquid eyes never left hers.

"When a knight meets his true lady," he urged, "he honors her like the Goddess-Mother Herself. He does not make his way to her bed because the boundaries of her kingdom lie next to his. He does not take her like a slave girl for his pleasure, then pass her on to his knights."

Isolde's stomach lurched, and she tried to compose herself. *Don't be a fool! He's telling you honestly that a king may court a woman out of policy, and a ruler must choose a partner for the good of the land. And he's saying that he's loved other women before. That's the way of men, you've known that all your life.* She gritted her teeth. *Fool again, girl, to think that somewhere a man is waiting for no one but you as you have been waiting for him—waiting to enter the dream—*

"And for a lady—a pure lady," the dark voice went on, "the love of a man can be a blessing indeed. His joy becomes her joy when they are joined as one, and he teaches her all she needs to know. She gives her soul to him and he cares for it like a bird with a broken wing. All his life he will love and shelter that little bird."

Little bird?

Isolde's senses raced. *I come from a line of battle hawks, warrior queens. My foremothers kept the Romans at bay, and never an iron sandal trod these shores.*

But somehow his fingers had found their way into the hollow of her hand and her palm was growing damp with springing dew. Her mind swam in the heady scent of his pomade, all the perfumes of Arabia, oil of lemon, sandalwood, and myrrh—

"Let me woo you, lady. Take me for your own."

His voice wound its way through her scattered thoughts as his fingers traced his wishes on her hand. "I will throw kings and kingdoms at your feet. I will rain the treasures of the Orient on your head, pearls for your tears, sapphires for your eyes. Let me take you to the black tents of my tribe. Admit me to the red pavilion of your heart!"

He kissed the inside of her wrist and whispered in her ear. She was softening, he knew it, she was taking his imprint like wax.

Her thoughts were swarming like a hive of bees.

A queen needs a champion—

—and the kingdom needs an heir—

He is a king and a very valiant knight.

—and babies have to be made lying down with men—

Babies—

She froze. Made with touches and kisses like this, and these odd sensations in her breasts and thighs? Was this what the maidens did at Beltain when they crept to their beds on the hillside with a man they did not know?

Suddenly she was riding a hot wave of shame. *I cannot do it!* Tears sprang to her eyes. *He has known slave girls and queens and I'm still a virgin, a wretched slow beginner in the game!*

Except to him, it seemed. The sensual words went on. She watched the red moist mouth moving to and fro, and glimpsed his thick tongue behind his fine white teeth. A sick sensation gripped her, and she could not breathe. *Make a baby with this man? Never!*

"Thank you, my lord." She pulled back and broke away. "You honor me, but I cannot offer you the same honor in return."

His eyes dilated. "Do not say so!" he said harshly. "We will talk of this again at a better time."

Isolde shook her head. "I must take care of the Queen. And I have a duty to my country, too. She and I are married to the land."

"You do not mean it!" He clutched his breast as though he had been stabbed. "You are my lady, and I am your knight!"

Isolde looked away. "I will know my knight when he comes." Unconsciously her fingers sought her father's ring.

"Who is he?" he cried jealously. "How will you know?"

"I learned it—" She caught herself up. She should not share such things with the Saracen knight. "No matter. You must go your way, sir, while I go mine."

"Princess, this cannot be!"

She looked up into an expression she had never seen before, black and scowling, cold and set. Her back stiffened. "My lord, I—"

"You will learn I am not to be scorned," he interrupted, staring intently into her eyes. "You are my—"

"Lady, a ship, a ship!"

There was a distant cry from far below and a bustle of sudden action down on the shore. The evening landscape was fading before their eyes, and a veil of silver mist lay over the sea.

Sir Palomides leaned forward, peering into the dusk. "A stranger ship at the dock," he announced suspiciously. Then he stiffened, and his lustrous eyes grew opaque. "They have come for you."

She started. She had heard that the men of his race had the gift of Sight. "For me—why?"

He turned his unseeing gaze upon the ship. "Its sails are dark, like death," he said at last. "And you—" he fell silent, staring down the twisting road of time. "You," he resumed, "are life. You are what they seek." He gave a bitter laugh, and she knew he had seen more than he would say. "Death seeks life as the land seeks the sea."

"Lady!" came the distant cry again.

She looked at the stranger ship with its black sails. A small group was struggling down the gangplank, carrying the body of an unconscious man. Behind them limped a crooked old pilgrim, waving his arms and trying to take charge. She hastened down the path to meet them with Sir Palomides on her heels.

Halfway between land and sea she encountered the ragged procession moving slowly through the gathering dusk. Coming toward her were four sailors bearing a rough litter and, lying on it, the figure of a man. The glimmering light played over his sleeping face and one battle-scarred hand rested lightly on his heart. She heard a rushing in the skies like the wind off the sea. *Who are you, sir?*

She moved forward like a woman in a dream. The stranger was dressed in the humble garb of a pilgrim, with a few traces of a more distinguished past. A cunning bronze brooch held his robe in place, and a fillet of gold held back his thick fair hair. By his side lay a harp and a broadsword in a plain leather sheath, and he wore an emerald ring on the little finger of one hand. In good health, she could see, he would be a fine-looking man. Now his skin was gray, his breathing was harsh, and his skin was like clay to the touch. Around him hung the stink of impending death.

Did it matter? No. Never had she seen a man more beautiful. The moonlight lovingly caressed his face, sharpening the strong lines of his jaw, etching his cheekbones, deepening the shadows of thought around his eyes. His thick, glossy hair fell back from a broad forehead and a thousand little lovelights gleamed around his mouth.

Oh—

The world faded, and she trembled from head to foot. The old pilgrim thrust his way forward and bent over the man on the litter, and she saw his lips working but could not follow a word. Dropping through the veils of evening came one sound alone, a low, rich voice from distant Avalon. *Hear me, Isolde—you will know your knight when he comes.*

And now her mother's voice sounded again in the great quiet all around.

When the doors of the Otherworld stand open for love, a woman awakens to the man of the dream—

A man from another country, tall and unsmiling, shining in the dark—

Far away she heard the slow, sad roar of the incoming tide. Suddenly she was salmon and dolphin, sea-wife and mermaid, at home by land and sea. Her sisters were the kittiwakes crying in the air, and her brothers the otters whistling from their dam. Written in the sand she saw the footprints of a man, alone, unseen, coming her way. A wind from the Otherworld brushed her face, and she felt the approach of the great wave at the ending of the world.

Goddess, Mother, tell me—

Can it be?

She looked up and saw a ring around the moon. A sweet mist rose from the sea and the tall stranger lay on the litter, shining before her eyes. But he was sick, he was dying, perhaps already gone. She laid her hand on his forehead and he stirred and looked up with the sweetness of a child. Then his wondrous lips parted and he laughed.

She heard the tuneful ringing of the stars echoing the music of her heart. She threw back her head, holding down a famished howl of fear and hope. *"Who are you?"* she cried.

chapter
19

He asked them to lay him with his mother, and he thought they had. He knew it must be her, because he remembered the touch of her hand, and the look in her eyes as she watched him, full of pain. She had asked him, *Who are you?* and he did not know. He saw her now with stars flaming round her head, all robed in clouds. Then he heard her voice, and knew that he was wrong. She was not his mother. She was a spirit, a saint.

"Who is this knight?" her voice said.

"No knight, lady, but a poor pilgrim like myself," came an old man's whine. "We were sailing to the land of the Picts when a drunken sailor stabbed him with a poisoned knife. He gave me the last of his gold to bring him here."

Did I do that? wondered Tristan. Perhaps I did. He felt the light touch again, and laughed for joy.

"Can you save him, Princess? He's a lovely lad," the old man moaned.

Who was this ancient, who seemed to know more about him than he did himself? It seemed to Tristan that he had heard the voice before. But that had been an old beggar on a clifftop when he saw the Lady of the Sea, not a pilgrim at all. His mind wandered off. It was all too hard.

"Believe me, old sir, we will do all we can."

The lady's footsteps retreated and he drifted peacefully again. Then he heard the old man's voice hissing in his ear. "Hear me! You are in Ireland, the land of your mortal foes. If you want to live, forget all you were. You are Tantris the pilgrim now, harper and bard."

Tantris? He wanted to laugh. But the old man's voice came again, whispering inside his head like the sweet silver song of the sea. *Sleep, Tantris, sleep—*

Suddenly there was nothing else he wanted to do.

Sleep, Tantris, sleep—

Kneeling beside Tristan's litter, Merlin watched the fluttering eyelids as the young knight slipped away. Then he tugged his pilgrim's gown tighter around his thin chest and got to his feet. So far, so good—now would the Princess come to Tristan's aid?

He stiffened. Who was this gorgeous pampered stranger coming up? Merlin eyed the newcomer and felt the hackles rising on his neck. He knew with an animal certainty that the Saracen knight was his enemy and Tristan's, too, and bared his teeth in a feral grin.

Who was that ancient loon? With a surge of anger, Palomides returned the glare and strode over to Isolde's side.

"Let me help you, Princess," he said solicitously. He turned and raised a hand to summon his knights. "We can take care of these men."

Isolde gave him a smile. *He means well—and I should treat him well.*

"Thank you, sir." She gestured toward the litter. "This man is very sick. Let's get him and the old pilgrim up to the castle as fast as we can."

Palomides's eyes widened. "You mistake me, lady," he said. "You must have nothing to do with riffraff like this. My knights will deal with them."

Isolde stared. "But he's come to me to be healed."

Palomides waved a contemptuous hand. "He's a dead man, Princess—the only thing to do is send him back to his ship."

She could feel her face flaming. "If we help him fast enough, he might live."

"And bring diseases to Dubh Lein that would kill us all." Palomides's eye flickered over Merlin in his shabby robes. "Like his unsavory friend. Why concern yourself with wretches like these?"

She drew a breath. "Sir Palomides, you are a stranger here at court. In my own country, I know what to do."

His anger now was plain. "I tell you, Princess, they are not for you."

He tells me?

Gods and Great Ones!

Her temper flared. "This man is dying while we wrangle here!" She turned to the sailors and pointed the way up the hill. "Sirs, bring him up to the castle. We'll take care of him."

"I'll prepare the infirmary, lady," Brangwain said, moving briskly away.

"Till tomorrow then, Princess." Sir Palomides was taking a furious leave, tugging at the point of his beard.

Isolde shivered. *Did I think this man could be my knight?* The next thought was even colder. *And the stranger, too—what was I thinking of?*

A lonely wind was coming in off the sea. Torn, ragged clouds were fleeting across the sky, and the moon was gone.

It was madness—moon madness—I lost my mind. Lost my mind to a dream, not to love itself. When my knight comes, he will not be a dream.

The castle lay ahead in the gathering dusk. The lights of the infirmary beckoned through the dark, countless tiny swan lamps flickering like stars. She forced herself to move up the castle hill.

Hurry, hurry—

The infirmary was blazing with light through the open door. "Are we ready, Brangwain?"

"Vervain, antinomy, lady," the maid called, "all here. And we've taken care of the old man who brought him in. He was offered a bed for the night, but he wanted to be on his way."

Hastily Isolde wrapped herself in a clean apron as Brangwain bound up her hair. She hurried over to the figure on the table in the center of the room. "How is he?"

Brangwain followed. "The wound's in his leg, they say."

"Let me see."

He lay on his back, his eyes closed and his face as pale as his shirt. A rough length of linen lay across his loins, and his legs were bare. A shallow pulse was fluttering in his neck, and he had a huge engorged wound in the front of his thigh. The flesh around it looked like a rotten plum, and she could see the quick of the sore, black and festering.

She stood irresolute. Never had she missed her Druid father as she did now. *What if I fail and he dies like Marhaus?*

Brangwain's voice came again. "We're ready, lady," she said steadily. "The men are standing by to hold him down."

Isolde drew a breath. "Good." She rolled up her sleeves and reached for her instruments. "Then let's begin."

AFTERWARD TRISTAN COULD remember crying out, but only in the caverns of his mind. He knew he must not flinch or make a sound as the small steely fingers probed his wound, in case the grip faltered on which his life now turned. He floated out of his body on a sea of pain and his spirit grew strong as it roamed the air. With his senses heightened beyond their normal pitch he could hear the two women murmuring as they worked, and rested in the soft cat's cradle of their voices weaving to and fro.

At the end he could feel their sadness in the air like dew. You have done your best, he wanted to say, but could not. His whole being dwindled down to a pinpoint of pain, and he drifted away.

Goddess, Mother, save him—

Holding his wrist, Isolde felt the feeble pulse fluttering in and out, and threw down her instruments in distress.

"It's not enough!" she cried. "The poison has entered his bones, and nothing will cure the flesh that does not scour the whole body to drive the evil out."

She turned to the shelves along the walls of the room. The light from the swan lamps shone over bottles and jars of greenish glass. She moved between them, her fingers remembering their contents from their smooth, cold sides: juniper, sundew, foxglove, wild bryony—

"Every poison has its opposite," she said stubbornly. "Somewhere in here lies the answer to his grief."

Her sight shivered and she saw a woody dell, deeply overshadowed by a thick forest roof. Nothing grew in the gloom but nightshade, hemlock, and yew, and she knew she was looking into a poison grove. In the center a small yellow many-headed flower burned with a sickly flame, and its thin leaves groped like witches' fingers in the air. Its little mouths turned to her with a venomous grin. *Do you know me, Isolde?*

Isolde smiled. Yellow spurge. *Oh yes, I do. I know your name, my dear.*

The lamplight danced in and out of the bright fluids on the shelf. Her hand went to a pale liquid the color of life itself. "This is the antidote."

She looked back toward the table and her smile vanished. "Hurry, Brangwain, hurry," she panted, reaching for the jar, "while there's still time."

THE LAMPS IN the infirmary burned late that night, and for many nights. And outside, Palomides prowled the shadows like a watcher of the deep while Isolde never left the sick pilgrim's side. At last the Saracen could bear it no longer. Pale and heavy-eyed after a night of fitful sleep, he rose early and dressed with unusual care. Then he crossed the courtyard, surrounded by his knights, and knocked at the door of the Queen's House to see the Queen.

The distraught, thin-faced girl who answered looked as if she had not slept for a week. She stared at Sir Palomides with fear in her eyes. No, the Queen could not—she dared not—the Queen had forbidden any visitors—she'd be whipped—

Only when he threatened to have her whipped himself did she conduct them to the Queen's chamber and vanish inside. There was an interminable wait in the drafty corridor, then the maid's pale eyes reappeared round the door, a finger beckoned, and he was within.

The chamber stretched before him like a cave. The maid closed the door behind him and whisked away. Black drapes blocked the windows and the only light came from a few flickering swan lamps hidden in holes round the walls. A moment of doubt darkened the Saracen's soul. This was a house of mourning—why was he here?

The air in the chamber lay heavy, like a pall. Slowly his eyes grew accustomed to the light, and he picked up the signs of mourning everywhere. Headdresses and jewels lay scattered on the floor. A tray beside the door held an empty flagon of wine and a few crusts of bread, clearly all that was keeping the Queen alive. Farther in, a great stand of armor dominated one wall, displaying a winged helmet of gold, a great shield of bronze, and a breastplate carved with swans in silver and gold.

He caught his breath. The workmanship was far in advance of anything he had seen before. Made for Marhaus, of course, to reward the champion when he came back in triumph to the Queen. He reached out in wonder.

A furious howl came slicing through the air. "Don't dare to touch!"

He whipped round and blanched at what he saw. "Your Majesty—"

The Queen lay huddled on the bed, her long plum-colored hair torn out by the handful and tumbling around her like blood. Her face was scored with the marks of her nails and tears stood in her bruised and swollen eyes. As he watched, she began to beat her breast.

"Are you looking for my love?" she keened, throwing back her head. "Don't you know he's gone?"

Alas, poor lady—

Palomides felt his soul dissolving in grief. He fingered the hilt of his sword. "All the world knows, madam," he rejoined sorrowfully, "when a hero has gone."

"Yesss!" She lunged forward, then drew herself up like a queen. "You're a sensible man," she said grandly, peering through the gloom. "And I know who you are." Her red-rimmed eyes narrowed. "Why are you here?"

"To win your help," he said abruptly. He shook his head hopelessly and spread his hands. "I have courted your daughter, and failed."

"Failed?" Her red-black eyes shot fire. "How?"

"I offered to make her my queen, and she refused." He bared his teeth. "She said that, like you, she was married to the land."

"Not so!" The Queen leaned forward with a savage laugh. "If she were, she would have taken a consort by now. We would have a young princess to follow after her, and a brood of other children around the throne." She spat with disgust. "But she will not make the choice."

Palomides's large eyes darkened. "Sooner or later, all women must make the choice. And no woman refuses a knight of the Saracens or a king of my tribe." He turned his gaze on the Queen. "Give her to me, Majesty, or I must take her by force. She has dishonored me!"

The Queen favored him with a sardonic smile. "In our country, sir, women may choose and refuse. And sooner or later, a queen has to choose." She laughed harshly. "Never fear, sir, I've destined her for your bed."

He started. "What?"

The Queen threw back her hair. "I shall hold a great tournament for her hand, with many knights."

His face cleared like sunrise at sea. "And I shall win," he said simply. "God will fight for me."

The Queen smiled like a mother tiger on her cub. "And when you do, Isolde must choose you. The champion will become the chosen one. Isolde must have a consort, because she must have a child."

What a woman!

"Majesty—"

Palomides's huge eyes took on a fervent glow and he looked at the Queen in awe. His mind flew back to the senior sultanas who ruled his father's household when he was a boy, women of ancient knowledge and brooding power. Such would this lady be as time went on.

And she had planned all this. Isolde would be his! The dark chamber faded and he saw ahead long days of happiness and nights of bliss, galloping beside Isolde across burning sands, lifting the dusky veil of her pavilion under a desert moon. . . .

"Sir—"

He came to himself with a start. The Queen was bearing down on him through the gloom. She was near enough now for him to smell the salt of her tears.

"See, lord, see?"

She opened her hand. Lying on the palm was a fine sliver of metal glinting in the dim light. He knew at once what it was. All Dubh Lein now knew how Marhaus had died. But why would the Queen treasure such an ill-omened thing?

Keening to herself, the Queen turned on him again.

"Revenge," she moaned, "will I have my revenge?"

Palomides shook his head. "Lady, lady," he said sorrowfully, "who can say?"

chapter
20

ere, Sweyn! Over here!"

The Earl pricked up his ears. That sounded like Gawain. And the boy should be there too, if what the horse master had told him was true.

He quickened his pace into the stable yard, impervious to the blooming of a glorious day. And there they were, in a whirl of horses and grooms, Gawain and Lucan busy mounting up, calling to young Sweyn as Lienore crossed the courtyard toward them with her son by the hand.

"Good lad!" Lucan laughed, flashing his even white teeth. "You did well last time. We'll make a knight of you, young Sweyn, never fear."

Lienore dropped her eyes modestly to the ground. "Be good to him, sirs," she said in a soft, musical voice. "The Mother Herself will bless you for taking care of a fatherless child."

"This way then, young man!"

The two knights clattered out of the stable yard with young Sweyn and his pony between them, the small boy overshadowed by their bulk. Armed with his own small helmet, shield, and lance, he was a miniature knight from head to foot. Transfixed, the Earl did not hear Lienore approaching till her voice dropped into his ear.

"Well, Father?"

He came to himself with a start. "What d'you mean?" he snapped.

"I mean things are going well," she returned, undeterred. "Guenevere thought she'd thwart us by sending for Merlin, but while they waited, they've all fallen for young Sweyn."

"And some of them for you," the Earl retorted savagely. "I've seen Gawain and the others sniffing around you like dogs." He glared at her. "We want no more bastards, d'you hear?"

She raised one shoulder in a careless shrug. "Not even if it's the King's?"

"What?" His eyes bulged. "Are you saying . . ."

Lienore surveyed the horizon and savored the pause. "No," she said. "Not yet."

"But you mean—"

She fixed him with eyes that matched her dainty blue gown. "Oh yes, Father," she said serenely. "It needs only time."

"Time!" The Earl fought down a nervous laugh. Seducing the King— Gods above, would another bastard endear them to the King? Or would King and court see her for the trollop she was?

"Look, Lienore," he began, with a menacing frown.

"Look yourself," she replied indifferently, pointing toward the gate. A withered old man in a threadbare pilgrim's gown was making his way into the courtyard with slow, limping steps. The Earl hastened forward with his whip upraised.

"Be off with you!" he roared. "We want no beggars here!"

The old man turned, and smiled into his eyes. He raised a hand, and the Earl found he could not move. As he stood motionless, frozen in rage, the pilgrim threw back his hood and straightened up. Shaking out his rich gray locks, he seemed to swell and grow, no longer a crippled beggar but a calm and stately old man.

His golden gaze fell on Earl Sweyn and he smiled. "Good day, my lord," he said courteously. "Will you take me to the King?"

❧

"MERLIN!"

Arthur's joyful bellow split the air. "God only knows how dearly we've longed for you here!"

Behind Arthur, Guenevere's lovely face was wreathed in smiles. "You are welcome, sir."

Merlin disengaged himself from Arthur's embrace and paused to cast an unfavorable eye over the low sofas with their yellowing sheepskin pelts, the battered tables, and worm-eaten chairs. His mouth twisted in a sardonic grin. Yes, time I was here.

"You have heard the news from Cornwall?" Arthur began. "They have fought off the threat from Ireland, for now, it seems. We intend to press on to King Mark to make sure."

Merlin nodded. "But that, I think, is not your main concern now?"

"No." Arthur took a deep breath. "Merlin, there's a child here they say is my son."

Guenevere leaned forward, as pale as a lily in her silken gown. "I do not trust the woman," she said tremulously. "But the child—"

"He's a wonder, Merlin," Arthur said simply, unable to keep the pride out of his voice.

Merlin strolled away to the window. "I have seen the boy."

Arthur started forward. "Where?"

Merlin waved a hand. "Just now, in the courtyard, riding out with Lucan and Gawain." A gleam of something like malice crossed the ancient face. "He has a princely air. And a man needs a son."

Guenevere's lips compressed into a thin line. She knew that Merlin was jibing at her and had never felt her childlessness more painfully than now. "Only if his mother is to be believed."

Arthur winced under his wife's baleful stare. "Did I lie with her, Merlin?" he cried desperately. "Is the boy my son?"

There was a pause, then Merlin shook his head. "Ask the Old Ones, boy. This is beyond the reach of my simple art."

Simple art! Guenevere's eyes searched the old enchanter's face. "But surely you can tell if he's Arthur's son?"

Merlin's eyes were opaque. "My stars are dark. I cannot see so far." He spread his sinewy hands and shrugged resentfully. "Even a Lord of Light does not know everything!"

Arthur's face was filmed with sweat. "Help me, Merlin," he said in a voice not his own. "What shall I do?"

"Ah, there I can guide you, boy." Merlin stepped forward and took Arthur's arm, bowing to Guenevere. "Will you excuse us, lady? I shall walk with the King until dinner, then I must be gone." He steered Arthur possessively out the door.

Guenevere watched them go, then turned back to the room. Her large eyes were welling with distress, but her mouth was set in an attitude the companions knew. "Lord Merlin does not know the truth of this, it seems. We must look elsewhere."

Bedivere rose to his feet. "What shall we do, madam? Give us your commands."

Guenevere paused. "One woman knows." Her voice was implacable. "You must get it out of her."

Kay stared. "Madam, the Lady Lienore won't tell us the truth! She'll stick to her story like blood to a rusty knife."

"Not Lienore." Guenevere forced a smile. "The fortune-teller. Travel far, travel wide, but track her down."

Gawain's jaw dropped. "She could be anywhere!"

Lucan seconded him. "They're traveling people, madam. They don't stay in the same place from month to month."

"They don't, it's true." Kay shook his head. Slowly an idea was forming in his brain. "But they always take the same routes."

An answering light was dawning in Lucan's eye. "Tracks they've been following since time began. If we went back to where the tournament was held, we could trace them from there—"

"Yes!" Bedivere cried. "We could at least try."

The blood rushed to Lucan's head. If they took to the road, they'd be knights errant and have adventures again. They'd get at the truth and clear the King's name.

He pounded Gawain on the back, then punched the air. "To horse!" he cried. "To horse!"

chapter 21

h e came to himself in deep water, drowning in the sea. Then the face of his uncle swam toward him through the glass-green waves and he knew that King Mark was drowning, too.

"Sir Tristan," the bloodless lips intoned, "do you swear to honor me above all others to your dying day?"

"I do!" he cried, willing it away.

But the spectral form seized him by the neck and drew him down. "Ah, Tristan!" cried Mark, in a voice full of tears. "Now you are mine till death!"

Then a small, strong hand cupped the back of his neck and raised his head. He heard again the voice he had heard before, saying, "Drink this." He had no sensation of drinking, but after a while he grew warm. Then he sank again, but into a different sea.

Icy currents kissed his face and froze his limbs. The spirit shape of his uncle howled and writhed around, and he knew it had come to drag him back down to the depths. With the last working part of his mind, he knew he was only reliving the oath to King Mark because it was the last thing he remembered in the world of light. But the darkness had claimed him now. A mortal chill settled around his heart, and the briny taste of death filled his mouth.

Then a woman's form came between him and King Mark. Through the surging waters he caught the gleam of a face like a lily, and a halo of bright hair. He looked up from the depths into a pair of bright eyes that danced like sunlight on waves, and forgot his oath.

Meanwhile, the voices around him became more cheerful by the day. One was an older woman from the Welshlands by her sharp, lilting tones. The other sounded like birdsong on a May morning or the rising sun breaking through the clouds. Soon he knew that the voice of gold belonged to the owner of the hard, clever little hands. Sometimes when she was nursing him a strand of her hair brushed his pillow or he felt the edge of her veil.

She smelled of the outdoors, fresh and clean and sweet, and always she carried with her the tang of the sea. When he sank, as he did, down to the cold dark place, he thought she swam after him and brought him back.

At last he awoke to a morning as fresh as the days when the Shining Ones ruled the world. Beside his bed stood a girl with smiling eyes and a flowing mane of hair, red as the sunset and golden as the dawn. She wore a sea-green gown and a fine fillet of gold with a simple white veil holding back her clustering curls. His mind was as clear as his flesh felt now, and he knew he was lying in bed because he was ill.

Lying . . .

He was lying in Ireland, whose champion he had killed. And nothing but lying and more lying lay ahead if he was to live.

"Who are you, sir?" came the girl's sparkling voice.

And he turned his face away because he could not lie.

*

"WHAT'S WRONG WITH him, Brangwain? Why won't he speak to me?"

Brangwain raised her head from the task of sorting herbs. "I don't know, madam." She favored Isolde with an unfathomable look. "It's hard to tell what he thinks, he's so brave."

"Yes, isn't he?" Isolde cried. "He never flinched when I searched his wound, only smiled and closed his eyes."

Brangwain gave her another piercing look, while her busy hands worked. "And he's young and handsome, and for sure he's gently born."

"Yes, he doesn't seem like a poor pilgrim," she enthused. "He looks like the son of a king."

"He's a fine young man." Brangwain took a deep breath, willing Isolde to understand. "But he's still a poor pilgrim, my lady, a sick man, and not used to royalty. So it wouldn't be surprising if he was over-whelmed."

An unpleasant sensation caught Isolde unawares. "Not by me!"

"As you say, lady." Brangwain dropped her head and busied herself with the fragrant foliage passing through her hands. "Now let's see, savory, all-heal—"

"It's just that he won't speak."

"—vervain, thyme—"

Isolde paused. Whatever Brangwain said, there was always a lurking truth.

She shuddered. *I will not be too much for any man.*

All her life she had seen that in her mother, and vowed to be different. She must be cooler with the patient, more reserved. He was only a pilgrim passing through, after all.

So she watched him recover and grow strong, but at a distance, holding back her smiles. Yet there was so much about him that interested her, from the deep-set, thoughtful eyes to the long, clever fingers of his strong brown hands. One day after dressing his wound, she laid her hand on the harp beside the bed. "Are you a bard, sir?"

He laughed. "No, lady, I harp for my own pleasure."

Would you play for mine? came strangely into her mind. But it was one of many things she did not say.

THEN CAME THE day when he left his bed. She saw the sweat break out on his forehead as he set his hurt leg to the floor, but he made no sound. With his arms around the shoulders of two burly serving men, he dragged himself around the chamber till she was forced to order him back to his couch. Even then he was on his feet again within hours. Every day after that he practiced till he could move without pain.

Soon it was time, she decided, to walk on the beach. They left the castle on a bright, raw morning with the melancholy tang of autumn in the air. The gathering birds were twittering in the skies and the first yellow leaves were mourning the summer's end. Four sturdy attendants followed with a carrying chair. But she could tell from the set of his chin that he would walk or die.

There was no wind as they approached the shore and the sea lay before them like a sheet of glass. Isolde saw a handful of boats clustered in the harbor and felt a shadow fall across the dawn. Soon the stranger

would sail away and be gone, no more to her than one of the clouds floating on the glossy surface of the sea. She shook her head. What was it
to her?

His voice behind her sounded a somber note. "When the sea is calm
like this, who could believe the fury hidden in its depths?"

She turned. He was staring out over the bay, its green waters cradled
in the arms of the land. Great flocks of waders huddled on one leg in the
shallows, their dark brown bodies as motionless as stones. A silver sun
shone over the slumbering mountains and its light fingers caressed his
face. With a rush of pride she saw that his pain-ravaged features were
returning to health.

"You are a pilgrim, sir?" she observed conversationally. "Where lies
your pilgrimage?"

She saw a shadow pass across his face.

"Here and there," he replied with difficulty. "I have not set a goal."

"What do you seek?"

The voice of her old master Gwydion came into her head. *Every man
seeks the woman of the dream.*

She flushed at the thought, and struggled to sound natural again.
"Wherever your path lies, you are welcome in Ireland, sir."

And once more the guarded look shadowed his face. "Thank you," he
said.

"My mother the Queen will receive you as soon as she can. She is not
well. She has suffered a great loss. Her champion was killed—"

"I am sorry to hear it," he broke in. "More than I can say."

His face was glistening, and she feared he was in pain. "Are you well,
sir?"

"Never better!" he cried hoarsely.

She did not believe him. "I am afraid we have overtaxed your
strength."

Overruling his protests, she insisted they turn back. As they left, she
cast one last glance behind her over the bay. Far out at sea a little boat
rode at anchor and it came to her, *We could sail away together, I could leave
with him now.*

Sail away?

She frowned.

Leave with him?

What is this?
She hardly knew the man.

LATER SHE TOOK him out riding, to try his strength on a horse. She chose a stately old stallion for him, well past his wicked days, and she rode her own white mare with the cornflower blue eyes, as the Queens of the Western Isle had done since time began. Leaving the castle they turned inland, away from the sea, and took a sheltered path into the forest where they could be at peace.

The morning sun was pale now in the sky, and the dew hung trembling on the turning leaves. The mournful chill of autumn enveloped them and again the fleeting thought shot through her head, *Winter is coming and he will soon be gone.* She shook her head, annoyed with herself. Of course he would. His well-shaped face was bright with renewed hope, and his flesh glowed with life and health. Why should he stay?

The air in the forest was crisp and the horses trod eagerly forward under the trees. His hands on the reins were loving, quiet, and firm, and she could see years of horse mastery in his gentle touch.

"You may like to go down to the tiltyard," she ventured. "One of our knights would be happy to try a pass with you."

"Thank you, no," he said with deep reserve. "I do not fight. I am a man of peace."

Isolde felt him drawing back and looked away. *Tread carefully. You do not know this man.*

At the edge of the path, great ferns were uncoiling their fronds, and trailing woodbine mantled the trees with gold. In the soft sunlit gloom, the grass glowed with a vivid green and she saw his eyes feeding hungrily on the emerald growth.

"Does it rain much here?" he inquired.

"Only as much as we need," she replied merrily. "And the sun shines, too."

"So you must have rainbows?"

"Like the morning of the world." Her face lit up. "The Mother is always shining through her tears."

"You keep the Old Faith here?"

She looked at him sternly. "We keep the only faith." Her face softened. "But we also give home to the Christians and all who come. The Mother teaches us that all faith is love. And love is life itself, that's why we should never kill."

"Never kill?"

An impulse of distress passed over his face, and again she had an awkward feeling of trespassing where she should not. "Where do you come from, sir?" she asked, turning the conversation into an easier path.

But still the odd constraint hung over him, and an impenetrable glance darkened his eyes. "From—from Terre Foraine," he said awkwardly.

"The land of King Pelles?" she asked eagerly. "They say he's had a prophecy that the most peerless knight in the world will come to claim his daughter as a virgin bride. Then the son she will bear will find the Holy Grail, so for all Christians, the Princess is the vessel who will redeem their sin."

He shifted in the saddle. "I have no knowledge of this," he said dismissively, turning his head away.

Isolde stared. "But surely, if you come from Terre Foraine—"

He closed his eyes. "I do not know the girl."

"But your father must—"

"My father is dead. And my mother, too."

He was sweating again. She must not press him like this. Perhaps his parents had died suddenly, leaving him alone, and that was the sorrowful cause of his pilgrimage. She set her mouth in a slender line and resolved to be quiet.

But her questions had unlocked something deep in him.

"I was a child of sorrow," he said. "My mother died in the forest as I was born."

She frowned. "In the forest? What was she doing there?"

"Her pains came on before her time." He gestured to the ring on his little finger, where a fireburst of emeralds flashed and sang in the sun. "This is the only remembrance I have of her. My father gave it to her when they were betrothed."

Isolde felt a pain beyond words. "So you never knew her at all?"

"Oh, yes, I did." His face was blooming with a mystic light. "My nurse told me that my mother held me from the moment I was born, and would not be parted from me till she died. So I knew her for many hours before her soul slipped its shell."

He was speaking to her, but she could see from his eyes that he was far away. "Then she passed into the Beyond," he went on in a low voice, "and I never saw her again. But sometimes I think that she comes back to me at sunrise or sunset, or when I cannot sleep. Then through the veils of night I see her face, as I saw it before."

She had so much pain around her heart that she could hardly speak. "It is a sorrowful tale."

His smile was luminous. "I do not find it so. My mother loved me. Not all men can say that."

"It's true." She thought of her own mother with a peculiar pang. "A mother's love can be like a chain."

"You're a forest doe," he said with an insight as sharp as pain, "and for you, capture is death."

Her mood lifted, and she laughed merrily. "You're the woodland creature; I'm a child of the sea. I lived in the water from the time I was born."

He could not help catching her newfound sense of fun. "With waves for playfellows." He grinned. "And the dolphins to guard you when you swam far out."

"Whereas you," she teased, "were born in a deep dark wood, and grew like an oak tree, rooted in the land." She paused, suddenly serious. "You're the land, I'm the sea. Land and sea together—" she broke off.

"—make the whole earth," he finished quietly.

The haunting fragrance of honeysuckle filled the air. Confused, she tore a leaf of ivy from a nearby tree and its sharp, dark scent mingled with the honeyed sweetness and drowned out her senses. She tried to speak, but did not know what to say. The deep silence hung heavily between them all the way back.

Yet after that they rode out every day, sometimes late into the night. Often they found themselves returning after dusk, as the evenings were darkening down earlier now. Sometimes they heard the sound of the fairy hunt, and she could see that the horns of the Fair Ones spoke to him in tunes that she could not hear. Other times they caught fleeting laughter and flickering lights, and saw slender, shadowy shapes dancing beneath the trees. But as soon as they heard the high, tinkling revelry, they changed their direction to leave the Fair Ones in peace.

All this time he made no move to leave and she forgot her own warnings, *Soon he will be gone.* Autumn blazed through the woods in flaming red and gold, and she drifted through timeless, sunlit hours, long days of dreaming and nights sweeter than any before. One day he took up his harp and sang for her, melodies that lingered long after their sound had gone. They talked of everything and nothing under Brangwain's loving eye, and found a new world in each other's thoughts.

It seemed that the glory of those golden days would never end. And so they continued till the day when Brangwain came running to tell her that the Queen had called a tournament, and Isolde was the prize.

chapter 22

a tournament, madam?"

"Isolde!"

The Queen uncoiled her lean frame and sprang up from the couch. As she came forward, her mourning silks frothed sadly around her feet. She was calmer than she had been, Isolde saw. But the marks of her suffering had not left her face.

"Yes, a tournament, Isolde!" she cried. "You know it's time."

Outside the Queen's House a livid sun was sinking into the sea. A strange red and yellow light danced off the waves, filling the cavernous room with glints of pus and blood. With rising alarm, Isolde caught an unpleasant odor seeping through the air, and saw a foul, shapeless mass among the ashes on the hearth. Her stomach turned. The Queen had been raising her old gods of blood and bone. There would be no way now to turn her back from her desires.

Isolde groaned. "Mother, what have you done?"

The Queen clapped her hands, and her dark face danced. "The heralds have been sent out far and wide. The tournament will take place at the full moon."

Isolde felt tears of despair biting the back of her throat. "But why?" she cried. "Mother, tell me why!"

"You know why!" The Queen's eyes flashed with fire. "I am the Queen of a great Mother-right and my only daughter refuses to go the way of the Mother, the way of all womankind!"

No, Mother, that's not true—you don't know—

Isolde bit her lip. "But why now?" she demanded desperately.

The Queen tossed her head and whirled away. "Now is as good a time as any," she cried airily. "There are many knights here to choose from, great fighters and fine men, too—kings, champions, you may take your pick."

Kings, champions?

Palomides!

Isolde struck her head. She could have torn her hair. *Fool, fool!* she berated herself, *Three times fool!* How could she have forgotten him all this time, when she knew in her heart that he would not forget her?

How often in these last weeks had she seen him crossing the court-yard to the Queen's House, surrounded by his knights, and been only too glad to believe that the noble Saracen was unselfishly consoling her mother in her loss? Why had she never thought that he might be fur-thering a scheme of his own?

And her mother—lonely and still mourning her lover's death—she could hardly have been more vulnerable to a handsome young man. Gen-erous, too, she thought bitterly, looking at her mother with mounting rage. That girdle of gold, that chain of tiger's eyes, the black pearl ear-rings so sweetly kissing the long neck—all these glittering baubles must have come from Palomides.

"Isolde, my dear." Her mother was at her side, taking her hand, touch-ing her cheek with a tremulous smile. "You know the tournament is announced," she said beseechingly. "We can't stop it now. Let those who answer the challenge fight over you, and see who wins. Then you can take all the time you want to choose your knight."

"Mother—"

She wanted to weep, to shout, to push her mother away. The Queen was never to be trusted when she took this wheedling tone. *What are you plotting, Mother?* she cried inwardly. *Have you promised me to Palomides if he wins?*

She nerved herself up to destroy her mother's dream. "Let us hold the tournament then," she said steadily, "and give a true Irish welcome to all who come. But—"

A wild look of triumph crossed her mother's face. "Why, there's a girl!" she cried. She swooped on Isolde and folded her in her arms. "I knew I was right! You'll be happy, I swear to you." A shower of kisses fell on Isolde's face. "Oh, dearest, as soon as you know the love of a man—"

Isolde disengaged herself as gently as she could. "Mother, let me speak!" She stepped back and looked her mother in the eye. "Whoever wins, I will not take the champion for my love."

"Oh, you will, Isolde, you will!"

Isolde froze with shock. She had braced herself for wild tears and reproaches, but her mother's triumph was open and unalloyed.

"You forget, my dear," the Queen said in a voice vibrating with satisfaction and menace alike, "the Queen's Tournament is attended by lords and crannog-dwellers, by the highest in the land and those from the farthest bog and fen. I have sent to every hidden corner of the island, even to the Land Kin, the lost folk who were here before the Old Ones and mated with them when they came." She gave a high, dangerous laugh. "Why, the Fair Ones themselves will step out of their hills and hollows to see who wins the love of the future Queen."

Her voice took on an incantatory note. "All the people of the Western Isle will be there—your people, Isolde, those who will take you as their Queen. They will watch from dawn to dusk as each knight sheds his blood for you, breaks his bones, risks his life. At the end of the day, one man will stand alone, the champion of champions, a consort fit for a queen. That man will be a worthy partner of your bed and sword. The people will see him as your chosen one. And when they demand it of you—*how will you refuse?*"

***

A TOURNAMENT?

And the Princess to marry the champion, come what may?

Tristan paced the floor of his chamber and fought down his rage. Only a moment ago, it seemed, they had been riding in the forest without a care, then a white-faced Brangwain had confronted them with the news that had sent Isolde running to the Queen's House, tight-lipped and trembling with shock.

"Wait for me," she had said. "I shall return."

Since then he had been tossing on a sea of anger and dread. It was intolerable to see the Princess treated like this. What should he do?

A dull ache began at the top of his leg and his fingers flew to the throbbing in his thigh. His injury was not fully healed, he knew, and traces of the poison still lingered in his bones. Any exertion, and the wound would break out again. Why torment himself, then? It was nothing to him what the Princess and her mother did. He'd be leaving the island as soon as he was well.

All true, murmured another part of his mind. *But you have remained here long after you could have gone. You have seen the sun rise and set in a merry face and a cloud of bright hair. You have gazed into eyes of such mystery that the man who once looked into them would never cease to hope.*

"I have sworn my allegiance to King Mark!" he cried in his soul. "I have to go back."

Leave here? the inner voice went on. *Here where you have found a welcome that has fed your heart's desire, and known again the warmth of a mother's touch?*

He groaned aloud. "But I'm here under false pretenses, I'm lying to her with every word I say."

And in danger of your life every moment, if the truth is known. Yes, a hard fate, my dear.

"No harder than hers, if this tournament takes place!" He resumed his distracted pacing. "She has no knight. And I'm here as a pilgrim, without armor or horse—Gods above!" He could have torn his hair.

Think, man! he besought himself thickly, only think! You still have Glaeve. . . . He paused to consider the mighty sword lying idle among his baggage, and hurried on. Glaeve's time would come. They had shed enough blood for now.

But Isolde—

There was a light step in the corridor and a knock at the door. "Excuse me, sir—" She was standing outside the door with her head bowed. "Will you walk in the garden?" she said in a low voice.

"At your wish, madam," he returned hurriedly. He knew she could not enter his chamber alone.

At the end of the passageway Brangwain curtsied to him and followed as Isolde led the way silently down the stairs. In the Queen's garden an autumn sun filled all the air with gold, and the last roses gamboled around the walls.

She came to a halt beneath a rustic arch where ivy and honeysuckle met overhead. The sun was warm on his back, but he could feel his fever rising and began to shiver again. He gazed at her imploringly, but she would not look up.

"It is true," she said in the same listless tone. "The Queen has called a tournament to determine which knight is fittest for my hand."

The blood drained from his heart. "It is no surprise," he said hollowly. "You will have to marry, if you are to be Queen." He could hear his voice sounding sicker with every note. "And you must have many admirers." He turned away. *A beautiful woman like you,* he did not say.

She colored and dropped her gaze. His soul congealed.

"This tournament—" he began, and broke off. He could not bear to see her brought so low. He wanted to kill all the combatants and overthrow the Queen.

He fingered the wound on his thigh. "I'd fight for you myself," he said passionately, "but for this." He gave a furious laugh. "I'd give your supposed champion a beating he wouldn't forget!"

"But you said—" She stared at him, alarmed. "You told me you don't fight—you're a man of peace."

"Yes, yes, so I am." The blood flooded his face. "But once—long ago, I—" He stumbled to a halt. "No matter," he resumed with difficulty. "That's all over now."

"And besides—"

He could see her struggling to get back to the world they had known.

"You're not well enough yet to think of anything like that. You've been very ill." She gave him a gaze that would have melted stone. A welter of wild impulses seized him and he fought them down.

"Well, lady, what must be, must be," he said harshly. "So, a tournament then—and may the best man win!"

❧

"YOU CAN'T SAIL tonight?"

Merlin bared his teeth, and clenched his crabbed hands like an eagle snatching a lamb. "Can't or won't?" he demanded threateningly.

But the weather-beaten figure before him was not to be put down. "Same thing, sir," he said stolidly, "when the weather's like this." He nodded at the sky, where oily, ragged clouds were driving furiously before the wind. His battered face set in determined lines. "No going out tonight."

Merlin tried another tack. "You're a man of wide experience, I know," he said flatteringly. "And knowledge has its price." He felt for the leather pouch in the bosom of his gown and allowed the captain to hear its suggestive chink. "There's gold here, man, redder than any sky. How much would it take for you to put out tonight?"

The man chuckled. "You may set your life at whatever price you like, sir." He rolled his eyes. "But there's no money on earth to buy mine."

"But my business calls me to the Western Isle!" Merlin stared out in a frenzy over the wind-lashed waves. "A sudden turn of events—there's danger there, even disaster, and I cannot delay." He turned and met the steady, sea-washed gaze. "Surely there's a man here who would go—"

He gestured toward the little cluster of white stone dwellings huddled round the bay. But even as he spoke, the hope died on his lips.

The wind now was whipping the words out of his mouth and drowning them in a high, rising whine. He did not catch the captain's dry farewell as the man departed, rolling with the gale. Drooping, Merlin turned his face into the storm and sent his spirit winging through the void.

"May your Gods be with you, boy," he growled hopelessly. "And your Princess, too. May the Mother fight for her now—I cannot!"

chapter 23

t the end of the day, one man will stand alone, a worthy partner of your bed and sword. The people will see him as your chosen one. And when they demand it of you—how will you refuse?

She had tossed all night with her mother's words hissing and whispering through her broken dreams. Yet still the day of the tournament dawned too soon. Lingering in her chamber, Isolde drove Brangwain to sharp-tongued irritation as she fretted over every gown the maid brought out for her to wear. First she chose a simple silk as white as bone, only to throw it off in favor of something stronger and less maidenly. Then she thought that the dark indigo velvet made her look too austere, like the women Druids of the ancient days, and off that came in a frenzy, too.

At last she settled on her favorite emerald green, with a cloak of gold and a veil of silver gauze. A deep diadem of pearls held back her unruly hair, and crystals and pearls shone at her neck and waist. Brangwain had insisted on a glimmer of coral on her lips and cheeks, and the maid at least was pleased with the result. But Isolde had never felt more unhappy in her life.

As they left the castle, she could not contain her rage. *How dare you, Mother, how dare you do this? The tournaments I remember were golden days of glory and of grief. But today, while the knights are fighting for their lives, you and I have a battle of our own. For I will never consent to this scheme of yours!*

The day was fine for the tournament, dry and clear, but every step brought a darker cast to her thoughts. Now even her skill as a healer was failing, it seemed. The pilgrim's wound had broken out again when the tournament was announced, and a low fever returned to all his limbs.

This morning she had found him pale and shaking in a sweat-soaked bed, and he would surely be worse by the end of the day.

Goddess, Mother, help him, she prayed distractedly. *I should be with him now—I should be at his side.*

Outside the castle walls, an excited throng streamed around them on all sides. While her guard struggled to hold the people back, within minutes, farmers were pushing their plump, red-faced wives forward to greet her, and mothers were holding out their children for her to bless.

"That's the Princess!" she heard on countless lips. "Today she'll have a champion and a chosen one!"

Again the unspoken fury filled her veins. *Mother, I cannot—I will not submit to this.*

Now the jousting field lay before them in the sun, its rough grass new-mown for the day's events. The meadow beside it was dotted with brightly colored pavilions, and humming with pages and squires running to and fro. Many of the knights turned out to bow and salute her with admiration in their eyes, but Isolde passed them all by with scarcely a glance. *At the end of the day, one of these will stand alone.* Well, so be it. Whoever he was, he would be nothing to her. She gave a crooked grin. *How will I refuse, Mother? Wait and see!*

On the far side of the field, the Queen's gallery loomed up darkly in the eye of the sun. Tensely Isolde climbed the wooden tower, feeling her resentment mounting with every step. She could hear her mother's laughter as she approached, and its strident echo set her teeth on edge.

"D'you hear that, Brangwain?" she demanded despairingly.

"Courage, lady!" the maid shot back under her breath.

In the center of the gallery, the Queen stood wide-eyed and glittering, surrounded by her knights. She had thrown off her dusky mourning attire and blossomed in crimson and red like a damask rose. Looking at the tall young men in their silver coats, Isolde felt a rush of raw distaste. With Sir Marhaus gone, they would all be sniffing round her mother: Sir Claig, Sir Finneail, Sir Tolen, which of them would bed her now? The next moment she felt the weight of all their eyes as every head swiveled intently toward her. Who will win you today, Princess? Who will we have to honor as your chosen one? was written in every gaze, and she cursed her mother again for doing this.

"Princess Isolde!"

It was the Queen's councillor Sir Gilhan, marking her appearance with a sweeping bow. The same question was hovering in his eyes.

You, too? she wanted to say, but her heart failed. With a murmured word of greeting, she turned away.

"Isolde, come here!" the Queen called with a triumphant smile, imperiously beckoning Isolde to her side. "You said it was too late in the season for a tournament, but see for yourself..."

One wild, white arm moved out over the field below. Gritting her teeth, Isolde forced herself to look. Now she could see that there were far more pavilions than she had thought, their flags blazoning their knights' origins from far and wide.

"See, Isolde?" came her mother's voice in her ear. "The King of the Blacklands, King Faramon of the Green, the Lord of the Isles, they're all here." She smiled exultantly. "And Sir Palomides, of course. Whoever wins will be a worthy choice."

Isolde did not trust herself to speak. Below them the knights were already pouring onto the field, lean, eager figures in red and silver, blue, white, and gold. Like brilliant birds of prey they stalked the field, fighting to hold their horses back from the charge. The roaring crowd greeted each one with delight, loudly cheering their heroes on by name.

"This way, sirs!"

Marshaled by the heralds, the combatants formed a procession to parade round the field and bow before the Queen.

"Isolde, look!"

The Queen was in ecstasy, her sensual soul responding to every move. One by one she scanned the nodding plumes and multicolored banners flying in the sun.

"Look, there's Sir Tennel!" she cried, clutching at Isolde's arm. "And Sir Saffir and Sir Epin of the Glen."

A gleaming figure bounded onto the field, resplendent in armor and trappings of mulberry black.

Isolde nodded. "And Sir Palomides, of course."

She could not keep the caustic tone out of her voice. From his blood-black crest to his sinister, glistening spurs, the Saracen king outstripped every other knight. His sword was of shining silver, a gold crown adorned his helmet, and a crescent moon of solid gold gleamed on his shield. When he rode up before them, he was careful to show all due reverence to the Queen. But Isolde read the glint in his eyes and knew his mind. *Not yet, sir,* she told herself through gritted teeth. *You may not yet look at me like that and think "You're mine!"*

Slowly the procession wound its way round the grassy arena, passing before the viewing tower to greet the Queen. One by one she welcomed each knight by name, and bowed to those who came with their fellow knights as a troupe. A dashing band from Little Britain galloped in with their blue and white banners held aloft, loudly proclaiming that a knight of France would surely carry the flag.

"Pour l'amour des dames!" they caroled as they cantered past. "For the love of the ladies, we will do splendid things!"

Behind them came a dozen or so men with wind-burned skins and brilliant, staring eyes. At their head rode a boy of twelve or fourteen, tall and well-built, showing teeth as white as a wolf's in a fearless laugh. Like all his men, he wore a length of checkered plaid, kilted round his waist and passing over his shoulder to hang down his back. His only armor was a set of oxhide guards on his forearms and shins, and an ancient breastplate of molded and figured bronze.

Yet still he had a kingly air of command, and a gold coronet held back his thick, curling hair. As he drew up before the viewing tower, he stared at her as if he had never seen a woman before. All this she saw and hardly noticed as her eyes took in the strangest thing of all. The faces of all the men entering were tattooed with blue.

Blue, purple, and more: scrolls of rose and amber, indigo, black, and red began on their cheekbones and ran down their necks, shoulders, and arms. Laughing, they bantered to and fro in an unknown tongue, a high guttural sound like the call of otters or foxes coughing in a distant den.

Isolde leaned forward, entranced. "Who are they, Brangwain?"

"Picts, lady!" Brangwain laughed. "Our ancient enemies from the far north of the island of the Britons across the sea." She nodded to the boy riding at their head. "That's Darath, their young prince. They say he's a promising boy. They'll have brought him here to flesh his sword." She gave a reassuring smile. "They're here for the sport, lady, not to win your hand."

The heralds' cry rang out around the field. "Let the contest begin!"

At the sound of the trumpets the grassy arena erupted in a free-for-all, as each knight took on the nearest opponent and tried to beat him down. Some conflicts were swiftly decided, as age and treachery outwitted youth and hope. Isolde watched one wily old warrior baffle a series of novices by drawing them out to heroic, exhausting deeds, yet always evading the point of each flailing sword. But no sooner had he tumbled his last young foe to the ground than he was humbled in turn by another knight, who rode head and shoulders above the rest.

"That's Sir Byrrell the Big," murmured Brangwain in her ear. "His father was a giant, did you know?"

Isolde shook her head. She neither knew nor cared. She was watching Palomides, and what she saw made her sicker as the day went on.

For the Saracen knight was unbeatable, it seemed. With his stallion rock-solid beneath him, he was holding his ground and winning every bout. While others roared and bellowed and charged about, he simply cut and thrust, remaining uninjured by staying clear of the fray. Fighting shrewdly, he drew out his opponents to feats of pointless excess, then knocked them from their horses in one contemptuous sweep.

As she watched, she could tell that he chose every bout with care, allowing the better knights to defeat and exhaust one another while he took on lesser foes. In truth his chivalry was only skin deep, it seemed. When the young prince of the Picts attacked him boldly and pressed him hard, she saw Palomides goading his stallion to rear up and strike the boy down.

The next instant the biggest of the Picts drove his horse forward to thrust the young prince out of the way, while the rest formed a ring around him and rushed him from the field. Isolde shook her head. Palomides was lucky that the warrior who had taken the full force of the falling hooves was more intent on protection than revenge. As the knight galloped after his fellows, bleeding from the head and with one arm hanging uselessly by his side, she knew that the Picts would not overlook such treachery again.

But the heralds had not seen Palomides spurring his horse, and took the beast's rearing as an accident of war. So they noted down another win for the Saracen, and his tally now placed him at the head of the field. The last few of the knights attacked bravely, but Palomides beat them all down. One by one he disposed of the survivors, steadily, savagely, like a slaughterman at play.

At last he held the field alone as the champion, bathed in the angry light of the setting sun. In a dream of disgust she watched him ride up to the Queen's tower, raise his visor, and make a deep bow. His face was that of a stranger, masked with dust and sweat.

Isolde stared. *And this man seeks my hand?* Loathing gripped her guts and ran like fire through her blood.

"Your Majesty!" he cried. "I claim the victory here—and the prize!"

The Queen rose to her feet, flashing Isolde a look of triumph and delight. "Sir Palomides," she crowed, "you have fought well—"

"Hold there!"

A stranger knight was galloping down the field. He was clad from head to foot in silver-white armor burnished like a pearl, and a mighty silver sword swung by his side. But his shield was unmarked, and he carried no banner or flag. Beneath the snowy plumes of his helmet, as white as the wings of a swan, a sharp visor like a metal beak concealed his face.

Isolde felt the hand of fate constrict her heart. *Who are you, stranger?* her inner voice cried out.

The newcomer came to a halt facing Palomides.

"I challenge you to single combat," he called in a muffled voice, "for the hand of the Princess, who will be Queen of this isle!"

"No!"

Black clouds of anguish covered the Queen's face. She leaned over the gallery rail, her eyes raining daggers on the scene below.

"Heralds!" she shrilled, "close the lists! The tournament is over. This knight may not compete!"

The herald marshal stepped forward. "Majesty, the lists are still open till the new champion is proclaimed. This challenge is within the rules of the day."

"Quit the field, coward!" the Queen howled to the newcomer. "Sir Palomides has been fighting all day. It is against the laws of chivalry to offer battle to an overbattled knight."

"True, madam," the stranger called back. "But today I have fought hard battles of my own. The knight and I will find ourselves well matched. And he alone will decide on my challenge now." He turned to Palomides with a courteous bow and raised his voice until all could hear. "Sir, I know you for a noble king and a man of might. You hear the heralds: I challenge you to the field."

Palomides curled his lips in an elegant snarl. "And I know you for a knight with no name. I have beaten every man on the field today. When I have you down, I shall not be merciful."

The stranger waved a gauntleted hand. "I offer single combat till the loser yields up his sword." He paused. "The winner to extract any forfeit that the loser must swear to pay."

Any forfeit . . .

A savage sense of triumph swept Palomides's soul. His God was with him, he could feel it in his bones. He would win this battle and make this knight his slave. The fool had forfeited his life out of his own mouth, and what better way to end a victorious day? The Queen already cherished him like a son. And as soon as he had Isolde in his grasp, he would make himself more than a son to his new mother-in-law. . . .

He focused again on the stranger knight and smiled like a panther marking down its prey. "You will do battle, sir?"

"I will. Swear to accept my terms!"

"I swear." Palomides slapped down his visor. "Have at you, then!"

Isolde never knew how long the two knights fought. The clash and thud of their weapons, the smell of the trampled grass and then of their blood, the screams of the charging horses, all blended in a dream of misery that gripped her, body and soul. In growing dread she tracked the sun down the sky, and dared not contemplate the moment when darkness would come. The day was dying in a burst of gold and red, and soon it seemed that her new champion's bold challenge was fading, too.

For his strength was ebbing with the light, and every blow he took weakened him. At last Palomides's swinging sword swept him from his horse, and he lay on his back on the ground, unable to move.

"So!"

With a sardonic laugh, Palomides vaulted from his horse and approached the fallen knight.

"You are mine now, sir," he cried gloatingly. "By your own oath, you have forfeited your life to me. It is my will to enslave you for the rest of your life."

There was no answer from the figure lying on the grass. Palomides frowned and stepped nearer.

"D'you hear me, sir?" he cried. He hefted his sword and brought the point to the stranger's throat. "Answer, slave, or you'll never speak again."

The next moment he felt the sword wrenched out of his hand and a cold metal gauntlet close like a vise on his wrist. Pulled forward, he lost his balance and found himself flipped over onto his back while the stranger leapt up and stood over him, sword in hand. Gibbering, he felt the point pierce the flesh beneath his chin, and a warm trickle of blood ran slowly down his neck. With the fragments of his mind he saw the red seeping through the joints of the pearl-pale armor and knew that his enemy was bleeding heavily, too. But he could only babble, "My life!— spare my life—let me live—"

"Sir, you may live, and love," came the sorrowful voice. "But never-more here. You must leave the Island of the West, never to return. You must forsake the Lady Isolde and never write to her, talk to her, or see her again."

"No!"

A howl of fury racked the Queen. Eyes bulging, she leapt forward and gripped the rail. "I decree otherwise! And I am Queen here still!"

Isolde embraced her mother in a sadness almost too great to bear. "Madam, it may not be—Sir Palomides gave his word."

The new champion looked up at the Queen and began again. "Sir, the same is true for all the ladies of this land," he intoned, leaning heavily on his sword. "You must swear to leave them all for the rest of your life, on your honor as a knight."

"I swear!"

Screaming, Palomides seized the dagger in his belt and slashed at the straps that held his armor in place.

"See, see!" he howled, hurling his heavy breastplate to the ground. "I shall never bear arms in this cursed land again!" He looked up at the gallery and held out his arms. "This is for you, Princess," he wept. "All for you! Bid me farewell to a life of sorrow, for I shall never find joy in love again."

Isolde's heart stirred. "Sir, for every man there is the woman of the dream," she called back. "Your true love waits for you, hopes for you, longs for you, even as I speak."

His huge and beautiful eyes filled with tears. "She will be you, my Princess, in another skin." His bow swept the ground. "Farewell."

"Farewell." She raised her hand. "May your God bring you safely back to your own land."

She bowed, and gravely watched him walk away. Out of the corner of her eye she saw the stranger knight heavily remounting his horse, preparing to approach. *Goddess, Mother, spare me—have I escaped a knight I knew for a man with no name, no face?*

"Isolde, what shall we do?"

Her mother was weeping piteously by her side. "We must have new blood!" she muttered madly. "The land needs new blood to keep our line alive." Closing her eyes, she began on a mumbled prayer.

"Mother—"

The sound of departing hooves took Isolde by surprise. She turned. The stranger knight was galloping off the field. *What, gone already, stranger, without a word? Wounded, too, when I should have taken care of you? Will I ever know who you are, or be able to thank you for setting me free?*

Isolde drew a deep breath and her spirits soared. The stranger had gone, but so had Palomides. Now she could hurry back to the pilgrim and tell him that the clouds hanging over her had vanished clean away.

The pilgrim . . .

Suddenly she saw his face with new clarity, and found herself longing to see him, to be at his side. If the threat of the tournament had made him take to his bed, then would these glad tidings make him better again?

Impatiently she endured the delay as the tournament dispersed and the Queen processed back to the castle, attended by her knights. At last she was hastening to the pilgrim's chamber with Brangwain on her heels. From the end of the corridor, she could see that his door was ajar.

"Sir?" she called joyfully, as she knocked and hesitated only a moment before stepping through.

There was no light in the chamber, and she thought he must be asleep. A silver moon shone in through the window and gently traced the still outline on the bed. Moving forward as her eyes adjusted, she could not believe what she saw. The pilgrim lay on his back in a pool of blood and there was no sign of life in his clouded eyes.

chapter
24

M *arhaus, why did you leave me?*

Who can I trust now? Who will tell me what I need to know?

Snarling, the Queen prowled her chamber, black thoughts flying around her mind like bats. Who was the stranger knight, and what did he want? Where had he found the courage to defy a Queen?

She groaned aloud, tearing at her gown. And why did he leave? Isolde was his as soon as he beat Palomides. Why didn't he stay to claim her as his prize?

She bit her knuckles to stop herself from crying out. Outside the window a quiet moon was sailing over a lazy sea, and she should be sleeping, too. Instead she was walking the floor, walking the floor....

Gods, she missed Marhaus! Unconsciously she reached for the silken pouch she wore round her neck and felt inside for the fatal sliver of metal, the last trace of him she had. If you hadn't left me, my love, she mourned, you'd have saved me now. When Palomides failed me, you would have challenged the stranger and beaten him to the ground.

Palomides...

Curses filled her heart and choked her throat. The handsome Saracen should be sitting here with her now, feasting in her chamber as her son-in-law elect, roast boar crackling on the hearth and the ripe juice of peaches running down his chin. Then he and Isolde would have made the feast of the flesh, and Goddess, Mother, *yesss*, what a coupling that would have been!

And then next summer, when the neap tides rose, there would have been a new queen for the Western Isle, another Isolde, a true child of the dream, a baby with huge dark eyes and hair as bright as corn—the Queen paused—if the earth magic she made for them that night was powerful enough, if her Gods were with her when Isolde lay down with Palomides and trod the path of womankind since the dawn of time.

But now—

Now the Saracen was wailing his way back East, and Isolde was dancing off with a light in her eye—to look in on the sick pilgrim—or so she said—

The pilgrim?

The Queen came to a sudden halt and closed her eyes.

Goddess, Mother, no!

Not that wretched invalid, that poor gray-coated thing, a miserable beggar, a man on a pilgrimage? No, no, it was impossible, Isolde couldn't care for him! Every woman knew that a holy man was only half a man, and this one was more than half dead!

But Isolde knew nothing—and something—or someone—had captured her mind and heart.

Frowning, the Queen tried to remember the tall figure she had seen at a distance, riding out with Isolde. If he was young and handsome, with a body most women would bed, any girl could love the first man she saw. And if Isolde liked him, she would be stubborn enough to want her own way—

The pilgrim?

The thought worked through her like poison, body and mind. She bunched her fists and kneaded her heaving gut. "Help me!" she groaned.

"My lady?"

A tall young knight reclined at his ease on the bed. Against the blood-red hangings his eyes were bright with promise, and his long body pulsed with feral grace. He preened himself visibly as she turned, then smiled and held out a hand.

"Will you join me, madam?"

"Sir Tolen!"

She bit back a curse. Mother of all confusions, why had she sent for him to keep her company? True, his clan was the finest in the isle, and many of his forefathers had been chosen ones. The lad himself had shown a careless glory in battle and his tall, rangy body promised much in bed.

But Gods above!

She wanted to tear her hair and lay open her skin. Better a lonely dinner of bread and herbs than flesh and wine with a witless boy! Or worse than witless—a youth with a scheme to advance himself through her, to love her and master her as Marhaus had done.

Marhaus, my love, my love . . .

"Majesty?"

He was watching her closely, more insistent now. Soon he would be reaching for her hand, thrusting himself on her, pulling her down—

He gave an insolent grin. "I am your knight, let me serve you," he insinuated, staring into her eyes.

"What?" She forced a laugh. "You are too young!" A frenzy seized her. They were all too young, now that Marhaus was gone.

He laughed and pushed back his hair. "Try me," he said.

Her eyes raked him, torn between need and despair. His teeth were very white, and his gaze held hers with all the raw confidence of his twenty years. She imagined her fingers brushing the soft stubble of his chin and cupping his hard young jaw to feed on his mouth. His chest would be smooth, his flanks lean and firm, and, young as he was, he would bear battle scars. Already she could feel the long silvery sword puckers brushing against her skin, and smell his young manhood, hot and raw and strong. Yes, she thought, *yesss!*

But first . . .

She nodded to him abruptly. "Wait here," she said.

She left the chamber and passed through a series of inner rooms, where her gowns hung in splendor from ceilings and walls, and little side tables groaned under combs and mirrors, scents and lotions and countless face colorings in their bowls of jeweled glass. In the last room of all, she picked up a swan lamp and lifted a hanging to reveal a hidden door. The key hung on a silken thread around her neck, and she locked it carefully behind her as she went through.

The light of the lamp shone upward into the dark. The worn stone steps wound upward through the thickness of the castle wall and she felt her way forward to another door at the top. As she opened it a dark cloud of birds rose in screeching flurries and swirled around her head. Unperturbed, she moved forward into the clamor of wings and flying claws, put down the swan lamp, and settled herself in a chair beside the hearth.

Slowly the room returned to its previous calm. When all was still, a hundred or so jackdaws filled the abandoned chamber, perched on tables and the backs of broken chairs, roosting in the ragged hangings of the bed and perched along the beams. The walls and floor were covered with birdlime and the rotting remains of their prey littered the floor, but the Queen bore the slime and the stench without concern. Here in her divination chamber she would know the truth.

High on a beam in the center of the room stood the grandfather of all jackdaws, huge, ancient, and decayed. His molting feathers were patched with white and gray, and his bulging eyes had lost their coal-black gleam. But time had not taken the edge off his piercing, pitiless stare and she knew he could see beyond mortal sight.

So? The great bird emitted a raucous cry, hunched his skinny shoulders in question, and stood still.

She laughed. "No, Old Father, I have nothing for you today."

She laughed again as she thought of the times she had offered him raw meat in her mouth and his wings had kissed her cheek as he took the food. Next time she must bring him a plump mouse, or better still, a rat. But tonight—

"Tonight I must know the truth."

The jackdaw stared intently. *The truth,* he echoed, shifting from claw to claw.

"The pilgrim Isolde healed," she asked urgently, "does she love him?"

The mangy head nodded. *Love him, love him.*

"I knew it!" She clutched at her temples. "Will he bring us good, or harm?"

The harsh cry came at once. *Harm, harm.*

"If I gave him money, would he go away?" she persisted. "Or would he come back?"

The great bird clacked and shuffled his bulk around. *Come back, come back, come back.*

The Queen groaned. "For Isolde, yes?"

Isolde, yes.

Cold apprehension clawed at the Queen's gut. "And she'd have him?"

She'd have him, she'd have him, she'd have him.

"Goddess, Mother, no!" she bit the back of her hand. "She'd mate with him, instead of Palomides?" Her mind darted madly back to the tournament. "And the stranger knight, Old Father, what d'you know about him? Is he a famous knight? The son of a king?"

A famous knight. The son of a king.

"A worthy partner then! But my daughter cared nothing for him." She gave a sardonic laugh. "Isolde prefers a pilgrim to a knight, and a beggar to a king?"

The great creature cocked his head and fixed her with an Otherworldly look. *Pilgrim, knight,* he rasped, *beggar, king.*

The Queen froze. The bird clacked importantly and strutted up and down. *Pilgrimknight,* he crowed louder now on one breath, *beggarking.*

"What are you telling me?" She gasped for breath. "That the pilgrim and the knight were one? The beggar beat the king?"

The bird began a triumphant jig, cawing with every step, *Pilgrim-knightbeggarking—*

"No!"

The Queen snatched up the lamp and flew down the staircase, careless of her life. In her chamber Sir Tolen still sprawled at his ease on the bed till her commands brought him leaping to his feet.

"Assemble a band of knights! Bring them with swords drawn to the Guest House and meet me there!"

He was already racing through the door. "Lady, it is done!"

Muttering and crying, she swooped through the palace to the Guest House, traversing courtyards and cloisters like a spirit of the night. In the pilgrim's chamber, a maid was stripping the bed. The dirty linen lay bundled on the floor, the bed was empty, and the room was bare.

The Queen hovered on the threshold like a thundercloud. "Where is the pilgrim?" she cried. "Speak, simpleton, or I'll have you whipped!"

The little maid's face flooded with panic. "The—the infirmary," the girl stammered. "The Princess took him there—"

The Queen dismissed her with a toss of her head. "Leave me!"

The maid scrambled for the door, her round pale eyes like cartwheels in the dark. Hissing, the Queen pounced on the pile of linen and threw it about. Great bloodstains marked the whiteness of the sheets. Whoever lay in this bed had been wounded, and where but at the tournament? She nodded madly to herself and heard the jackdaw's words anew. *The pilgrim is the knight. The beggar is the king.*

King of where? Gasping, she tried to trace her way through. If the pilgrim were in truth a great knight and the son of a king—if Isolde truly loved him—and if this pilgrimage was not his life's vocation but merely a fleeting vow he had to fulfill—

A precious dawn of hope sprang in her heart. Then Isolde could love him and take him to her bed. She would go the way of all women and have a child. A new queen would be born, and a clutch of young princes, too. . . . Her mind blossomed with a garland of tender thoughts and dreams. She smiled, and her face shed ten years. Sturdy boys and rosy, blooming girls. New life—new love—

She prowled the spare white chamber, thrilling with joy. Who was the pilgrim? Now she had to know. She threw open the chest that held his effects and laughed for joy. Inside lay the pearl-white armor of the stranger knight, bloodstained and battered, but unmistakable.

"So, sir!" The blood coursed through her veins. "Who are you?" she breathed. "Tell me your name?"

Beneath the bed was a battered saddlebag of ox hide. It held a shirt or two and a spare pair of shoes, a thick woollen cloak and a cap for the rain. His pilgrim's apparel—nothing more. She tossed it aside.

In the last corner stood a stout cupboard, locked now and the key gone. The Queen laughed. In her own palace, the key she carried opened every door. She was still laughing when the door swung back and she saw inside.

A great sword stood upright on the point of its scabbard, crying out softly in a high, urgent whine. Hearing the sound, the Queen began to shake. For the metal in the pouch around her neck was calling out too.

In a trance she opened the pouch and the silver sliver within quivered like raw flesh at her touch. The truth was here, she knew it, she could smell Marhaus's blood. With both hands she reached for the scabbard and drew out the sword. Halfway down, there was a jagged gap in the blade.

The truth, the truth—

Trembling violently, she pulled the shard of metal from its pouch and fitted it to the gap. With a sigh, the great sword shivered and took back its own. As the Queen watched transfixed, the blade embraced the broken piece and the jagged edges came together as if they had never been apart.

"No!"

The Queen whirled the sword around her head and hurled it from the room. Then she fell to her knees, babbling Marhaus's name.

"This is the sword of Tristan of Lyonesse. He killed my love, and I will have revenge!"

chapter 25

Overhead the owls called from the bell tower and a harvest moon proclaimed a cloudless night. In the quiet of the infirmary, Isolde and Brangwain had finished binding up the pilgrim's wounds. The lamp light shone on many new gashes on his shoulders and arms, and he was gray from loss of blood. But pale, weak, and shivering, he was alive.

Goddess, Mother, thanks. Isolde reached for a vial of cordial and tried to smile.

When she found him near death in his chamber, she had one thought only, to try to stanch his wounds. But as she tore back the sheet, the glory of his long pale body dazzled her eyes, and a dancing, singing bliss pervaded her heart. *Trust to your knight,* Cormac had said. *He will come.* She wanted the music within her to play through the world. *I trusted to him, and he came.*

At the time, Brangwain had made short work of calling up the servants and getting him to the infirmary, leaving a maid to tidy up his room. Now Brangwain was tactfully occupying herself elsewhere in the room and they might have been alone in the universe.

I will know my knight when he comes—

He lay before her in the moonlight and the beauty of him made her soul ache. She saw his strong, well-featured face, full of haunting angles and shadowed planes, and wanted to run her finger around his long, full mouth. In repose his eyelids were as pale as harebells, and she could count every one of the veins beneath the delicate skin. His thick hair fell around his shoulders, and he smelled of willow and heartsease, all the herbs she had used to cleanse and heal his hurts.

I could . . . I could . . . I could . . .

Watching him, she slipped into a gentle dream. *Goddess, Mother, tell me—is this love?*

He opened his eyes. She saw him swiftly review his surroundings, then struggle to sit up. She came forward with the cordial to revive his heart.

"Drink this, sir," she said. She did not say, *Who are you? I know you are my knight.*

"Thank you." He raised his head, took a sip of the drink, and gave her a pallid smile. "Once again, lady, I owe you my life."

"And I owe you more," she replied fervently. "My life and freedom from Palomides." The joy of it ran coursing through her veins. "How did you come to fight for me? I left you sick in your bed."

He shook his head. "I walked out along the high road, looking for knights on their way to the tournament. Most of them were too small for me, or poorly armed. Then a good big knight came along and I offered him all the money I had to lend me his horse and trappings for the day." He smiled wanly. "He told me he wanted to fight for the Princess himself. So I fought him unarmed till he yielded to me."

"Unarmed?" Her eyes widened. "So you were injured before the tournament began?"

"Yes. But Palomides had been fighting all afternoon, so that made it fair."

"You're a true knight indeed," Isolde said, glowing with pride.

He winced and drew back. "I'm a pilgrim," he said awkwardly. "Not a knight."

She gave a merry laugh. "Any knight could learn from you!" Then she saw his face and grew serious. "But you must have had some knighthood training at least. Where did you learn your chivalry?"

He stared at the ceiling, and seemed to be composing his thoughts. "My father was . . . a poor man," he ventured at last. "But he put me to service in a college of knights. Watching them, I picked up all I know."

"Oh, sir—"

Suddenly she did not care if he was a poor harpist or the runaway son of a king. *I am your lady,* she was about to say, *and you are my knight.* Then she would lean down and seal the bargain with a kiss.

"What now, lady?" he said abruptly, before she could speak. She saw he was watching the door, his eyes hard and wary and his face set.

"What do you mean?" she said, offended by his tone. "You are safe here with me."

"Not for long, lady," he rasped, "when the Queen your mother learns what I have done."

Gods above, yes! How could I forget? She bowed her head, struggling with feelings she could not name.

"She will be angry," she acknowledged reluctantly, "but there's nothing to fear. You acted within the rules of chivalry. The Queen will not threaten you in any way."

"What?" He stared at her in wild disbelief. "She will try to take my life!"

How dare he? The angry color flooded her cheeks. "We are not savages, sir, in the Western Isle. Believe me, my mother is a lady and a Queen!"

I do not believe you, said his level, gray-eyed stare. *And in this world, ladies and queens both kill.*

Fury flooded her. "Believe me, pilgrim," she said hotly, "hospitality is sacred in the Western Isle. Our queens do not make war upon their guests—"

She broke off. Standing in the doorway was a bedraggled maid clutching a sword almost as long as herself. Her mouth was working and she trembled piteously.

"What—" The pilgrim reared up with a strangled cry, staring at the sword.

"The Queen!" the girl gabbled, beginning to weep.

"Now don't upset yourself, child!" Brangwain crossed the room in two or three strides. She drew the servant forward, patting her hand. "Tell the Princess what you saw."

Isolde watched the little drudge approaching, her mind aflame. What had the Queen discovered? What did she know?

The girl was babbling out her tale through her tears. "The Queen came in raging for the pilgrim and sent me away but I was too feared to go. She was quiet at first, talking to her Gods. Then she went into the chest of armor and chuckled and laughed."

Isolde looked at the pilgrim. His face was covered in a sick sheen of fear. "So she knows you were the stranger knight."

The servant sniveled and wiped her nose with her hand. "Then she came to the cupboard behind the door and laughed again. It was locked, but she's the Queen, she had the key." She nodded her greasy head up and down. "And she found this sword."

Isolde saw her patient shudder, his eyes out on stalks.

"Enough!" he cried.

The maid turned to Isolde. "But I heard her, lady, crying for murder and vengeance and naming—"

"No more!" the pilgrim shouted. "Be gone!" He leapt from the bed and seized Isolde's hand. "Lady, you see now why I have to leave?"

A chasm seemed to open at her feet. *I did not know my mother could be like this.* "Yes," she said hollowly. "It seems the Queen is more angry than I thought."

He was very pale. "I beat Palomides and thwarted her plan for you. Now she seeks vengeance and she wants my blood."

Isolde drew a long shuddering breath. "There'll be a ship in the harbor. We must get you away."

Brangwain swung into action. "Fetch a lamp, girl," she cried.

Fearfully they huddled the pilgrim into a cloak and made their way out of the infirmary and down to the quay. A ship was leaving on the night tide, and if the captain had any qualms about the muffled passenger, his conscience was eased by the exchange of gold. Brangwain made her farewells to the pilgrim and left with the maid. Before Isolde knew it, the ship was ready to sail and they stood on the edge of the dock to say good-bye.

The rising wind was heavy with salt tears and sobbing in the shrouds like a soul forlorn. He stood before her swaying on his feet, the outlines of his face etched with moonlight and pain. She reached up and touched his cheek.

"I was your lady," she said. "You were my knight."

"Every man seeks the woman of the dream," he said huskily. "And I have dreamed of you my whole life long." He drew the ring off his finger and took her hand. "Wear this for me. I shall give it to only one woman in my life."

It was the circlet of emeralds she had seen on his hand when he first arrived. *I knew even then it was a woman's ring. I never knew it was mine.*

The green stones flashed and danced in the starlight's glow. "Emeralds for the greenwood, and for the sea," he said. "And for your emerald eyes." He slipped it onto the fourth finger of her left hand and gave a desperate laugh. "And now your mother hates me, and I have to go." She could see his eyes gleaming with an unearthly light. "But for that, I would never leave your side."

She nodded, in a dream of sickness. *I shall never be well again, now that you have gone.* "Nor would I leave you," she cried.

"Tide's turning, sir," the captain cried from the ship. "All aboard!"

He groaned like a tree torn up by its roots. "Must I go? It's like parting the sea from the land—it cannot be—"

"It must be," she said dully. "When hospitality fails, revenge is sacred in the Western Isle. If my mother has sworn an oath, she will never take it back."

"I shall return!" he cried desperately.

She heard the night wind sighing round the ship and her heart grew cold. The sailors were loosening the gangplank from the quay.

"Do not say so, sir," she forced out. "If the Queen hates you so much, it cannot be. The future for us is written in water and blood. The Mother Herself cannot turn back the tide."

"Aboard, sir—come aboard!"

Somewhere in the palace she could hear wolfhounds baying on a steady, hunting note. In the darkness above, torches were springing up, and the searchers would soon find their way down to the shore. She lifted her head.

"You must go," she said.

He caught her hand and brought it to her lips. "Lady, lady," he muttered frantically, "I can't leave till I've told you the truth."

The cold now had possessed her, body and soul. "What d'you mean?"

He closed his eyes. He was trembling from head to foot. "I told you I was born a child of grief. I didn't tell you that my mother named me for her sadness when I was born. When she thought of her sorrow, her *tristesse,* she called me—

"—*Tristan!*"

Isolde groaned. A lightning bolt of understanding split her brain. "You are Sir Tristan of Lyonesse, the Cornish champion!"

He gripped her hands. "And I killed Sir Marhaus, the Queen's chosen one!"

She tore herself away. Fury flooded her. "And then came here to gloat?"

"No, no!" he cried in anguish. "Merlin prophesied—"

"Merlin, Merlin!"

She was beside herself. "You came here as our enemy and deceived us all! You passed yourself off as a beggar when you're the son of a king. Even today—" She could hardly speak for rage. "'My father was a poor man, I am not a knight!'" she mimicked savagely. "'I come from Terre Foraine.' Gods above, every word you said was a lie!"

"Not every word," he said. He was very pale. "When I told you—"

"Enough!" she cried. She gestured toward the sea. "Sir Tristan, there lies your way. Be thankful my mother has been cheated of her revenge. Take your wretched life, and try to live better elsewhere."

His mother's ring flashed in the cold moonlight, the emeralds reproaching her with every winking green flame.

"Go!" she howled, mad with grief. "Go! You are nothing to me." She turned and strode away. "Farewell!"

"Lady, lady—" His agony rang off the headland and knocked against the sky.

"Farewell, sir," she shouted as she went. She did not look back.

From the headland above the bay, she watched the ship sail away, beating down the silvery avenue of the moon. Her fire had faded and she felt cold and sick. Muttering to herself, she tried to raise a curse to pursue his ship and haunt his days and nights. But her mind could reprise only one haunting refrain.

I have lost my knight. I have lost the only true love in the world.

chapter 26

*L*ost—

All lost—

The cold on the headland chilled her body to the bone. The rain ran down her face and soaked into her flesh, till every part of her was weeping for the man who had gone. Weeping? She heard her own laughter above the rising storm. Weeping for a man whose name she never knew? *Tantris—Tristan—taunter—trickster*—whoever he was, did it matter now?

Behind her she could hear the wolfhounds closing in. Turning, she saw a line of torches with her mother at the head. Her gown and headdress fluttering in the wind, the Queen flew into view like an avenging saint.

"Where is he, Isolde?" she howled. "Where has he gone?"

The face in the torchlight was childlike, naked, crazed. Isolde felt her heart heaving in her breast.

"He's gone, Mother," she said, crushing her feelings down. "Gone, and he'll never trouble us again."

"Gone?" The Queen gasped. Her eyes rolled like a woman in a fit. "You helped him get away?"

"Mother, I had no choice," she said dully. "The Goddess forbids us to take the life of a guest. Whatever he did, he came here in peace, and such a man is sacred, you know that."

"I swore to have revenge." The Queen's lovely face shone upward through her tears.

"The Mother teaches us to welcome all who come," Isolde insisted. "As she welcomes and feeds us with the four holy things."

"The four..." She could see the Queen struggling to comprehend.

"The Cauldron of Plenty and the Loving Cup—the Sword of Power and the Spear of Light?"

"Yes." Isolde raised her eyes to the dark void above. "These are our lodestars from the days of the Shining Ones." She felt like a dry husk. "And we must keep the faith."

"Oh, Isolde," the Queen cried. She clutched at Isolde and reeled like a bird in the wind. "He killed Marhaus!"

The Queen's scream was lost in the baying of the hounds. The smell of torches, dogs, and men was all round them now. Over the Queen's shoulder she could see a band of knights, every one armed to the teeth, sword and dagger in hand. In the forefront, Sir Tolen stood ready for action, a brutal, stupid look on his handsome young face.

"Death to the traitor!" he cried, rattling his sword. "Where is he, Princess?"

"Oh, sir—"

Gently but firmly she disengaged herself from the Queen. "Call off your dogs, madam," she said in a low, insistent tone. "Their quarry has gone."

"My knights? No!" The Queen's face crumpled. "I can't do that." Her eyes were huge and wild. "Without them, we have no one!"

"Madam, we have ourselves!"

But the Queen did not hear. Her voice rose to a shriek. "We've lost all our men, all of them, every one. Your father was the first." She brought her fists to her mouth, and cried like a child. "I thought we could conquer the land of the warlike Picts. But my folly sent him down to the House of Death. Then Marhaus was killed, and now"—she was keening as women did over the dead—"now we've lost Palomides and your pilgrim, too!"

Gods above! Was there no end to her mother's changefulness?

Isolde clenched her teeth. "A faithless man can never be a loss! And you hated him, madam, for what he did. How could I love your mortal enemy?"

"Aahh—" The Queen flared her nostrils and tossed her head about. "Love and hate are all the same in the end."

Mother, Mother, is that true?

"Always the same." A look of sleepy cunning settled on the tortured face. "But I know—I know about the pilgrim!" She wagged her finger strangely in the air.

Isolde stared. *She is losing her mind,* came in a hideous flash. *Goddess, Mother, save her, keep her whole—*

But her mother was running on. "I know, I was in the divination chamber tonight! My spirit father told me the stranger was a noble knight and the son of a king." A furious sadness crossed her mobile face. "Couldn't you have loved him, Isolde? A little bit?"

She stared at the Queen, aghast. "Mother, he killed Marhaus!"

"Men kill all the time. Marhaus would have killed him if he could. But he would have given us new life to repair that loss!"

She could have torn her hair. Only moments ago her mother was vowing vengeance, howling for Tristan's blood. Now as soon as he was gone, she wanted him back. Isolde gasped with rage. "He's a man of deceit. He lied to me!"

"Oh, Isolde." Suddenly the Queen looked a thousand years old. "Men always lie, even the best of them."

Is that true?

Isolde felt the ground slipping beneath her feet. "But we don't!" she cried. "Women don't!"

"Ah, little one—"

Now it was the Queen's turn to fold her in her arms. "We do it all the time," she murmured. "All the time."

Isolde felt herself dissolving into tears. "I never will." She wept fiercely on her mother's breast. "Never on this earth!"

"Be careful, child!" Suddenly her mother's hard brown finger was on her lips. "Never is too long a word to say."

This is madness. I must not listen to this. The thought catapulted Isolde out of her tears. "Madam, I—"

"The pilgrim." The Queen's voice took on a strange, incantatory note. "He was a worthy knight and the son of a king. You were the beautiful daughter I knew I would have. You came from the love I had for such a man. I only wanted the joy of that for you."

"Joy, madam?" Isolde felt older than the Old Ones themselves. "You mean lying down with a man? Has it brought joy to you?"

The Queen's eyes slid sideways. "Joy and pain. They weave together in the loom of life."

More madness. Isolde pressed her fists to the side of her head.

"I dream of spirit children," the Queen sang on. "Little ones in white and gold who smile and laugh and play about the throne. Your children, Isolde—when they come to us." She smiled roguishly. "And till then—"

Till then, what?

With a sick lurch, Isolde saw her mother looking at Sir Tolen, who smirked and braced himself and sheathed his sword. Any minute now he would take the Queen from her arms and carry her back to the castle for the brief feast of oblivion she found in men's flesh.

And tomorrow, what, Mother?

Sir Tolen in the place of Sir Marhaus?

A new chosen one young enough to be your son?

She turned to the knights muttering in the rear.

"Put up your swords," she called strongly, "and escort us home." She looked Sir Tolen in the eye and waved him away. "You are free to go about your business, sir. The Queen will sleep in my quarters tonight."

"Alas, lady—"

He stepped forward with a foxy stare, and showed his white teeth in a confident grin. "Her Majesty commanded my attendance tonight."

Isolde turned to the Queen. "Madam?" she ground out.

The Queen flared her eyes, fluttering her hands like a child lost in the dark. "Isolde?" she murmured through her tears.

Isolde could not breathe. *Is this my burden, written in the stars? I must be mother to my mother, even though that makes me a motherless child?*

She felt a wind from Avalon and heard a voice dropping lightly from the astral plane. *Have pity. Always have pity. There is only faith and love.*

It was the very sound of Avalon, the mellow teaching of the Lady of the Lake. *We must each take up our burden of pity and love.*

She bowed her head. *So be it.*

She looked again at Sir Tolen and saw the confused fighting boy beneath the swaggering knight.

"As you see, sir," she said as gently as she could, "the Queen is indisposed. When she is herself again, she will think of you."

"Yes, yes!" the Queen fluttered eagerly, leaning against Isolde for support.

Isolde reached out her arm and embraced the trembling form.

Take up the pitiful burden.

She turned her face toward the castle and saw its windows shining through the dark.

Home. I must get her home.

She put her arm around her mother's waist. "Come, Mother," she said. "Let me take you home."

chapter
27

*a*valon, Avalon, sacred island, home—
Who is Queen here, Isolde, I or you?

In a frenzy, Isolde roamed the Queen's House, wrestling with her thoughts. A fitful moon tracked her steps from room to room, and the stars were cold companions for her fears. She had brought her mother home safe and seen her asleep, but where would she find a safe place for herself? There was nowhere for her since she left Avalon.

Once again she saw the sacred island, the green hill rising from its shining lake, its sleeping flanks crowned with apple blossoms, its orchards alive with the flutter of white wings and the call of doves. There she had lived and studied with the Lady and her maidens, there she had found the love of the Mother and discovered herself. Now Avalon was very far away. *Goddess, Mother, help me. What shall I do?*

Earlier that night the Queen had been eager to lay down her royalty and give Isolde command. Now she was at peace, sleeping like a child, and while the Queen slept, all the world slept, too. But tomorrow—who knows?

Whooo knows? echoed the owls in the bell tower as Isolde roamed on. Tomorrow the council would meet on affairs of state. Would her mother be fit to attend, and if she did, fit to rule?

Outside the window a lone ship was sailing down the pathway of the moon. *Where is he now?* floated into her mind. She forced the thought away. The pilgrim was nothing to her from now on. Her life lay here in Ireland, his in—

Cornwall!

She groaned aloud. Her mother had challenged the Cornish King for his throne. At the last council meeting, Sir Gilhan and others had insisted that given such provocation, any ruler could seize the chance to counterattack. King Mark might be planning his revenge against Ireland now. *Oh, Mother, Mother, those who start a war should know how to end it—did we?*

She had come to the door of the Throne Room, where the council would meet. Looking into the chamber, her anxiety soared. Tomorrow this cool space could echo again with angry voices calling for war. Sir Gilhan and the wiser souls might find it very hard to keep the peace.

Gods and Great Ones, when will we have peace?

Brooding, she stroked her father's ring to give her strength and drifted unhappily into the vast space. The great chamber loomed stark in the moonlight, the black beams of its vaulted roof like a petrified forest, its white walls stretching away into the gloom. Ahead of her the throne stood alone on the dais, communing with itself in a powerful hum. The pale moon gilded its great gaunt shape and cast a shadow behind it as dark as night. Made of black bog oak as ancient and hard as rock, it gleamed and breathed like a living thing. Whoever had fashioned it, where it had come from was a mystery.

Beneath it lay the greatest wonder of all, a stone that had been old when the world was young. Serene and slumbering, the stone of destiny for all Ireland's queens never failed to cry out under any true ruler of the isle, and without its blessing, none of them could thrive. Till now this seat had always been her mother's place, its high back carved with scenes of the Goddess, its mighty arms ending in great crystals like the one the Queen bore as a symbol of her power. Now for the first time Isolde saw herself seated there and felt the stone calling her, *I am Lia Faill, the Stone of Destiny, approach, Isolde, draw near.*

Unhesitatingly she obeyed. Entering its circle, she felt a long-forgotten calm and joy around her heart. This was one of her favorite stories, first learned at her mother's knee, years ago. In the shadow of the throne, she heard again her mother's thrilling voice from the time when she herself could hardly speak.

D'you hear me, little one?

I hear you, Mawther.

Long, long ago, when the world was young, the Shining Ones made our island out of sunshine and rain. Then the Great One Herself came here to live and called it Erin the Fair, because there was no finer land in all the world.

Erin, Mawther?

She gave it her own name. Then other lands cried for her, and she had to go. When she left, the Shining Ones left us, too, to live forever on the astral plane. Now they shine down on us from the world between the worlds, and we mortals struggle on as best we can. But they left us the sunshine and rain, and when these two kiss, the rainbow they bear is the Mother's word to us all.

Word of what?

Religion should be kindness. Faith is love.

Behind the throne a low arch led down to the Dark Pool below. Once, long ago, her mother had taken her there, but she had been too young to know what she saw.

You will return, Isolde, her mother had said then, *when the time comes.* Now another voice floated into her head. *The time is here.*

Taking a torch from the wall, she passed behind the dais and down the stone steps beyond. As she felt her way carefully forward into the dark, the sweet smell of holy water rose to meet her and draw her on. Down she went and down into the fragrant gloom.

At the foot of the steps her feet encountered sand. Beyond it she saw a lake as smooth as glass. Above her arched a rounded roof of rock and around the edge of the water, boulders lay scattered here and there. Heartsick, she planted her torch in the sand and sat down. Here at least she would have peace to think.

How long she sat there musing she never knew. The low cave was warm, and its red-brown primeval rock welcomed and enfolded her like a living thing. Slowly her fears subsided and she slipped into a waking dream. She felt the soft pulse of the water keeping time with the song in her veins while kindly things rustled in the velvet air. Far off she heard the sea's eternal roar and caught the endless beat of life itself.

Now she knew that she was not alone, but part of earth's turning circle since time began. Staring into the dark, she saw all three worlds in one, the world that was, the world that is, and the world yet to come. When the waters parted, she did not see the silent head that broke the surface, and the beckoning hand. All she felt was a brief sensation of bright eyes and the memory of a smile that tugged at her hungry heart. *Avalon,* she wept, *Avalon, mystic island, home—*

The water was moving again in the middle of the lake. A dark head surfaced, and for the second time she felt a keen, bright glance and a welcoming smile. A hand called her forward, and the faint cry, *Come!* sounded insistently through the cavern's perpetual night. But still she sat entranced, unable to move.

The head vanished, and once more she was alone. Slowly, slowly, she felt her senses stir. *If the swimmer returns, this time will be the last.* She stood up and breathed deeply in the warm, scented air.

Ahead of her the lake rippled and she saw the head and shoulders of a laughing young girl. Her gray eyes twinkled, as friendly as a young seal's, and her long hair spread out around her like a cloak of seaweed. As she broke the surface, one long white arm rose straight into the air.

"Come!" she called clearly, in a strange, rusty voice. "Isolde, come!"

Then she dove and was gone.

Isolde ran forward to the edge of the lake.

Can I get back to Avalon? ran through her mind.

There is no going back, came the echo from her soul. *Forward, always forward, is the way of truth.*

Feverishly she tore off her overgown. Like a woman in a dream, she fumbled with her headdress, kirtle, and shoes till she stood on the edge of the water in her shift. The lake lay black and unsmiling at her feet.

Goddess, Mother, save me, she prayed, then, flipping up like an otter, threw herself in.

chapter
28

the chill of the water cleansed her soul like balm. As she broke the surface, caught her breath, and looked around, the joy of the swimmer's laugh still echoed in her ears. Already she could see her guide swimming strongly away. Filling her lungs with air, Isolde doubled over and followed her down.

In the silent world beneath the lake, her body was filled with the faraway sound of the sea, and its rhythmic pull drew her forward through the dark. Ahead of her she could see the swimmer's fluttering feet as her passing disturbed the water and made it glow. Supple as a mermaid, Isolde followed the scattered flakes of light without fear. They led her down to a deep channel through the rock, and as they went, she tasted salt.

Now her chest felt hollow under the weight of the water all around. The rocky roof of the tunnel was inches above her head. *How much farther?* flickered through her mind as she drove herself on. And still she seemed to hear *Come!* ringing around her head.

On . . .

How much farther?

On . . .

Don't breathe! she exhorted herself shrilly as her lungs contracted, loading every movement with pain. And still the rippling form ahead carved onward into the dark. Powered by desperation, she hung on to the fleeting vision with her last vestige of strength. At last she saw her guide turn upward and vanish into a shadowy pool of light. Moments later, trembling with relief, she broke the surface herself, gasping for air.

She was in a lagoon of warm water, in a low, quiet cave. Far away she could hear the cold rattle of shingle against the cliff as the sea howled round the shore. But here the air was soft and welcoming, like the warmth off the seashore on a summer night. As she found her feet and waded out of the pool, a beach of white sand ran back to a dark tangle of boulders around the walls. From the roof of the cavern to the floor, the red folds of living rock embraced her fondly, like a long-lost child. With the dull, muffled throb of the waves like a heartbeat far away, she might have been inside the womb of the world.

Around the edge of the water, a host of small fires bloomed in the rosy dark, and the salt tang of burning driftwood filled the air. As her eyes adjusted to the light, she saw white blossoms of spindrift wreathed around blood-red walls, and chests groaning with the riches of the sea. Her soul surged with wonder and delight. *I am in the house of the Mother. I have come to the place where the Great Ones live.*

"Isolde!"

She thought it was the voice of the maiden who had guided her here. But the slender, seal-gray form was nowhere to be seen, already lost in the gloaming at the back of the cave, where a dozen or so young women clustered round the walls.

"Isolde!"

The voice came again, a rich cascade of sounds, sweet like spring water over stones, mellow like the roaring of the deep. "Draw near the fire, Isolde—draw near."

Dazzled, she looked around. In front of her burned the largest of the fires, its red-gold flames keeping time with the music of the voice. In the shadow behind it she saw a domed alcove carved out of the living rock, with a stream in full spate sighing and whispering at its feet.

Through the leaping flames she saw an oddly shaped throne and the misty shape of a woman, veiled from head to foot in Otherworldly light. Her cloak gleamed with the silver of a salmon's skin, and her filmy robes shone like the sea at night. In her right hand she held a scepter of red coral, and her left bore the ring of the Goddess, set with pearls. Pearls of moon-white, shell-pink, smoky gray, and black shone from her head-dress, neck, and waist, and Isolde thought she was seeing the Great One Herself.

"No, Isolde," came the musical voice, a hint of gentle amusement in its tone. "I am only a servant of the Great One, one of the Three. The Lady of Avalon is my second sister, and the youngest is the Lady of Broceliande. I am the oldest of the sisters, indeed, I am the oldest in the world. The sea was here before all things and from its womb came life itself."

Understanding came to Isolde like the dawn. "You are the Lady of the Sea?"

The Lady inclined her head. "My sister knew you were in sorrow, and sent you to me."

"Your sister—the Lady of the Lake?" Isolde marveled. Joyous memories of Avalon flooded her brain. "You all dwell by water?"

"The way to the Otherworld lies across water, and only by water can we reach the world between the worlds." The Lady paused. "But you are a child of water, you know that." She leaned forward, and Isolde felt the full force of her unseen gaze. "Tell me, Isolde—what troubles you?"

"My country." Isolde did not hesitate. "Our land. We have made an enemy of Cornwall. What will happen to us? I have to know."

There was a silence. "Ah, little one," the Lady sighed, "is that all?"

"Yes!" Isolde trembled. *No!* thundered through her mind.

She clenched her fists. "I do not ask for myself. My mother the Queen is not..." *Not herself? Not well? What can I say?* Hopelessly she shook her head. "I don't know what to do."

"The Mother knows. That is not your concern." The sea-green draperies fluttered. "You are here to ask about your faraway love."

"He is not my love!" Isolde colored hotly and her fingers flew to Tristan's emerald ring on her hand. "No, Lady, I told you—the Queen—and the land—"

"Hear this, then." The resonant voice carried the ghost of a smile. "The Queen makes powerful earth magic with her young men. But your spirit will walk the mountains of the moon."

Isolde was entranced. "Lady, tell me how!"

The Lady rose from her throne. "Follow!"

Suddenly she was gone. Gathering up her shift, Isolde leapt over the fire and stepped across the rushing stream. Then she saw that the alcove housing the throne gave onto a fold in the rock leading through a natural archway to an unseen place beyond. From within came a pearly glow and a silence too deep for joy. Taking a breath, Isolde ventured in.

The Lady stood in a cavern of white quartz, each glittering fragment shining like a thousand stars. Her arms were outstretched as if to embrace the world, and her shapely figure swayed rhythmically from side to side. Her voice was as old as the hills.

"Look carefully, Isolde. This is your fate."

Within the circle of her outstretched arms stood an ancient altar half as old as time. On it rested four antique objects forged in massive gold.

"Look, look, Isolde," the Lady crooned. "The Hallows of the Sea—the sacred relics of our worship since time began. These are the four treasures of the Goddess, left behind by the Shining Ones for our delight." One by one the gauzy arm drifted over the treasured things. "The Cauldron of Plenty from which the Mother feeds all who come. The Loving Cup, to succor all who thirst. Her Spear of Light, to guide the way for the strong. Her Sword of Power, to champion the weak."

The Lady stirred, and the sands shifted around her feet. "These are your fate and your task. You must defend the Mother-right in the Western Isle. In doing so, you will make desperate enemies. You will need powerful moon magic to fight your cause."

Isolde brought her hands to her mouth. "Is it all dark for me, Lady, ahead?"

"We all walk in darkness. We all seek the light." Suddenly the great womb-like chamber was filled with love. "Courage and strength in life are demanded of men. Women bring wisdom and power to life's feast. The best of men and women join hand and heart to share all these and more. Then the circle contains all being and no one may break it, just as no force on earth can hold back the sea."

The best of men—

"The pilgrim has gone." She made her voice sound strong. "I thought I loved him. I was wrong!"

"Ah, Isolde, do not speak too soon. A great and mighty love will come to you." She paused. "But at a great price. The Great Ones wrote this in the stars before you were born."

She could not bear it. "Will I have my love? Or will I have to die to be with him in the Otherworld?"

"Ah, little one, death wedded love a long time ago. But a green fire runs through your veins, and you will come at last to the land of your heart's desire."

That will be when I die. Isolde felt her heart splitting in two. "Lady, will I ever get back to Avalon?"

"All waters run to Avalon in the end."

The cry surged up from the depths of her soul. "What must I do?"

"Watch the bubble rising in the foam. When it breaks, follow its path to the sea." She paused, and Isolde felt the great eyes shining through the veil. "My maidens will guide you back to the Dark Pool. Tomorrow you will think all this was a dream. But remember, the Mother gave you and your foremothers the sovereignty of the isle. You are married to the land."

The Lady's words hovered in the warm windless air. Isolde groaned. "When will I find peace?"

"Do right by your country, and you will find peace."

The vast brooding figure was fading before Isolde's eyes. She stretched out her arms and the emerald ring on her finger glowed with pale fire. "How will I know?"

The sonorous voice reached her faintly through the rising mist. "You will awake from your dreaming and be that which you have dreamed."

So be it!

Isolde pulled the emerald ring off her finger, kissed it, and laid it on the altar with the Hallows of the Sea.

I am married to the land. I give this to the sea. Turning, she left the crystal chamber and did not look back.

chapter 29

The clearing lay open to the fading light. Reining in his horse, Kay looked at his companions and gave a triumphant grin. In the center of the grass lay a bed of ashes surrounded by a ring of blackened stones. Other traces of habitation told the same tale—the remains of a Gypsy encampment, without a doubt.

Gawain's broad face lit up. "They were here!"

"Here and gone," Lucan complained.

Gods, give me patience! Kay suppressed a furious groan. "But we're catching up with them all the time, you know that."

"The sooner the better," said Bedivere quietly.

Kay nodded. For mile after mile they had tracked the band of Gypsies on their time-honored routes, and they were closing on them now. But unless they encountered them soon, they would have to give up. The autumn chill was beginning to bite, and soon winter would put an end to adventuring for the year, unless they wanted to freeze to death as they slept.

Even now, before they began to wake to the glitter of frost crystals mantling their blankets, a bed would be more than welcome, Kay had to admit. He was not made of rough outdoor stuff. But nothing mattered if they could find the fortune-teller and put an end to Arthur's misery. Kay's heart lurched. For a vivid moment he was back in the castle of Earl Sweyn, hearing again Lienore's smirking boast, *You fathered this child,* and watching the shadows gather around Arthur's noble head. He could not bear to see him in such pain.

So, find the Gypsies, and fast! He caught Gawain's eye and nodded toward the path leading out of the clearing. "That way. We'll follow them till night falls."

They plunged into the forest. The day grew darker now with every step, and a dismal rain drove needle points of drizzle into their faces and clothes. Hunched into their cloaks, they did not see the swineherd at the side of the path till he bellowed, "Welcome, masters!" and tugged off his battered hood. The toothless grin split a pockmarked face and he was clothed in hairy pig hide from head to foot. His charges snuffled happily round his legs, as much a part of the woodland as the herdsman himself.

"So, churl," said Kay, wrinkling his nose at the ripe odor, "who's your lord round here?"

"It's Sir Turquin, sirs, the lord of Castle Malheur." The swineherd waved a hand. "But see for yourselves—the castle's hard by."

Warm water and a bed—Kay's spirits rose. He reached into his pouch for a coin to reward the man. "Here's for your pains."

"Sir Turquin?" puzzled Gawain as they rode away. "Have I heard that name?"

Lucan grinned. "Only rumors that he has no chivalry—that knights are lost on the road around here and never seen again."

"A rogue knight?" pondered Gawain. The blood lust of the Orkneys filled his veins. "Let's take him on, then! We're four against one."

Kay's black eyes snapped. "We're knights of King Arthur, on a mission for the King. He won't meddle with us. Ride on, I say!"

"KNIGHTS OF KING Arthur? We are honored, sirs. Open the gates there! Let the lords ride in."

At the castle, the warmth of the welcome more than made up for the cold journey there. Attentive servants divested them of their sodden clothes, helped them to unarm, and wrapped them in fine gowns of velvet and fur. Soon they were standing in a lofty hall with fires of oak and holly roaring on the hearths, and half a dozen knights standing around the walls.

And the man hastening toward them looked far more knight than rogue, with a jovial smile and a lean face of indeterminate age. He had the body of a man in his thirties who had lived sparingly and fought hard, and was dressed for the tiltyard, in short tunic and silver mail. Only a pair of odd and colorless eyes and an old sword wound on his forehead marred his appearance in the mellow candlelight.

"Knights of the Round Table?" He came forward eagerly, spreading wide his arms. "I am Turquin of Malheur. Welcome, welcome! Will you feast with me tonight?"

Afterward Kay could hardly remember the meal, as platter after platter of venison, pork, and duck poured through the hall, each salty broth or rich, herb-laden brawn more flavorful than the last. Four roast hogs' heads, each with an apple in its tusked mouth, glared sulfurously as their host carved for the four knights in turn. Then the jellies, the custards, the figs, the nuts, and the wine—above all, the wine, flowing in gold and ruby streams from flagons that never ran dry—Kay's head began to swim.

Across the table from Kay, seated at the right hand of their host, Gawain, too, had been freely indulging himself.

"Our thanks to you, sir!" he cried expansively, raising his goblet to Sir Turquin in a toast. "We are in your debt. Call upon us in honor, and we shall repay."

"Indeed I shall." Sir Turquin leaned forward, his thin face suddenly alive. He gestured to his men standing around the walls. "We're all knights here, wedded to honor and the sport of arms. I have devised a game that will amuse you, sirs, a custom I follow in the name of chivalry." He smiled. "All my guests are my prisoners till I set them free. They must fight for their freedom, in single combat with me."

Lucan's hand flew to his side and he furiously cursed the absence of his sword. "You'll hold us to ransom?"

"No, no!" Sir Turquin laughed openly, showing his teeth. "Let others trade bodies for gold, that doesn't interest me." His odd eyes rolled, and he spread his hands. "Prowess, lords, that's the only thing."

Gawain knuckled his eyes and tried to clear his head. Gods above, if only he hadn't had so much to drink!

"So you challenge one of us?" A slow smile spread across the Orkneyman's face. He would take on this fight, and Sir Turquin would regret the day he was born.

"Gawain—" Kay began warningly.

But Gawain did not hear. "We accept your challenge, sir!"

"Gawain, no!" Kay cried in dread. "We don't know what the challenge is!"

"Kay, one Orkneyman is worth any ten men alive!" Gawain chortled. "I'll fight him for our freedom, and beat him bloody, too!"

"Ah, Sir Gawain," sighed Sir Turquin, grinning like a death's head, "if only you could! But you are in my power, and therefore I set the terms. I choose whom to fight—and my choice is not you." His eyes left Gawain, and alighted on the weakest man in the hall. "I choose Sir Kay."

Kay gagged with fear. "What?" He looked at Sir Turquin's knights, their mailed bodies planted as if for attack, their hands on the hilts of their swords. Some were grinning openly, others were simply bored, and he could see they had watched this scene many times before.

"What's going on?" Gawain's mouth fell open. He looked around in bafflement and his small eyes sharpened in a sudden glare.

"You only fight battles you can win?" Lucan stared at Turquin with undisguised contempt. "And this is your prowess?"

"Yes, indeed, sir," Turquin agreed. "In honor of the great fellowship where one day I will sit."

Bedivere gasped. "At the Round Table?"

"Yes, indeed." Turquin smiled again. "You are its heroes now. But I am readying myself to take your place."

"By treachery?" Bedivere choked, wishing in despair he had not given up his sword.

Sir Turquin laughed and stroked his pointed nose. "By chivalry," he said patiently, as if to a child. "First I'll defeat the knight I can dispatch, then imprison the rest of you till I can beat you, too."

"You'd fight us at our weakest," scoffed Lucan, "and call it knight-hood?"

"Prowess, sir," came the gentle correction. "Every knight must build his reputation by the sport of arms."

Kay could take no more. "Hold your tongue, sir," he snapped. "If I must fight you, tomorrow you shall have your sport. But we've heard enough from you for one day!"

"Now, Kay," Gawain chided thickly, "don't be unchivalrous." The great fair head wagged drunkenly from side to side. "Our host makes the challenge, so he has the right to set the terms."

Three pairs of eyes turned on Gawain in rage.

"Gawain—" threatened Lucan.

"No, no, it's what d'you call it? Prowess?" Gawain protested loudly. He reached for his goblet, took a deep swig of his wine, then stumbled to his feet. His left hand fumbled around his body, reaching into his breeches to scratch himself as unself-consciously as a child. "A toast!" he brayed. "A toast!"

"Gawain, sit down!" Kay yelped in a blind rage. He could see the knights around the wall nudging each other and sniggering, and he smarted with shame.

"Iss all right, Kay," Gawain mumbled, closing his eyes. "Our host's a man of honor an' a true knight." He waved his goblet at Sir Turquin and swayed dangerously. "Sir, lemme shake your hand."

Sir Turquin gave a scornful laugh and held up his hand in reproof. "Sir Gawain, you're in no fit state—"

"No, no, man of honor." Gawain set down his goblet, lunged forward, and grabbed Turquin's hand. "Shake," he mouthed.

"What—?" The next moment Turquin found himself jerked forward violently as Gawain pinned his arm to the table, and with his free hand sank the point of a dagger behind Turquin's ear.

"Where's your prowess now?" the big knight exulted in a voice suddenly not drunken at all. "It's all over, Turquin—give up your challenge, or die!"

Turning, Kay saw Turquin's knights spring into horrified action, swords in hand. "Drop your weapons, all of you," he shouted, "or your lord dies!"

The leading knight hesitated. "My lord?" he appealed at last.

Turquin swiveled his ill-matched eyes, dumb with shock.

"He dies!" Gawain sang out joyfully. The battle cry of the Orkneys rang in his ears. He pushed Turquin's head down on the table and twisted the knife.

"Drop your swords!" came a shriek from the prostrate form.

One by one the knights' weapons fell to the ground. Lucan and Bedivere leapt to their feet and gathered them up. Exuberantly Gawain jabbed the dagger into Turquin's neck and grinned to see the bright spout of blood.

"Make your choice, villain!" he cried. "What is it—yield, or die?"

There was an endless pause. Then it came, like a dying gasp. "I yield."

Almost regretfully, Gawain lowered his dagger. Lucan and Bedivere seized Turquin by the arms and heaved him to his feet. Turquin's face was twisted with rage, and his unmatched eyes were spinning like wheels of fire.

"Well, sirs," he gasped. "You have beaten me." Breathing deeply, he struggled to find a normal voice. "The terms of my challenge are fulfilled. You are free to go."

There was a pause. "Alas, sir, no," came Bedivere's quiet voice. "You are no longer lord of Castle Malheur. It is Gawain's now, by the fortunes of war."

"And I yield it to the King," Gawain cried.

Kay nodded, a flush of wonder filling his sallow face. Gods above, Gawain had done well! He turned to face Turquin's knights. "From now on, you are knights of King Arthur and owe your duty to him."

"At the Round Table?" breathed the leader openmouthed, a world of new visions dancing before his eyes.

"Perhaps, in time." Kay waved him away. "Lead your men to Camelot to swear allegiance to the King and Queen."

"Yes, sir!" He knelt to kiss Kay's hand, then, with a word of command, led the knights from the hall.

Kay turned back to Sir Turquin. "You'll spend the night with us, under armed guard. Tomorrow you will go to King Arthur, too, and submit yourself to judgment at the King's hands." He looked at the tortured face, and felt his pity stir. "He and Queen Guenevere have sworn to rid the land of rogue knights. But if you truly wish to learn chivalry, you may find it there."

Lucan turned to Gawain. "And in the meantime, my friend," he said admiringly, clapping the big knight on the back, "you can tell us how you did it. I thought you were drunk!"

Gawain laughed. "No more than usual," he said magnanimously. "And never too drunk to take an insult to the Round Table lying down."

"But the dagger," Bedivere puzzled. "They unarmed us when we came in. Where did that come from?"

Kay looked fondly at Gawain. "You had it up your sleeve."

"Ah, Kay," roared Gawain gleefully. "Never ask an Orkneyman where he keeps his secret weapon—in the name of chivalry!"

chapter
30

ady, lady—"

Farewell, she had said.

Again and again he heard her voice ringing over the headland, and knew that she had put her heart into that parting cry.

Farewell.

There was no way back for him to the Western Isle.

All he could do was hope to forget—not Isolde herself, but the worst of the pain. On the voyage back, he kept to his cabin while his wounds healed, and the captain, a decent man, left him alone. The cliffs of Cornwall greeted him through veils of mist and rain, and there was a melancholy comfort in coming home. But there was no home for him till he could lay his head on Isolde's breast.

Lying in his chamber in Castle Dore, Tristan gazed out on a November landscape as drear as his hopes. Like the gray, sunless dawn, everything was dead to him now. Even Cornwall, once loved as much as his own land of Lyonesse, was drab and meaningless, a foreign place. He thought of the Western Isle and his sorrow welled up afresh. To be in Ireland now with the woman of the dream . . .

But she does not dream of you, came his inner voice.

She could! he protested vainly, soul in hand.

Once, perhaps. Not now.

Goddess, Mother, just to hold her, to rest in her arms! Grief as sharp as elf arrows struck him to the heart. *Farewell,* she had said, and *You are nothing to me now.* He would never touch her, kiss her, see her bright eyes again.

He leapt to his feet, every breath a torment to his aching soul. The spacious chamber Mark had furnished for him felt like a cell. The warm loam-colored walls, the beeswax-scented boards, the fire laid ready on the hearth all mocked him with a comfort he could not feel. Out, he thought numbly, I must get out. He would walk or ride, he would go with the King to the hunt. He would take a turn in the tiltyard to build up his strength.

He would ... he would ... Tears filled his eyes.

Would he always be a poor thing now that she had gone? He stumbled toward the door, feeling his big body a burden, his whole being a barrier to his dreams. Outside the window lay a dank and wintry day. But even a wet and windy ride was better than this.

Oh, my lady—my love—

Visions of her came back to him like knives, the sun on her shiny hair, her smiling eyes, her green gown. One by one the losses crowded in. I left Glaeve behind, and my silver harp, he mourned. But what were they against losing her? Dully he tried to choke the remembrance back. He was gagging with misery, hardly able to breathe.

Out—he must get out—

Standing by the door were his riding boots, whip, and cloak. He had not eaten for days, and knew he should break his fast. But whatever he ate felt like dust and ashes in his mouth. Surging blindly out of his chamber, he took the nearest way to the stable yard, desperate to miss King Mark and all the court. As he rushed round a corner he saw too late the very thing that he wanted to avoid. Outside the Council Chamber he blundered into the King and his knights and lords, some also headed for the stable yard, to judge by their dress.

"Nephew!" caroled Mark, throwing wide his arms.

Tristan pulled up, a flush of embarrassment staining his face. "My lord!" he cried awkwardly, fumbling a bow.

He was suddenly aware of Sir Nabon, Sir Wisbeck, and others clustering round Mark, their expressions dark. With them stood Sir Andred, his face studiously blank.

"I was just about to send for you to the hunt!" Mark stepped forward and hugged Tristan to his chest. His moist eyes filled with tears. "By sweet Jesus, nephew, you are welcome to me."

Sir Nabon frowned and exchanged a glance with Quirian, signaling his impatience to be gone. Tristan sensed a tense and hostile atmosphere, and knew that for the barons at least, the council had not gone well. He forced a smile.

"You honor me, sire." With a sinking heart he saw Andred's dark stare turning his way. Let me go! he cried inside, I am not wanted here.

Mark peered at Tristan, dimly noting his gray face and desolate air. "Fully recovered, no? They tell me you do well in the tiltyard these days." He laughed jovially to cover his perplexity, and waved at his lords. "I'll have to send all my knights to take lessons from you!"

Now Andred's gaze was matched by twenty and more cold stares. Tristan could not meet the wall of eyes. "As you say, sire," he muttered.

Out—must get out—pounded inside his head. He knew he should have eaten. Too late now. He closed his eyes and felt the world rushing away. Out—out of this forever—never to return—

"Nephew, are you well?"

He felt a hand gripping his forearm and opened his eyes on his uncle's fearful face. He shook his head, unable to reply.

Mark cast a glance around at his knights and lords and waved them away. "Leave me, all of you!" he cried. "Wait for me in the stable yard, those of you who will hunt."

Murmuring, the pack moved off. Mark drew Tristan back into the Council Chamber and closed the door. The remains of a dying fire smoked on the hearth and the room was still thick with the angry arguments of those who had gone. Tristan's empty stomach betrayed him, and his gorge rose.

Mark leaned forward anxiously. "What's the matter, nephew? You look sick again!"

Tristan tried to collect himself. "I'm not sick, sire," he began huskily.

"But not well either!" Mark moved around the chamber with a jerky, resentful stride. "God's blood, I'd give my kingdom to see you right again!"

Tristan flinched. I shall never be right again now that she has gone.

"I thought your wounds were healed in Ireland," Mark rambled on. "Was it a bad place for you, after all?"

Bad? Tristan heard himself laugh.

"It is the fairest place on all the earth," he said, struggling to rouse himself from his misery. "They have green meadows fed by sunshine and watered by soft rain, and upland pastures breathing clover and shamrock to the air. The coastline there is even lovelier than ours, sheltered harbors, bold headlands, and a silver sea—"

His soul filled till he knew it would overflow. "Believe me, sire," he said choking, "all the world is there!"

"But you went there to get well," Mark said peevishly. "And you're not." He wagged his head fretfully, wishing he was out in the saddle, not having to deal with this. "When we sent you to that healer—what's her name?"

"Isolde," said Tristan numbly.

"Yes, that's it." Mark laughed dismissively. "They said she was the best in all the isles. And now look at you."

How dare he? Tristan felt an ugly flush on the back of his neck. Anger flooded him, and he found his voice. "She's truly a wonder, sire. The people call her La Belle Isolde for her goodness to them. And she healed me."

"What ails you, then?" Mark cried.

Tristan tried to still the roaring in his ears. "I have a—a trouble, sire," he said with difficulty.

"Why, so have I!" said Mark. His mind roamed back to the stormy meeting with his councillors, and his owlish eyes opened wide. "What's yours, nephew?"

Goddess, Mother, where can I begin? "Forgive me, sire," he mumbled, "it's a deep thing—"

"Mine, too!" Mark burst out.

"Then Your Majesty should speak first."

"Yes, yes, I will."

A glorious scheme was hatching in Mark's cloudy brain. Now he would show them all what a king could do! He would settle Tristan's troubles and his own, and still be out on horseback before the hour was through.

"Come, nephew," he said impulsively. "I'm King here after all! If you help me, I swear I'll see you get your heart's desire."

My . . . ?

Can it be?

Tristan's soul staggered with the shock of sudden hope. Isolde, Isolde, flooded his veins. He could hardly speak. "What is your trouble, sire—and what is your will?"

Mark threw himself into a chair like a spoiled child. "Nabon and the others give me no peace! They want me to marry, and I've got to do something, I know. I thought when you came back they'd let it go, but they're as bad as before." He attempted a careless laugh. "They say I must give the kingdom a son of my own. Always jabbering like jackdaws, there's no end to it."

"Sire—" Tristan shook his head. He did not know what to say.

"And I should marry, I suppose," moaned Mark. "But where? Who?" He rolled his eyes. "Help me with that, nephew," he added sarcastically, "and I dare swear I can solve any trouble of yours."

Can it be? Tristan felt his hopes swelling into life. He took his soul into his hands. "In Ireland, sire," he forced out. "There's a lady—the one who healed me, the Princess Isolde—"

"In Ireland?" Mark stared at him. "The Princess? Aha!" He gave a peculiar laugh. "She's a healer, you say, but is she healthy herself?"

"Sire?" Tristan's brain reeled. "What do you mean?"

A sly look crept over Mark's dull face. "I mean young, well-fleshed, a good breeder—long, strong limbs like mine, all her own teeth—"

What's he thinking of? Tristan thought numbly. "Yes, indeed, sir," he mumbled, at a loss.

"And what about the mother?"

Gods above, what now? Tristan tried to gather his wits. "The Queen, sire?" The old wound on his thigh was beginning to ache. "A great beauty, and a famous warrior."

"How old?"

How old? Tristan gasped. How did he know? He caught at the nearest straw. "About your years, sire."

"Pouf!" Mark threw his long legs around, muttering to himself, then returned to the attack. "Sole ruler, no?"

"Established by the Mother-right," Tristan said. "And a queen of great power."

"So the rule passes down from queen to queen?" Mark mused.

Tristan saw an odd light in his uncle's eye. "Without challenge, sire," he said wonderingly. "They keep the Old Faith in the Western Isle."

"Tell me, nephew—" Mark began in a strange voice.

Tristan stared. Smiling, twitching, Mark was trembling in every limb.

Attend, Tristan, attend, cried his inner voice. Something is happening—something Mark himself does not know—

A look of infinite cunning crossed Mark's foolish face. "What would you say . . . " He laughed excitedly. "What would my barons say . . . to a union of dynasties?"

Tristan felt a cold breath from the Otherworld. "A union?" he stuttered. I am losing my mind. "With whom, sir?"

"With Ireland!" Mark cried, flushing bright red. He pounded Tristan's shoulder. "What d'you think of that?"

He wants to marry the Queen! Goddess, Mother, praise and thanks!

A world of joy opened before Tristan's eyes. New hopes ran babbling through him like a woodland stream. If he marries the Queen, any danger of war is at an end. With Mark as her husband, the Queen must forgive us for the death of Marhaus, and I will see my only love again—

Dimly he heard Mark's voice running on. "She's a fine woman, you say."

A tall shape in red and black, fluttering silks and velvet, glowing with garnet and jet swam across Tristan's mind. He closed his eyes. "The finest," he breathed.

"And no fool, if all you say of her is true."

"All true, and more."

"But will she agree?" Mark surged on fretfully. "There must be other men—"

A hundred at least—maybe more, Tristan thought, amused. He cleared his throat. "But none like you, sire," he said truthfully. "A ruling king. No one else can offer her Cornwall, this land of ours—"

"Our country, yes, what a prize for the Western Isle," Mark declaimed. Sentimental tears stood in his eyes. "And no more war! We shall give them and ourselves a future of love and peace!"

Tristan hastened to agree. "With this marriage, sire, our two lands are one."

He could hear music on the astral plane. I will come to Isolde! he rejoiced. She will come to me. He closed his eyes, and hardly heard his uncle's closing words.

"This is my desire, Tristan. Swear to it now and, by God Almighty, whatever it is, I swear you will have yours!"

"Sire, I gladly swear!" Joy overcame him, and he could not hold back. "I swear by the Great Ones and the Mother of them all to fulfill your desire." He laughed in ecstasy. "I swear on the life and soul of the woman I love. I swear by my hopes of the future and my dearest memories of the past."

Tristan, Tristan, hold on—

He thought he heard a voice from far away, but he could not stop now. "I swear this on my beloved mother's grave."

"Then this marriage must be!" Mark's joyful voice reached him from miles away. "She cannot refuse!"

Tristan was delirious. *My love, Isolde my love, I shall see you again—*

"You have sworn your oath, then, Tristan, and you will not fail," Mark boomed in his ear. "The Queen will surely be glad to give us her daughter's hand. I know you will bring back Isolde as my bride."

chapter
31

The horizon was lost in a line of blinding spray. The ship bucked and reared in the storm like a runaway horse, as wall after wall of water broke over her prow. The wind howled through the rigging and all around him the sailors were scrambling up and down, some white-faced and silent, some volubly cursing their gods. Turning, Tristan left the deck and went down to his cabin, praying for death.

But the little ship would survive the storm, he knew. The tough Cornish craft had seen worse seas than this. It was late in the season to sail, and the voyage was hard. But no one doubted they would reach Dubh Lein alive.

He was chilled to the bone. His lips were cracked, and he could taste the salt spray on his face like tears. Shivering, he pulled off his wet clothes and threw himself down on his bed. The coarse blanket hardly warmed him, but he did not care, for these things were mere pinpricks now. Every day without joy, or hope of joy, was his fate.

And all done by his own hand!

He tossed on his hard narrow bunk like a man with the plague. His last meeting with Mark came back to him in waves of shame and rage. Thoughts of death descended on him again. How could any man be so foolish and hope to live?

Wild laughter rose in his throat and he choked it back. He had seen the odd looks the sailors were giving him now, and knew they had heard him raging and talking to himself. Any more of this madness, and they'd take him for a jinx on board. And that would mean mariners' harsh justice, rough hands in the night, a startled scream, and a swift passage to the sea's dark embrace, even if he was Prince Tristan of Lyonesse and the nephew of the King. No, no more strange noises now.

But Goddess, Mother, how to contain the grief? He thrust a fist in his mouth and gnawed on the side of his hand. How to forget the moment when Mark spoke out?

I know you will bring back Isolde as my bride.

Without warning he was back in Cornwall, hearing his love, his life, all blasted by the words from his uncle's mouth. The chamber where he stood gaping at Mark, the dying fire, the King's ashen face and staring eyes, had all dissolved in that moment of blind doom.

"No, no," he had gasped, and "Surely, sire, you don't mean—" But he had known the truth at once. He had sworn on Isolde's life, on his mother's grave, to woo and win his dear love for another man.

His stomach heaved. He had traded his life and Isolde's for Mark's offer of help, and would never make a more infamous bargain in his life. Mark would never help him in any way. The King had no interest in anyone but himself.

And seeing Tristan falter had sent his uncle into a frenzy of rage. As the young man floundered in panic, trying to take back his oath, Mark had shown a side of himself that filled Tristan with despair.

"You have given me your word," Mark had said, his voice trembling with spite. "If you break it now, I'll drive you from the land. I'll blacken your name from here to the Orkneys and beyond, and all the world will know you're a knight who is false to his lord."

"I am not false!" cried Tristan, his soul splitting in two.

"Prove it!" Mark's face quivered. "Or else live a rogue and a recreant all your days."

"But consider, sire!" He could hear his voice rising in despair. "The Queen of Ireland's a beauty—not past childbearing—and she rules in her own right—"

"Tristan, you're a bigger fool than I thought!" Mark's mouth twisted with contempt. "Why should I take the old woman when I could have the girl? Tall and well-fleshed, a good breeder, you said—that means fine haunches and fat breasts—any man would enjoy securing the succession with that."

A look Tristan dared not contemplate stole over his uncle's face. His gut revolted, and he could have spat at Mark's feet.

To think of Isolde with Mark—

That Mark should even think of her that way—

It was vile, beyond vile. It stank to heaven and above.

He loathed himself. How could he have been so rash?

But there was no turning back. Mark had charged ahead, summoning his council to draw up the terms of the treaty, ordering up gifts to present to his hoped-for bride. Reeling with shock, Tristan had gone through the preparations in a trance and taken ship, armed with Mark's formal offer of marriage and the barons' warm consent.

"Bring her back, Tristan! Cornwall needs a queen," a jovial Sir Nabon had rallied him. "And don't forget to look for a bride for yourself!"

"Sir—" He had mustered a feeble smile. But how he refrained from punching the smiling lord, he never knew.

And now . . . He bit madly on his fist again. Despite the bad weather, the ship would make Dubh Lein soon. He would march up to the palace as Cornwall's ambassador, flying all her flags. In formal audience he would ask the Queen of Ireland for her daughter's hand. And in that moment he would earn Isolde's hatred for the rest of his life.

Hatred?

He leapt up from his bed and paced around the tiny cabin, berating himself. No, worse—she'd despise him, see him as a loathsome thing. The best he could seem to her was a pitiful fool. The worst—an odious trickster and a liar, a man ready to pander to his uncle and betray his love on command—

No!

No more!

He howled with despair. He did not care who heard him anymore. He was on the road to madness, yearning for darkness at the end of the day.

But he had sworn to make this offer, and must endure the ordeal to the dregs. His only consolation was that Isolde would refuse. Not out of love for him—he had thrown that away. But she must surely love herself enough to laugh Mark's offer in the face.

Yes, Isolde would reject him out of hand. Then he'd sail back to Cornwall and make his farewells there. Mark would blame Tristan for her refusal, and would never want to see him again.

And then—

Without his love, without his country or his kin—what then?

Then he would be alone, and no creature on earth would care if he lived or died.

So be it.

He stared out through the porthole at the heaving gray waves. Well, the world was wide. And all journeys in the end led back to the sea.

You are here to ask about your faraway love?

He is not my love! I thought I loved him, Lady, but I was wrong.

Isolde prowled her chamber, lost to herself. Through one window lay mountainous gray seas and skies, through another the barren land in the gray grip of winter all round. Every tree had lost its leaves and, through-out the palace gardens, not a bird sang. On the shore, the only sound was the heartsick cry of gulls, and every night, black frost was in the air. But nothing could match the bleakness she felt within.

The night she had seen the Lady, she had felt alive. But now the bright fires in the cavern, the cold thrill of the sea on her flesh, the warmth of the Lady's love, all these had gone as if they had never been. In their place was a hollow where her heart should be.

And her mind, too—she could neither think nor feel. When she thought of the pilgrim now, he had no face.

Tristan, you were called. But I never knew you at all.

In truth, she could hardly remember him. A vague sense of a tall, well-made form, a strong face, a firm hand, swirled around her head and made her body ache. When she yearned like this, words like *I love him* came into her mind. Then she thought of the tales he had told and the gossamer web of falsehood he had spun. And then *He lied, he deceived me* drove all thoughts of love away.

She moved back from the window and the grayness followed her.

Yes, that's it, I hate him, she said to herself. And in time she'd forget, people did, she knew. With luck, they would never hear of Cornwall again. Especially now that her mother had given up all thoughts of war.

Could it be? Isolde wondered, leaden with lack of hope. Could they put all this behind them and forget?

Forget.

The voice came chiming from another plane, an echo from her girl-hood days on Avalon. *The more you forget, the less there is to forgive.*

She squared her shoulders and got to her feet. *Forget, then. Start now.*

There is work to be done. No more lurking here, hiding from the world. No more thoughts of Cornwall—of the past—of him—

"Lady, lady!"

Brangwain whirled through the door, an Otherworldly light on her dark face.

"There's a ship sailing into the harbor, lady," she said urgently. "It's come from Cornwall to judge by the black sails, and the flag of Lyonesse is flying from its mast!"

a ship from Cornwall? Have they come in peace?"

The Queen burst out of her inner chamber like a bark in full sail. Her tall headdress shivered as she surged about the room and the jet at her waist and wrists rattled angrily.

"Has King Mark sent his champion to challenge us?" she demanded with a dangerous laugh. "Must we fight Cornwall after all?"

"No, no, Majesty." With the worn, weary love of long years, Sir Gilhan took in the tall, queenly frame, the expressive hands, the eyes like dark stars. Even now, he thought, she can still set all hearts alight. His face creased in a smile. "It seems that Cornwall has another offer in mind."

"What?" She stopped in her tracks and whirled around. "Sir Tristan is here, you say?"

"Moored at the quay, under flag of embassy," the old knight confirmed. "He has come in peace."

"For the hand of Isolde, it must be!" she cried huskily. Her eyes were like moons in her head.

"Whatever he's here for, madam, we must respect the flag," Sir Gilhan repeated carefully. "If Your Majesty feels any enmity toward him now—"

"Ah..."

The Queen paused, and struggled in her soul. In truth she still thought of avenging herself on Tristan, but her fury had faded along with her grief. Sir Tolen was not Marhaus, but he cheered her loneliness every time he warmed her bed. Tristan was less and less to her with every passing day. And, like it or not, here at last was a man Isolde could love. Gods above! Without that, there would be no lying down for the girl, no earth magic, no new life.

"Enmity? None!" The Queen waved an impatient hand and stalked away. "That's all in the past."

Sir Gilhan probed on. "So if the King wants a treaty to unite his country and ours . . . ?"

"We must rise above vengeance," the Queen proclaimed grandly, "for the good of the land!"

"As you say, Majesty, for the good of the land."

Sir Gilhan inclined his head. Privately he suspected that the Queen's newfound magnanimity had more to do with the afterglow left by Sir Tolen, whose nocturnal movements he made it his business to know, but that was her affair.

"You will receive Sir Tristan then?" he queried.

"But not alone!" The Queen whirled around again and joyfully clapped her hands. "Send for Princess Isolde," she cried as the servant appeared. "Say the Queen begs her dear daughter's presence in the Great Hall at once!"

MY KNIGHT HAS come.

My love has come to me.

But he lied, he deceived! Can he be truthful now?

Joy and misgivings alike thronged Isolde's mind. Then a flash of emerald fire came to her from a dark altar in an ancient place.

His ring.

I left his mother's ring with the Lady, I gave it away.

Gods above, will he ever forgive me?

"A little color, lady, for your cheeks—and a touch of carmine on your lips."

Isolde opened her eyes as the maid's cool fingertips danced over her skin. "What are you doing, Brangwain?"

The maid dipped into a pot of rosy madder and returned to the attack. "Just making you ready for the audience, madam. You're so pale."

Isolde stared at the unfamiliar image in the mirror as the maid fussed at her face. She hardly knew what she saw—a spirit, a woodland goddess?—in the gorgeous stranger all in green and gold. Rising to the occasion, Brangwain had picked out a gown of bright green velvet the color of hawthorn buds in March. Gold filigree gleamed on the bodice, and cloth of gold lined the long sleeves of the green silk overgown. A froth of gold lace like starlight fell from the circlet of emeralds on her head, and great ropes of emeralds shimmered at her waist and neck. Brangwain gave a last loving touch to the carefully looped and braided hair. "So beautiful, lady," she said softly. "So fine."

Isolde looked into the mirror and their eyes met. Fine enough, Brangwain did not say, for a marriage, but the whole castle knew what was in the air. No one quite knew how, for Sir Gilhan was the soul of discretion and he had spoken to the Queen alone. But from the lords of the council to the kitchen lad who turned the spit, every soul in the palace knew that the knight of Cornwall had come to offer for the Princess's hand.

Some who saw the young man himself pacing feverishly around the deck had seen him before, and hastened to tell that, too.

"It's the pilgrim!" panted one stout fishwife to her husband, bustling up from the quay.

"Go on!" The blacksmith paused in the act of pumping up his bellows, then resumed his work. "Not that beggar the Princess healed?"

"It's him, I tell you!"

He grunted, unimpressed. "What, come back as a knight?"

"And a great prince, and the nephew of Cornwall's king!" A lusty smile spread over the woman's face. "A good looker, too, and a fine body of a man. I don't think our Princess'll kick him out of bed."

The blacksmith raised his hammer and seized hold of a horseshoe to beat. "You'll be telling me he's the King of the Fair Ones next." He pounded resentfully. "What's wrong with you, woman? You've lost your mind!"

"Better than some as have no mind at all!" the aggrieved wife shot back. "Go and see for yourself, you great lubbock—don't believe me!"

Flouncing out, she rejoined the crowd already gathering to watch the knight and his followers march up from the quay. Young and old lined the route to the castle and many voices sought to unravel the exciting tale.

"It's the pilgrim come back!"

"No, it's not him, it's the King of Cornwall himself."

"It's his nephew, I swear—come for our Princess's hand."

Snatches of the hubbub greeted Isolde as she made her way to the Great Hall. Eager clusters of servants and courtiers thronged the passages as she went, bowing or curtseying and wishing her well.

"Bless you, lady!"

"May the Mother speed you to the place you deserve!"

"Thank you—thank you—"

She greeted them all in a dream of fear and joy. She did not know that she was now La Belle Isolde as they would always remember her, luminous with hope and radiant with desire. Beneath her smiles lay doubts she could not dispel. But she knew she had been released from the prison of despair and gave thanks for her delivery every step of the way.

I will not look back. I will take his coming as a gift of the Gods, begin again, forgive and forget.

She did not feel the flagstones beneath her feet as she hastened into the Great Hall and made her way through the vaulted space. A surge of confidence seized her. *Goddess, Mother, bring me to my love—*

Shafts of pale sunlight as glorious as her hopes poured through the windows and lay in golden pools on the floor. Ahead of her loomed the dais, with the Queen on her throne and Isolde's smaller throne standing at its side.

Any fears she had had of her mother vanished at once. The Queen's dark, handsome face was glinting with secret delight. She was robed as if for an audience of High Kings, resplendent in dusky silks like a night-flying moth, carmine and crimson, damson and mulberry black. The great diadem of the Queens of the Island shone on her head, and her wrists were laden with garnets like pigeon's eggs.

She reached out to embrace Isolde with arms of love.

"Welcome, little one," she whispered tremulously, patting Isolde's hand. She gestured toward her lords standing around the dais and the bright bevy of knights and ladies in the hall. "You know why we are all here?"

Isolde tried to speak, but could not find her voice. She felt like a goblet brimming over, her whole being pregnant with untapped bliss.

The Queen smiled into the large earnest eyes. "You have heard about the offer we are to receive?"

Isolde nodded. Her smiling eyes left no doubt about her reply.

"Good! Good!"

Sighing with satisfaction, the Queen waved Isolde to her place and settled herself on her throne.

"Send for the knight from Cornwall." She signaled to the chamberlain. "We will admit him now."

"Your Majesty." The chamberlain bowed and obeyed.

Afterward it seemed to Isolde that this was the last time she was ever truly happy or free from fear. The courtiers stood silent and still in the wintry sun, and even the tiniest motes of dust hung suspended in the shining air. In the deep silence, Isolde heard her heart singing like the birds on Avalon where winter never comes. She was feeding on bliss, gorging her poor, starved heart, till her soul left her body for the astral void.

And there he came to her, in the world beyond the worlds. Glimmering, she saw his tall body clad in starlight, his immortal face, the light of kindness blooming in his eyes. He took her in his spirit arms, and softly laid her down. She felt his kiss on her face like moondust, his warm hand on her breast, and she gave him in return her heart in his hand.

You are mine now, he said, *my lady and my love. From now on, we shall never be apart.*

She lay in his long, strong arms and marveled at his touch, his love, the miracle of him. She reached up and brushed his lips in a phantom kiss.

You are mine now, she promised him. *You are my knight and my love. From now on, we shall never be apart.*

Through the window she could see a glossy green ivy clinging to the wall. Entwined in its leafy branches, winding tightly around every stem, was a sturdy honeysuckle, dormant now for winter, but part of the evergreen's life.

So shall we be, Tristan, you and I, she told him on the starlit plane. *Now our lives are one, our spirits are entwined. Like the ivy and the honeysuckle, we shall never be apart.*

She hardly heard the trumpets calling as the doors opened and the embassy appeared. Down the hall marched a forest of banners and proud flags, silver, white, and blue. Behind them came a troop of bearers heaving great chests and boxes to lay before the throne. They were followed by a band of knights in blue and silver, a moving wall of bright lances held erect. *But where is he?* With every passing moment, her yearning grew.

At last the figure she longed for stood framed in the door. Her eyes burned for him, her famished heart was hungry for his sight. With a shock she saw she was looking at a different man. In place of the simple pilgrim's habit, he was arrayed in glittering silver mail and cloth of gold. A rich red velvet cloak swung from his shoulders and a broad coronet of gold held back his hair. She did not recognize her gentle friend in gray in the gorgeous stranger advancing down the hall.

Fear came to her then, and a scalding shame. Why had she parted with his mother's ring? What would he think when he saw it was gone? In a panic, she covered her left hand with her right. But the next moment she saw that he would not miss the ring because in truth, he would not look at her at all.

His eyes were everywhere but on her. With a deeper dread, she saw he was deathly pale. *Have you been ill, my love? I can heal you as I did before.* But nothing could allay the sudden sickness at her heart. *Something is wrong. Look at me, look at me now!*

He stalked toward her like a man facing death. As he reached the dais, he fixed his gaze on the Queen, and his bow declared he meant to deal with her mother, not with her. Now the clamor of her thwarted hopes could not be stilled. *He will betray me. He lied and deceived before.*

The Queen rose to her feet. "Welcome, Sir Tristan, to the Western Isle."

"Your Majesty, I am sent by the King of Cornwall to propose a union of our two kingdoms, the joining of our lands."

A union—

Isolde closed her eyes. Relief flooded her, sweetening her spirit, loosening every joint.

Yes, a union, my love, she promised him. *A true marriage of souls and minds.* For an endless moment she passed to the sweet place where souls wandered hand in hand, where kisses meant more than words and there were no more tears. Then she listened again and knew that something was truly wrong, everything was wrong.

His mouth was still making fine noises, but the words were hollow, as empty as the air. *Peace, gracious Queen,* she heard, and *free passage between our kingdoms,* and *mutual goodwill,* and much more of the same.

His white face glistened with strain as he strove ever harder to put his speech across. And still his words slipped through her mind and burst like the bubbles on the sea. What was he talking about? And all this time, he never looked her way.

She knew then that whatever he had come for, it was not for her. She was seized by a fury of grief. *You don't love me! Did you ever love me at all?* Then came the return to the darkness she thought she had escaped.

He is false.

All my hopes were false.

He is as false now as he was before.

Anguish ripped through her and the world diminished again before her eyes. She saw his drawn face, his lips still moving, but she could not hear what he said. She was lost in a dark place, far away and alone.

Lost—

I have lost my knight.

Lost my love, my joy, my life, my only hope.

So she looked on in deadness as he threw open boxes and chests of gifts and offered up silks soft as twilight, satin shiny as a summer's day, blue tourmalines like owl-light, yellow agates, tigereyes. And she sat by, calm and raging at the same time, in belief and black disbelief, as he stepped forward and opened his pale, traitorous mouth.

"These gifts I bring from Cornwall, by command of King Mark. I am here to lay his heart at Princess Isolde's feet. He begs the hand of the Princess as his bride, and I am ordered to escort her to Cornwall to be wed."

chapter 33

I am ordered, he had told her, that ought to have been clear enough.

By command of the King, he'd repeated that, too.

And *I am sent,* and *the King bids me say,* and much more. But still he knew that she had not understood. She thought he had betrayed her of his own free will.

Trembling as he had never trembled in his life, Tristan finished his speech with a deep, formal bow. On the dais, the Queen was regarding him with something dark and hostile in her deep-set eyes. But all he could feel was Isolde's pain. He knew without looking at her that she was suffering a thousand piercing sorrows, fury, grief, and betrayal, all at once.

At last he forced himself to turn his eyes on her. Glittering in vivid greens, crowned and veiled in gold, she sat as remote as an idol on a painted throne. She even wore a different, painted face and her lovely hair was tortured into strange shapes. He did not recognize his dear friend of so many woodland rides in the gorgeous stranger seated on the throne.

And the ring!

White-hot rage gripped him, piercing flesh and bone, as he saw through her tightly clasped hands to the naked finger beneath.

I gave you the best thing I had and you threw it away. What have you done with it? he gasped inwardly, speechless with pain.

He wanted to leap onto the dais, shake the answer from the garish rouged lips, take her by the throat. Did you throw it in the sea? Did you give it to a beggar or a Gypsy queen? He could not breathe.

But now their griefs were equal—now she, too, had dealt him a wound that would never heal. There was nothing but to leave as soon as he could. So he took his dismissal with thanks when the Queen rose to her feet. Every moment was torture till he could turn back to Cornwall and be free.

❦

IN THE QUEEN's privy chamber, the bread and mulled wine had come and gone, along with the cold meats and sweetmeats, the best of winter's fare. Three times now the fires had been stoked up, and still the Queen's councillors would not be dislodged. The Queen had taken to yawning loudly and prowling about. These old fools have not had such excitement in years, she thought with scorn. She was sick of their earnest faces and prating mouths.

But Goddess, Mother, what are we to do? her dark soul demanded frantically, adrift in confusion and fear. Why was marriage with Mark the question, when Tristan was the man? She would never forget Isolde's face as Tristan spoke and could not bear to look at her daughter now. Seated like a statue at the table, Isolde was a ghost of herself, no more.

What to do? The Queen covered her eyes. If only Marhaus were here! Tolen was a perfect companion for her horizontal hours, but no match for Marhaus at any other time. But you know what Marhaus would say! she rallied herself. He'd say marry her, marry her off. Who counts here, Isolde or you? Remember who is Queen.

And would that be so bad? It would certainly be a good match, perhaps even a great one in time. The Queen's fertile mind bloomed. With a union like this, Isolde would be Queen of two kingdoms as time went by. And if Arthur and Guenevere failed to have an heir, Isolde could even become High Queen of all the Islands in their place....

But could Cornwall's King be a worthy partner for her? Frowning, the Queen tried to remember what she knew of Mark. A weakling, Marhaus had said when he wanted to attack. A cowardly knight who was afraid to fight. Yet a man could be too bold, Marhaus, she mourned. If you had been more of a coward, I would have you still. But you rushed headlong into the House of Death.

And weak? her swift mind ran on. That was a good fault in a man. With a weak husband, a woman could have her own way. Isolde could rule the King and his kingdom and take lovers where she liked, Tristan perhaps?

A glimmer as old as the world lit her midnight eyes. Yes, she thought with deep certainty, he'd be the first. And if Isolde bore him a child, who would question that? Both Ireland and Cornwall obeyed the rule of Queens. Where the Mother-right ruled, the mother was the only parent who counted.

The Queen's clouded face relaxed into a secret smile. *If Isolde marries the King, she'll have husband, kingdom, lover, and children, too. The Western Isle will have another homeland across the sea, and I shall have new life—new life at last!*

Tears started to her eyes and a bevy of spirit children skipped through her dreams. *Yes, things might yet turn out as she had hoped, better even, the best!*

She turned back to the table. *Time to get rid of these gray-beards full of wind.*

"—for the good of the country," she heard.

Sir Gilhan was lecturing Isolde across the green baize while she listened, pallid and staring, without a sound. "You will be Queen, lady, and a queen must marry, after all."

The Queen came forward and raised her hand. "Thank you, my lords, for your good counsel here. The Princess and I will discuss the King's offer. It is time to decide."

Time to decide—

Isolde stirred. She knew without thinking what the Queen would say. Sir Gilhan's words, too, were coursing through her mind. A good marriage, with a ruling king—a union of equals—for the good of the country and the promise of peace.

She drew a deep breath.

Remember, Isolde—you are married to the land. Do right by your country, and you will find peace.

A cold strand of comfort wrapped itself round her heart. The land would never leave her, lie or betray. And inner peace must be her only goal now.

She stuck out her chin. "Your Majesty, why delay?" She rose to her feet and spoke as coldly as she ever had in her life. "The King of Cornwall has offered for my hand. We shall tell the Cornish envoy that I accept."

THE WORD WENT around the palace like lightning from mouth to mouth. Waiting in Isolde's chamber, Brangwain was the first to hear it from Isolde herself.

"Make ready, Brangwain, organize all my effects, books, papers, everything, not just my clothes. We are leaving for Cornwall. We sail on the fairest tide."

Brangwain stared at the frozen face. "For Cornwall, madam?"

"To marry the King."

Brangwain suppressed a gasp. "You would do this?"

"It is decided." Isolde's voice was cold.

The maid was stupefied. "You will marry the King?"

Isolde fixed her with a frozen eye. "It is not what you'd think. We don't follow the Man-God from the East, so I won't have to grovel to my husband and promise to obey him as Christians do. King Mark holds his lands as a vassal of Queen Igraine, and as long as I can follow the Mother-right, I can be my own woman in Cornwall just as I am here. And besides"—she paused indifferently—"I can always come back to Ireland whenever I like."

She has no idea what marriage means, thought Brangwain, whose own lively sense of the blessed state had kept her firmly single all her life. If you love your husband, you won't want to leave. And if you don't, he'll do all in his power to force you to stay.

"Indeed, lady," said Brangwain unhappily, "it's true that Ireland will always be your home. But marriage?"

"Within there!"

The voice of the guard sounded at the door. Brangwain hastened to open it, and returned, veiling the hope in her eyes. "It's the knight from Cornwall, madam. Sir Tristan has heard your decision and begs an audience with you."

Isolde waved a hand. "I will not see him."

"But, my lady—"

Isolde did not hear. "I will make this marriage, tell him that. And Cornwall and Ireland will be allies for all time." She stared out of the window at the grey veils of fog blotting out the horizon and making the whole world one.

My country—

The land—

Whatever the future, whatever her false knight had done, the island was hers, both now and evermore. Its dark earth was her flesh, its shining waters flowed through her every vein, its seas fed her soul. Its trees were her sisters, its hills her brothers, its waves her playfellows, its people and their shy, tousled children her closest kin. *Gods and heroes chose this place as their home, and we petty mortals are blessed to call it ours.*

In the darkest place of her soul, she made a vow. *Western Isle, sacred isle, land of Erin, home—from now on, you must be lover and mother, tutor and nurse to me. I will never love again, now this love is dead. I will guide my steps by you, and you will lead me to the light.*

Later she was to think, How could I have been so blind—so uncaring—thoughtless—willful—rash?

But she was young then and drunk with sorrow, and it was nothing to her to throw her life away.

chapter
34

There were many good things about being one hundred years old. Or
two hundred, or three, whatever she told them she was.

The wizened creature in the chair folded her papery hands and
grinned. In truth, she had no idea how old she was. When she was born,
no one around her could count. But she knew she was older than anyone else alive. And old enough for them all to fear a woman who could
not die.

The old woman closed her lizard eyes and smiled. In truth, that was
the best of her tricks, convincing the people that her powers could defy
time. And when the Dark Lord came for her, as she knew he must, they
would all still believe that her spirit lived on, and would go on obeying
her teachings as they did now. Then indeed she would have cheated
death.

Which would come whenever the Dark Lord decreed. And it could
not be long. Her body had wasted till she was now more cricket than
woman, a crooked thing of leathery skin stretched over fragile bones.
Her wrinkled skull had long ago shed its hair, and she could not remember what it was to have teeth. Even her eyebrows and eyelashes had vanished and she knew she looked like a monstrous baby, ancient yet
newborn.

But as close to the grave as she was, life could still be good. There
were many worse things than to sit by a fire like this, holding out her
hands and drawing the warmth of the flames into her crumbling bones.
The darkness in the cavern was good, too, because her old eyes could
pierce the gloom, though for decades now she had told them she was
blind. Even better was to be cared for in the hardest of winters when

others starved, and carried everywhere so that her feet never touched the ground. Best of all was to have outlived every other wise woman on the island, and become the Nain, the one who held power from the Mother Herself and was the mother of every soul alive.

She grinned again. She loved being the Nain. The Nain smiled upon marriages, or divorced warring couples with a frown. She gave babies to childless women and revived flagging unions with the help of a range of liquors to arouse the weakest spouse.

That was life. The Nain dealt in death, too. She blinked indifferently.

You conceived a child while your husband was away?

Take this.

You thought your moon times were over and childbearing done?

Take that.

She never hesitated to give these unwilling mothers a draft of the liquor that meant death for the child. Far better an instant passage to the Otherworld than life as the family dog, beaten and cursed. And if the child still insisted on being born, it was the Nain who unflinchingly drew the newborn from the womb and plunged it facedown in the birthing box before it could draw breath.

The Nain grunted. The fine ashes of the birthing box were an easy delivery from life compared with some. And once it slipped its earthly shell, every soul was free to walk the astral plane and return at will. As she would very soon.

But till then—

She leered out into the cave. On the other side of the fire, three old women dozed and muttered, their heads drooping like dead flowers awaiting winter's scythe. The Nain stared and blinked her eyes. As they felt her cold milky gaze, the three helpers twitched and mumbled and jerked themselves awake. The Nain had heard something, they knew.

And here it came again, a faraway rustling high above. Soon they could hear rapid footsteps and frantic, frothing silks, feel the troubled soul forging its turbulent way till a wavering swan light loomed up out of the dark. Behind it stood the Queen, panting with haste. She set down the swan lamp and advanced, holding out her hands.

"Help me, Nain," she implored. "Isolde is sailing to Cornwall to marry the King. The first time a woman lies down with a man, it should be one her heart longs for and adores. Or else the dark stranger at Beltain, when the fires call through the darkness and all the world sings."

She shivered, besieged by hot memories of a wide hillside dotted with points of flame, warm shadows, beds of bracken, and the night vibrating with dancing and drumming and lovers' moans. How often had she turned aside herself, ravished by a wild beauty, to lie with a man of no country, tall and shining in the night? It stabbed her to the heart that her own flesh, her daughter, would never know such bliss.

"She'll have to lie down with a man she does not love. But she might! She still could," the Queen cried feverishly, "if you'll help her now."

The Nain glimmered at her. Yes, a woman's first lying down should indeed be the first of the three joys the Mother gave to women, the bliss of love, the fulfillment of children, and the satisfaction of a life well lived.

"Can you do it, Nain?" The Queen brought her hands together in prayer. "A drink to make her love her husband and forget the man of her heart?"

"You want an elixir—a distillation of desire?" The Nain bared her gums in a smile of assent. Already her three crones were moving round the cave. One assembled a metal tripod over the fire, the second hung a small cauldron on it, while the third unerringly sorted through a tangle of pink, red, and tumescent purple flowers.

"Weeping-heart," she chanted, tossing them into the pot. "Love-lies-bleeding, marry-me-quick."

Her sister crone approached with a deep glass of ruby liquid pulsing with inner light. "The souls of red roses," she intoned, "distilled from the desert sands—attar of the heart of a princess of Araby, who died because her lover was hated by her kin." Chanting, she poured it into the cauldron to cover the flowers.

The third came forward with a flagon of red wine. "The soul of the grape, to make the best drink these lovers ever had."

Chanting, the three old ones went to and fro. Strange roots and fragments of bone, bitter herbs and aromatic gums, powders of haunting fragrance and drops of nameless liquor found their way into the pot. Over a slow flame, the contents swelled to a low, rolling boil, and the smell of rising heat filled the air.

The chant went on. The Queen pressed her fingers to her temples and a drugged and dreamy look passed over her face.

Yesss—

In all her years of making earth magic, she had never found a man who excited her as Tolen did now. He did not know how to adore her body, as Marhaus had done, nor did he care to learn. But every time he rolled off her, groaning and sweating, the touch of his hand or the sight of his narrow hips made her want him again. The very ways he satisfied her hunger left her hungering for more.

A fine frenzy gripped her. Already she could feel his hands on her breasts, his head between her thighs.

"Hurry, hurry," she moaned, her eyes growing dark with desire. "There's not much time—they sail on the evening tide."

"Patience," crooned the Nain. "Sooooon—"

Now the cauldron was humming to itself in low, gurgling tones. The ruby liquid convulsed and called out in the voice of an underground sea.

Now—

Standing over the cauldron, the Nain held out her crumpled hands and began the words of power. The air throbbed and thickened, and the Queen found herself struggling to breathe as the Nain drew down all nature's force into the pulsating elements.

"Alla purim ut philaranon manag robis elter dan—"

Was the spell sounding in the cave, or inside her head? Was it even on this human plane at all? The Queen caught her breath. The force was building, building—she wanted to cry out. Suddenly the darkness of the cave was split by thunder and lightning, and a scream issued from the center of the earth. The Queen hugged herself in fear. When the power of nature was harnessed to pervert true love, the very voice of nature would protest. The Nain had indeed torn the elements apart as she made them release their secrets in her quest to counterfeit true desire.

"It is done."

The liquid in the cauldron released a plume of glassy smoke and subsided with a sigh. The Nain collapsed into the arms of two of her supporters, and was carried back to her chair. The third lifted the cauldron from the fire, carefully decanted its contents into a flask, and pressed it into the hands of the Queen.

The flask was of old red gold, with a great ruby for a stopper and thick bands of ancient rubies round its waist. The Queen clasped it to her breast and knelt before the Nain.

"Thanks to the Mother," she whispered, her tears falling like rain.

"Thank yourself," the Nain said in her worn-out voice. "For giving your daughter Isolde what she deserves. Thanks to you, she will know the love of a man—a love greater than you and she can dream. Whoever drinks this drink will share a lifelong faith and truth. Hatred will never part them, and their love will never die." Her voice rose to an eldritch scream and she closed her eyes. "Either shall love the other all the days of their lives!"

"Bless you, bless you, bless you!"

Weeping, the Queen took a pearl ring from her finger and pressed it onto the Nain. Then she hastened from the cave.

Hurry, hurry—up to the world above—

The tide is rising—they'll be taking ship soon—

"Brangwain!"

She found the maid in her own chamber, packing her effects for the voyage. Seeing the maid standing amid heaps of boxes and hampers, the Queen checked her impetuous rush and drew back.

"Oh, Brangwain," she said sorrowfully, "what have we done?"

Brangwain's black eyes crackled with fire. Madam, you began all this when you let your love for Sir Marhaus defeat your duty to the land, her dark gaze said louder than any words. But too late for reproaches now.

She dropped the Queen a cold curtsy. "Madam?" she said.

The Queen looked away. "I do not trust you," she muttered. "You are Merlin's kin."

"Like all the Welsh, lady." Brangwain gave a crooked smile. "It is in our blood."

The Queen held out the gold flagon, its ruby eyes gleaming dully in the evening light. "This must go with Isolde when she sails."

Brangwain eyed it warily. "What is it?"

"A cordial to compose her on her wedding day. To settle her stomach and ease her virgin pains. She must share it with her husband when he comes to her bed." The Queen paused, watching Brangwain closely. "It is a mother's gift to her daughter for her first lying down."

Brangwain hesitated. "It is a hard thing she is going to."

The Queen nodded. "And this can help her. I know you love your mistress," she said insinuatingly. "So you will not deny her that."

Brangwain made up her mind. "I'll take it, madam." She held out her hand. "For her wedding day, you say?"

"Yes! To compose her. And to keep his love all her life." The Queen thrust the flask at Brangwain. "Be sure to give it to her just as I said."

Brangwain took the heavy gold object and clasped it to her heart. "I will."

It is done as the Nain promised, thought the Queen, trembling with relief. Brangwain is as true as steel, she won't fail. When Isolde marries King Mark, she will know a love greater than she or I could dream. Together they will share a lifelong faith and truth. Hatred will never part them, and their love will never die. Dreamily she recalled the Nain's last cry: "Either shall love the other all the days of their lives!"

So rejoicing, she went out into the night. And overhead all the demons of death and destruction came to life and danced with delight at the feast of evil ahead.

chapter
35

*n*ew life—

A new country, marriage to a stranger, another world—

Bending her head against the bitter wind, Isolde felt for the handrail and made her way onto the ship. A thin sleet seeded the wind with pinpoints of ice and she could feel the gangplank slipping beneath her feet. Soon they must face the mountainous wintry seas, but wherever they landed, there would be no safe harbor for her. She was leaving Ireland, her mother, everything she called home. And with a man she hated and despised.

*Tantris—Tristan—taunter—trickster—*whatever he called himself, the man she had never known. But whoever he was, she would never know him now.

As soon as they reached Cornwall, she decided, they would never be alone again. They would keep a dignified distance and whatever had passed between them would fade and die. She would become King Mark's wife, and everything else would be subordinated to that. As she passed these thoughts through her mind, it came to her that she did not know what marriage to King Mark would mean. But women married all the time, she could surely do it, too. She would meet her husband at the dock and be married at once. There was no turning back.

Then this springtime love for the pilgrim will be gone.

As he is gone already, and this hateful gaudy stranger come to take his place.

She could see him now, waiting for her on the deck, acting the lordly master of the ship. She watched him give the captain and crew orders to cast off, then turn with a bow to welcome her on board. As *welcoming as a man can be,* she thought, simmering with disgust, *with a frozen sneer on his face and a distant gaze that never meets my own.*

"This way, my lady."

Only the sleet in her face was icier than his tone. Bowing, he ushered her forward along the deck, and down a narrow flight of steps to the space below deck. Oddly, it was colder here than out in the wind.

Taunter—trickster—pilgrim—liar—

"Go ahead, sir."

She waved him on, squared her shoulders, and followed, her head held high. *Soon I shall be alone.*

The low passageway smelled of wood soaked by the sea, the tang of brine as sharp and salty as tears. *Where's Brangwain?* she thought querulously. *Surely she's seen all the boxes on board by now?*

"The Queen's cabin."

Striding ahead, he threw open a door. "King Mark has had this fitted out for you." She was not to know that this was all Tristan's work after Mark had handed over everything to him, and he would never tell her now.

"Thank you."

She followed him over the threshold into a low spacious cabin. Rows of gleaming portholes ran along each side, all smoldering with the fiery remains of the day. The sleet had stopped and the dying sun poured its red and gold into a bright, warm boudoir, lovingly made for a queen. Beechwood tables and chairs, all bolted to the floor in case of storms, clustered against the walls, and plump sheepskin couches huddled around a blazing stove. At the back of the cabin a great bed took up an entire bulkhead, curtained and canopied in Cornwall's royal blue.

The air was fragrant with burning applewood. Did she like it? She did not seem to care. Hovering tensely, Tristan watched as Isolde moved forward and took off her wrap. Instantly he noted her mournful gown of dark winter green. Why was she making herself dull and ugly like this? In his mind he saw her again as he had known her first, riding out in a green gown like springtime, when the daffodils come.

A wild yearning seized him for the muffled figure, the long strong limbs, the cloud of fiery hair. He wanted to peel off her thick woollen wrappings, bend her rigid body till it softened into his, submit himself in turn to the tyranny of her touch. He felt her brush past him in the narrow space, and had to fight down a wave of savage desire. The next impulse was a gasp of disgust. *Gods above, man, she's your uncle's promised wife!*

And she hates you.

He could not keep that thought at bay. She will not want to see you or talk to you. She is only enduring this voyage till she reaches Cornwall and can bid you a frozen farewell. When you tried to see her in Ireland, how many times did she send you away without a civil word? He stifled a bitter laugh. Keep your distance, then.

He opened the door, and bowed. "Excuse me, my lady." Time to be gone.

"Be careful, there! Watch what you're doing, lads!"

Shaking the sleet from her cloak, a lean dark form blew through the door, alternately scolding and urging on the hapless boy who was struggling along in her wake with a massive trunk. Behind him came others burdened with boxes and traps, who followed him into the cabin and set down their load.

"Good lads! Now off you go." A smiling Brangwain pressed silver into their hands and ushered them out.

Tristan watched them all disappear and bowed to Isolde again. "Farewell."

"A moment, sir." Isolde snapped. She signaled to Brangwain.

The maid crossed to the nearest box and opened it. Inside the box lay two objects wrapped in silk, one above the other, carefully cushioned in fine straw.

Tristan froze. A faint sound wove its way into the room, two high voices calling in ethereal harmony. Isolde nodded. She could see at once he knew what they were.

"Glaeve?" he said in disbelief. "And my harp?" Tears started to his eyes.

She stared at him. "Did you think we'd keep them? We're not savages in Ireland, sir!"

The soft, sweet sound grew higher and more intense. Hidden in their veils of silk, the two treasured objects were crying out for his hand.

Isolde struggled for breath.

The touch of his hand—
Oh, the feel of him—
And I am married to the land.

"Well, there they are, sir." She turned away. "You are free to go."

Behind them, Brangwain was moving quietly about the cabin,

unpacking boxes and bundles and clearing the floor. The silence was broken by a sudden stir and running feet on the boards overhead.

"Cast off, there! Hoist the mizzen!" came the captain's cry. Groaning, the ship left the dock and slipped into the swift pull of the tide.

"No holding her, sir!" hollered the first mate. "Running fair and free."

"Into the sunset, then, mister," the captain sang back. "Let her go!"

"Aye, aye, sir! All the way home!"

Tristan looked up. Isolde's eyes were huge, blind pools. Her mouth had lost its shape, and her fingers were pulling her skirt.

"Leave us, Brangwain," he said quietly.

The maid gave one startled glance, then vanished through the door.

Isolde looked around. Her mind felt like lead. *Where's Brangwain?*

He stepped forward, all his coldness gone. "Why are you making this marriage?" he said earnestly.

"You—you dare to challenge me?" Her anger flared. "When you lied to me—deceived me—led me astray—"

To her horror, her voice cracked and broke.

But he held her gaze and his steadfast voice went on. "I do not excuse the lies I told to you. But I never planned to deceive you, or even to come here at all." He gave a grim smile. "I passed out after fighting Sir Marhaus, and came around to find myself in the stronghold of his Queen. I was half dead, and in the hands of my mortal enemy. I woke up with a false name, and all I could do was live by it, or die."

Goddess, Mother, yes—

With a pang she saw him lying injured on the bed, his suffering eyes casting wildly round the room, his sheets soaked with sweat as he fought to move his limbs. *Waking in the arms of the enemy, too weak to move—he must have been in terror for his life.* She felt a creeping shame. *And I blamed him for that? What would I have done?*

"And then you and I—" He paused and cleared his throat. "You—we—we rode out together and became friends."

Friends? she pondered. *Was that it?* A great dreariness seized her. *No. More, much more. I thought you were my true love and my knight.*

"More than friends," he said in the same low, earnest voice. "So I ask you again—why are you marrying King Mark?"

Fury cracked her indifference, and stung her to retort. "Tell me why I should not!"

She saw him take a long breath. "The King is marrying only because his barons are insisting that he take a queen," he said at last. "So he needs to be married, but he does not want a wife."

He does not want me? "But he must want a child!"

"That, too, is more his barons' idea than his own. As far as Mark's concerned, he has an heir." He laughed harshly. "He has two. You'll meet my cousin Andred, his brother's son. And I stand before Andred in the Mother-right."

Isolde felt the ground shifting beneath her feet. "This is a dynastic alliance," she said stoutly, "to secure peace."

Tristan gave an irritated laugh. "Our King will not attack Ireland! And would your Queen be tempted to challenge Cornwall again?" His face darkened with scorn. "I do not think so, Princess."

In spite of herself, she rose to meet his ire.

"Princess indeed, sir," she spat, "and a princess must marry, too. The King of Cornwall is a good match for me." She thrust her chin in the air. "And I have no doubt that he will love and respect me in time—that we will come to an understanding as man and wife—"

"Goddess, Mother!" he muttered. He knew there was no way to soften this. "King Mark has a mistress," he said brutally. "She cares for all such needs."

Isolde froze. "Who is she?"

"The wife of one of his barons. She is the leading lady of the court." The Lady Elva's long white face and virulent black stare came into his mind, and a new fear was born. "She will be jealous of you. She will hate you for supplanting her."

Jealousy, hate, and another faithless man—

Palomides, Tristan, Mark—Goddess, Mother, is there no man in the world I can call my own?

"Gods above," she burst out. *And I never thought of this?* She raged round the cabin in a spasm of self-hate. "I thought—" *Gods above, how could I be so rash—so blind?* For the first time, she turned and looked him in the eye. "I thought—no, it was madness—I did not think!"

"Oh, lady," he groaned, "this is all my blindness, my evil doing, my stupidity."

She had never seen anything as deep and dark as his eyes. "I don't understand." She felt a growing dread. "What did you do?"

"Lady, lady," he cried. "I betrayed you to this! I told my uncle about you—praised you to the skies. He spoke of an alliance with Ireland, and I thought he meant your mother the Queen. So I pledged him that I would win him his heart's desire." Loathing choked him, but he forced himself to go on. "I swore it on the soul of the one I love. Then I found out he wanted to marry you!"

She felt her heart, her mind tearing at once. "And you had given him your oath?"

He was the picture of misery. "Sworn to him as my liege lord, my King, my kin. A threefold promise I can never break."

Horror seized her. *On the soul of the one you love—you were talking about me!*

You swore to win me as his bride when you could have come back for me yourself.

We could be sailing now as man and wife.

And instead—

Darkness covered her eyes and she felt a roaring in her head. The floor groaned and buckled beneath her feet.

"Lady, lady!"

She felt his hand beneath her elbow and his arm round her waist. He supported her across the cabin and lowered her onto the couch. Sick to her soul, she leaned back against the cushions and gave herself up to grief.

"Hold on, lady—I'll get you something."

She could hear him searching the cabin, muttering to himself. Then he crossed back toward her and sat down at her side. He took her hand and the cold rim of a drinking flask nudged her lips.

"Drink this," his voice said in her ear. "Brangwain must have brought it in case you were sick."

The scent enveloped her and she felt herself sailing high above the earth, riding the billowing clouds. Golden clearings beckoned from the heart of dark forests, tiny boats rocked sweetly on long, rolling waves, coracles of love for bodies and souls entwined. Somewhere a dark fear stirred, and a cloud like a warning hand passed over the sky. Then his voice came again. "Drink."

She drank, and was a child at her mother's breast, then a woman feasting on her lover's mouth. She tasted sunlight and dancing, tears and eternal night. She saw into the chambers of his heart and walked with him through the caverns of his mind. His hand in hers was all the strength she sought, all she needed to sustain her life. His sorrows smote her like a sword, and his joys were the greatest she could know.

She saw again the green ivy and trusting honeysuckle as they entwined together on the castle wall. *Two lives, one love. Two bodies, one green soul.*

So.

It is done.

She opened her eyes. Her head swam in a fine ether, she felt fresh and new. Tristan sat beside her, holding her hand. For the first time she saw his fine tunic of pearly leather studded with gold, his white silk shirt, his silver girdle and the gold torque of knighthood round his neck. *This is not vanity,* she thought. *He did this for me.*

"Lady, lady—" he said brokenly.

She pressed the flask into his hands. His beauty was too much for her to bear. "Drink."

He took it unquestioningly, like a child. As he drank, she saw on his face all she had felt, and more. She traveled with him to the place where he began, alone in the dark wood when his mother died.

Great tears stood in his eyes. She reached out to kiss them with her fingertips.

"Oh—oh!" he gasped. "You're warm—"

He took both her hands in his, and brought them to his lips. As he looked up, he gave her his soul in his eyes.

"You are the woman of the dream," he said.

She had waited to hear him say this from the time before time. "And you are my knight."

She knew they had been touched by the Goddess, and would remember this trembling moment all their lives. He stretched out his hand and touched her face.

"I love you," he said, feeling how strange and wonderful the words were in his mouth. "More than life itself."

"And I love you." It sounded like a prayer. "More than all three worlds."

He held her soul in his hands, and she could not breathe. His fingertips brushed her eyes, and suddenly she was melting, dissolving, like the waters of Avalon.

"This love will never leave us now," she wept, "neither for weal nor for woe."

His heart was weeping, too. "Enough, lady," he said huskily. Then, kissing her tears away, he led her to the bed.

chapter
36

Into the sunset, mister—running fair and free—

His arms around her felt like coming home. His hands were firm and quiet, as they had been on the reins of his horse when they rode in the woodland in the springtime of their love. With every touch she felt her love for him wrapping itself round her heart like a briar rose, thorns and sweetness together, piercing deep down into her heart's blood.

Deftly he parted the heavy folds of her gown. *He has done this before,* floated through her mind, but she did not care. Her whole body was trembling, hoping for him now. As he reared above her, his eyes, his face, flared red and gold in the sun's dying fire. Now she saw signs of his birth in the wild woodland, the blind lovelights lifting the corners of his eyes, his ears like a faun's, his strong white teeth.

His lips were kissing away the last of her tears. "My sword is yours," he breathed, "my soul, my body are yours."

The hot green scent of the midsummer forest rose from him, filling the wintry chamber with delight, and she caught the scent of the great roe deer in his pride. The joy of him, the unspeakable wonder of him, stopped her breath. She wanted to bury her face in his long, tangled hair, worship his bigness, take him to her soul.

All around she could hear the roaring of the sea. Laughter coursed through her, and she took his face in her hands. Like a hungry orphan she fed on its hard planes and boundaries, rejoicing in the pricking of his stubble, his hard jaw, his full, strong lips. Kissing him, she knew that she had never dreamed of knowing his mouth as she did now.

"Oh, my lady—my love—"

He had never imagined how sweet she would be. Marveling, Tristan floated in the world between the worlds. All his loves of the past shrank to nothing against the loveliness that fell from Isolde like light. Watching her face as he held her, he felt every one of her quicksilver changes and basked in her gentle joy. In wonderment he traced the tiny lights glimmering on her temples, her cheekbones, at the corners of her mouth. Surely the Fair Ones had kissed her in her cradle as she slept?

Lying in his arms she smelled sweeter than mown grass in summer, as clean and fresh as a waterfall in spring. Beneath the gloomy gown of winter green she wore a soft shift of palest lace and lawn. Trembling, he loosed its countless ribbons and ties, then shrugged out of his clothes so that they both were free.

Naked, he could worship her body's sweet hills and hollows, the honeysuckle ripeness of her breasts, their delicate rose-pink tips and creamy skin. Her body was fuller and richer than he had dared to hope, her whole frame flushing warmly under his kiss, her breath changing as he touched the silky softness at the top of her legs.

He gentled her for a long, loving time, and she felt the clock of life itself suspended as she waited for each caress. At last he came into her in one swift, sure move, and she cried out in pain. Then a dark glory seized her, and she gripped his flanks, drawing him deep into her as he shuddered and called to her in throes of his own. Panting, they clung together, two bodies, one soul, surging and soaring in a sightless sea.

Had he come from the Otherworld? She had known tall men in plenty, though few as big-built as he was, with such gentleness. Other knights, too, had his nobility, and would give their lives to succor orphans and the aged and those weaker than themselves.

But no other soul in the world burned with his special grace. She knew without knowing that the Old Ones had been with him at his birth. Drowsing, she dared to hope that She who was the Mother of them all had held his poor mother in Her arms as she labored and died.

And now this man-child of sadness was hers to love, hers to care for and worship her whole life through. Curling into the shelter of his arms, she fell asleep.

TRISTAN WOKE SHIVERING, in a frozen dawn. The potbellied stove had gone out, and bright shards of frost spangled the portholes where last night's sun had shone. Beside him Isolde lay as golden as a dormouse at harvest, curled up in its nest. Love and terror fell on him in one blow. *What have we done? What are we to do?*

Her eyes opened sleepily, as if he had spoken aloud. "We must tell the King," she said, covering a yawn.

"Tell him what?"

His tone was sharper than he meant, and she looked at him, huge-eyed. "The truth."

"And shame him through all the world?" He laughed in despair at her simplicity. "The wedding's in hand and the priest is rehearsing the vows. The King's clerks will have sent to King Arthur and every other king in the islands and beyond—the Kings of France, of Gaul, of Little Britain, will be on their way to Castle Dore. Once you're married, there will be feasting and tournaments, a month of festivities at least."

Her eyes darkened like rock pools at low tide. "I didn't know—"

Tristan drove on. "He'll be waiting to greet you himself when the ship gets in. All the court will be there, his confessor, his advisers, his knights. And you'll tell him that the marriage is over before it's begun? That the man who won him his wife also took her away—his own nephew and sworn knight?"

"He'd kill you," she said with bleak certainty.

"Or I'd have to kill him. And then—" He groaned as if his soul would burst. "Then Andred and his nobles must pursue me to the death. A blood feud demands it. There is no escape."

She threw her arms round him and hugged his head to her chest. "We could flee away!" she cried, but as she spoke, her inner voice demanded, *Where?*

They were so close now that he heard her thought. "Alone, I could go. A poor knight can hope to lose himself in the world. But you were born to be a queen. Where does a queen hide her head?"

"I'd rather be a milkmaid for your love!"

"Queens are not milkmaids," he returned stubbornly. "The King would track us down. And queen or no, he would kill you, too."

"What?" Her hand flew to her mouth. "Goddess, Mother, what kind of man is he?"

"Like all men, lady," he said heavily. "Ready to kill when he's been betrayed."

"Gods above, Tristan!" she burst out. "D'you want me to marry him?"

"No!"

But the thought hung between them, *What else can we do?*

She clung to him fiercely. "Say you'll never leave me!" Yet even as she said it, she knew it was a lie.

THEY STOOD SIDE by side on the topmost deck. Behind them Brangwain held herself upright against the wind and tried not to show the sorrow in her heart. One glance at Isolde had told her what had passed, even before Isolde had nodded and held out her hands, asking for whatever comfort the maid could give.

The empty cabin itself spelled its own tale, from the still-sputtering fire Tristan had tried to light before he left, to the tangled sheets on the disordered bed. The white linen was stained with drops of red, proof positive in an enemy's hands that Isolde had given up her maidenhood in this bed and was no virgin when she came to marry the King. That at least Brangwain had swiftly taken care of, bundling the sheets into the stove to burn. But there was nothing to be done about the flask of the Queen's elixir, standing empty at the side of the couch. How was she to tell the Queen that the liquor had reached the wrong couple, and Isolde's fate was sealed? And Goddess, Mother, how was she to tell Isolde herself?

In silence she had robed Isolde for the day. For a princess encountering a king, a bride meeting her husband, a queen-to-be greeting her future court, nothing was too good. So Brangwain had made her mistress a glory to behold, except for the wounded mouth and dream-dazzled eyes. And now the call had come, "Land ahoy!"

Around them the wind lashed at the restless sea as a troubled dawn broke over the tortured waves. White mares crested the sighing, yearning surge and galloped feverishly toward the shore. From the sea, the long quay was almost hidden by the spray, but there was no mistaking the bright cloaks and silver mail of those waiting there. All the court seemed to be here, and the townsfolk, too. In front of the busy crowd stood the heralds in their multicolored coats, trumpets at the ready for a royal fanfare.

"The welcome party is out in force." Tristan pointed bitterly ahead. "That's King Mark in the center, in the red," he said through chattering teeth. "My cousin Andred on the right, in royal blue."

Isolde stared at the tiny figures and nodded dully. "And the one in black is the priest?"

"Father Dominian," Tristan confirmed. He did not name the tall, upright woman standing next to Dominian in jealous green, though he knew that Isolde had seen her striking form. She would know the Lady Elva soon enough.

Isolde looked at her rival and closed her eyes. *Goddess, Mother, show us what to do!*

The wind changed and the clouds parted above their heads. A great white bird flew toward them out of the sun, circled the ship, and landed lightly on the topmost mast.

"It is the Mother." Isolde could hardly speak.

"Or Her messenger." Tristan held his breath. "Bringing Her blessing on us before we part."

With a long, soft call, the bird spread her white wings and clapped them gently together, one, two, three. A sound of unspeakable sweetness fell through the air.

There is no gift but love.

No joy but love.

No pain, no bane, no cost, no loss but love.

There is no life but love.

They both heard it, low and clear, breathing from Avalon, sighing from the deep heart of the sea.

She could not take his hand in sight of the shore. But she answered with one clear thought, and knew he heard it, too. *This love will never leave us now, neither for weal nor for woe.*

Steadily the ship drew nearer to the dock till the sailors were leaping out with landlines to secure the prow. Then came the thud of the gangplank and her legs took her forward, though she could not feel her feet. The next moment she saw a great gangling figure in a blur of royal red, and caught a self-satisfied smile and a clumsy bow. The brazen snarl of the trumpets split the air and a rough hand grabbed hers.

"Princess Isolde!" roared Mark above the fanfare. "Welcome to Cornwall, my bride—my wife!"

chapter
37

There. Over there."

Lucan leaned forward over his horse's neck and pointed through the trees.

"We've got them!" Gawain cried.

They could all see it now, a faint flicker of firelight dancing through the wood. As they watched, other fires sprang up around the first. A good-sized group was making camp ahead. They had run the Gypsies to earth, and none too soon.

"You're right, Lucan." Kay looked around at the dank, dripping pines and the dense undergrowth in the last of its autumn decay. Tonight they would sleep with the travelers and there would be yet more nights on the road before the bliss of clean linen, lavendered sheets, and a warm, curtained bed. But this was the end of the trail.

"On, then," Kay said urgently.

Step by step the deep forest thinned out till the tunnel of knotted pines widened into an open, grassy space. Ahead of them burned the largest of the fires, a great blaze of red and gold lighting up the sky. Around it dusky figures came and went, some throwing down cushions and rugs, others tending the flames. The wide clearing was dotted with rough tents, and between them, the Gypsies' stubby ponies grazed at will.

The knights dismounted and led their horses toward the fire. Twenty or so of the travelers were taking their places around the leaping flames, men and women of all ages settling down with their children and dogs. One dark-faced man toyed with a strange instrument, making odd flights of melancholy sound, while another softly tinkered on a drum.

"Sirs!"

A tall figure rose to his feet as the knights approached. He was loosely clad in a short jerkin of leather over a full white shirt and voluminous breeches tucked into high leather boots. A gold ring pierced one ear and the handsome, swarthy face was lit by a humorous smile.

"You have found us at last!" He chuckled. "You have been long on the way."

Kay grinned mirthlessly. "You knew we were following you?"

"We are the Roma. We know everything," said the Gypsy airily. "I am Zrladic, the king of this tribe. Tonight you will feast with us and sleep in our tents." He bowed courteously to a young woman lounging at his feet. "And if the Gods are with us A'isha will dance for you. Now, let my men take your horses, and tell us why you have come."

With a flourish, Zrladic returned to his cushion by the fire.

Uneasily Kay complied, all too aware of A'isha's hard gaze. He tried not to look at her sensual, olive-skinned face and tumbling black hair, hennaed nails, full body, and light, low-cut gown.

"We are knights of King Arthur," he began, "on a quest for the King. Years ago, at a tournament, one of your women told fortunes in a tent. We need to speak with her." He looked around. "Is she here?"

"She is everywhere." Zrladic gave a bland, impenetrable smile. "The woman you saw was the Old Mother of our people, and she has the Sight. You want to talk to her?"

"Yes," said Kay firmly.

The musician raised his head, languid as a harebell on its stalk, and struck a sardonic chord. "But will she speak to you?"

"Why not?" Kay demanded defensively.

A'isha laughed derisively, pursing her mulberry mouth. "The Old Mother would say, why should she?"

Kay paused, taking time to collect himself. "A child was born," he said stiffly. "We need to know how it came about."

"How it came about?" Zrladic grinned. He threw a sly glance at A'isha, who laughed back. "Our women can show you how babies come about, if you don't know."

Kay stared at him, seething. "We need to find out who fathered this child!"

"A child belongs to its mother." A'isha rolled her hips carelessly from side to side. "What does it matter who the father is?"

Kay's eyes bulged. "It matters to the man!"

"Women don't need men." A'isha shrugged. "Men betray."

Bedivere flushed and thought of his first and only love. "Ah, lady, women do, too."

"We're here to get at the truth!" Gawain cried.

A'isha yawned and got up, stretching her long brown arms above her head. Her breasts writhed luxuriously inside her bodice, and the dark hairs in her armpits moved like living things. Gawain looked at her and struggled to hold on to his mind.

"The truth, you say, Sir Gawain?"

A'isha laughed huskily and spat on the ground. "Truth is the stranger who always comes to stay. Admit him to your tent, you have him for the rest of your life." Her black eyes stabbed through the night. "Are you sure you want to know?"

Gawain stared at her suspiciously. "D'you think I'm a fool?"

Lucan snorted with mirth. "Gawain, don't ask!" He fingered his long red locks and flashed his widest smile. "Forgive us, lady," he said winningly. "We only seek the truth for the sake of our King."

"So, sirs." A'isha surveyed the knights. "Will the Old Mother see you?" She looked at Zrladic and something dark and veiled passed between their eyes.

"Let us ask her!" he cried. He jumped to his feet. "She alone will say. And while we wait, you will eat and drink!"

He clapped his hands, shouting orders in a language they did not know. Attendants slipped up to the knights and thrust goblets of crude red wine into their hands, the liquor as thick and meaty as bull's blood. Strange pieces of roasted meat followed, along with heels of chewy black bread and handfuls of dried herbs.

A sudden crashing chord split the peace of the night. Zrladic waved his wooden goblet in the air. "You are in luck, Arthur's knights!" he shouted. "A'isha will dance for you!"

The drummer struck out a heartbeat and the musician followed with cascades of rhythmic notes. A'isha sprang to her feet and, pacing, whirling, tossing her long hair around, began a lament. She sang of joy and death, of the hard love between men and women, of trust betrayed and faith and hope built anew. As she danced, she became the maiden at her first lying down, the mother cradling her newborn child, the wise woman reconciling life's sorrows at the end of her days. Kay saw the candles blooming around the bed of love, touched the soft down on the tiny sleeping head, shared the winter's dying fire.

In the light of the fire, A'isha's limbs flowed like liquid bronze. As she threw her long arms around her head, Gawain saw her red-black talons flicking through the dark and imagined their hennaed points raking his chest and back. Mesmerized, he stared at her breasts straining through her gown, and watched the dark fleshy globes bobbing and swinging till his head spun.

Dimly he heard Lucan laughing, and Kay's furious hiss. "Remember who we are! Don't disgrace us, Gawain!"

The music ended, and A'isha vanished into the night.

"Now, sirs," cried Zrladic, "you came to consult the Old Mother. Let us see if she will hear you." He jumped to his feet. "This way."

In silence they followed him over the darkened field. The Old Mother's tent stood removed from all the rest, dark and brooding against the forest wall. From its long, high ridge to the rich hangings over the door, it was clearly the home of one treasured by the tribe. *But does she know who lay with Lienore on that dreadful night?* Kay tormented himself. *And will she tell us if she does?*

"Enter, sirs."

Zrladic lifted the thick drapes over the opening and led them in. They filed into a low, fragrant space, lit by fires in small braziers set against the walls. Zrladic crossed to the nearest and fed the glowing coals from a box at the side. It's the same stuff, Kay thought in terror, inhaling the scented smoke. It's the incense she was using the night we were there!

For a second he was back in the ill-fated tent, feeling love approaching to feed him with both hands. Tender hopes blasted him, and fragile joys, and for the first time he saw how the fortune-teller's fumes had preyed on their senses and stolen their minds away. He fought to hold on to himself.

"So, the Old Mother?" he demanded in a high-pitched tone.

Zrladic pointed forward without a word. At the far end of the dimly lit space, a gossamer curtain fell from ceiling to floor. "You may speak to the Old One. But she will not let herself be seen."

"Why not?" demanded Gawain roughly.

Zrladic smiled. "She will not give you her eyes."

Kay licked his dry lips. Was there no end to the tricks? Bravely he approached the curtain, leaving his companions in the rear.

"We come with a question, Old Mother," he called. "Will you answer it?"

The voice from behind the curtain was no more than a growl. "Ask."

Kay could see a shadowy presence behind the veil. "Our King is said to be the father of a child. We need to know if this is true."

The low growl came again. "Why do you need to know? A child belongs to the mother, not to any man."

"This child will be heir to a kingdom."

The voice was deeper now. "What if you never know?"

Kay shook his head. Desperation seized him. "We must know!"

A sigh like the hissing of a snake fluttered the veil. "Alas, you never will."

Kay's calm deserted him. "Never?" he shouted. "I don't believe you. You're just playing games." He sprang forward until stopped by Zrladic's arm. "Tell us the truth!"

There was an endless silence. Then Zrladic caught a sound they could not hear. He listened, then nodded to Kay. "If you must know, the Mother says you may." He drew the curtain back.

Reclining on a great heap of cushions lay A'isha, with a cluster of dogs by her side.

"Yes, sirs." She smiled, registering their shock.

Lucan was the first to find his voice. "Who are you?"

"I am the Old Mother you seek." She held his gaze with a world of kindness in her smile. "The Old Mother is always the leader of our tribe, our undying queen. When the earth goes over her eyes, her daughter takes her place."

"But Zrladic—the king?" stammered Bedivere.

"My father. My mother's first lover and husband when she was queen." She glinted at Zrladic, who grinned cheerfully back. "King till one of the young bloods kills him for his crown and a place in my bed."

"But the woman at the tournament—the fortune-teller?" Kay was beside himself. "*Where is she?*" he yelped.

"My mother?" A'isha laid both her hands lengthwise across her eyes. "Gone down to the House of Shadows. Penn Annywn is her lover and husband now."

"The Dark Lord," muttered Bedivere. "King of the Underworld."

Lucan gasped. "You're saying that she's dead?"

A'isha pursed her damask lips defiantly. *"Dead* is not a word the Roma say. She will come again." She smacked her palm against her breast, and her huge eyes welled. "My mother was more than a mother to us all. She must come back!"

"But not in this lifetime."

A terrible sadness filled Kay, and his stomach turned. I have failed you, Arthur, he mourned to the night air. "We must send to the King," he said dully. "He'll have to be told."

Gawain knuckled his head. "What'll he do?"

Kay frowned. "You know Arthur's sense of honor, he'll acknowledge the boy. Then we'll have Sweyns round our necks for the rest of our lives."

Lucan drew a deep breath. "But at least he can leave Castle Sweyn. He'll be able to push on to Cornwall now to see King Mark."

"You're right." Kay tried to rally himself. "We should make for Cornwall ourselves and catch up with him there." He eyed Gawain's brightening face and tried not to be sour. "There'll be no war for you, Gawain, that's over and done. But there's sure to be tournaments and jousts galore."

"By the Gods, yes!"

Gawain surged to his feet. Already he could hear the call to the lists, feel the muscular thrum of the horse between his thighs, smell the broken grass of the arena sweetening the winter air. Then another, warmer thought softened his smile. "And young Sweyn, the boy—he'll be with Arthur, too. Our kin don't abandon their kin."

"So you'll have a playmate, Gawain." Lucan chuckled and punched his friend's shoulder fondly. "All boys together, you'll be."

At the head of the tent, A'isha was still lounging at her ease, watching the knights with eyes as old as time. Gawain turned to her, took a full survey of her inviting flesh, and could not resist.

"Lady," he said hopefully, "as knights of King Arthur, we offer you our thanks." He flashed his eyes and teeth as he had seen Lucan do. "And as a prince of the Orkneys, I lay my sword at your feet. A lady as lovely as you should not be alone. Allow me to come to your couch, and serve you tonight!"

chapter 38

Welcome to Cornwall—my bride—my wife—

They were married in the chapel on the rock, a cell so ancient, the little priest told her, that it would bless their marriage ever afterward. It had been built, stone by stone, by one of the earliest holy men in these parts, a hermit so pure that he could not live near lesser humanity, loaded with its sins.

Isolde shivered. Even the candles and the heady incense on the altar could bring no warmth or welcome to this desperate place. This cell would bless their union? To her it was a stark housing of cold stone on the edge of a cliff, perched over a dizzying drop to the sea below. Who but a Christian would choose such a drear, lonely site? Why did they have to make everything so hard?

Jubilate Deo—rejoice, rejoice in the Lord—

Half a dozen boys in white robes stood before a rough stone altar, caroling away. In front of them, the little priest was chanting the marriage rites. With his poor hunched body, black gown, and Christian vestments, Isolde knew him as the King's confessor, Father Dominian. But the others, the courtiers who now packed the cold space behind her and spilled out of the door and onto the clifftop beyond—who were they, all the people of this strange new world?

Sir Nabon she would recognize again—the King's chief councillor had knelt to kiss her hand and sworn, "Lady, I am now your servant, as I am the King's." She had looked into Nabon's shrewd eyes and known it was true. Here at least was one man she could trust.

And Elva, the King's mistress, there was no mistaking her. As Isolde had alighted on the quay and all the court ladies curtsied and bowed

223

their heads, one alone had lifted her long neck above the rest and cursed her with a pair of mad, spangled eyes.

But all these others—who are they? She huddled under her veil and dared not look around.

She thought she would know the King's nephew Andred again. She could still hear Tristan's hollow voice at her shoulder, "This is my cousin, madam," but the man himself was a blur. She saw the swing of a royal blue cloak and a flash of black hair as he pulled off his cap and bowed. But she could remember no more of him than that.

All she had seen was King Mark, her husband-to-be, a man like an overgrown schoolboy with an ungainly body and odd, middle-aged ways. The Gods had given him muddy skin and dull sandy hair, and his rapid blinking did nothing to enhance his looks. But if he had been the King of the Fair Ones himself, she would not have looked at him. Because he was not Tristan—and could never be.

"Beloved in Christ, we are gathered here . . ."

The cold of the flagstones was weeping up through her shoes. Mark stood beside her at the frozen altar, his head held high. His lanky body was lavishly decked out in a blood-red gown, trimmed with red fox fur. A long ceremonial sword tapped at his heels, and an ornate silver dagger swung from his belt. On his left hand he wore his coronation ring, a deep blue band of lapis lazuli and gold, and a heavy show of jewels encrusted his right. Proudly he sported Cornwall's ancient crown of gold, and a massive gold chain shone on his chest.

Yes—

I came here to make this marriage, and make it I must.

Isolde's will revived. Standing to attention in front of the priest, Mark looked decent enough, a marriageable man. Alone last night in the darkness of the Queen's House in Castle Dore, tenderly taking stock of her body now it was no longer her own, she had nursed her future in her arms and made a solemn vow. What had happened with Tristan must lie in the past. The sacred moment on the ship was outside the world she would inhabit now. She must marry King Mark and live with him as his wife.

Already Mark had shown a respect that had given her hope. After meeting her on the quay with a fanfare of trumpets and drums, he had brought her at once to the castle, where the Queen's House, finely furnished, waited for her. Striding awkwardly around, throwing his arms about, he had shown no signs of forcing himself on her, indeed no eagerness to be alone with her. Crying, "Tomorrow, lady, I shall bring you to the church!" he had vanished, commanding his lords to follow him to the hunt. And that was all she had seen of her husband till now.

My husband.

Yes.

I am marrying this man.

Outside the unglazed window, she could see a winter sun as pale as sea-washed bone. A biting wind blew in through the slit in the wall, bringing with it a random flurry of snow. In a dream she watched the white flakes drifting to the ground. *If I'd married in my own country, the maidens would have rained rose petals on my head and laid garlands beneath my feet. But I am fated to be a winter queen, cold hands, cold heart—*

"Kneel—all kneel to hear the word of the Lord!" intoned the priest.

Goddess, Mother, help me—

Sinking to her knees beside Mark, she tried to pray. The web of sound wove on.

"*Clamavi in toto corde meo ad te, Domine*—I have called upon you with all my heart, Lord God—" sang Dominian in his strong, clear tones.

"We call upon you, God our Lord, we bear witness to your truth—"

A pace behind him, Simeon struck up the antiphony in a clear tenor, the young voice almost unbroken from his boyhood days.

"Who gives this woman to be married to this man?"

"I do."

Stiffly Tristan stepped up to Isolde's veiled form, took her hand, and passed it to the King.

"Do you, Mark, take this woman?" Dominian asked.

The red-clad figure at the altar bellowed, "I do!"

Simeon came forward with a cushion bearing a ring. She was suddenly conscious of her father's ring on her right hand—should she have given Mark that? *No—impossible.* She watched as Mark took the wedding ring from Simeon and clumsily tried to force it onto her hand. But it stuck at the knuckle, and would not fit. She told herself not to care. *What did he expect? He never knew the size.*

"Well!" Mark huffed with annoyance in her ear. She clenched her fist to keep the ring in place as Dominian loudly pronounced them man and wife.

"Man and wife! Jesu Maria, we are one!" Chortling, Mark led her on his arm from the chapel, to the cheers of the crowd outside.

"Man and wife!" he chuckled all the way back to the castle, alternately pounding her hand and nudging her in the ribs.

Where am I? She was adrift on a sea of grief. *And where is Tristan?* she mourned. *Why did he give me away?* She had to ask him that.

But it was not until they reached Castle Dore for the wedding feast that she saw him again, standing with the other young bloods at the knights' table in the center of the hall. As she looked, she thought he threw her a glance of inexpressible pain. But he was so far away that she could not tell.

And where's Brangwain? Seated somewhere among the ladies, the maid was nowhere in sight. One hostile presence, however, was all too near. Sitting next to a finely dressed lord, surely her husband, to judge from his fat and complacent air, sat the Lady Elva, in a headdress taller than any other in the hall. Her gown was of a luxurious mottled silk, flashing green and yellow in the candlelight and clinging closer to her body than a snake's skin.

From her place at the High Table, enthroned at Mark's side, Isolde distantly noted the array of agates and emeralds, jasper, beryl, and gold adorning Elva's hands, neck, and bosom, and dripping from her ears and waist. *They must all be from the King,* she thought vaguely. *Will he still go on bedding her and rewarding her now that he's married to me? And if he does, will I care?*

Seeing Elva decked out like a queen was a sharp reminder of how little she had cared to dress like one herself. For the wedding, her mother had given her a magnificent gown of gold encrusted with emeralds shaped like Ireland's trefoils, with a cloak of gold and a veil of gold to match. But she had had no stomach for such array.

Disregarding Brangwain, who produced a dozen gowns almost as fine, she had chosen a simple shift of ivory as pale as a lily, lightly seeded with pearls. Over it she wore a simple cream cloak of wool, and a gossamer veil. She did not know that the plainness of her dress enhanced her alabaster skin and the amber and copper lights shining in her hair.

She did not see, in her misery, that unadorned as she was, she was still the most beautiful woman in the room.

What she caught was a glance of pure poison from Elva's quivering eyes.

She hates me! She will kill me! flashed into her mind.

The next second, Elva was smiling brightly all around. Isolde held her breath as the rest of the guests swirled into the hall. A sprightly figure paused to greet Elva as he made his way across the hall, and she recognized the King's nephew, Andred, by his flourishing bow. Suddenly the two dark heads were together and whispering, and now it seemed to her that two pairs of hate-filled eyes were staring her way.

They are planning my death dropped into her mind with the force of a stone down a well. Her head reeled. *I am not myself.*

A servant appeared at her elbow. "Wine, Your Majesty?"

"Fill the Queen's glass!" ordered Mark at her side. He leaned over importantly. "Drink up, sweetheart," he chirped, "you need some color in your cheeks! And be cheerful, you're Queen of Cornwall now!"

Relaxing, he wagged a jovial finger at Sir Nabon sitting opposite, and took a deep swig of his own goblet of wine. "See, Nabon, you all thought I'd go a bachelor to my grave. But this beauty brought me to the altar in the end!"

He means well, Isolde told herself, and she forced her face to smile.

"As you say, sire," murmured Nabon imperturbably. He raised his goblet. "We drink to you and your bride."

Farther down the table, the venerable Sir Wisbeck, Sir Quirian, and others joined in the toast. Mark drank again, spilling his wine down his chin. He gave a raucous laugh, nudged her, and winked round the table, leering at his knights. "And I'll call her to account before the night is out!"

Before the night is out— Resolutely Isolde seized her goblet and drained it down.

The feast wore on. Then suddenly Mark was on his feet, red-faced and swaying, pounding the table with his fist.

"Bring the bride to bed!" he shouted thickly. "Time to make a new heir for Cornwall—Cornwall's next king!"

"At once, Your Majesty."

There was a flurry in the body of the hall. To Isolde's horror, the Lady

Elva rose to her feet, and all the court ladies gathered in her wake. Isolde drew a furious breath of disbelief. Already she could see Elva and her cronies swarming into her bedchamber, stripping her of her clothes, scattering flowers and fooling with spells and charms, then rushing out squealing, as Mark and his knights strode in. She had heard of these rituals at other courts, where all the married women joined together to have fun at the expense of the bride. *She is the leading lady of the court,* Tristan had said. Isolde's face set like stone. *Not any more!*

She reached for a smile of command, and stood up.

"I thank you, sir," she cried in a ringing tone, "and the court ladies, too. But we keep a different custom in the Western Isle. My maid alone will make me ready tonight."

With a brief curtsy, she strode seething away. From the corner of her eye she saw Brangwain rise hurriedly to her feet in the body of the hall and make for her side.

Mark's loud, boastful cry followed her down the hall.

"Prepare yourself, sweetheart—I shall soon be there!"

chapter 39

Prepare yourself, sweetheart—I shall soon be there!

How dare he make a filthy joke of this?

Trembling, Isolde strode down the hall with Mark's sally ringing in her ears. In its wake came a burst of coarse laughter, and she knew that the traditional wedding jests were flying to and fro. As the wine went round the tables and the candles burned down, the most sacred moment between two souls struggling to become one would become the subject of vile laughter and drunken mirth. Rage flooded her. *Why did I not see how this would be?*

"My lady—"

Brangwain caught up with her before she left the hall. As the guards bowed and flung wide the great carved doors, the two women plunged out into the darkness of the night. An icy wind whined and whipped round the courtyard and they gained the shelter of the Queen's House with relief. *But there's no sanctuary here for me,* was Isolde's next thought. *My husband is coming to claim his rights.*

Her stomach turned. *Goddess, Mother, what to do?*

The door swung open on a bevy of smiling faces and curtsying girls. Fluttering around like moths, the maids could not contain their excitement as she came in.

"Oh, my lady!"

"Ssshhhh—she's the Queen now, it's 'Your Majesty'!"

"Let the Queen pass," commanded Brangwain as they hurried through, "and keep watch for the King!"

In the great bedchamber, a bright fire burned halfway up the wall, commanded by Brangwain before the feast began. Isolde stood before it in silence as Brangwain unrobed her to her shift, then helped her into a loose chamber gown. Above the sea-green brocade, her eyes were as wild as the ocean, and against the white sable collar, her skin was deathly pale.

Never had Brangwain seen her looking like this. Oh my lady, she grieved—my poor girl—

"Here, madam."

She drew up a chair and settled Isolde by the fire. Then she found a stool, and sat down at her mistress's feet. "Before the King comes, lady—"

"Yes!" Isolde roused herself from her daze. "I won't have his knights in here when they come to bring the bride to bed, d'you hear?"

"I know, lady, I know—leave it to me. But there's something else you must know." She looked at Isolde and hesitated. Was this a good time to speak? No—but Isolde had to hear what she had to say. She took a deep breath and plunged in. "When we left Ireland, your mother gave me a flask—you saw it, lady, in the cabin on the ship."

Isolde sighed. "The small one—made of gold?"

Brangwain nodded unhappily. "The Queen got it from the Nain. She wanted me to give it to you on your wedding night—to share with the King before you lay down with him."

"So?" Isolde tensed. "Why?"

"To settle you to your marriage and King Mark. And your husband would love you all the days of your life."

Isolde's sight faded. A chasm opened at her feet and she saw the cavern, her mother, the elixir, the Nain herself. The hundred-year-old voice, rustling like dried leaves, dropped through the silence of the night.

Whoever drinks this drink will share a lifelong faith and truth. Hatred will never part them, and their love will never die.

She heard the Old One's whisper rise to a scream as the chanting of the attendants sounded behind. *Either shall love the other all the days of their lives!*

Brangwain's voice came from very far away. "I brought it onto the ship so you could decide for yourself what to do."

Isolde closed her eyes. *But Tristan found it before I knew, and we drank it together—*

And that is our fate.

We are bound together for life.

Our love will never die.

"Holla within there!"

There was a fearful pounding at the door below. Brangwain listened aghast to the drunken roaring of the knights and the breathless giggles of the maids as they let them in.

Mark's loud cry rang out above the fray. "Give entrance to your King! Bring me to my bride!"

Brangwain's black eyes snapped. "Leave this to me, lady!" she cried as she sped from the room.

Isolde sat without moving, staring into the fire. Her spirit was drifting off into the unknown. She knew she was like a cup about to crack, running over with the fullness of despair. *Could any other woman have been so wrong as this? Dug a grave for her heart and jumped in so blindly?*

"Your Majesty! My lords!"

Brangwain's sharp reproof resounded below. The hubbub subsided, and was followed by a flurry of sheepish farewells and the tramping of booted feet. Brangwain had dispatched the knights, it seemed. But not even she had the power to dismiss a king.

And here he was, announcing his presence with a rousing knock on the door.

"My lady Isolde?" Without waiting for a reply, Mark came striding in.

She got to her feet and faced him in front of the fire. His eyes were round and his cheeks inflamed with wine. Traces of the night's carousing were spilled all down his fine tunic, and the stale scent of drink came rolling toward her as he approached.

"Waiting for me, sweetheart?" He chuckled, in a boisterous imitation of a ladies' man. But already she could see the manly swagger melting away.

He is lost, like a child, came to her with a pang of pity and distress. She made him a gentle curtsy. "How are you, sir?"

"Never better!" he cried thickly, waving his hands in the air. But she could see his eyes darting unhappily to and fro, and her awkwardness grew.

There was a strained silence. She gestured around the room. "Many thanks to you for making the Queen's House so fine." She stepped away from him. "Would you care to see?"

"Yes, why not?"

Obediently he followed her around the chamber, admiring the new wainscot, the fine hangings, the bright rugs. She could tell he had never seen them before. *Who fitted out the place so lovingly, then? Tristan?*

At the far end of the room, like a great ship at anchor, loomed the bed of state. She turned her back on it and led the way to the couch. "Be seated, my lord."

Nervously Mark complied, stumbling a little as he did. "Did I offend you, lady, coming with my knights?" A foolish look settled on his face, and he gave a blustering laugh. "Your lady-in-waiting was very stern with us!"

"No offense, sir." She spread her hands. "But our ways are very different in the Island of the West. Where the Goddess rules, women are—"

"Yes, yes," Mark broke in impatiently, clutching his head. God Almighty, he hadn't come here for a lecture on his wedding night! His shrinking brain was instantly prey to another lowering thought. With all the wine he'd been pouring down his throat, if he didn't act soon, there'd be no wedding night at all.

He brought his wandering eyes together and focused them fiercely on the woman at his side. She was good enough to be his bride. It shouldn't be hard then to do what had to be done. True, she was still a stranger—he'd hardly seen her since she arrived. But she was a damned fine woman, and every red-blooded male at court would like to be in his shoes tonight.

He laughed hollowly, and rolled a roguish eye.

"I'm a lucky man!" he told her, feeling for her knee. But she might have had legs of stone for all the joy they gave. With the very touch of her, his heart quailed.

Why isn't she Elva? came the mad, inner wail. Elva knew what to do! When she took him in hand, everything happened as it should. She only had to lay open the front of her gown, tease him with a flash of her small, hard breasts, and there he was—

Thinking of Elva, his flagging hopes revived. He screwed his eyes onto Isolde again, cloudily assessing her loose shift and open gown, and felt his sluggish manhood stir. If he could get her clothes off, see her naked, that'd do the trick. He threw a long arm round her shoulder and began to fumble at her breast.

"Come here," he muttered thickly in her ear.

The heat in the chamber fanned her face like fire. Through the window she could see a black and starless night. *Even the moon is hiding from me now. The Mother has turned her back on me—on us—*

Where are you, Tristan? Were you here with the knights before, to witness my shame? Or have you abandoned me, too?

Snuffling, Mark was mouthing her ear, paddling at her neck and feeling her breasts, pulling up her shift to expose her knees, her bare legs. Nausea broke over her and she could not breathe. She took Mark's hand from her gown and disengaged his arm.

"Excuse me, sir—" She pulled away.

"What?" Mark lifted his head, staring stupidly.

Her hands moved to her stomach. "I am not well."

Mark twitched and recoiled. "Is it catching?" he cried.

His fear was so real she could almost have pitied him. "No, sir," she replied. "I—I have a condition of women." *A condition most women have, I can't give my body to a man I don't love—*

She could see him torn between wounded self-importance and a sudden sharp dislike. "A women's indisposition?" He floundered. "Well, you're certainly as pale as a lily! What, a—a loss of blood, you mean, that sort of thing?"

That sort of thing, indeed. I am bleeding from the heart, from the deepest part of my soul. She breathed deeply. "Then Your Majesty understands."

He goggled and licked his lips. "Well—"

"Thank you, sir."

Mark rubbed his head. What was going on?

Isolde took a breath. "I must crave your indulgence to postpone our wedding night—"

"What?"

"—for a good while, I fear." She paused. "I don't know when this will end."

"So? Well! Humph!"

Mark frowned, puzzling it out. He knew he ought to feel angry, cheated of his bride. But all he could feel was a spreading glow of relief.

Dimly he saw that Isolde felt it, too, and his mood changed. By God, she was his wife! She owed him obedience and respect, not a put-off like this. And what if it got about? He'd be a laughingstock throughout the land. His knights were all carousing in the Knights' Hall, toasting his wedding night. The whole of Castle Dore thought he was making a new heir for Cornwall now. And instead—

He leaned forward and gripped her wrist with a meaningful smile. "Well and good, lady—I release you from your duty for a little while. But remember, not a word of this to a soul!" Without warning, he dropped his jovial grin and an unmistakable hint of menace filled the air. "Don't make me look a fool!"

Or else I will make you pay for shaming me. . . .

The unspoken thought hovered between them like a threat. *He means it!* She looked into the pebbly eyes and knew it was true.

"Rely on me, sir," she said steadily. "In our island, when a man and woman come together as one, these are the holiest mysteries the Goddess gives. We never cheapen them with common talk." *Still less the vile jokes of men who fear women, and cover their dread with drink and cruel mirth,* she could have said, but did not.

Mark shook his aching head. Goddess—holy mysteries—what was she talking about?

"Did you hear what I said?" he said irritably.

"I heard you, sir." Isolde drew a breath. *Try again.* "And I must tell you this. I care for my own reputation as much as yours. What passes here is between us alone."

"Good! Good! Well, I've been here long enough."

Mark heaved himself to his feet. Thankfully he found his way to the door. Still time to rejoin the carousing in the Knights' Hall—boast about Cornwall invading virgin lands, conquering the Island of the West—

And tomorrow he could hunt in the morning as he always did, any bride would want time alone to rest—

"Farewell, sweetheart," he caroled as he clattered down the stairs. "I will leave you in peace!"

Leave me, just leave me, sir—

Already she knew she would know no peace that night, only a dry-eyed communion with the creatures of the dark. Screech owls and flitter-bats would be her companions now, alone and sleepless in her marriage bed.

chapter 40

There is no gift but love.
No pain, no bane, but love—

He was at a standstill now, after raging and weeping till there were no more tears to shed. At midnight he had flung out of the palace and taken his sleepy, startled horse for a breakneck ride. Returning at dawn, exhausted and covered in mud, he dropped onto his pallet in his clothes and fell asleep.

Or rather into a drowse, tormented by bad dreams. He saw again the tall veiled figure in the church turning its sightless head to him in reproach. *You, Tristan?* Isolde seemed to say. *Why did you have to give me away?* But why not? She had no father, no uncle, no brother to her name. He was the only one in Cornwall who knew her at all. Didn't she know he'd have to give her away?

And again at the wedding feast—from the dais, she'd given him the same sense of her overwhelming disappointment and distress. He sweated with shame. *Did I fail you, lady, did I fail?*

Of course you did, fool! You betrayed your only love! A black bat of despair flew around his head, shrieking, and he fought it off. *Lay me with my mother*, was his last dreaming thought. *Shroud me with my true love, I shall not awake.*

But he woke in a lowering noon to see a sickly yellow sun hanging in the sky. The mud from his late-night ride had fouled his sheets, and his bed stank of horses and sweat and grief. All the fears of the small hours rose up to ambush him again.

Mark had had her body—how many times by now? He was her husband, after all, entitled to enjoy her in bed. Any man with red blood in his veins would do all that, and more. Memories of loving Isolde himself brought new torments, new jabbing pains. *Did she do for him what she did for me—did he—did they—*

His mind revolted.

No! She loves you, not him.

He leapt up from his bed and strode around his chamber to ward off evil thoughts. *She loves you, fool!* There was a little comfort in that, for a short while.

Mark could have forced her, though, if she tried to refuse. This new fear came all too soon. His uncle was certainly capable of that and more, especially if his wounded pride was at stake. Groaning, Tristan saw Mark's hand raised in anger, his powerful arms pinning Isolde down, his body bucking and driving like a stag in rut, and Isolde's fists vainly pounding his naked back. He ground his knuckles into his eyes to drive the sight away.

But what if Mark didn't have to force her, if Isolde opened her arms to him willingly, joyfully spread her legs? More black bats came screeching around Tristan's head. Did she greet Mark with wine, perfume the chamber with fragrance, blandish him to her bed? He forced himself to go on. She wasn't a virgin any longer, after all. She had lain down with him, she could lie down again. After loving him, she might have feared a child was on the way. To make her new husband free of her body would be a perfect cover for that fear, that shame. If she gave birth after this, whose child would it be? Would he spend a lifetime bowing and scraping to a supposed son of the King, when in fact the boy was his own? How would he ever know?

Dark thoughts attacked him like a swarm of bees. Goddess, Mother, would he ever forget the horror of the wedding feast, trapped at the knights' table under Andred's curious gaze? The constant fear of betraying himself, when he felt sure that his cousin must have noticed something amiss. The grim aftermath when Mark and Isolde had left, forced to go on drinking with the knights, glassily pretending to join in the good cheer.

Then just as he thought he could slip away, there was Mark bouncing back into the Knights' Hall in triumph, returning from the Queen's House with his tail up like a farmyard dog. Hours then of Mark's vile boasting of his triumph between the sheets and the knights' drunken mirth, toasting the Queen's health with loud ribaldry. Mark's arm like lead round his shoulders, wine running down his chin, and his sodden insistence that Tristan drink along. His own loathing compliance, for fear of betraying himself.

And betraying her.

But tonight she had betrayed him with Mark.

No! His was the first betrayal when he sold her to Mark. All the rest came from that.

And now she was married, she was Mark's, and there was no escape. But did he have to stand by from now on and see her bedded every night? Could he even pretend to be a loyal knight to the King when he was longing every second to beat him to death?

Time to leave court then, to take to the road. A lone knight could lose himself out in the world. He had done it before, he would gladly do it again. It was a good clean life, riding from tournament to tournament, living on his winnings, sleeping on his shield—and more than good enough for a man who had nothing else.

On the way, then, out of this stinking sty. He cast a look at his bed. Better than stewing here like a pig in his own filth. Get cleaned up, bid farewell to her, then beg the King's leave to depart. He glanced at the sky. Half the day was wasted, blown away, gone. But still he could be miles down the road before night fell.

<hr />

"HOW ARE YOU, lady?"

Pressing into the silent chamber, Brangwain scarcely dared ask. Many hours had passed since she had admitted the King, and not long afterward curtsied him out again. When Mark left, she had waited a long while in the antechamber in case Isolde needed her, before creeping to her own bed. Now noon had come and gone, and there was still no sound from within.

But she had to disturb her mistress if Sir Tristan was here. Whatever had happened between her and the King, Isolde would want to be told that.

"Good morning, madam."

Fixing a smile on her lips, Brangwain sailed in. Isolde was sitting motionless beside the hearth. The fire was long dead and the room was dank and drear. But the still figure by the fireside was beyond feeling cold.

Brangwain dropped to her knees with a cry. "Oh, my lady—did he—"

A wan smile lifted Isolde's lips. "No."

"Then—"

Isolde nodded like a child. "I am safe for the moment."

How safe? For how long? Brangwain bit back her thoughts. "Sir Tristan is here to see you," she said quietly. "He has come to say good-bye."

"Good-bye?"

Brangwain nodded. "He is leaving court."

She stared in disbelief. "He can't!"

"Tell him so, madam. He is waiting outside."

Isolde sprang to her feet. "Let him in!"

"At once."

The door opened and closed as the maid complied. He came toward her all curled and groomed, as spruce as a bridegroom on his wedding day. The sight of him hurt her eyes—*how dare he look so fine?*

And how dare he look so cold, so indifferent? Has he forgotten all we said and did? Is he glad I'm married and out of his way?

She had no time for greetings. "In the church yesterday," she said bleakly, "by what right did you give me away?"

He smiled grimly to himself. He could not help betraying her, it seemed. "The service requires the bride to be given away. There was no one else to do that for you."

"Ah, your Christian rituals!" A smile of contempt twisted her pale lips. "In my faith, sir, women give themselves. We do not belong to men to be traded like sheep."

He was in no mood for this. He could not bear to look at her, hollow-eyed as she was from last night's exertions, marked and bruised by sex, gray from lack of sleep.

"The King ordered it," he said shortly, glancing at the door.

He can't even talk to me! He can't wait to get away. Her temper flared. "And do you always do what the King wants?"

"No longer, lady," he said crisply. "I am going away."

She had not believed it. "What?"

"I am leaving court."

She fought for breath. "Why?"

"To seek tournaments and deeds of arms. No prowess is to be gained by lingering here."

"You said there'd be tournaments here," she said madly, "a month of celebrations at least, with King Arthur and many other kings and knights."

He gave an impatient sigh. "That much is true. King Mark has proclaimed a tournament, and they are all on their way."

She thrust out her chin. "Are you too proud to fight in such company?"

He felt his temper rise. "Yes, madam," he said evenly, "such company is indeed too much for me." He swept her a sudden bow. "Your Majesty will excuse me. I am going to the King—your husband—to beg leave to go."

"Go?" she said, possessed with a terrible dread. "Go where?"

Still he would not meet her eye. "Anywhere."

"Tell me the truth," she said huskily. "Do you have to go?"

He looked at her for the first time. "Does it matter?"

"It matters to me." She stepped forward and engaged his eyes. "I have given you my love. And it will never leave me now for weal nor woe."

He recoiled. "You can't mean it anymore! You're married to the King!"

"By the rites of the Christians." She gave a bitter laugh. "Indeed, you were there. But to those who follow the Goddess, it was no marriage at all."

He could not bear it. "Your husband the King tells a different tale."

She colored as if he had struck her in the face. "So Mark has been boasting of his prowess last night? Tales of our amorous exploits are all over Castle Dore?"

He covered his eyes with his hand and turned away, ashamed. "Yes."

She flew at him like a wildcat. "And you believed him?"

"No!" He wheeled back to face her, and met her eyes. "Yes," he mumbled, dropping his own.

"Tristan, how could you? You know what the King is like!" She broke away from him and began to weep.

"And I believed him!" He threw his arms in the air. "Gods above," he cried, "I have betrayed you again!"

"After the love we shared—" She looked at him, drowning in grief. "How could you trust in him and not in me?"

"He is my King. I have sworn him my oath."

"When we lay together, you swore your truth to me."

He was almost beside himself. "I have to honor him. He's my only kin!"

She stared at him. "I thought you had a father. Is he dead?"

He gave a high, cracked laugh. "Dead to me!"

She sat up. "How so?"

He clenched his fists and took a pace or two away. "When my mother died, he took another wife. She hated me, though I never did her harm. She wanted her own son to be king in my place."

Isolde gasped. "So she—"

"She tried to poison me. But her own son took the cup by accident and fell down dead. She was sentenced to be burned, but when they brought her to the stake, I begged my father to spare her life."

"And he granted it?"

Tristan nodded. "He told me I could save her from the fire. But afterward he had to take her as his wife again." His mouth twisted painfully. "So he sent me away."

Her anger rose. "He sent *you* away?"

"He sent me into France to learn deeds of arms. And that was the start of my life in chivalry." Tristan looked at her and his face began to burn. "And without that," he said intensely, "I would never have found you."

Oh, my love—my love—

She held out her arms and he came to her without words. She drew him down to her side and took both his hands. "I am all your kin now, and you are mine. You are my chosen one. Say you won't leave me—you won't go away!"

"You are my lady," he said huskily. "I will not leave you now. You are the spirit I was born to serve."

"You walked with me in the world before the worlds. I will be at your side through the worlds to come." She looked down at their hands, closely entwined. "You pledged your love to me with your mother's ring. I have not lost it. It is in a safe place, far away. One day we shall have it back again."

He gave a broken smile. "Till you do, love, you must wear it in your heart."

For the last time she stroked her father's ring, then drew the heavy gold band off her finger and threaded it onto his. "Wear this for me," she said.

"I will." He brought it to his lips. "I beg you, lady, be handfast with me?"

Her eyes filled with tears. "I will."

They cupped their right hands together, palm to palm, then clasped their fingers firmly around each other's thumbs.

"Fast hand, fast heart," Isolde prayed, closing her eyes. "From now on, I am yours."

"Heartfast, handfast," Tristan echoed. "From now on, I am yours, your servant, your knight, your champion to the death."

"Handfast, we are married now by the most ancient rite. The Goddess loves a handfast above all." She took him in her arms and kissed him on the lips. "Oh, my love—come to bed."

chapter
41

*G*ods above, what was Isolde thinking of?

Pacing the antechamber, Brangwain hardly dared to ask. She was a married woman now—the only man who should be admitted to the Queen's bedchamber was the King! And Sir Tristan had been closeted with her for how long?

The maid smiled grimly. Long enough for a very long good-bye. She crossed to the window and watched the sun sinking in a sky as yellow as bile. Madam, madam, she prayed, wringing her hands, we're not in Ireland now. Send Sir Tristan out of your chamber and out of the house! The Gods only know what will happen if you don't—

"Holla there! Is the Queen within?"

Brangwain froze. She did not know who was banging on the court-yard door below. But she could tell that the imperious female voice would not be denied. She heard the visitor admitted, and moments later came the loud clacking of a fashionable lady's painted wooden heels on the stairs. With an effort, Brangwain collected herself and threw open the chamber door.

Stalking down the corridor, her head held high and her long body ramrod straight, came the Lady Elva with her maids in tow. Seeing Brangwain, she gave a glittering smile and surged past her into the chamber as if it were her own.

"So?" she said unpleasantly, looking around. "This is your lady's chamber—her special place?"

Brangwain looked at her, struggling to wipe her feelings from her face. Gods above, did the King's mistress ever wear anything but that vile green? And not even the sweet woodland shades of summer or spring, but mottled colors like the skin of a sick snake?

Yet if she, of all the souls at court—if she saw Sir Tristan—knew he was here in the inner room with the Queen—

"The Queen is indisposed," she announced trenchantly, still holding the outer door open, willing the wretched woman to leave.

"So." Elva nosed round the room, fingering the fine hangings, staring at her long face in the mirror against the wall.

What did she want? Scraps of gossip filtered back to Brangwain from the servants' hall. She loved King Mark, they said, laughing behind their hands. She'd give anything to be Queen. Sharpened by fear, Brangwain read the message of the furious back and interfering hands. She thinks she ought to be here—this is her place.

"Your mistress is indisposed?" Elva gave a final twirl before settling herself elegantly in a chair. Her two maids took up their stand behind her, eyes everywhere. "She will see me, I think."

Brangwain stared straight ahead. "She has given orders not to be disturbed."

Elva's lips parted in a contemptuous smile. "Not even for the King?" she said silkily.

Brangwain felt herself flush. "I don't understand, lady."

"I am here on his orders." Elva's eyes were suddenly ablaze. "To call on the Queen and pay my respects."

Was it true? There was no way to know. Brangwain took a few rapid breaths. "The Queen will be sorry to miss you," she said, clasping and unclasping her hands. "I shall give her your greetings and tell her you came."

"No need for that," Elva cocked an ear toward the inner door and gave another venomous smile. "I can hear her stirring. I'll wait till she comes out."

Goddess, Mother—comes out with Tristan? Hanging on his arm, kissing him farewell? There were definite sounds of movement in the inner room. Brangwain's heart sank like a stone.

Elva reached out a hand to a side table holding a copper bowl bright with winter berries and red and gold dried leaves. Beside it lay a little box of ivory, finely carved. Elva's snaky fingers pounced on it as her maids cooed with admiration in the rear.

"Did the King give her this?" she demanded, looking up.

Her eyes, her mouth were shot through with pain. Brangwain's heart heaved. *She's jealous, she hates us, she'll do anything to ruin us now.*

Desperation sharpened Brangwain's wits. She closed the door and came forward with a knowing smile. "Oh, that and much more," she said gaily, waving her hand round the room. "He dotes on her, lady. I never saw a man so in love."

"In love?" Shock thundered across Elva's face. "The King?"

That's not what he's told her! Brangwain thought with savage glee. She picked up a pair of leather gloves, a present from Isolde's mother before they left. "Look at these, madam," she gushed, "lined with kidskin, and so finely stitched! He lavishes gifts on her every day."

From the look on Elva's face, every word was poison to her ears. For a moment at least, Brangwain knew she had distracted her from the sounds of movement within. But if Isolde and Tristan came out together, drowsy with love—

Ruthlessly Brangwain pressed her advantage home. "You should see her, lady, and you will," she cried. "Why, her skin's blooming—and her eyes, her hair—it's good for a woman to be loved the way the King loves her, every mortal inch—"

"Hold your tongue, wretch!" Elva sprang to her feet.

Wretch, yourself, thought Brangwain triumphantly. *You came to crow over my lady, and got what you deserved. We'll show you that you aren't queen here anymore!*

"Give your mistress my greeting," Elva hissed. Shafts of rage were flashing across her face. Crossing the room in a couple of strides, she could not wait to get through the door.

Eyes down, her two maids scurried after her like mice. Brangwain closed the door behind them, then began to shake. The sounds from the inner room were clearer now, murmuring voices soft with laughter and sleepy delight.

"Brangwain?" Isolde called. "Are you there?"

Brangwain watched in a trance as the inner door opened and Isolde stood on the threshold with Tristan, rosy with love. His arm lay across her shoulders and their every lineament breathed their satisfied desire.

Love had clothed them in stardust, transported them out of this everyday world to a better place. Then Isolde saw Brangwain's face and the glory fled away.

"What is it, Brangwain?" she cried. "Tell me at once!"

Outside in the courtyard, Elva flew away into the dusk. All she could think of was the scene ahead with Mark, when she would thrust all his lies down his faithless throat. He didn't love Isolde at all, he loved only her? Well, she knew better now!

Only later, after hours of jealous rage, did something occur to Elva that she had not thought of before. Why, if Isolde was so glowing with love, was she too indisposed to receive visitors? If her mistress was as happy as Brangwain claimed, why was the maid so tense? And why, if everything was perfect, was she pacing up and down and twisting her hands till her knuckles were white?

THEY WOULD NEVER after forget the terror of that moment, when Brangwain told them how near they had come to betraying themselves. So while Isolde retreated to the safety of her chamber, Tristan strode away from prying eyes, careful to look as cold and angry as when he came in. Isolde appeared for dinner in the Great Hall that night, resplendent in royal blue, crystals, and pearls, and set herself to smile and be gracious to the King. She knew she could play the part of Cornwall's Queen. Now that she and Tristan were one, she could do anything.

Every evening, then, in the glow of the candlelight, Mark rejoiced in his new bride. When she smiled on him like this, all the court believed he had made himself a hero in her bed. It was easy enough, he had found, to pass the night in the Queen's House with only himself and Isolde knowing that nothing took place. And if Elva wanted to be jealous without cause, accusing him of showering Isolde with gifts, then he would ignore her completely till she mended her ways. That would teach her a lesson and put her in her place.

He could trust Isolde, he knew that now. She would not betray them to the scorn of the court, still less to the mirth and derision of foreign kings. For they were all on their way to celebrate with him, the kings of France and Gaul and Little Britain, and many petty kings and knights besides. Arrangements for a great tournament were in hand, and even

King Arthur would attend, it seemed. And with knights and kings on the way to the tournament and a new bride to flaunt when they came, Mark was happy enough.

Like all women in such marriages, Isolde soon found that she could be happy as long as her husband was engrossed elsewhere. And so they continued till the old moon waned, and Isolde woke in the knowledge that the new moon was here and her moon-time had not come.

chapter 42

oddess, Mother, help me—help me now—

They were near the top of the cliff, they both knew that. The sound of the sea was calling them, step by step, and the thunder of the surge could be felt beneath their feet. But the going was hard, and they could not see their way. The track they had followed through the woodland petered out here, and the ground rose steeply ahead. They were surrounded by dense thickets of conker-colored bracken and wild briar on all sides.

Could this be the place? They could go no farther on horseback, that was plain. Stifling her misgivings, Brangwain helped Isolde to dismount, and tied the horses to a tree. At least they had the best of a fine winter day. A genial sun smiled down from a pearly sky and, with the forest behind them, the wintry air was even warm.

It's here somewhere, I know it, Brangwain muttered to herself. She suppressed a sigh. Isolde must never suspect what it had cost to get her here. But from the moment they knew Isolde had missed her time of the month, Brangwain had been searching tirelessly for help.

The dread of disclosure dogged their every step. If the Queen called for the King's doctors, every soul in Castle Dore would know it within hours. If she sent for a wise woman, the story would be the same. So Brangwain had to ask in Isolde's place, and far away from Castle Dore. For weeks now she had been slipping out quietly, riding to distant settlements to seek help as if she wanted it for herself.

Brangwain shuddered. How many wretched old women had she encountered on her search? Half-mad, toothless old crones scratching for herbs by the wayside, whose one hope was a handful of something to eke out their daily bread, and whose wildest dream was a rabbit for the pot?

If she had expected help from them, she found none. They all saw through her pretense, and in the midst of their own hard lives, had little kindness to spare. Some even enjoyed her discomfort as they questioned her.

"So your fine lady's in trouble, eh? She needs help?"

"From someone who knows herbs." Brangwain responded as coldly as she dared. "Do you—"

"Not I, lady! My green fingers are all thumbs!"

Cackling, one old crone held up her stumpy hands, enjoying seeing the fine lady shiver as they always did. Arthritis, leprosy, all the diseases of the old and poor, what did they know of such things, court ladies in velvet gowns?

Sometimes, it was worse.

"So your lady has played belly-to-belly and her tail-flowers haven't come? What is she, a pretend virgin who's getting a babe for her basket before a husband for her bed? Or a pious widow with a good name to keep up? Or one of the Christian sisterhood who have forsworn men, all except for the lusty lad who comes in to chop the wood?"

And on, and on. But the maid persevered. At last, taking a bite of supper in a faraway inn, she had ventured to question the landlord's daughter, a big, bold wench with jutting breasts and an inviting eye. If Brangwain knew anything about young women, this one would have had good reason to seek out the service they needed now.

"You're looking for a wise woman—one who knows about . . . Not I, lady—I never heard of such a thing!"

Brangwain listened to the wide-eyed girl's overemphatic denial, and knew she was near. So she was not surprised when a group of woodmen quietly downing their ale in a corner volunteered news of just such a woman, if she could find her.

"Up beyond here," said the oldest, waving a callused hand, "where the forest lies up to the edge of the cliff and the briar's above your head." He shook his head. "But it's a wild place. Some say she hides her door in the hillside if she doesn't want to be found. She lives by the hawthorn, below the top of the cliff—"

"No, not by the hawthorn," guffawed a hoary-headed ancient with a friendly eye. "It's past the stand of oaks where the owlets roost—"

"No, no."

You follow the track from the valley, they agreed in the end. Up the hillside, till you can't go anymore. Then left and left again, widdershins all the way. Not much of a path at the top, hardly anything at all. But you get to the face of the rock and there she is.

And there she is? thought Brangwain, staring grimly at the wilderness ahead. Bramble, elder, bracken, and stinging nettles rioted away before them, all taller than head height in the glory of their winter red and black. Aloud she said, "We're nearly there, lady. Let me lead the way." Then, with more conviction than she felt, she gathered up her skirts and forced her way in.

Isolde followed. Brangwain's keen eyes must have seen a track through the clinging thorns, and, having come so far, she was not going to falter now. But the briars slashing at her face and hands and catching at her skirts only deepened the anxiety in her heart. *Tristan's child—a love child—could it be?*

And if it is, whatever shall I do?

Slowly they forced their way uphill, foot by foot. Overhead the sun shone down and crisp bracken curled above their heads. The rich smell of the loam rose from the earth as they went. But a brisk salt breeze was blowing straight off the sea. The seductive beat of the surge was very close now.

Ahead of them the undergrowth ran right up to a wall of rock. Beyond it, Isolde guessed, the edge of the cliff plunged down to the sea below. A dank disappointment settled on her heart. Why did she think they would find the old woman's house? No one could live here.

Reaching the rock wall, Brangwain plunged off the side and began working her way along it, casting to and fro. Sick at heart, Isolde watched the maid disappear from view. Beside her, two little gilded flies were dancing in the sun. When the frost came they would be gone, swept away by winter's giant hand. *And so will we,* she thought.

Irritation seized her. What was she doing here? Fishing for moonbeams with nothing but wild hopes for bait. Well, it was over. She had to face the truth. Time to go.

She stepped forward. "Brangwain," she called, "the afternoon's almost gone. We must turn back."

"Here, lady! It's here!" There was no mistaking the triumph in Brangwain's voice.

Isolde started and felt a pang of fear. In this wild place?

Reluctantly she followed the maid's call. Rounding a corner, she came upon Brangwain standing by the cliff face. Beside her, half hidden by tangles of ivy and woodbine, was an odd little door set into the hillside, so gnarled and low that it could hardly be seen.

"Good luck, my lady," Brangwain whispered stoutly, pushing open the door. "I'll be with the horses when you're done."

Isolde ducked her head and moved forward in a dream. Inside the door, a shallow flight of stairs led down to a warm, firelit space below. All around her she could hear the sound of the sea and as she felt her way through the gloom its sweet sigh and rhythmic call seemed stronger now. Slowly her eyes grew accustomed to the light. She was in a small, round, underground chamber with smooth walls of rock and a floor of dry, packed earth. A sea fire chuckled to itself on a rough hearth, and the smell of burning driftwood caught at her throat. Suddenly she was a child again, an imp dancing on the seashore in her golden days when she had no more cares than a wave of the sea.

The salt flames leapt up to greet her as she came in, rose-red, orange, and blue. By the fire sat a crooked old woman with wrinkled, work-worn hands. She was poorly clad in ragged, sea-stained black, and a battered black hat crowned her disordered hair. But beneath the tangled fringe Isolde saw a small kindly face with eyes like those of a porpoise, clever, bright, and sweet.

"Your maid did well to find me," she said in a voice like the wind on the sea. "But then, she is Merlin's kin." She patted the stool at her side. "Come and sit by me."

Isolde obeyed. The leaping fire threw its light here and there, making unseen things gleam and disappear and creating warm pools of rosy darkness all around. The old woman's shadowy garments seemed like part of the night and the rhythmic throb of the sea filled the room.

The old woman sighed. "What do you seek?"

Isolde felt a flush starting up her neck. "I have missed my monthly course."

The old woman squinted through her tangled hair. "And if you're with child, what then?"

Isolde saw herself growing heavier day by day, unable to conceal the deed of love, forced to carry her great belly before her as a mark of shame. She closed her eyes and dropped her head in her hands.

The old woman's voice sharpened. "If there is a child, shall we make it away?"

Isolde's stomach heaved. "Ohh—"

"It's easy to do," the old woman cackled. "There are twenty ways."

"Not for me." A sudden clarity flooded her like light. "Not for my child."

"But if you cannot own the father—" The old woman cocked her head inquisitively to one side. "Will you sleep with your husband, then, to father the newborn on him?"

"No!" Isolde recoiled. She had a sudden shaming urge to be sick. "Never," she said thickly. "I'd kill us both first."

There was a silence. When the old woman spoke again, her voice had changed. "What will you do?"

She did not need to think. "This is a child of love, and I will love it dear."

"If there is a child," the old woman corrected her with sudden gentleness. "You are in a strange country, with many trials to bear. At such times a young woman's moon days are easily disturbed." Behind the veil of hair, her eyes were as clear as a wave. "Let us see."

A gleaming globe of rock crystal lay on a table beside her, crooning to itself with its own light. The old woman cradled it tenderly in her wrinkled hands and stared into it, answering its song with a soundless hum of her own. Isolde watched in a dream of fear as unseen things danced and flickered in its liquid depths.

At last the old woman raised her ragged head. "There is no child."

No child—

A storm of tears swept over Isolde like a weeping cloud.

The bright eyes were watching her closely. "If you want a child, lady, it can always be."

Tristan's child?

"I cannot." She dared not think it. "A child needs a father and a home. I can give it neither, as things are."

There was an endless pause. "Then you must take the way of the Mother to close up your womb."

Isolde started. "What?"

The tangled head nodded inexorably. "Or a child will come."

Goddess, Mother—

Isolde shook her head. "Close up my womb? How?"

Outside, the wind howled, the sea moaned, and the air grew chill. Inside the cave, the fire shivered and sank down. The old woman took a tiny bottle from the table beside her, and held it out. "Drink this, and the Mother will seal up the seedbed of life in you."

Isolde heard the weeping of childless women everywhere. "Forever?" she gasped. "If I take it, will I ever have a child? Or will I be barren for the rest of my life?"

"Ah, Isolde—"

The old woman's sigh came from Avalon and beyond. "Not even the Mother herself can answer that."

Now the crying of children was sounding in her ears, weeping in vain from the world between the worlds, a legion of spirit children waiting to be born. *New life,* her mother always said when she prayed for a child. *No life,* could she choose that?

She stroked her temples with trembling fingers and tried to think. If she lay with Tristan, sooner or later a child must come. In truth, she should be grateful she was not carrying now. Complete avoidance of Tristan would keep her safe. Yet how could she bear never to love him again?

She clutched her head in pain. Loving Tristan should mean bearing his children, not having to be barren for his love. Yet to bring a child of sorrow into the world? Surely there was enough suffering, they should not make more—

Goddess, Mother, tell me what to do!

"You must choose for the need you have now," came the old woman's voice.

The need I have now?

Anguish shot through her. She needed to be safe, and this was her chance. If she refused the old woman, would she ever find this place again?

"Choose," the old woman chimed softly again. She held out her hand.

Tristan—

I choose you.

The little bottle of red-black liquor lay between them, pulsing with the banked-down force of life. Isolde reached out an unsteady hand and brought it to her lips.

Goddess, Mother, help me—

The salt fumes made her gasp, but she drank it down. The raw tang of bitter alum filled her mouth, and she tasted the skin and bone of dead things and the ashes of green fires. Behind it came the fatal trace of foxglove, and she felt her senses swirl. *She has poisoned me*, came to her, and her body convulsed. *I will die here!*

Wild terror swept her, and unspeakable fears. *Mark has had me followed. Elva has paid this woman to make me away.* Then, worst and maddest of all, *This is Tristan's doing, all his work! He wants me dead so he can be at one with his uncle again—he made her do this to me—*

The old woman's voice darkened in pain and reproof. "For shame, Isolde! Tristan is true to you."

"How do I know?" she cried in panic.

"Ah, little one—do you not know me?"

The old woman was dissolving before her eyes. In her place rose a great gleaming figure clad in Otherworldly light. Her blue-green robes ebbed and flowed around her feet and she was veiled in stardust from head to foot. She smiled and the cave filled with a glow like the moon on the sea.

"Lady, Lady," Isolde cried, tears pouring down her face, "how can you be here? I left you in Dubh Lein!"

The Lady gave a low musical laugh. "Some meet me in Dubh Lein, some in Tintagel and some in Castle Dore. Others find me half a world away. The sea is everywhere." She paused and her voice grew deeper. "I am here now. Ask what you need to know."

"Help me, Lady!" Isolde could hardly speak. "I love Tristan and I'm married to King Mark. Will I ever be together with my love?"

The cloudy shape lifted her head. "The land and the sea are one, but always apart."

Always apart? She cried out in pain. "How shall we bear it?"

"Remember you come from a line of warrior queens." The Lady's rich voice rang out. "Be strong in them for yourself and for your love."

A new fear was born. "Why for him?"

"He was born in sorrow, as all men are. Cast out of the circle of the Goddess, they are fated to spend their lives in the quest to return."

"He was born of a great love, too," Isolde cried. "His mother ran wild in the woods for the love of her lord."

The Lady sighed her thousand-year-old sigh. "Ah, little one, even the greatest love has sorrow at its heart. And the deeper the love, the deeper the grief it brings."

"Grief?" Another shaft of fear. "Will I lose him, Lady? Will he die?"

"That is not the trial you will face."

"Will he betray me, then? Will he fail?"

"Only the Mother never fails. The rest must fade and vanish, just as all life in the end ebbs away to the sea."

"What must I do?"

The great foamy shape pulsed like the wind on the waves. "Embrace the fate that has brought you to this place. Child of the sea though you are, you chose a landsman to love. Married to the land, you must be a sea-wife, too. Therefore sorrow and joy must be yours till you come to the place where they are one."

Embrace your fate. Isolde bowed her head. "So be it."

The Lady's deep, rhythmical tones beat onward like the tide. "But remember, Isolde—those who follow the Goddess can always enter the dream."

Through the leaping flames, she saw a rising mist. The tall figure was growing and expanding, filling the room. The luminous eyes lingered fondly on Isolde in a last blessing: "May you dream your dream and become all that you have dreamed."

"Lady, don't leave me—don't go!"

Weeping, Isolde held out her hands. The muffled shape was fading into the shadows, and the room itself was melting into the mist. She felt the wind brush her face and a chilly dew from the sea settled on her skin.

A low call echoed through the night. "Farewell."

The sea sighed and the Lady was gone. The air softly mourned her passing, and a flock of night birds called from the hillside, long wailing cries of woe. Isolde felt herself welling over with grief. These were the children she would never have, lamenting that she would never bring them to life. Then wreaths of silver-white fog, drifting shapes of gray, blue, green, and black, rose up around her and she saw no more.

She came to herself alone on the cold hillside. Thorns and briars tore at her skirt, and a mist off the sea was drifting down like rain. The first lights of evening were appearing in the sky, and the love star on the horizon bloomed with a steadfast fire.

Farewell, she heard from a faraway place. *May the Mother go with you everywhere you go.*

She gathered herself up and rose stiffly to her feet.

Embrace your fate, the Lady said.

So be it.

My soul is given to Tristan and I am married to the land.

My children must be the good deeds I can do.

Down the hillside she could hear the horses whickering softly to each other and Brangwain conversing quietly with both of them.

"Brangwain?" she called. "Are you there? I'm coming down."

chapter
43

Cornwall at last! After all this time on the road. Kay leaned forward in the saddle for the first sight of Castle Dore. Would there be a bed here to comfort his road-weary bones? With a feather mattress and fine linen sheets—all a man could dream of at the end of a wild-goose chase, trailing halfway around the country with nothing but failure at the end?

"King Mark's palace, is it?" grunted Lucan, riding at Kay's side. He kicked his feet out of the stirrups and stretched out his legs. "Well, so far, so good."

Did Lucan mean the fine castle up ahead, all decked out with banners for the tournament? wondered Kay. Or the way in which Arthur had taken the news? Either way, what the red-haired knight said was true.

Castle Dore beckoned warmly in the distance, sitting snugly on its round hilltop, smiling in the sun. Behind it a lazy sea washed the rocky shore, freshening the air with a welcome salt breeze. The flags of many countries hung from the battlements and the bright standards of kings and knights flew from every tower. And Arthur was riding calmly ahead of them now, apparently unruffled by what he had heard. If only, Kay mourned, we could have brought better news . . .

But Arthur had shown a truly noble resignation when Kay reported that the fortune-teller was dead. Guenevere, too, had loyally hidden her disappointment that the truth of young Sweyn's birth would never be revealed, and bowed to Arthur's ruling that a knight must acknowledge his own. The Sweyns would return to Camelot with him, Arthur decreed. There he would notify his council of barons that young Sweyn should be officially recognized as the High King's son.

Somewhere riding in the rear, then—Kay gnashed his teeth at the thought—were the hated Sweyn family, every one of them. Gods above, how he detested the smug, slippery Earl and his polecat of a daughter with her bastard brat. Darkness and devils, was young Sweyn to be the King's son now?

Enough!

Kay shook himself fiercely, and filled his lungs with the clean briny air. He had to stop thinking like this, put it out of his mind. He had tried to save the King and he had failed. He couldn't go on reproaching himself for the rest of his life.

The little knight shifted his travel-worn bones in the saddle, reaching for what crumbs of comfort he could find. The sun was shining, and the weather had been clear for days, so the journey from Castle Sweyn had been quick. And, as always, he took pride in riding behind Arthur, following his great foster brother as he had done all his life. Approvingly he surveyed the knights of the fellowship of the Table, who would lay down their lives for one another or the King. Yes, there was something great here, something great. He felt his sore heart turn.

And this tournament of King Mark's would surely bring more cheer. There'd be knights here from far and wide, old friends not seen for years, fond reunions and joyful candlelit cups of wine late into the night. All these things meant far more than charging into a ring to knock over as many men as you could!

Not that Gawain would ever think that way, Kay thought with a sardonic grin. But the rumbunctious Orkneyan could be gentle, too, and in the course of this journey he had made a new best friend. There he was now, riding with young Sweyn, yarning expansively while the boy hung on his every word.

Kay had to laugh. Well, those two were happy enough, boys together for all eternity. And ahead now he could see a great group on the terrace in front of the palace, waiting to welcome them with trumpets and drums. That must be King Mark in red, with his Queen at his side, and was that his nephew, the fair young man in blue towering over him?

The path began to wind down toward Castle Dore. Kay shook his head, feeling better in spite of himself. He closed his eyes, caught midway between hope and prayer. Gods and Great Ones, all might yet be well!

Looking out from the terrace at the stately procession winding its way up the hill, Tristan shielded his eyes as he stared into the sun. So that was the High King, Arthur himself, the great figure in red, head and shoulders above the rest? And behind him in the block of glittering lances borne by the knights, the big, burly knight riding with a child—that must be Gawain, the King's first companion and his closest kin.

And the short, dapper figure in fine armor? Sir Kay, of course, and next to him, Bedivere. With deep excitement, Tristan put names to faces he had not seen since he was a youth. In those days, when he traveled to tournaments as his father's squire, the great men of the Round Table had seemed heroes beyond his ken. Had he ever thought that within a few short years, he would be competing with them on equal terms? Or more than equal? He grinned to himself, knowing that he could sweep ten knights like Kay from their saddles in one thrust.

And he would, too, as soon as the tournament began. But how would his uncle rise to the challenge of entertaining Arthur and a dozen vassal kings? King Mark looked royal enough, he saw with some relief, in a fine red tunic edged with fur and a richly furred cloak to match. The crown of Cornwall kept down his awkward hair, and he was waiting calmly for Arthur to arrive. Tristan took a breath. This was a friendly event, a celebration indeed. Mark should do quite well.

Behind Mark, Andred, too, was finely dressed, from the feather in his cap to his soft black leather boots, and both Prince and King were set off by their eternal black shadow, the priestly Dominian. Around Mark were all his councillors, led by Sir Nabon, Sir Wisbeck, and Sir Quirian, every one arrayed to greet a king. Someone—Tristan suspected Sir Nabon—had a keen eye for the occasion and knew what Cornwall should do. So the heralds stood ready in their multicolored tabards, the trumpets had their instruments to their lips, and the drummers were poised to second them with a thunderous roll. Tristan sighed and relaxed. He did not know that he outshone them all in a tunic of Lyonesse blue, with the gold torque of knighthood round his neck and a simple fillet of gold holding back his hair.

Away to his left stood Isolde at the head of her ladies, waiting to greet Guenevere. She, too, was clad in flowing sea-blue today, with ropes of blue-green peridots round her waist. A tall headdress rose above her crown, and a gossamer veil frothed behind her to the ground. The pale winter sun caught her marigold hair and a radiance came from her like the brightness of the sea. Seeing her was a blessing, and Tristan blessed her silently with humble love.

She turned and smiled at him, and in spite of himself he was suddenly smiling, too. This was one of the best parts of loving her, the infectious joy they gave one another freely, as a gift. The next second he made himself look sharply away. Fool! If he wanted to guard against discovery, he must not be seen gazing at her like this, misty-eyed with love.

But to look at her and not look at her with love—it was hard! With every day that passed, he loved her more. True, she often sighed and wept in his arms, and he had had to learn that the merry girl he loved had another side to her nature and struggled with secrets he could not share. A while ago she had been pale and huge-eyed with concern, and it had taken a day-long ride with Brangwain to restore her spirits again. She was better now, but he knew there would be no such simple answer to the grief at the heart of their love. Their times together were snatched and always too short, and it was a running sore to see Mark at her side.

But the King would not force himself on her, they both knew that now. And Mark himself had insisted on making Tristan Isolde's knight.

"Take care of the Queen for me, nephew," he had proclaimed. "With matters of state to attend to, I can't be with her as much as I'd like. And women need attention, you know that. They're not like men."

"Women are not like men?" Tristan bowed, wondering what other insights would fall from his uncle's lips. "If you say so, sire."

The sudden bray of the trumpets brought him back to himself. The procession was drawing up to the terrace and the greetings began.

"Your Majesty! We are honored."

Mark knelt to King Arthur in fealty and kissed his hand. To his left, Isolde was welcoming Guenevere with a formality that did not conceal her bubbling delight. Tristan nodded. Of course—the two Queens had been girls together on Avalon, studying with the Lady in the House of Maidens there.

Tristan bowed to Arthur with a trace of awe. Then his attention was caught by a hatchet-faced man in the rear. His burnt-velvet riding habit and fine whip and boots proclaimed him a lord, but the sorry nag he was riding said a poor one, too. Yet he was clearly a force to be reckoned with.

But the girl at his side did not seem to care. She was young enough to be the lord's daughter, but, to Tristan's eye, she treated her father with unfilial contempt. Still, she had every good reason to be pleased with herself. The face she turned up to the heavens had the bloom of a renegade angel, and when she smiled, her soft peony mouth showed a set of perfect, white, small teeth.

Tristan looked at the father again. Had he seen him before in France or Little Britain, when he left Lyonesse and went adventuring? Or before that, when he was too young to compete, while he was still a squire?

Lost in thought, he looked up to see the young woman's eyes fixed on him in frank appraisal, and knew with deep discomfort that she was assessing him sexually, raking him up and down. Stung, he noticed that her gown was cut so low that if she coughed, she would fall out of it. She locked her gaze on his and the tip of a rosy pink tongue peeped out through her lips. Flushing with annoyance, he thought, I have seen you before, madam, and you did not see me.

He was suddenly aware of Sir Nabon at his side. The councillor nodded smoothly toward the girl. "A fine young woman, no?" he said, staring at Tristan with interest.

No! Tristan wanted to retort, but could not. "Fine indeed," he said shortly, trying to move away.

To his annoyance, Nabon moved in closer, assessing the red flush he knew was coloring his cheeks. "The lady Lienore, daughter of Earl Sweyn," he said, still scrutinizing Tristan's face. "You know her of old?"

"Not I," said Tristan, more vehemently than he meant. What's it to you, sir? he wondered irritably, then regretted it at once. A knight should always honor an older knight.

"Come, sir!" he said as cheerfully as he could. "Let me escort you in."

The guests were all dismounting in a happy hubbub, and the procession was beginning to wend its way indoors.

"This way, sirs! We mean to feast you royally in Castle Dore." Keeping up a welcoming banter, Andred chatted easily with Kay as he ushered the companion knights into the hall. But following the exchange he had just witnessed, his sharp eyes and keen mind were busy elsewhere.

So Nabon had suspected that Tristan might like the girl? Andred dismissed the idea with contempt. Not Tristan. He took no interest in the ladies of the court, still less a piece like that. From what Andred had seen, the young hunter of Lyonesse had no eye for the game.

Andred shook his head, puzzled. It was odd that the handsome young knight cared so little for women or girls. Tristan was a man of the world, after all. Indeed, he had spent his life knocking round tournaments, where there was plenty of such excitement as a matter of course.

Andred paused. When a man showed no interest in women, his desire could lie with other men—common enough between knights—but he'd swear not in Tristan's case. More often, it meant that the knight's heart was already given away, pledged to the woman of the dream.

Ha! Did that mean Tristan was stalking other prey? In another part of the forest—and if not among the court ladies, perhaps even in the royal demesne?

No, surely not! Andred found himself holding his breath. Could Tristan—even for a moment—be thinking that way of the Queen?

Just now he had seen Tristan look at Isolde, then hastily look away again. *Could it be?*

He shook himself roughly. Who knows? It was only a glance, after all. But stranger things happened—and it never hurt to keep watch.

Yes, he would watch Tristan closely—no, both of them, Tristan and the Queen. Elva would be a good ally, too, for she could follow Isolde where he could not.

The fertile mind spun on. Within minutes his thoughts were hatched. And all the spirits of evil awoke in their slimy lairs, yawned, stretched, laughed, and prepared to act.

chapter
44

the tournament would be fine after all. Beforehand, it had rained for days and the winds off the sea made it hard to set up the knights' pavilions and the heralds' booths. Tallest of all, the great open-fronted viewing galleries for the kings and queens cost the workmen many a hammered thumb and muttered curse. But despite all fears, the day itself dawned bright and clear, and the grassy arena had never looked more green, moist, and gleaming in the morning sun.

The far meadows were dotted with pavilions in every hue, each small round tent its owner's home from home. Inside, sweating squires and pages toiled from early dawn, scouring their knights' armor and burnishing swords and spears. Farther in, eager groups of combatants were gathering in the knights' enclosure on the edge of the field, ready for the fray. Greetings and curses flew in equal measure as the horses bounced into one another in their excitement, bucking and rearing and dancing up and down.

The townspeople were thronging merrily out of the town, all work suspended in honor of the great event. For most, it was their first chance to see the new Queen, and anticipation ran high.

"She's Queen of the Western Isle, they say," volunteered one busy young mother, struggling along with a child on her hip and three others in tow. "In her own right."

"That's her mother," returned her husband, deftly fishing his first-born from under the hooves of a passing knight. As one of the carpenters, he cast a professional eye over the two galleries facing each other across the arena, ready for the kings and queens. Not a bad job, considering... "She won't be Queen of Ireland till her mother dies."

"And is she the beauty they say?"

"What, the Queen?"

He turned his mind back to the tall, elegant figure who had come down to the field in the worst of the weather to cheer the workmen on. A beauty? Yes, but that wasn't it—

His mind struggled with a hundred tender thoughts. How could he put into words that shining cloud of joy she brought with her and the airy sense of delight she left behind? How could a man even talk about her without making other women feel like common clay? He looked at his dear wife's raw red cheeks and gap-mouthed grin, a tooth lost for every child, and nodded up ahead.

"See for yourself," he said fondly. "There she comes."

A party of ladies was making its way over the grass, chattering like birds. At its head Isolde led Guenevere up the steps into the Queen's viewing gallery, where two tall thrones stood looking down on the field below.

"The way, sire!"

Across the arena Mark was effusively welcoming Arthur into the King's gallery with the older lords. Isolde bowed to Arthur politely and tried not to stare, but since Guenevere had confided in her last night, the story absorbed her mind. Could that noble presence in red and gold, that gracious young King with the frank, open face, have unknowingly fathered a child?

Unthinkable. She shook her head, bewildered. But if Guenevere said so, it had to be true. And there was worse, it seemed. Now the mother had appeared from nowhere, and Arthur felt honor bound to take the child as his own. As soon as the woman was named, Isolde knew her at once. She had noticed the girl the moment the procession arrived, and distrusted her on sight.

The girl was to the fore again at the feast that night and Isolde disliked her more. But why? As she showed Guenevere to her seat and took her own, Isolde struggled to be fair. Was it the girl's little blonde head held so appealingly to one side, or the wide-eyed innocent smile? The surreptitious way she assessed all the men or the disturbingly low-cut gown? Whatever it was, the young woman had her own strange aura and carried it with her everywhere, like a cat. And there she was now, farther down the balcony, standing demurely among the ladies but making Isolde uneasy with her every breath. Well, Castle Dore would soon be rid of her. But Guenevere would have this burden to bear for the rest of her life.

At least she had Arthur, though. A sudden stab of envy pierced Isolde so sharply that she gasped. Arthur may have strayed once as a youth, but the great kindly-eyed warrior was Guenevere's for life. Whereas she . . . Isolde clenched her fists and willed herself to hold back her tears.

For the love between Arthur and Guenevere was hard to bear. Castle Dore was overrun now with guests, but amid all the hurly-burly, the devotion between them was plain. They sat together at dinner in the Great Hall, murmuring and smiling, sharing their every thought. Meanwhile, the man at Isolde's side boasted and drank too much, laughed too loudly, and made foolish jokes, while the man of her heart was away at the Knights' Table, nowhere to be seen. All she could do was hold her head high and smile. And smile, and smile, defying the cruel hour.

But Guenevere had noticed much and guessed more. Almost without words, Isolde found the shadows around her secret gently illuminated, and her sadness shared. With the utmost delicacy Guenevere conveyed her understanding that a man like King Mark could never be Isolde's chosen one. With a husband so hard to love, it went without saying, a woman must love elsewhere.

Nothing more was said, but Isolde's sore heart was eased. She knew from her days on Avalon that she could trust Guenevere. And Guenevere knew that a woman must always choose, and a queen must have her knights. Where the Mother-right ruled, thigh-freedom was never in doubt.

Freedom to love where she chose—

Oh, my love, my love, where are you?

Brangwain's voice sounded in her ear. "They're starting, madam!"

"Thank you, Brangwain."

The trumpeters and heralds were beginning their circuit of the field. Isolde leaned forward to watch, thankful that the loyal maid was at her back. Somewhere among the court ladies lurked the King's mistress and her coterie. Isolde shivered. She could go nowhere these days without meeting Elva's inky gaze and serpentine smile. Like Lienore in Guenevere's life, the fateful Elva would not go away.

"Hear ye!"

The sudden bray of trumpets split the air. The herald marshal strode out into the expectant hush and surveyed the crowd with an imperious eye.

"One joust for all," he bellowed, "by order of the King! A general melee, all knights admitted at once. The winner to be the knight who stands his ground and holds the field alone when all are done."

A general melee—

Oh, my love, my love—

Isolde knew at once what this would mean. In single combat, Tristan could beat any knight on the field, even three at a time. But in a general free-for-all, the best of the knights became targets for many spears. Tristan could be attacked from behind, unhorsed and trampled, even killed—

She was suddenly aware that she was making little whimpering noises of distress. She turned to see Guenevere's eyes on her, luminous with sympathy.

Guenevere leaned forward. "You fear for your knight?"

How did she know? Isolde nodded wanly. "Yes, I do."

The herald marshal split his lungs again. "The King's tournament for his marriage will begin, in honor of the Queen!" he brayed. "The winner to be acclaimed as Queen's champion, by right of his prowess. All who challenge for the Queen's favor come now into the ring!"

The great gates of the knights' enclosure swung back and the contestants poured onto the field, each furiously galloping forward to take a stand. The grassy space filled with a hundred armored figures and became a sea of flying banners, bobbing plumes, and thundering hooves.

Then a last, lone figure bounded onto the field. Both horse and rider were magnificently clad in Ireland's colors, emerald green and gold. On his sleeve the knight sported a rosette of white trefoils, the flower of the Western Isle. His silver breastplate was adorned with two fighting swans and his helmet bore a pair of swan's wings, their every feather lovingly worked in gold. Even the trappings of his horse, from the green plumes on its head to the gold threads woven into its tail, echoed his armor and declared his love.

Tristan, my own—

Isolde laughed, in spite of herself. She might have known that he would enter last, yielding up his natural advantage to give others a better chance. Already the rain-soaked field had turned to mud, and the hardiest competitors had seized the best stands around the edges of the field. Tristan, she saw, had no such options now. He was out in the center of the arena, undefended and alone.

Oh, my lord—my love—

"The Queen's champion!" roared the delighted crowd.

King Mark leaned out of the King's gallery. "Oh, clever!" he shouted gleefully. "Well done, sir!"

He turned to King Arthur. "See the Queen's colors, sire?" he boasted. "And her emblem, the fighting swans? That's my nephew, Tristan, the best knight of them all. I told him to look after my Queen—and see how he has!"

Already the melee was heaving like a living thing.

"Have at you!" Tristan cried through the thin wintry air, as he set spurs to his horse and charged into the press. With his first rush, she saw four knights cannon into one another and fall from their saddles, toppling like pins.

"Away, the Orkneys! Away, away!"

At the other end of the field, Gawain was thrashing about him, roaring like a bull. Pausing to laugh at his friend, Lucan found himself taken in the side by a knight half his size, and paid for his amusement with a heavy fall.

Goddess, Mother, my father would be proud of me!

With his back to a corner, Kay was doing better than he dared to hope. Years of knighthood training with his father, Sir Ector of Gore, could not compensate for the little knight's lack of stature, but the tactics Sir Ector had taught him were clear and sound. Ducking and weaving, Kay had kept his lance firm and straight, and marveled at how many wild enthusiasts had run onto his point. He only had to withstand the impact and their own momentum would send them flying backward off their horses, spinning through the air.

Gods above, am I learning to joust at last?

Kay was still enjoying his newfound skill as two knights charged him together and had him down.

At the heart of the melee, Tristan plunged and thrust, light spinning from Glaeve's busy point. He was the only man on the field with the strength to fight two-handed, his spear in his right hand and his sword in his left, but despite his prowess, his chivalry never failed. Time and again Isolde saw him spare a weaker opponent, or pull back from the melee to avoid spilling blood.

Now the field was beginning to thin out, and those who survived fought on in a sea of mud. The fallen knights picked themselves up and limped off with rueful groans while the riderless horses kicked up their heels and galloped blithely off the field. With her face set in a cheerful public smile, Isolde watched anxiously as Tristan began to work his way around the edge of the field where the strongest had taken their stands.

But wherever Tristan was, the melee followed him, stronger and weaker knights alike jostling to take him on. Amid the heaving throng, no one would have noticed the knight in dark armor, stalking Tristan like a shadow in the rear. But with the sixth sense of the hunter, Tristan tensed and swerved to the side, just in time to avoid a spear point from behind.

The melee parted as Tristan wheeled around and the attacker was exposed. Andred was driving toward Tristan, his spear aimed at Tristan's back. Spurring forward, Tristan bounded toward Andred, bellowing with rage. With more fury than skill, he hooked the point of his spear under Andred's breastplate and tossed the smaller knight backward over his stallion's rump. Under the eyes of the crowd, Andred hit the ground with a crash calculated to knock all the breath from his body, and lay on his back, spread-eagled in the mud.

In the King's gallery, Mark's eyes bulged like a schoolboy's, and he jeered with coarse delight.

"You asked for that, Andred," he yelled. "You tried to take him by stealth—unchivalrous, sir!"

Waving feebly, Andred raised his visor and picked himself up. His face was pale, and the silver trace of his harelip throbbed vividly as he spoke. But still a courageous smile played over his lips. He gestured ruefully to his battered armor and the fine silk banner trailing in the mud.

"Beaten by a better man!" he sang out.

Isolde stiffened. *He hates us. Elva does, too. You don't know that,* she chided herself, *you have no proof.* Yet why could she not believe a word Andred said?

With the other beaten warriors, Andred was making a graceful exit from the field, bowing to the cheering crowds as he left. In the center of the arena, only two great figures remained, as Tristan and Gawain held the field alone.

"Away, the Orkneys! Away, away, away!"

Yelping like a wolfhound in full cry, Gawain charged. Tristan eased toward him at a slow canter, apparently oblivious to his enemy's furious approach. Only at the last minute did he touch his spurs to his horse's sides. The willing beast gave a massive leap forward just as Gawain prepared to lunge. Tristan's lance slipped under Gawain's guard, found the center of his breastplate, and dealt him a resounding blow. Unhorsed, the big knight fell heavily to the ground.

The trumpets sounded. "Sir Tristan it is! Sir Tristan!" the heralds declaimed.

"The champion! The Queen's champion!" caroled the delirious throng.

Panting, Tristan drew up below the Queen's gallery, his quivering, snorting horse throwing sweat and foam. Isolde rose to her feet to greet him, trembling with joy. He tugged off his helmet and made a formal bow.

"On behalf of the King," he proclaimed, "I lay my victory at your feet."

"On behalf of the King," Isolde cried, "I accept your triumph, sir."

"Sir Tristan—!" came an unexpected voice.

Isolde turned. Farther down the gallery, cooing like a dove and leaning seductively over the edge, was—

Lienore!

The girl was almost falling out of her gown. Her pouting breasts could have kissed Tristan's startled face. Isolde stared in fury and opened her mouth to speak. But Lienore was impervious to reproof.

"Sir Tristan, you have fought well," she called, unabashed. She reached into her low-cut gown and fished out a scrap of lace. "The ladies salute you. Here's for you, sir—from us all!"

The handkerchief fluttered slowly to the ground. Tristan sat on his horse like a man of stone and Lienore's voice chimed on shamelessly as they all stood by. "Sir, I look forward to renewing our acquaintance today. Call on me to honor the Queen's champion as he deserves."

Her acquaintance with Tristan? What did the trollop mean?

This is too much!

With smiling calm, Isolde moved forward to take charge.

"Sir Tristan, go with the blessing of us all!" she cried as warmly as she could. "The Queen accepts your championship with grateful pride!"

❧

HOURS PASSED BEFORE she could talk to Tristan alone. The evening came on with feasting in the Great Hall, then long hours of dancing and talk as the fires roared up the chimneys and the candles burned down. She saw him passing by many times, meeting former friends from foreign tournaments, or conversing with Sir Nabon and the lords. Sometimes he was speaking with court ladies, though never, as far as she could see, with Lienore. She herself was constantly with King Mark, as Mark attended on the High King and Queen.

At last she drew aside for a moment, drawing breath in an alcove of the Great Hall with the faithful Brangwain.

"It's late, Brangwain," she said. "Time for bed?"

"Madam?"

They had not heard him come. She forgave his cold and formal bow as he stepped in—even at this hour, the court was still awake, the musicians played on, there were prying eyes.

"Sir Tristan." She nodded formally. "You are welcome here."

He moved toward her, turning his face away. She could smell his manhood scent, musky and strong. *Why didn't he speak?*

"The Lady Lienore—" she heard him say.

"Tell me," she said.

Staring out at the dancers, he addressed her from the side of his mouth. "Whatever she said, I never knew her before."

He's lying! flashed madly into her mind.

"Never?" she said graciously, keeping up her public smile. "She claimed acquaintance with you."

"Not as you'd call it—"

"Oh, sir—"

Isolde's smile grew sweeter, and she acknowledged in passing a departing courtier's bow. "What would you call it, then?"

He shook his head. "On my oath as a knight—"

Wild fears flooded her. *He knew her before, and he loves her still. He will go to her quarters tonight, while I'm in the Queen's House alone—*

The smoke from the candelabra stung her eyes. "What?"

He was very pale. "I may not tell you."

"May not?" she hissed.

"Lady, I have sworn an oath of chivalry—"

"And you have sworn a deeper oath to me!" Suddenly she was beside herself. "Tell me what you mean, or leave me at once!"

Stepping forward, he dropped to one knee, and began a muttered tale. She watched as his color changed to an unhappy red, then back to a pallor again.

"I have broken my oath as a knight to tell you this," he said with dull fury at the end. "I swore to myself that I would not breathe a word. But that is how I know the Lady Lienore."

So that is how you know the Lady Lienore.

Isolde could not help herself. "Sir—"

She was laughing, a rich, full-throated, gurgling sound. Tristan raised his head.

"Lady, what?" The last thing he expected was this.

She was staring at him strangely, smiling down at him.

"Would you say that again," she inquired, with light he did not know dancing in her eyes. "Tell the King all you just told me?"

He started. "Tell it to Mark? Why would he want to know?"

"No, no." She shook her head with the same mysterious delight. "Tell the High King. King Arthur himself."

chapter
45

The next day dawned with a rank December chill. A weeping mist rolled in from the sea, and all Castle Dore shivered in its sad embrace. But Isolde awoke with a wicked grin in her heart. *There is justice. And there is faith and truth.*

She sent to Guenevere as soon as it was light. The little page was soon back with beads of mist shining in his hair. The Queen would see them in the Guest House at once. Before long she was crossing the courtyard with Tristan at her side.

They had hardly spoken, and she could see he had not slept. He hated this, she knew. But as she stole a look at his face through the white, writhing fog, she knew he would not fail.

The best apartment in the Guest House had been given to the High King and Queen. The low audience chamber was newly furnished, its walls as white as a fresh fall of snow, its satin floors scenting the air with the golden smell of beeswax and summer in its prime. Copper pots full of berries brightened the wintry rooms, and a sea-coal fire burned with a cheerful flame. Isolde stepped in with a steady heart. *Yes, this is right. This is what we should do.*

At the end of the room, a grave-faced Arthur sat on a low dais beside Guenevere, with the four companion knights standing at his side. Across from them, Isolde saw with an unpleasant sensation, were Lienore and her hard-faced father, Earl Sweyn. She drew a deep breath. What else had she expected? Sooner or later they would have to know.

King Arthur leaned forward, beckoning them to approach.

"Welcome to you both," he said in a troubled voice. "My Queen tells me you have knowledge to share with us." He gestured earnestly to the

Sweyns standing at his side. "I invited the Earl and his daughter to be here because this concerns them, too. You all know each other, I think."

"We do, sire," cried the Earl fulsomely, grinning like a rat. Isolde could see he was ready to jump out of his skin with delight. At last, said his nods and smiles, a reliable witness who will confirm all Lienore said!

Arthur turned back to Tristan. "You were at the tournament in question, eight years ago?"

Tristan bowed stiffly. "Sire, I was, though not yet as a knight. The lord I served then was fighting at the tournament, and I followed the crowd to the fortune-teller's tent."

"What?" Kay twitched with excitement. "You saw us there?"

"I saw all of you." He laughed self-consciously. "I was only a squire. You would not have noticed me."

Arthur nodded gravely, and indicated Lienore with the utmost courtesy. "But you saw this lady."

Tristan colored. "I did."

He made a confused bow toward Lienore. "I saw everything," he said stoutly. Only Isolde could hear the reluctance in his voice. "There was a great crowd of people in the tent. The Gypsies had partitioned it with hangings to make different rooms. Knights and ladies were meeting and talking in the main part, while the Gypsy women sang and danced and sold them ale."

"What else?" demanded Arthur hoarsely.

"The tent was dark, even though it was midday," Tristan went on with difficulty, at a loss to describe the rich silk hangings shutting out the daylight, the strange lamps here and there, the shining, scented gloom. "But there were braziers giving some light and making sweet fumes. One by one, those who wanted to have their fortunes told were taken off to another part of the tent. And from time to time I saw a knight give a Gypsy some money, and lead a lady away."

"Aha!"

Earl Sweyn strutted forward, flourishing like a barnyard cock. He paused, holding them hostage to the moment, savoring his power. "So you saw my daughter leave, escorted by the King."

"Alas!" Arthur muttered. He bowed his head and covered his eyes with his hand. Guenevere straightened her back and changed color as she braced herself for what was to come.

Isolde stared at Tristan and briefly caught his eye. *Go on.*

He cleared his throat. "No, sir."

There was a stunned silence.

Earl Sweyn turned a livid shade of gray. "No? You're lying!" he shouted, fumbling for his sword. "Someone's paid you to deny it! I'll make you say who it is!"

Guenevere half rose from her throne. Beside her Arthur was staring like a man in a dream. "My lord," she cried angrily, "remember where you are!"

Tristan threw back his head. "Believe me, sir," he said sadly. "The Lady Lienore did not withdraw with the King. King Arthur stayed with the others in the tent. He did not leave."

Earl Sweyn let out a howl of disbelief. "Not the King?"

He turned on Lienore, his face suffused with rage. For a moment Isolde feared for her, then she marveled to see the girl holding her head up, perfectly unafraid.

"Did you know?" the Earl cried.

Lienore shrugged. "It could have been him." She paused with a secretive smile. "It had to be one of them."

"One of them!" Earl Sweyn clutched at his head. "There must have been fifty men there. A hundred at least!"

He could not contain his rage. They were back where they were, only worse. Claiming false kinship with the King, they'd be the laughingstock of the whole kingdom now. "So I've got a fatherless bastard on my hands again—"

"Not so."

Tristan's voice chimed through the air like a bell. "Young Sweyn has a father, and a worthy one, too."

Kay started. "He knows!" he hissed to Bedivere.

Bedivere nodded slowly. "Of course he would!" he muttered. "He was there."

"Tell us, sir," said Arthur with grave authority.

Tristan shook his head. "Sire, I may not," he said desperately, "on my oath as a knight. I swore to honor every lady and act as a brother toward every knight. I cannot betray a fellow knight."

"He's right!" Gawain whispered loudly, punching Lucan on the arm. "A knight must keep his—"

Lucan punched him back. "Quiet, Gawain!"

Arthur frowned. "But you also swore fealty to your King, did you not?"

Tristan paled. "I did."

"And your King obeys the High King?"

Tristan bowed his head. It pained Isolde to see him torn like this. "Yes, sire."

"Then obey your High King's command!" ordered Arthur peremptorily. "Did you see who left the tent with the Lady Lienore?"

"I did."

"And did you know him?"

"I did, sire."

Arthur's eyes flashed dangerously. "Then on your sword, Sir Tristan, tell us who it was!"

Tristan's eyes turned to Gawain, Kay, Lucan, and Bedivere. The four companion knights stiffened in surprise.

"Forgive me," Tristan said sadly, then looked away. He took a step toward Arthur and knelt before the throne. "On your command, sire. The knight I saw leaving with the lady was . . . Sir Gawain."

No one moved. Gawain's jaw dropped and his eyes almost fell out of his head. He looked at Tristan, then at Lienore and at Tristan again.

"I?" he croaked. He shook his great body wildly and tried again. "You mean I had the joy of this lady's"—he collected himself—"company, and I never knew?"

Tristan nodded painfully. "That day in the tent," he said, "no one knew what was happening. You were all in a mist."

"I've got it!" Kay clicked his fingers. "It was the fumes from the brazier, wasn't it? They filled the tent."

"No, sir." Tristan shook his head. "It was the drink. I saw one of the Gypsy girls laughing as she poured the wine, and she winked and told me they put a spirit of forgetfulness into it."

"And you, sir?" Guenevere asked earnestly. "How did you escape?"

Tristan's smile made him look very young. "I was only a boy then, Your Majesty. I did not drink."

Isolde's heart swelled. *Oh, Tristan—oh, my love—*

Arthur's face was clearing like sunshine after rain. "Well, Gawain?"

"Sire." Gawain shook his great head and struggled to adopt a noble attitude. "A true knight accepts his own. I am honored to be the father of such a child."

He made a gallant bow to Earl Sweyn and his blue eyes lit up lasciviously as they fastened on Lienore. "And doubly honored in the embrace of a lady such as this." He turned to the King with another lavish bow, ogling the smiling Lienore in shameless lust. "Give me your permission, sire, to bring the boy and his mother to court."

"The boy, yes," Arthur agreed. His mouth twitched and Isolde could have sworn she detected suppressed amusement in the measured tones. "But young Sweyn must leave the house of women and become a man. And indeed a prince—for a son of the royal Orkneys is my cousin, too." He nodded gently to Lienore. "Lady, you will always be welcome as a visitor at court. But as soon as we have settled your son with us, we shall give you leave to return to Castle Sweyn."

He turned courteously to Earl Sweyn, standing speechless at Lienore's side. "And you, sir, will be glad to have your daughter with you as you raise the men and money we require of you. Each lord must pay his due to keep the Saxons at bay. We shall be sending overseers to assess your lands."

Another hint of a smile crossed Arthur's lips. "We have heard much about your poverty, sir. We look forward to finding out that it is not as bad as we feared. Farewell." He rose to his feet and offered Guenevere his hand. "Come, my Queen."

"Sir—" The look Guenevere gave him in return left no doubt that the royal couple would lose no time in celebrating the morning's discovery and renewing their love.

Gawain looked round chortling, as Arthur and Guenevere left the room.

"A son, eh?" he cried, marveling at himself. He poked Lucan in the ribs, then dragged all the companion knights away. "Come on, then! Let's go and see my son!"

Goddess, Mother, thanks—

"Shall we walk, sir?" Isolde followed the procession joyfully, leaning on Tristan's arm. She smiled into his eyes. Now, where in Castle Dore could they be alone?

Standing in the empty room, Earl Sweyn refused to look at Lienore. "You knew, didn't you?" he said thickly.

Lienore lifted first one creamy shoulder then the other in a glorious shrug. "I knew it was one of them."

"Couldn't you tell?" he screeched.

Another shrug. "All men are big in the dark." Or think they are, said her lascivious eyes.

He was gasping for breath. "You played me for a fool!"

"No more than you played yourself, Father," she said carelessly. "You wanted Sweyn to be the son of the King." Her white teeth showed again in a derisive grin. "I knew they wouldn't remember. And I didn't think they'd find out."

"Did it ever occur to you to tell the truth?"

She laughed openly at that. "You called me Lienore, Father! I was born to lie down wherever I liked, and lie about it afterward."

"Well, Lienore, you'll have a long time to enjoy the joke," he struck back. "As soon as we get home, I'll have you put in a convent for the rest of your life." He began to feel better. "And with a large enough endowment from me, I daresay the holy sisters will find you a cell all to yourself. They should also assist your penance with a diet of bread and water and vary your confinement with the liberal use of the whip!"

Lienore treated him to her sunniest of smiles.

"You can't do that, Father," she said innocently. "If you do, I'll tell the King how much land and money you've really got. Then he'll make you hand over far more than you want to to keep the Saxons at bay."

She leaned forward and whispered lovingly in his ear. "I think you should give some of it to me—for your grandson, of course. His father's a prince of the Orkneys, after all, we don't want to look mean. Or else Arthur might learn exactly what you're worth. Just tell me what you'd like to do, Father dear."

chapter
46

The first snow of winter fell silently overnight. The white flakes floated down like goose feathers, till all the earth lay in an enchanted sleep. The sun rose on a white wonderland, and all the world seemed spellbound and made anew. In the stable yard, the lads were playing joyfully in the snow; the older grooms were bantering as they settled to their work and Andred took his horse and rode out with evil in his heart.

And no finer day for it, he thought with darksome glee, as he turned his horse's head toward the wood. Since Tristan had come, his path had been marked by storms. Now at last, the future was set fair.

Andred grinned mirthlessly. Tristan would never know what he had done. Andred snatched down deep breaths of the sharp, frosty air and shivered, but not with cold. Once again he relived the shameful fall at the tournament when he had been so contemptuously tossed over his horse's backside. Mark's jeering laugh would ring in his ears till he died.

He lifted his head sharply. He could hear it now, echoing around the wood. *You asked for that, Andred!* Any moment the leafless trees would be craning their bare branches to sneer at him and snigger behind his back. He stiffened his resolve. Nothing to do but press on.

With a touch of his spurs, he signaled to his sleepy horse to pick up the pace. In the still, white heart of the forest lay the remedy for all his pains. No one else ever came to the old hermitage, moldering beneath its mound of dead leaves and earth. The healer who lived there had long ago passed beyond mortal aid, taken back to the arms of the Mother who gave him birth. But his were not the skills that Andred sought. There were more ways than one of healing life's deadly wounds.

The forest was silent, awaiting his approach. He threaded his way through the trees, ducking beneath frost-spangled branches, trusting his horse to keep on the narrow path. The snow showed passing traces of weasel, stoat, and fox, but otherwise the white wilderness was his. Tristan, Tristan, he thought, I will have you, you are mine.

The hermitage lay beyond a gaunt stand of pine, its low, domed roof scarcely higher than the snowdrifts around it. Behind it a white horse waited patiently, tied to a tree. Andred smiled. His remedy was here. He might have known that his doctor would not fail.

But which was the healer, which the sufferer now? came to him as he dismounted and tied up his horse. Both of us, he heard in his inmost heart. We are both the same, and together we shall prevail.

He stooped to enter the low doorway, noticing the familiar footprint on the threshold, the mark of a gloved hand on the latch. The tall, muffled figure inside hovered for a moment in the half-light, then came into his arms in a wordless embrace.

"Elva! Oh, Elva!" he sighed.

They held each other for a long time, their heads brushing the low roof. Then he put her away from him and stared into her eyes. As she gave him her gaze, her fire crackled into him and he forgot the cold. She smelled like a vixen in her lair and he could feel her narrow hips, her sharp, rangy bones, even through her furs. For a moment he thought of taking her now, on the bare earthen floor, and he could see from her hungry gaze that she felt it, too. But they both knew that there was work to be done. With a raw sigh, she pushed him off and paced away.

"So," he said softly. "What have we learned?"

Behind her, the wall of the cell glittered with snow crystals in a thousand intricate forms. But her eyes were a thousand times brighter as she smiled at him. "He does not sleep with her!"

"How do you know?"

"One of my women has a niece in the Queen's House—one of the maids. I've been paying her to watch and listen as the King comes and goes. When he enters Isolde's apartments, he does nothing but talk. And the maid insists he has never been in her bed."

"So—"

Andred paused. It was no more than he had heard already from the servants in his pay. But a wise man never told a woman all he knew. And what was happening now called for all the wisdom he had. He looked back at Elva with a peculiar pain.

"If he does not enjoy the Queen's body," he said levelly, "you must think the King will return to your arms again?"

She flared her eyes. "Yes!" she thrilled.

A dull ache began in Andred's heart: What a fool I was, what a fool. He and Elva had been lovers for so long that he thought nothing could break their secret bond. If she made advances to Mark, he told her, then between them, they could take control of the King. From the first she had protested that she loved only him, and he had had to work hard to wear her resistance down. In the end he convinced her that it would only strengthen their love. That at least had proved true. But it never occurred to him that she could love the King as well. What a fool I was—such a fool—

"What about the Queen?" He looked at her searchingly.

"Oh, she's happy enough!" said Elva with a relish that made him stare.

"What do you mean?"

Now she knew she was bringing him fresh news. "Who else is happy these days?" she asked teasingly.

He dared not let himself hope. "Who?"

"Tristan!" she shrilled, clapping her hands with delight.

"Lovers?" He could hardly breathe. "You have proof?"

"Not yet. But we can get it easily."

Darkness and devils—the blood roared in Andred's head. "Tell me," he said.

"He does not call on her in the Queen's House—they are too clever for that. But she walks every day in the solarium, and he goes to her there."

"The solarium?"

Yes, he knew the long gallery at the top of Castle Dore, built to catch the summer sun on a dull or rainy day. His mind ran on. "Now it's winter, they must have the place to themselves."

Elva nodded. "Her maid keeps watch on the stairs, and they're in there alone. They talk to each other for hours. Only talk," she added, with an obscure sense of loss that no man had ever wanted to do that with her. "They have other pastimes, too. They sing and he plays the harp."

The harp—

Andred sneered in his deepest soul. They must do more than talk. And how hard would it be to trap a harpist in love?

"But her maid only watches the way the courtiers come in," Elva pressed on. "There's a servants' staircase at the other end. It comes up behind the hanging on the far wall. You could bring the King to overhear them and catch them out."

Overhear them—fetch the King—catch them out—

Gods above, *yesss!*

It was at moments like this that he loved her beyond compare. One day, both Mark and her wretched husband would be no more. When he was King, she would rule at his side.

But not yet.

There were still too many obstacles in the way. He closed his eyes. Tristan was the greatest, and Isolde not far behind. If Elva was right, he could deal with them both in one fatal blow.

His heart soared. *When I am King—*

"They always go there around noon." He heard Elva's voice from very far away. "They'll be there now."

Now?

"This back way into the solarium," he heard himself say. "Tell me again."

COME TO ME, come to me, love!

The long gallery was filled with brilliant light. The sun sparkled off the snow outside and poured through the wide mullioned windows to warm the wintry air. Forgetting the letter in her hand, Isolde prowled the solarium with a joyful tread. Tristan was coming. That was all there was.

Goddess, Mother, thanks—

For surely the Great One was smiling on them now. The tournament had ended with feasting and goodwill and King Mark in a high good humor with himself and the world. Arthur and Guenevere had left Castle Dore rejoicing, Guenevere wearing the sleek, drowsy-eyed look of a woman who has been well loved. Now that the shadow hanging over Arthur had gone, Isolde could see that their delight in one another had been born again. It was no secret that the royal couple had renewed their love.

With them had gone Earl Sweyn, far from happy, but grimly accepting what he could not change. At his side rode the still-smiling Lienore, and behind them Gawain with young Sweyn, the big knight doting absurdly on his newfound son. With a sigh, Castle Dore settled down for its winter sleep, and Isolde was looking to the future and daring to hope.

She glanced around the long gallery and her confidence increased. Built over a pillared cloister, it was too high to be overlooked, yet for all its seclusion it was open to all and therefore free of the danger they faced in the Queen's House. As a place of retreat for the court on rainy days, it had tables and couches and alcoves and room to walk and talk. For those who preferred to sit, there were diversions galore, riddle books and counters and games to pass the time.

No one came here now that summer had gone. The great space was too cold for the courtiers when there was no fire. But waiting for Tristan was warmth enough for her. *Any moment now—*

"My lady!" came Brangwain's low warning from the stair. She heard footsteps bounding up from the cloister and the next moment he was striding through the door.

He cast off his cloak and came toward her, his eyes dark with love. "Forgive me, lady, if I kept you waiting here."

The smell of the wintry outdoors hung in his clothes and his beauty was almost too much for her to bear. His long hair was covered in drops of melted snow, and the cold had brought a rare color to his face. A golden down of stubble covered his cheeks, and she found herself pining for the taste of his kiss.

She felt suddenly shy.

"You are welcome, sir," she said.

He lifted his head like a pointer. "Is all well?"

More than well, now you are here, my love.

She lifted the letter she held. "From my mother."

He tensed. "Bad news?"

How little we know one another, passed through her mind. *You must think I fear her, as you do.*

"Not at all." She smiled at him and watched as his dear face cleared.

"The Queen is well?"

"Never better." She laughed. "Her new knight Sir Tolen is all that she desires—he even seems to have driven Sir Marhaus from her mind. Her only complaint is that she misses me. She has important matters to discuss, she says. She wants me to return for a royal visit, queen to queen."

"If you did, lady—" Tristan paused.

She heard his thought—*We could be together in a safer place than this.*

She would not think it. "We are safe enough here."

"I am not so sure." He took a pace away. "When I got to the stable this morning, Andred's horse had gone. And none of the grooms seemed to know where he went."

What was he talking about? "You were out riding early—why shouldn't he?"

He shook his head. "Perhaps I'm making something of nothing. It was a feeling—no more."

"Andred can't harm us," she said impatiently. "I am Queen here."

"Alas, lady—" He paused. "We are not in the Mother-country now."

She stared. "Why, what could Andred do?"

"He has the ear of the King," he said grimly. "And the King has the power to do whatever he wants."

She laughed, and waved a dismissive hand. "Mark could not touch me."

"Think, madam." He held his temper. "King Mark is no lover of women, there's a danger in that. He's ruled by the Christians, too, their priests are round him night and day. You know what they think of women—and what they do."

She shuddered. Every girl in the Western Isle knew how the Christians treated women in the name of their God. When their Good Book taught them that all evil came through Eve, men could punish women throughout eternity.

Her fragile mood veered like a weathervane. How could he stand there gleaming in white and gold, as tall and fine as a stag at the head of the glen, and talk like this?

"We only need to be careful," she said stubbornly.

He wanted to believe her. He loved her when she spoke as bravely as this. He saw her small chin set and his heart ached. "We shall be," he said.

Her spirits turned again. "If we are, then we have nothing to fear."

She looked into his face. She wanted to feed on his mouth and drown herself in his eyes. She felt the warmth blooming at her center, the raw feeling for him still strange and dangerous. Shivering, she longed for the safety of his arms.

She leaned toward him and gestured to the nearest couch. "Will you sit with me, my love?"

"Gladly I will." He bent down his head toward hers and gently touched the letter in her hand. "We must talk about this, lady."

"Later." She laid her hand on his. "Afterward."

High above, the sun paused in the sky, then hid behind the clouds. The sky darkened, and the muffled figure watching from the cloisters below saw the two heads meet in a tender intimacy, then draw back out of view. Sheltering in the shadows, he had endured the bitter cold without much hope that his vigil would bear fruit. But the couple he could see through the glass were far too close for a queen and her knight. Isolde and Tristan were lovers, and here was the proof.

Andred stood for a second to calm his heaving heart. Then he raced away, careless of the ice underfoot. One thought possessed him, beating through his rising blood.

Bring the King here—

Fetch the King—

Fetch the King!

chapter 47

Yes, yes, Father—the Lord's work, certainly."

Mark shifted irritably in his seat and tried to quell the resentful shuffling of his feet. God Almighty, what was wrong with these priests? Weeks of wind and rain, and now, when the sun was shining at last on fields covered in snow, when the horses were raring to get out and the game would be sportive from lack of food, then Father Dominian had to launch into a sermon apparently destined to go on for ever and ever, world without end, amen.

Dominian and his eternal shadow, Simeon. Mark gazed sourly at the youth waiting patiently for his master by the door. They were everywhere now, the black brothers of Dominian's community—why couldn't he read his infernal lectures to them?

"We must accept how narrowly we have won this land to the Christian faith," Dominian droned on. "Your Majesty must consider—"

Must, must, must!

Mark blocked his mental ears and turned his mind to better things. A day in the Trembling Forest, now, charging through the trees with the hounds in full cry—that was a sound to warm the meanest heart, better than choirs of angels all singing at once.

"—as Your Majesty must agree."

Must, must, must—

Sulkily Mark returned to reality. "What?"

"About Queen Igraine, sire," Dominian said forcefully. He had no compunction about bullying Mark in the name of the Lord.

"Igraine?" Mark spluttered madly, "What of her?"

Dominian stared at him implacably. "We need to win her to God and secure the Hallows of the Goddess for our own use."

"What?"

Mark gasped. Igraine was as old as Tintagel, older than the sea. Aloft in her palace on the rock, unseen by common folk, she had kept the worship of the Goddess for so long that many believed she was the Great One Herself. If Dominian thought that she would turn to Christ, he was madder than he thought. "What are you saying, man?"

Dominian's eyes were burning with a hard, bright flame. *Ecce nunc, Domine,* see, Lord, behold how I do thy will—

He leaned forward. "Sire, give me leave to write to Queen Igraine. She must have access to the Lady—she must know where the Hallows are. If we can open a dialogue, by degrees we can work these women to our Christian purposes." He bowed, and threw Mark the bribe. "If you agree, I'll have the letter ready to sign when you come back from the hunt."

The hunt, at last! Mark sighed with relief. Dominian was a sensible fellow after all. This plan of his should lead to interesting things.

"Good work!" Mark uncoiled his legs and stood up. "I agree—"

"Sire!"

Running feet sounded in the corridor, and Andred burst through the door. "Treason, sire!" he gasped.

Mark began to tremble. "What?"

Andred came to a halt, panting for breath. "My cousin Tristan is plotting with the Queen!"

"Tristan?" Mark gaped. "With the Queen?"

"They're together now, in the solarium."

Dominian stepped forward, his face alight with a wild curiosity. Dear God, could this be?

Mark stood rooted to the ground. "But why should the Queen—"

Andred showed his teeth in a savage grin. "Remember Ireland was our enemy, sire! To them, the death of Sir Marhaus went unavenged."

"What are they plotting?" Mark made a wild clutch at him. "Tell me, Andred, I have to know!"

"Queen Isolde's mother may want to invade again. Now Isolde's here, they have a spy within our gates." He gestured hastily to the door. "If we hurry we can—"

"Would Isolde betray me like this?" Stupefied, Mark hit his head. "Would Tristan?"

Death and damnation. Andred struggled for control. If he couldn't get Mark to the solarium, the lovers would get away!

"Sire." He chose his words with care. "Indeed, some of your courtiers, too, have reported strong concerns about the Queen and Sir Tristan."

"What about them?" cried Mark in desperation.

"They fear Sir Tristan has approached the Queen—in forbidden ways."

Mark's mouth fell open. A thousand fears went jangling through his brain. "You mean—?" he said thickly at last.

Andred nodded, looking agonized. "Alas, sire, that I had to tell you this!"

"Women are sinful creatures, we know that," Dominian put in tensely. "But—"

"Tristan?" Mark had gone very white. "And Isolde?" A look of vicious fury crossed his face. "I treated her so well! If she's done this to me—"

"They're in the solarium now, together, alone. You may overhear them there if you want, and not be seen." Andred leaned forward urgently. "What is your will?"

"God's body, Andred, d'you need to ask?" Mark snarled. He reached for his sword. "Take me to them! Lead the way!"

OUTSIDE THE SKY was dark with the threat of fresh snow, and the afternoon was well advanced. Heavily muffled, they slipped through frozen courtyards, and there was no one to see as they gained the solarium and stealthily climbed the back stairs. They crept up the narrow steps on silent feet, their swords drawn and ready in their hands. Give me Tristan, Andred clamored silently to his Gods, give him to me now!

At the top of the stairs was a small platform, and ahead of them a thick curtain reaching from ceiling to floor. The space they stepped into was cramped, fusty, and dark and they huddled together, craning for every sound. At first they could hear nothing but their own stifled breath and the beating of their hearts. Awkward as ever and hampered by his cloak, Mark had stumbled audibly on the top step and Andred was sure they would be discovered at once. But as their pulses slowed and their eyes adjusted to the gloom, he knew that the couple in the solarium had heard nothing at all.

For the two speakers were alive in a world of their own. The muffled voices reaching them in their gloomy hide were so interwoven with each other that nothing else could exist. The velvet murmurs and honeyed tones betrayed a couple in closest contact, drowsing head to head.

They're making love! Gods be thanked, caught in the act! Andred's venom peaked. I have you now, Tristan, you are in my hand. He sneaked a look at Mark. The King's eyes were bulging with concentration as he tried to make sense of the tender, fugitive sounds from within. Andred grinned to himself. The trap was laid, the prey deep in its toils. His finger was on the spring.

The lovers' words came faintly to their ears.

"—King in danger now—"

They heard Tristan laugh. "What's a King when a man holds the Queen?"

Then Isolde's voice, husky with love and the weight of satisfied desire. "And a queen has her knights."

"How so, lady?"

"The arrow finds the target, the hunter strikes down the stag—"

Tristan chuckled softly. "And the knight takes the King?"

What?

In the darkness behind the hanging, Mark's brain burst. They were lovers, they were plotting against him, just as Andred said. With this talk of arrows and killing, they were going to murder him, and make Isolde Queen. And here was his faithless wife wallowing in her treachery, vaunting her adultery with Tristan, with any of his knights she pleased—

"Traitors!"

Howling, Mark threw back the curtain and burst into the room. Hastily Andred leaped after him, quite unprepared. The wide gallery stretched away before them, flat as a field. Tucked into a side alcove midway down, Isolde and Tristan sat together at a table, their heads as close as those of lovebirds in their roost.

Not entwined in the act of love, Andred saw to his rage. What then?

The couple were poring over a black and white board. On the silver and ebony squares, pawns, knights, kings, and queens pranced to and fro, carved in crystal and jet. As he watched, Isolde's hand reached out and took Tristan's king. Gods' body, blood and bones, they were playing chess!

But Mark's jealous eyes saw what Andred did not, the light from another world in Isolde's smile. The same primordial pain stirred in his heart as when he first knew that Tristan was a fighter of great prowess. He would never win praise and honor like Tristan by deeds of renown. And now it came to him like a scream of rage that he would never enjoy that rapt love in a woman's gaze. Men like him commanded mirth, not adoration, and were laughed at wherever they went. He caught a tender chuckle. As these two were laughing now!

Isolde heard the sound of booted feet and raised her head. Over Tristan's shoulder she caught a dark, hurtling figure, sword upraised.

"Tristan!" she screamed.

"Lady—"

Behind the first cloaked attacker came another, but Tristan was in motion before she knew. Driven by blind instinct, Tristan leapt to his feet and turned on the intruders without thought. One furious blow sent the first flying to the floor, dropping his sword as Tristan struck him again. With the speed of a cat, Tristan snatched up the weapon and faced the second, disarming him, too. The first scrambled to his feet as Tristan, flaming with rage, set about his assailants with swinging blows. Lost in a fighting frenzy, he chased after the hooded figures down the hall, landing blow after blow on their retreating backs. At the top of the stairs he paused for breath and allowed the fleeing pair to get away.

"So!"

Tristan turned back toward Isolde in triumph, breathing heavily. Shaken, she watched the fighting fury leave him as he came to himself again. "Cowards!" he said thickly. "Did you see how they screamed and ran? I never heard such a noise in my life."

She was on her feet, stabbing him with her eyes. She threw back her head, her mouth twisted with anger and distress. "Gods above, Tristan, what have you done?"

His anger ebbed away like the tide. "What do you mean?"

"Do you know who they were?" He had never seen her look so deathly pale. "It was the King and Andred."

He threw down Mark's sword as if it stung his hand. "I attacked the King?"

Her face, her eyes, her lips were gray and bloodless now. "You beat him like a schoolboy. He will never forget the shame." She wrung her hands, striding up and down. "And it's treason. You tried to kill the King."

"Not so!" he cried angrily. "If I'd wanted to kill him, he'd be dead!"

She shook her head. "He'll never think that. He'll want you dead now."

"My armor." He bunched his shoulders and turned toward the door. "I must go and get ready to fight."

She wanted to scream. "Tristan, think! He'll never agree to single combat with you! He'll send a troop of men to take you by force. They're probably on their way now!"

He stared at her stupidly. "But a knight may not ambush another knight—"

"Mark doesn't care about the rules of chivalry!" she shrilled. "He thinks only of himself." She ran at him and struck him with her fist. "You must go!"

"Go?" He looked at her like a child. "Go where?"

Goddess, Mother, help me! "Mark is planning your death, I know it! You have to get away!"

He smiled and shook his head. "I will not flee."

"If you don't, you'll be dead by tonight!"

He looked at her. "I must take that chance," he said simply.

It was no use. Isolde took a breath. "Sir Tristan," she said, mastering her rage. "What am I to you?"

He gave a look of infinite sweetness. "You're my lady, my love, and my Queen."

"Then as your Queen, I order you to go."

He gasped and the blood left his face. "What?"

"Obey my command!" She could not look at him. "Leave Castle Dore this instant, and do not return."

There was a wind from Avalon and the sun shivered and fled. "If I must go, come with me!" he cried. "Let me take you away!"

Tears stood in her eyes. She shook her head. "I cannot. Go!"

Overhead the noonday sky grew black. Tristan stood for a second, like a man of stone. Then with a look of burning reproach, he caught up his cloak and sword, knelt to kiss her hand, and strode out of the hall.

She stood and watched the broad frame receding and his head disappearing down the stairs. One thought alone haunted her ravaged mind. *I have lost my knight. I have lost the only true love in the world.*

chapter
48

The love star was shining through the falling snow. From her window in the Queen's House, Isolde looked out over the courtyard and watched the busy lanterns going to and fro. Mark was summoning his lords to a council, that was plain. She had sent Brangwain to see what she could learn. But she had no idea what else to do.

Tristan—

She gasped with pain. Since he left, leaping down the stairs from the solarium without looking back, not a second had passed without the thought beating through her brain, *My love, where will you go?* She had no idea where he was. Fool, triple times fool! Why hadn't she thought to ask?

And to flee in weather like this—hopelessly she cursed each drifting flake of snow. *Where are you now, Tristan? Where will you lay your head?*

Her eyes were weary from staring out into the night. But at least she had done the right thing to send him away. Minutes after he had melted into the dusk, the tramping of booted feet had announced the arrival of the guard.

"King's orders, my lady," the captain had muttered, refusing to meet her eye. "Sir Tristan here?"

The men-at-arms had gone away after a cursory search but now she knew that Mark's malice was aroused and ready to strike.

And what next?

She turned away from the window, sick with despair. Any vestige of respect she had felt for Mark had vanished when she recognized the hooded figure as he screamed and ran away. Mark's humiliation was complete, and he would never forgive her or Tristan. He would move against her now and try to prove treachery, like a scorpion striking first. A wiser man would try to cover his shame. But Mark, once wounded, would not rest till he had discharged his venom in return.

And when he turns on you, chimed her inner voice, *how will you reply?*

The answer came at once, *With a pure heart.*

I have not betrayed you, Mark, she would tell him with her head held high, *because you and I are not man and wife. We are not married in body, heart, or mind. You love your Lady Elva and I love Tristan, and I never loved you and I never came into your bed.*

And as for treason, Tristan and I never intended you any harm.

Her eyes were burning with cold, watching the white flakes drifting to and fro. More calmly now she threaded the future through her mind. First she must face up to Mark, and get rid of this false charge of treason against Tristan and herself. Then she would ask Sir Nabon and the lords to reconcile Mark with Tristan and put their quarrel to rest. Sooner or later Tristan would want to come back, and Mark was still his uncle and his King. After that, her mother wanted her in Ireland and there was probably no better time to go. Not only for herself, she reflected grimly, but for the Queen and the kingdom, too. She knew from before that the whole of the Western Isle could suffer when the Queen was madly in love and had a new knight.

And then?

Should she bid farewell to Tristan, should they part? When she saw him again, should they agree never to love again, to be strangers evermore? The thought was like dancing on needles, but she could not stop. As long as he was her chosen one, he was breaking his oath to Mark. He had lost his mother and father—was it fair of her to come between him and his uncle, his only surviving kin?

When she saw him again—but what made her think she would? He could be gone forever, she might never see him alive at all after this. What if he'd taken to the forest and lost his way in the snow? Deep in the heart of the wood lay a world beyond greenways and tracks, and many men ventured there for safety, never to return. Or else there were outlaws in plenty on the roads, rogue knights and masterless men preying on travelers—what if they ambushed him? For all his strength, he could have died in a ditch with a dagger in his back—

Died—dead, my love?

She was gasping with fear. She forced herself to breathe. *Think! think! No tears, no fears—think and act—*

In the courtyard below a lean, muffled figure was pressing toward the Queen's House, head down through the snow. Moments later Brangwain came through the door, shaking off her cloak and brushing the melting snowflakes from her hair.

"As you thought, lady." The maid came forward with a frozen nod. "The King is in council now with all his lords."

"Well, there's comfort in that." Isolde reached for a smile. "They are all decent men. They will know that a game of chess is not a death plot against the King!"

"If he listens to them, lady."

Isolde felt a renewed chill. "What do you mean?"

The maid's sallow face was pinched with fear and cold. "There was a guard of men outside the council chamber, standing by."

"What?"

Anger convulsed Isolde and she bunched her fists. "This is Andred's doing! I must speak to the King."

Brangwain could hardly speak. "Lady, they told me the order came from the King himself. 'Wait till the end of the council, then go for the Queen.'"

Isolde stared, bewildered. "What for?"

"To take you to prison, lady—that's what they said."

THE COUNCIL CHAMBER was as cold as death. The wind sighed in the chimney and snow crystals frosted every pane of glass. There had been no time to light a decent fire, and the maid was still kneeling by the hearth, struggling with the smoldering wood. Sir Nabon rubbed his hands fiercely and resisted the impulse to blow on his fingernails.

"Gods above, sire," he said irritably, "why are we here?"

Mark's hollow chest puffed up like that of a pigeon in fright. "To try the Queen," he said loudly, "in the absence of Sir Tristan."

"To try the Queen?"

What pernicious nonsense was this? Nabon threw a disbelieving glance around the bleak, unprepared chamber, the dusty council board, and the awkward faces of his fellow lords.

"This is no court of trial," he said firmly. "Your Majesty has summoned your council, and we are ready to advise. Anything else will require the due process of law."

"Yes, indeed."

Seated opposite, the venerable Sir Wisbeck nodded his white head. But bobbing at Wisbeck's elbow, Sir Quirian was not so ready to give up his part in the excitement of the day. The short, self-important body swelled eagerly as he spoke.

"But our first duty is to the King, my lords. And His Majesty has grave concerns that we should deal with now."

"Yes!" cried Mark. He stared around the table, red-eyed. He had to teach his rogue wife a lesson, they must see that. "There's treason here, Andred and I overheard it, between Tristan and the Queen. And he tried to kill me! What more proof of treachery d'you want than that?"

"None, sire," murmured Andred from his place at Mark's right hand. Beneath his cloak he rolled his sore shoulders around, and his secret heart danced. Every blow he had taken was worth it to bring Tristan down.

Isolde, too!

Andred's triumph was complete. Isolde had committed the unspeakable sin of offending Mark's pride. Nothing would placate the King now but to see her disgraced. Tristan was already outlawed and on the run. Isolde would be accused to the lords and punished, by fire or the sword, then Mark must give him permission to hunt Tristan down.

Gods and Great Ones, thanks—

He was dimly aware that Sir Nabon was still droning on.

"These are grave charges, sire. We would all be sorry to think so ill of the Queen. And Sir Tristan is your nephew and an honored knight."

"Yes, sire." Wisbeck wagged a warning finger. "And as long as your Queen is childless, he's your principal heir. We cannot move against either of them without proof."

Andred smiled pleasantly at him, and made a vow. *When I am King, old fool, you will kiss iron and swallow my sword.*

"Proof?" Mark's eyes bulged. "I've given you the proof!" *Fools!* cried his struggling self, why didn't they understand? "Andred and I saw them plotting in the solarium, heads together, as close as bare legs in a bed! They were bandying insults, joking about kings and queens—"

"Words, sire, words!" Nabon cried heartily. "To hold a trial, there has to be more than this. Your Majesty will want to be just and fair above all. I propose a committee of barons to look into it."

A committee that would sit on this arrant nonsense till it all petered out, he did not say. But he could see from the faces around the table that they agreed.

All except one.

Dominian leaned forward, glowering at Nabon. "Look into what?" he demanded. "The Queen has already compromised herself with Sir Tristan. And the King's wife must be above reproach."

Mark looked at him, impressed. "That's right!"

"But woman is born to sin." Dominian pierced Nabon with his black, burning gaze, and stared into the darkness beyond the walls. "It is the sin of Eve," he said somberly.

"What, adultery?" Mark gave a start. Surely he remembered the story better than that? Adam was made first, then Eve came out of his rib—was there another sinner in God's garden, then? An adulterous young nephew, perhaps—a wandering knight?

"Treason!" Dominian intoned. "Treachery was Eve's sin and the downfall of man."

"Right again, Father!" Mark's face sharpened into an aggrieved self-righteousness. "The woman betrayed both God and her rightful Lord. Just like my Queen!"

Gods give me patience! Nabon took a breath. "But none of this is treason to the kingdom, sire. Nor to Your Majesty."

"Hear this, then!" Mark pounded the table with his fist. "Tristan fled from the solarium as soon as he could, then he ran to the stables and rode out like a devil from hell. Would an innocent man do that?"

Nabon sighed. "Sire, in your rage, you could have taken his life! Any man in reason may fear the wrath of a king and take flight to save himself."

Mark's foolish face flushed. "I may be King, but I'm a man of honor, too! He had no need to fear me."

"Indeed, sire, we know that," put in Quirian pompously. "You would have called him to account in single combat, as a knight should."

"Yes, exactly!" cried a preening Mark, unaware of the disbelief surrounding him now. "Single combat—knight to knight—I'd have faced him in the field. That's why the coward has run away!"

"And we still have to deal with the indiscretion of the Queen," Quirian huffed on. "She has undoubtedly compromised the dignity and safety of the throne. She should never have received Sir Tristan alone. Every man must be sure that his offspring are his alone—and still more a King! A Queen must be pure, and seen to be pure." He smirked. "Cornwall does not want a cuckoo in the royal nest."

"Within there!" None of them was prepared for the cry of the guards. "The Queen, my lords, the Queen!" The great double doors gaped and Isolde swept in.

Mark's mouth fell open in shock. "What?"

So, my lords? And my husband? What's afoot?

Isolde could see the surprise and consternation on every face. *Good, good!* She suppressed a savage smile. *It looks as if I got here just in time.*

"Good morning, sire."

She made her curtsy to Mark as brisk as politeness allowed, smiling down his livid glare. "And good day to you, my lords. You are dealing with matters concerning me, I think. I have come to assist your deliberations in any way I can."

No one moved. A paralyzed silence fell.

"Speak, one of you!" cried Mark, writhing madly on his throne. What was wrong with them all? This was the woman who had betrayed him, the traitor in their midst! Yet still there was a welcome for Isolde on every face. Surely they could see the wretched creature had no place here? How would he get them to condemn her now?

"By your leave, sire."

Dominian rose to his feet and nodded hotly to Isolde. "This is a Christian land, my lady, ruled by a Christian King. Cornwall keeps the rule of God under King Arthur, a Christian High King, too. In such a land, women may not follow their own will. Even queens must obey rules of purity, as you have not."

Isolde looked him up and down. Why had she ever tried to respect this man? At the wedding, he was wreathed in incense, but today he stank of old woollen nether garments and moldy cheese. *Your rules, priest, are for those who follow your faith. But your One way, One truth, One life is too narrow for me.* She laughed. "Who says so, sir?"

He felt her disdain and flushed. "Your lord and King!"

Mark jerked into action, furiously wagging his head. "By God, yes!" He waved at Dominian. "On, on!"

Dominian came forward with new energy. "Madam, His Majesty plans to set up a commission to investigate this."

A commission? Isolde made her voice sound strong. "On what grounds?"

"Grounds, my lady?" Andred joined the attack. "The King needs no grounds, he may do as he wants. You have given him good reason to question your purity. You live alone—"

Isolde waved a hand. "Alone with fifty or a hundred maidservants and men!"

"Who do not guard the freeways to your bed," Andred pushed on. "You sleep in a private chamber above the Queen's garden, where any lusty knight could climb the wall—"

"Enough," cried Isolde, reddening with rage. "I will not have my life picked over like this!"

"Forgive us indeed, Your Majesty."

It was Sir Nabon, rebuking Andred with a furious stare. "There's no need for such talk," he said angrily. "It was the question of treason that brought us here."

"Treason, my lords? Let me answer that." She paused and felt her power flowing through her veins. "The Island of the West was blessed by the Old Ones before Cornwall was born. When my mother dies, I will be its Queen. Why should I want your kingdom or plot against your King?"

"Why, lady?" Dominian broke in. "There's no answer to wickedness. Evil is its own God."

Isolde laughed. "Not in our worship, sir," she said scornfully. "Those who follow the Mother put their trust in faith and love." She raised her hand, making her voice ring out round the room. "On the soul of your God and mine, I never intended evil to the King!"

A long silence fell as she looked round the room. One by one the lords nodded and she smelled triumph—she could disregard Mark sulking on his throne. He would have to follow whatever his council agreed. She took a deep breath of delight. She had won!

The next moment she met Andred's hard black eyes. *You are mine, madam,* said his insolent stare. *Your paramour may have slipped through my hands, but the dearest thing he loves is still in my power. Prepare yourself, then. I mean to hurt and destroy.*

Behind her back, she made the sign against the Evil Eye. "Sir Andred—" she began boldly.

"Never intended any evil, you say?"

Andred favored her with a long, silky smile. "Then you can have no objection to the King's demand. This commission will clear your name and establish the truth." He turned back to the King. "Sire, give us permission to proceed and build up the case."

Build up the case—

Isolde heard a dark wind from afar.

There is no proof, but Andred will make it up. He will bribe my servants to say Tristan came to my bed—that they heard us plotting and saw us embracing, which no man ever did—

With a sudden bleak insight, she saw the whole game.

And there will be letters, too, that we never wrote. Letters from Tristan, promising to kill Mark. Replies from me promising to make Tristan King. Then the charge against me will be treason for sure, not simple suspicion as it is now.

Her heart almost burst in her breast.

No remedy but to strike first!

"Enough of your commission!" She turned on Mark. "I claim the right to clear my name!"

"Clear your name?" Andred sneered. "Madam, how?"

"Listen and learn!" she blazed. "And hold your tongue, Sir Andred, when your Queen speaks."

A hush fell on the room. She could see Mark frozen with fear in his seat, and it gave her strength. "I demand the right of ordeal!" She stared around at the lords, daring them to refuse. "Some of you will have seen it. You all know what it is."

Sir Nabon held his head and groaned aloud. "Madam, you don't know what you ask! This is not for a Queen—"

"Sir Nabon, a queen is the same as a goose girl before the law!" she said feverishly. "And I know the ordeals—earth, water, fire."

Nabon leaned forward and appealed to Mark. "You cannot permit this, sire!"

A look of childish cunning came over Mark's face. "What can't I permit?"

Nabon could have struck him. "The risk to the Queen!" he cried. "Sire, you know what this means!"

"Yes!" cried Mark in a fit. "Seven times through the fire, seven days in the earth, or seven times seventy underwater without air."

"I choose the ordeal by water!" Isolde threw back. "I demand it as my right!"

At last! Mark leapt to his feet in delight. The arrogant witch had played into his hand.

"Then you shall have it, madam!" he shouted. "In seven days' time! Till then, you'll be kept in the Queen's House under arrest."

He stalked to the door and turned back, his dull eyes alight. "You're not in Ireland now. Ask your Great Mother to save you from the Pool of Tears—for no man or woman has come out of it alive!"

chapter 49

Seven days from today, madam—at the Pool of Tears!"

Threatening and cursing, Mark stormed out of the council chamber, followed hurriedly by his lords.

In the courtyard outside, a lean, hooded form curtsied to the ground as the King swept past. She kept her head bowed too as the Queen was taken away, tall as she was, still dwarfed by the men-at-arms. Only when the courtyard was clear did Brangwain raise her head. In a week, the Queen would be thrown into the Pool of Tears to drown. Tristan could save her, if she could track him down. But where would she find him? Where would he have gone?

Anywhere! her anxious heart replied. Then the stubborn strain of the Welshlands came into play. No man disappears into thin air, least of all a big fellow like him. He loves my lady like his life. He'd never run away and leave her, he can't be far.

Brangwain sighed. Where would Tristan have gone? He fled the solarium only a step or two ahead of the guard. He'd need food and shelter and somewhere to take cover if the King went after him with his men-at-arms. So where? Not to the sea to take ship—that would carry him too far away from all he held dear. Nor would he find shelter on the shore—the beaches were too barren for a man to hide, and it would be all too easy to be trapped in a cave.

Think, now! she scolded herself feverishly. Where would he go?

It came to her like the dawn rising through the trees.

Where but the woodland?

Where else would a hunter hide?

GODDESS, MOTHER, PRAISE and blessings on your name!

The forester stepped out of his hut, lifted his face to the nip of the frosty air, and gave humble thanks. You're a fool, man, he grumbled cheerfully to himself as he set off with his dog at his heels. You should be praying for the Great Mother to take this away. All the other forest-dwellers hated the snow, cursing the hard weather that bound up the earth like stone, freezing the water and starving them of their food.

But he loved the mornings when he woke to find the well-worn paths and familiar scenes all white and shining, an enchanted land. He marveled at the way the Mother's hand lovingly redrew every branch of every tree, burnishing every twig, gilding each blade of grass. The woodland became to him then like the Great Hall of the Gods, every chamber opening onto other wide chambers of glittering white, all roofed with a stark tracery of dark branches, hung at night with stars.

His dog plunged off into the snow, yelping with glee. For a moment he yearned for four legs too, to romp through the forest like that. The cold pinched his face like a lover's caress, and he dragged it into his lungs with a primal need. Wondering, he watched the dawn breaking through the trees, the fine fingers of light striking fire from the ice and snow. Every mote in the air sparkled as it danced around his head. Winter killed many, he knew. But on mornings like this, he never felt more alive.

If only these early winter snows were not so short! Already he was lamenting the coming loss of this white kingdom, his wonderland. He felt the frost biting his ears and caught himself up with a laugh. Well and good for him to abide the groaning of his belly, but he couldn't inflict that on a weeping wife and a brood of bleating bairns. It was one of the things that had kept him single all these years. But a man needed a wife and children all the same.

Years afterward he thought that if he'd been a father then, he would have noticed the child. Or perhaps he'd have seen the boy if he hadn't been light-headed with hunger, floating on the fumes from his empty belly, dreaming his way through the trees. He only knew that when he passed the cloven oak, there was no one there. At the crossroads beyond, he whistled to his dog—now where had old Nipper gone?

"Good dawning to you, sir."

He turned with a start. At the side of the track behind him stood a child in woodland green. His pale, half-starved face was luminous with cold and his threadbare cloak hung off his skinny form. The thin boyish body was at odds with the child's wizened face, but many children of the forest grew old before their time. This one had a rabbit dangling from his hand. At least the family that had sent him out foraging would eat tonight. All well and good, the forester thought, till he met the child's staring eyes.

"Who are you, lad?" he said roughly, to cover his fear. "What's your name?"

"Emrys, sir."

His voice was as old-young as his little wrinkled face. Its high tones held the sound of the cataract on the black mountain and the upraised sea beating against the shore.

"Emrys," said the forester, to gain time. "One of the names of old Merlin, was it, in days gone by?"

"Merlin Emrys the Bard?" The child gave a strange, sweet smile. "It was and is."

"You're from the Welshlands, then?"

"Once." The child's eyes spun like cartwheels in his head. "Long ago."

The forester felt a sudden urge to be gone. "Well, I'll leave you, young sir."

The boy took no notice. "Have you seen a knight in the wood?"

The forester laughed in surprise. "Plenty, lad. Why d'you ask?"

A piteous eagerness flooded the scrawny face. "Tell me!"

"Why, the King hunts every day with his knights—"

"No, no!" cried the child tetchily, like an angry old man. "A Cornish knight. Here in the forest in the last few days, traveling on his own."

"What like?"

"Big-built, well-favored, tall and broad. But he moves like a hunter, and he's gentle with man and beast."

The forester felt an urge to know such a man. "No," he said with a curious sense of regret, "not a sign."

The child cried out sharply, as if he were in pain. "Not so much as a footprint in the snow?"

"None," the forester answered.

He was longing to say yes, and slowly it came to him that the child knew that. But how? Could he read his thoughts? A deep unease gripped him. Gods above, was he even a child? Who could say in the name of the Great Ones how old the boy was?

Suddenly the forester did not want to meet the staring gaze, the huge eyes containing all the colors of the world. Yet he could not avoid the scenes that unfolded there. He saw a pit beneath the earth and two dragons fighting, the red against the white. He saw a bloody battle raging till all the men of one kin lay in a valley, bleeding their hearts away, while a bard on the hillside above ran mad with grief. He saw a red dragon rampaging on a snowy field and blue-black dragons consuming their own kin. He saw more than he could think about for the rest of his life. And all this in a skinny young urchin's eyes?

"So you know the tales of Pendragon and their kin?" the child said softly. The forester flushed. Gods above, the boy was hearing his thoughts again.

The child's mood turned. "But Ronan, Ronan, you did not see the knight!" He struck his head. "He is lost, then. Grief upon me!" he cried. "Grief upon all of us!"

The forester gasped. How did the boy know his name?

"Never fear." The little ancient face stared into his. "You're a good man and good things will come to you."

"Be off with you!" he cried roughly, crossing his fingers against the Evil Eye.

A laugh like an old man's cackle leaked from the child's thin lips. "Gone already," he crowed, floating away.

Or that's how it seemed, when the forester pondered it afterward. All he saw was a sudden movement of the air, a flurry of snow, and the boy was gone. Like all the children of the forest, he knew how to steal away. But if he was truly one of them, why would he leave his rabbit at the forester's feet?

Goddess, Mother, thanks!

Tears started to the forester's eyes, and his head swam. He had had no idea how near to starving he was. Suddenly he knew that if he had not met the boy, he would never have gotten back to his hut tonight. Already he could taste the roasted rabbit, smell the herbs. Quick, then, he told himself, get home and eat! It took awhile to find his dog, cowering at a distance, and he knew it had witnessed something he could not see. But at last he coaxed it home and rewarded it with the parts of the rabbit that only dogs will eat.

At dusk he was by his fire, drowsing and replete, warm from the inside out, the best feeling in the world. Safe now in the faithful arms of his old wooden chair, he scoffed at himself for his starved fantasies.

Dragons and battles indeed! Why had he taken any notice of the boy? Then something came to him that banished sleep. Where the child had stood, there were no marks in the snow. The boy had come and gone without setting foot to earth. He had met a creature without being, without body at all—one of the Old Ones, the fathers of All-Being, the Lords of Light.

But who would believe him? He knew at once he could never tell a soul, not even the wife he dreamed of, the cheery, full-bosomed partner of his bed and board. If he did, he'd have to tell her what else he saw, the glories, the trumpets, the banners in the wind. And the big knight riding off in the fading light and the lady crying out and tearing her hair. . . .

He came to with a start. Drums and trumpets, and lovers in the mist? No, it was all too much. Men like him tended their traps and kept their homesteads tidy till they found a nice wife. They went to market on Wednesdays to look for a plump jolly bride, and winter or no, he'd go this very week. But no more visions, no more fetches after this! Nothing but his daily life and its daily deeds.

Which is why, when the court lady came by, asking for the knight, he said nothing of what he'd seen. He heard the accent of the Welshlands in her anxious voice, and wondered in passing if she and the child were kin, but he did not tell her that there was another on the same trail. He saw her grief and fear as she talked of her mistress, and would have helped her if he could. But already he had put the strange child out of his mind, and as soon as the lady left, forgot her, too.

Market day, now! That was the thing. When the farmers' wives came to market to sell their eggs, they brought their daughters, too. Somewhere, he knew, there was a plump chicken for his pot.

Till Wednesday, then . . . Dozing by his fire, he allowed himself to dream.

MEANWHILE THE HUNT went on. Mark led one troop of armed men into the forest and Andred another, searching to its very heart. All they learned was that an old man on a white mule had left the forest by one path, and a lady from the court had ridden away by another. None of them ever found Tristan, or knew where he went.

Only the seagulls flying over the rocky shore saw the tall, broad-shouldered figure coming down the cliff path. He made quite a stir as he rode through the village on the bay, catching all eyes. Even the busiest women stuck their heads out of their windows to take note of the stranger with the fine armor and handsome, ravaged face.

By the time he rode down to the harbor, half the village was watching him. They saw him dismount by a ship, talk to the captain, and lead his horse aboard. The village idlers hung about till the boat hoisted sail and headed into the wind. Some were still following its course far out to sea when night came down and the ship was lost to sight. With the lack of excitement in places as small as this, most regretted that the big knight had not stayed. But none missed him as badly as Isolde when Brangwain returned from the forest with the news that Tristan was lost and nowhere to be found.

chapter 50

No trace of him? You couldn't find him at all?"

"No, lady." Brangwain could feel the tears of weakness rising to her eyes. She was very tired. "I told you—" Her voice trailed off.

"Thank you, Brangwain."

Isolde took a pace away. Why couldn't she accept what Brangwain said? The maid had described in detail how she had searched the forest, asking everywhere. But Tristan was not there. Her knight had vanished as if he had never been.

She shook her head in despair. Seven days and nights alone, under guard in the Queen's House, must have softened her wits. What had she been hoping for? She drew a breath. *Only to know that my love has come to no harm.*

Well, Brangwain had answered that. Tristan had gone to earth as surely as a fox. And tomorrow at dawn Mark would come to take her to the Pool of Tears. So be it. There was no more time.

She could not bear to see the dread and disappointment in her maid's loyal eyes. She reached out and pressed her hand. "Oh, Brangwain—you're so good."

"It wasn't goodness, lady." The maid clenched her teeth. "I just don't want you to die."

"I won't die, Brangwain." Isolde smiled. "You know I can stay under water for as long as I like."

Brangwain nodded. It was true. Water had been a second mother to Isolde all her life. *Look at me, Brangwain!* A lithe, brown, laughing child bobbed up from her pool of memories and dived down again with a merry splash. She drew a ragged breath. "But the shame, lady! Being led out before all the people—I thought I could spare you from that."

Isolde's chin set. "No shame, Brangwain, when they see I'm innocent. Now, help me to prepare."

Dawn broke like thunder, hurling angry red flames up in the sky. When they came, she was ready for them, poised and calm. She wore her lightest shift beneath her overgown, and Brangwain had covered her in grease to ward off the cold. For the rest, she would trust to her skill and pray to the Gods. *Embrace your fate*, the Lady had said. She was ready for the water's cold kiss now that Tristan was gone.

From the stable yard, a distant clatter of hooves heralded Mark and his men. She stood in her window watching the love star fade.

Tristan, Tristan, when this is over, I shall search for you throughout the world.

And when I find you, we shall never part.

She took a last look round the chamber. "Come, Brangwain."

The cold in the courtyard bit her to the bone. Sharp gusts of wind flurried the snow on the ground. The cobbles, the mullions of the windows, every stone of the walls, were all outlined in thick tracings of hoarfrost and her breath was turning to ice in front of her face. For the first time she felt the sharp tooth of fear. *I chose the wrong ordeal. It's the worst time of the year.*

A lengthy procession was filing into the courtyard below. At its head rode Mark, Andred, and Dominian, the sun's red rays streaking their faces with blood. Behind them came Mark's knights, with a troop of men-at-arms riding in the rear. Holding himself aloof, Sir Nabon was looking as grim as ever in his life. From their set faces, Sir Wisbeck and most of the other lords shared his hatred of this, too. Isolde's spirits lifted. When this was over, she would have many new friends.

"This way, lady."

It was the burly captain of the guard. She mounted her horse and took her place in the procession with Brangwain at her side.

The way led down from Castle Dore, out of the town, and along the clifftop below. All the townspeople had turned out to line the road, men, women, and children buzzing with anger and disbelief. Mark and his men rode into a wall of silence, broken by hostile glares. Behind them, the muttered protests swelled and grew.

"What's all this about?" cried one hardy soul.

"What's she done?" "Nothing!" came from several throats.

"The King's mad!" shouted the bravest of all.

Mark colored, then wagged his finger at Andred. "Isolde won't go through with this, you'll see!" he ground out. "She'll confess and beg my forgiveness, then they'll know I was right!"

Riding behind the knights, Isolde saw sympathy on all sides. Many were weeping openly, and some could not help crowding into her path to touch her stirrup in blessing or kiss her hand.

"Bless you, lady!" sobbed a young mother, rocking her child in her arms. "May the Mother bring you safely through your ordeal!"

Her husband beside her shook a massive fist. "What's the King doing?"

"Listening to the Christians!" came an ironic cry.

A number of angry voices took up the refrain. "He's hag-ridden by his priests!"

At the head of the train, Dominian picked up the hubbub with a frozen smile. *Saepe expugnaverunt, Domine,* they have often fought against me, Lord, as I do thy work—but behold, how I triumph in the end!

The procession wound down through the town and set out along the cliff. A dense throng followed every step of the way, old and young, stray children and barking dogs. Before long they reached the rocky footpath leading down to the pool. The captain of the guard came forward to help her dismount.

The people surged forward, surrounding her, reaching out to touch her gown.

"Oh, my lady, it's cruel!" cried a woman in the crowd. Frightened by the commotion, a child began to cry. Turning to comfort her, Isolde did not see the beggar till she felt the blow. She only heard Brangwain's cry of horror and the shocked gasps of the crowd before a heavy body lurched into her and knocked her off her feet.

"Lady, lady, look out!" shouted Brangwain.

Goddess, Mother!

She cried out in fear. The next moment she felt herself caught up and cradled in a pair of sinewy arms.

"He's a leper, lady," she heard Brangwain scream. "Get away from him, get away!"

He smelled of blood and pus and rotting flesh. The arms holding her and the stumps of his hands were bound in bloodstained cloths, and his feet were shod in bloody rags. He wore the badge of leprosy on his breast and his beggar's gown was fouled beyond repair. Beneath his heavy cowl, Isolde saw a tangle of shaggy hair and a swath of bandages, and recoiled. Lepers lost their mouths and noses first of all. She could not bear to see what remained of his face.

"Get off, you vile wretch!"

"Put her down! Leave the Queen alone!"

With blows and curses, the men-at-arms came swarming to her aid. The crippled figure hastily set her on her feet and reeled back cringing, holding his stumps over his head to defend himself. Now she could see what had once been a noble physique in the stooping frame. Her heart stirred. The leper must have been a fine warrior once, perhaps even a knight, before age and disease had brought him to this.

"Leave him!" she commanded. "Don't beat a poor old man!"

Shamefaced, the guard pulled back. The leper hobbled off, his head buried between his hands, mumbling prayers for mercy between groans of pain.

"Gods above, lady!" It was Brangwain, fighting her way through the crowd.

Isolde smiled wanly and struggled to collect herself. "No harm done."

And perhaps some good?

Slowly an idea took shape in her brain. The ordeal to come required a solemn oath and there was no avoiding the interrogation ahead. She could swear innocence of treason, but what of her love for Tristan? Could this beggar stumbling against her in the crowd offer a way of escape? Was he perhaps even sent to her for this? Her frozen heart warmed. *Goddess, Mother, thanks!*

The clifftop stretched ahead, with the sea roaring below. A howling wind whipped over the iron-gray waves, and chased a running tide back out to sea. The path led down a steep incline, and every stone beneath her feet was slippery with ice. Already the cold was piercing her to the core. And she had volunteered to swim in weather like this? *And stay under water for seventy times seven besides—Goddess, Mother, help me, it will be hard.*

"Here, sire!" came a shout from up ahead. "The Pool of Tears."

The procession wound around a ragged bluff and drew to a halt.

Isolde stepped forward and felt a cold sheen of sweat. She could see at once how the place got its name.

At the bottom of the cliff, many feet below, lay a deep black pool surrounded by jagged rocks. It lay as still as a sheet of glass, though beneath the unruffled surface it must have been fed by the sea. But there was no bottom to be seen, and the sides were sheer. It looked like nothing so much as a well, a dark shaft to the world beneath.

She was suddenly sick with fear. If she managed to dive in without striking her head on the side, how would they ever get her out again? Mark's taunt came back to her with renewed force. *No man or woman had ever come out of there alive.* She closed her eyes. *Yes indeed, it is a place of tears.*

The King and his knights arranged themselves round the pool, and Mark motioned Dominian to speak. The priest stepped forward and threw up his short arms.

"God of justice," he declaimed, "take heed of this woman today! We have brought her here to face Your eternal tribunal where all human souls meet their doom. Vengeance is Thine, O Lord. We commit her to Thy hands!"

And remember, King of Kings, he intoned silently, *that this pagan Queen is the enemy of our faith. God, in your mercy, drown her like a rat!*

"In the name of the Lord, amen!"

"So, lady," Mark began. He was enjoying this. "You are here to meet your ordeal, and all alone. Did you know that the traitor Tristan, your paramour, has taken ship and fled?"

"Fled?" she muttered through cold lips.

"The whole village watched him sail away." A yelp of cruel delight escaped his lips. "He's gone, madam! Left you to your fate! Now what do you make of that?"

Isolde held herself very still.

Gone away, my love?

Far from Mark and Andred, safe from all of them?

"Thank you, sire." She dropped Mark a deep curtsy. "Your Majesty never gave me better news."

Mark nudged Andred in the ribs. "D'you hear that? I can tell she's ready to give in. At the last minute, I'll order the whole thing to stop. Then she'll be in my hands forever, she'll owe me her life." He slapped Andred triumphantly on the back. "I told you I had a plan!"

Gods above, is he mad? Stop the ordeal, when Isolde shows no sign of repenting or changing her mind? Andred fought down the urge to knock Mark himself into the pool. "Sire," he began, breathing deeply.

But Mark had moved on. "Where's the sergeant at arms?" he cried, waving his hand. "Do your office, man!"

"Here, sire!"

A tall figure clad in royal blue stepped forward with a scroll. "Hear me!" the sergeant proclaimed. "Any man or woman accused of a crime may claim the right of ordeal to clear their name. They must either pass seven times through the fire, or go under the earth and remain there for seven days, or take to the water and live seventy times seven without air."

Isolde listened calmly. *Seventy times seven*—she already knew what it was. Surviving the ordeal required those on the shore to count to seven times seventy with their hands on their hearts, listening for four hundred and more heartbeats, almost five. She could do it. She had swum under water often enough before and she was not frightened now. She stepped forward and threw off her outer clothes, willing herself not to shiver in her thin shift. No one must think she was afraid.

"Come, sir!" she cried. "I am ready. Hear my oath!"

The sergeant bowed. "We hear."

Isolde sent her voice ringing around the bay. "I swear by the Mother, by the Old Ones, and by the Shining Ones before them, by the three worlds and by the lives of all I love, that I never thought any treason to the King. I never intended it, planned it, dreamed it, or plotted it, and neither did Sir Tristan, on my mortal oath!"

Nevernevernever, agreed the echo off the rocks.

Dominian leaned forward fiercely. "You are not only accused of treason, lady. What of your other duty to the King?"

Isolde met his eye. "What of it, sir?"

Andred stepped in, speaking with insulting slowness, as to a child. "It is said that Sir Tristan has handled your person forbiddenly. We saw you with him, head to head and hand to hand. Swear that he never touched you in any way—"

"That is a foolish oath!" Isolde shouted. "Sir Tristan has handed me aboard ship and helped me mount my horse. And many men touch a woman, whether she wants it or not!" She laughed wildly, and gesticulated to the top of the cliff. "You all saw that beggar hold me in his arms! Does that make me false to the King? I will swear on my soul that no man born of woman has cheated the King of what is rightfully his. And I will go to my ordeal now to prove the truth!"

"Go then, madam!" bellowed Mark vengefully. When would she give up this charade? He'd show her that he was more than a match for all this. He waved to the guard. "Proceed!"

"My lady?"

Isolde turned. A man-at-arms was standing at her side, a bunch of short cords dangling from his hand.

Isolde's stomach seized. "What's this?"

The guard could not meet her eye. "You must be bound, as the ordeal requires."

"No!" Isolde found her voice. "The ordeal is to remain underwater for the count of seventy times seven. To do that, I need to swim!"

"No, lady."

Dominian stepped forward. If ever she had doubted the monk's malignant hate, she saw it now. "We Christians have refined this ordeal in the light of God's truth. To remain underwater and live, you must convince Almighty God that you are innocent. The ordeal tests innocence, not whether or not you can swim. Therefore you must be bound."

"Sire!"

Isolde turned frantically to Mark. "I chose this ordeal as I knew it in the Western Isle. With us, the accused have the use of their limbs."

Mark's face flamed. Good, now he had her, he was almost there! He thrust his chin forward aggressively. "And as I told you, madam, you're not in Ireland now!"

Isolde held out her hands. "Forbid this, Mark!" she shouted. "This is murder, not justice!"

"It's God's justice, sire!" Dominian hissed. "And your immortal soul. Which do you choose, this sinful woman or God?"

Mark stood in an agony of rage, twisting his awkward body to and fro. Don't weaken, man, he told himself, she'll have to give in now!

"If you kill me," Isolde spat, "it will be on your soul for all eternity!"

Mark flinched. "Bind her hands then, but not her feet!" He let loose a ridiculous laugh. "The judgment of Solomon, eh, Father?"

Andred nodded to the guard. "Get on!"

Already the man was fumbling at her hands. He secured one of her wrists, then the other, and tied them off. She could see from his face how he loathed what he had to do.

"Courage, soldier," she whispered. "The Mother will not blame you."

He glanced up with pitiful gratitude and backed away. Two burly men and their captain came forward now, their eyes downcast but their purpose plain. She laughed. She would not wait for their rough hands.

Tristan, be safe, be free! she cried in her soul. *And may the Mother bring me to you, wherever you are.*

Her heart sang.

I shall wait for you, love, where the three worlds meet. Where the silver trees blossom with gold and the stars sing in the high vaults of heaven, praising your name.

Wherever your road winds uphill, where your heart grows cold, where the wind scours your dear face, I shall be there. And when you come home at last to the Mother, nothing will part us evermore.

She threw back her head and her hair streamed in the wind. "Farewell," she shouted. "May the Mother forgive you all!" She ran to the edge of the pool and threw herself in.

A long moment of horror held the crowd transfixed. Then a babble of screams and curses filled the air.

Mark stood engulfed with terror. She hadn't, she couldn't have, surely not! God Almighty, she'd drown, and then everyone would hate him all his life!

And they'd—

And—

And—

The hideous list went on. Now the barons would have him even more in their power—even Elva would not forgive him for doing this—from now on, he'd never call his soul his own.

Mark clutched at his head in fury and began to moan. "Why didn't you stop me?" he wailed to Andred and Dominian. Andred would not meet his eye. But the little priest was incandescent with delight.

"Sire, this is God's plan!" Marveling, he peered down into the pool. For a second he saw the white shape plunging down, followed by its tail-stream of bright hair. Then the darkness swallowed her and she was gone. Glory be to You, O God! he crowed. Blessings on Your name!

High overhead, a raw scream pierced the air. "Hear me, King Mark! Hear me!"

An old crone teetered on the edge of the cliff, waving her withered arms in the air. Her poor and ragged garments fluttered in the wind, but there was a fearful grandeur to her sonorous chant. "In the name of the Mother I invoke the threefold curse. I call down on you the threefold death to come. May you die by water, earth, and fire for taking the Queen's life. May the Mother kill you by inches, as the Queen is dying now!"

Mark was trembling like a child. "Who is she?" he whispered hoarsely.

"And curses on you, too!" the old woman screeched. The withered finger pointed like an arrow, first at Andred, then at Dominian's heart. "The Dark Lord will punish you for what you have done! And remember, priest, even in the Christians' hell there's a special place for liars and men of deceit!"

"Who is she, sire?"

Dominian's face had turned a leprous white. "We know her all too well. She used to live by our settlement till we needed the land and had to drive her away. Give me leave to punish her for threatening you. We shall put her to the question and deal with her as a witch."

Mark's eyes bulged. Mary and Joseph, who was king here? Was he priest-ridden, as the people said?

"No more killing!" he howled. "Isn't one death enough?" He turned on Andred, shaking from head to foot. "This is all your fault! You made me mistrust her. And Tristan, too, my own flesh and blood!"

He tottered to the edge of the Pool of Tears, his outstretched arms embracing Andred, Dominian, and the men-at-arms.

"Forgive them, Lord," he cried, "for what they have done! And stretch out your hand to me, a man bereft. Thanks to them, I have lost my Queen! I have lost the only true woman in the world!"

chapter 51

down, down, down—

She hit the water like a rock and doubled over with pain. It was colder than she could have imagined, and every muscle in her body twitched and convulsed.

Don't gasp! Don't breathe in!

Swim, swim—

She had a desperate urge to break back to the surface, but unless she stayed under water, the ordeal would fail. *Down!* she harangued herself, *down—*

And swim—swim!

She thrust out her hands and found she could paddle like a dog, scooping the water toward her and kicking out strongly behind. Down she went and down, driving through the dark water, seeing strange shapes all around, gray phantoms that swirled away out of sight and were gone.

Count—don't forget to count—it has to be seventy times seven or the ordeal is void.

The water was very dark. As she went deeper, fine silky strands of seaweed pulsated through the depths like maidenhair and still she could not see the bottom of the shaft.

—twenty-one—twenty-two—find a rock—twenty-three—or a clump of sharp-edged mussels, use their shells to saw my hands free—

She swam to the side, feeling nothing but the smooth rocky shaft.

Down again—deeper—down—

The darkness enveloped her, vibrant and alive. *Down—down—*she had no fear. Since childhood she had known how to close off the soft back of her throat and swim underwater without air. Seven times seventy was a long time indeed, but she could do it, if she got her hands free. And swimming like this brought a joy few would ever know. In the deep water, the swimmer who was strong enough would reach the silence of the world that lay beyond sound, and touch the still place at the heart of the universe.

—fifty-nine—sixty—the first seventy!

Now the silence was alive, a strong rhythmic thrumming in her ears. It swelled into waves of unseen lightness, washing around her body and filling her head, supporting her as she swam, swallowing her up.

She felt the tug of the depths, and remembered the sea—the pool must be open somewhere to the tide. It was ebbing now, and the current would be strong. The deeper she went, the more strength it would take to swim back.

Eighty—ninety—

And still the count went on with every beat of her laboring heart. Her senses were shrinking and it was harder now to remember where she was, but she dared not forget for a second, or all was lost. She swam on, feeling her way round the sides of the pool. Her numb fingers met many rocky knobs and bumps, but nothing sharp enough to saw her wrists free.

A hundred—

Two hundred—

There must be a rock somewhere—

The water grew colder as she swam farther down.

Down—down—down—

With a shock of fear, she realized that her fingers were numb. *Goddess, Mother!* If she found the jagged rock she needed, she wouldn't feel it now. She wouldn't be able to use it to save her life.

Now her feet and legs were losing all feeling too. She tried to keep the blood flowing with a few vigorous kicks, but she was almost out of breath. As she forced herself ever downward, her chest buckled and her lungs shot through with fire. But then even the pain of that gave way to the cold.

Three hundred—

Three hundred and—three hundred—

Turn back—swim to the surface—abandon the ordeal—

Too late—

No more strength—

Her throat was frozen. She would never breathe again. It came to her that she could die here without pain. *Water is our first Mother, when we swim in our mothers' wombs. I am ready to return to the Mother for all time. Farewell, love. I will wait for you there.*

She could swim no more. She was sinking like a stone.

Cold—so cold—

Sleep then—

Three hundred—

Sleep—

Three—three—three—

There was a sudden swirl of water at her side, and a current of warmth brushed her like a lover's kiss. The freezing blackness pulsed then exploded in particles of light, all calling to one another through the dark. Then something was moving beside her in the singing dusk.

Three hundred and one—and two—

She could hear another voice, counting insistently in her head. She wanted to respond but she could not, and rolled and wallowed in the water like a dying thing. Then at her side was a shape in silky gray, and a pair of keen bright eyes shining through the gloom. She recognized the newcomer without surprise. It was one of the Maidens of the Lady, come to take her home.

A hand touched hers, and she felt a flicker of life. As the feeling returned to her fingers, little by little she found she could move her legs. Now she felt herself drawn forward through the water by the seal-like girl, in quite a different direction from before. The Maiden took her hands and drew her down. And there—*Goddess, Mother, thanks!*—was a jagged rock.

Four hundred and one—

Yes!

She set to work with a will, while her rescuer hovered at her side. Sawing away, she heard a distant roar and knew that her blood was thickening in her veins. As soon as there was no more air in her body, her lungs would collapse.

Four hundred and ten—four hundred and twenty-one—

Free!

With a last convulsive effort she snapped her bonds. Her head filled with jangling sounds and she knew she would swoon. She had left it too late. She had no more courage now.

Sleep—sleep—

Isolde, no! Listen to the count. Four hundred and thirty! Four hundred and thirty-one!

With a series of powerful kicks, the Maiden propelled herself forward and seized Isolde's hand. Then she struck out for the surface, continuing her wordless chant.

Four hundred and fifty! Four hundred and seventy-one!

Slowly the darkness thinned. As they left the frozen depths, the water began to feel warm. She could no longer tell if the lights flashing in her head were from the brightness above. But with every strong kick of the Maiden, she knew they were nearer to day.

Now she could dimly see daylight overhead. She could even make out the sun, a great disk as red as blood.

Farewell! Go with the Goddess! dropped into her ear. Then, giving her one last powerful upward thrust, the Maiden dove down and was gone.

"Five hundred!"

As her head broke the surface, she heard the roar of the crowd.

Dimly she felt their love, their loyalty. But all she could think of was trying to breathe again. Struggling, she unlocked her throat and gasped for air.

"Hold on, lady!" came the cry from above.

She looked up. Roped round the waist, one of the guard was making his way carefully down the side of the pool. High above, other willing hands were lowering him down. Someone—Sir Nabon, she guessed, seeing him lean over with a triumphant smile—had thought of getting her out when the time came.

"This way, lady!"

The man-at-arms was beckoning her urgently. She paddled her way toward him with feeble strokes. Deftly he passed a spare rope round her waist, then signaled to the men above to pull her up.

Up, up, up—

The rope caught her beneath her ribs, stopping her breath. But as she neared the top, strong hands reached down and lifted her up. The next second, Brangwain was at her side, chafing her frozen limbs, wrapping her in her cloak.

"Oh, lady—"

"The Queen! The Queen!"

The crowd around the pool was erupting with glee. Brangwain was silent amid the weeping, cheering mob, but Isolde could see from her bloodless face what the maid had endured.

"Isolde—"

Blubbering, Mark thrust Brangwain out of the way and seized Isolde clumsily in his arms. "I never doubted you, lady!" he mouthed, falling on her neck. "And I'll never mistrust you again, as long as I live."

He smelled of horse slobber and drink, treachery and fear. She pulled away and moved her frozen lips. "As you say, sire."

"I always loved you!" Mark shrilled, eyeing the crowd. The catcalls and hisses he had endured while Isolde was in the pool had taught him sharply to make much of her now. "And I'll prove it tonight. I'll give a great feast in your honor, what d'you think of that?" Whining, he launched off on another tack. "It was all Tristan's fault—he's to blame. He should never have beaten me and Andred and then run away. But we'll catch up with him. That's a blood feud at least, and Andred can't forget. He'll never forgive him till he sees him dead!"

"Not dead." She was shivering so badly now she could hardly stand. "No more killing," she whispered with the last of her strength. "For the sake of my ordeal, I beg you, spare Tristan's life."

Spare Tristan?

Mark paused, and called his cunning to his aid. "Let's discuss it after the feast, madam," he proclaimed with a flashing smile. "After the feast!"

chapter
52

"here's a health to Her Majesty!"

"The Queen! The Queen!"

"The Queen!"

Fifty—

Eighty-five—

How many more?

For the hundredth time, Isolde got to her feet and bowed, to the accompaniment of ragged cheering from the body of the hall. The toasts and drunken carousals had been going on for hours. When, oh when, could she slip away to her bed?

She could see Brangwain at a distant table, drowsing over her wine. She caught her eye, and nodded. *Soon, Brangwain, soon.* Both of them were dropping on their feet. But nobody in Castle Dore wanted the feast to end.

For the whole town was ablaze with joy tonight. The people were reveling in the streets, and even the dogs and horses were drunk on the free-flowing ale. Those who could not crowd into the Great Hall were feasting in the corridors, in the courtyards, even in the snow outside.

Inside the hall, every face had greeted her with smiles, every heart had rejoiced at her delivery. Sir Nabon had knelt before her with tears in his eyes and admitted that he had ordered the ropes for her rescue at the pool. Old Sir Wisbeck had kissed her hand, then kissed his sword, proclaiming himself her knight for evermore.

Even Andred had begged her forgiveness on his knees. "I was wrong, Your Majesty," he proclaimed, scattering great tears. "Can you find it in your heart to pity me?"

Could she pity him?

Yes.

Did she trust him?

Not in the least! Sir Andred had a hard road ahead if he wanted to win her esteem. But a handsome apology in front of all the court went a long way to repair the damage he had done. It was more than she'd had from Dominian, or was likely to have. As she emerged from the pool, threw back her dripping hair, and opened her eyes, she saw the livid face and misshapen body quivering with disbelief. Dominian had never expected her to live. Whatever bargain he had struck with his God had failed.

He had covered it well, of course. "A miracle!" he had cried. "Praise the Lord!"

But the townspeople had jeered him from the pool and the cowardly Mark had been quick to disown him, too.

"He misled me!" he cried to anyone who would hear. Blaming others was Mark's answer to everything now.

That, and getting drunk with his knights. He had long ago left her side to join his men in the hall, and it was a relief to her to see him go. She had remained at the High Table with the wiser lords, but her duty was almost done. *Soon, Brangwain, soon.*

The smoke from the guttering candles was stinging her eyes. The fires had burned down and the servants were dozing at their stations behind the hangings, dreaming of their beds. Even the dogs were snoring on the hearths, rumbling through eternal sunlit landscapes chasing rabbit and wild boar. She was free to go to her bed alone.

The hollowness of it all swept over her. *What now?* came the hammer beat of her heart. *Life here with Mark, and without my love?* For despite his earlier promise to discuss it after the feast, Mark had shown no interest in her plea for Tristan's life. As long as his fury still raged, she saw clearly now, Tristan must stay away. *And what life can I have when I don't know where he is?*

"Lady, come."

It was Brangwain at her elbow, helping her to her feet. The maid's sallow face was bruised with tiredness but her mouth was firm. "You have done enough for today. I beg, you, madam, come away to your bed."

Brangwain was right. Nodding, Isolde rose and made her farewells.

"Good night, sire. Good night, my lords."

"A health to the Queen!"

"And again!"

"The Queen! The Queen!" Peal after peal of cheers carried her from the hall.

The icy chill of the night would cut flesh from bone. Thankfully she gained her chamber and the comfort of a fire. She stood staring into the flames as Brangwain swiftly helped her out of her robes and wrapped her in a soft chamber gown.

"You triumphed twice today, lady, first at the ordeal, then at the feast," the maid said, her dark face flushed with pride. "You've made yourself Queen here indeed!"

"Yes," she said listlessly. It was true. Why did she feel so wan?

As ever, Brangwain picked up her mood. "I'll leave you, then, madam," she said quietly. "Send for me if you need me in the night."

"Thank you, Brangwain."

Wearily she watched the maid slip out of the door. She drifted to the window, too heartsick and weary to sleep. Where was the girl who had ridden out with Tristan on those dewy mornings in May? Gone like the green leaves of summer, years ago.

She had never felt so spent, so unhappy, so old. Her head was throbbing, and she could hardly move for pain. Stiffly she leaned her forehead against the window. *Goddess, Mother, help me—where is my love?*

Where? Where? mocked her reflection in the glass. She gazed out into the peace of the night. Legions of stars spangled the velvet sky, and the walled enclosure behind the Queen's House slumbered under a full moon. Thick frost-covered ivy mantled the four walls below, and all the lawns and paths were blanketed in white. The beauty, the midnight stillness, were balm to her grieving soul. She fancied she could see stars dancing on the shimmering lake of snow.

Where is my love?

She raised her eyes to the moon, aching in her soul. Then she saw a slight movement in the garden below. She looked and thought a shadow darker than the others slipped through a silver splash of moonlight between the trees.

She tensed, her senses aroused, but nothing moved. Impatient with herself, she turned away.

And there it was again, a gray shape flitting behind a bush. Softly she opened the window onto the night. The crouching figure moved as stealthily as a great cat. But this was a two-legged stalker, she was sure.

So which of the human predators was on the prowl? *Andred?* she thrilled, *or Mark?* She shook her head. Neither of them would do his own dirty work.

The shadow was silently approaching the foot of the wall. She could make out the shape clearly now, a man wrapped from head to foot in gray. He was dressed like a beggar or a pilgrim but he moved like a creature of the forest, without fear. Suddenly, strangely, she was quite unafraid.

Head down, the hooded stranger stood assessing the ivy, then began to climb. The massive old creeper groaned and strained under his weight. Foot by foot, hand over hand, he found the holds he needed and made his way confidently upward like a great cat.

Come to me—come—

As he reached the window, he threw back his hood. But already she knew the face that she would see.

Oh—oh—oh—

He jumped up onto the sill and then down into the room. His face was pale and shadowed with fatigue. But his eyes were the eyes she had seen in her dreams and his crooked smile was the sweetest thing on earth. Whimpering, she flew into his arms. He smelled of the snowy night and the dark outside. He smelled clean and fresh, he smelled of himself, of—

"Tristan!"

"Lady, lady," he soothed.

He stroked her cheek with a million tiny touches, each one food for her soul. She reached up and took his dear face between her hands. The light stubble on his jaw pricked her palms and she had never felt a more glorious thing in her life.

Kiss me, she wanted to say. But he was already lowering his wonderful head. They kissed till she was drowning, dying in his arms. She had forgotten the hardness of his lips.

Gasping, they broke apart. She found herself laughing with delight. "They told me you'd sailed away!"

He laughed softly in response. "I took a ship to throw Mark off the scent. But I paid the captain to sail only to the next bay."

Her mind was racing. "And you were the beggar who came to me at the pool!"

Tears stood in his eyes as he smiled back. "I have been beggar and pilgrim for your love."

"And a leper, too! What made you think of that?"

"I had a dream." He looked at her awkwardly. "A strange child with staring eyes came to me and told me what to do. I knew if I knocked you down then picked you up, you could swear on your oath that I had held you in my arms."

A strange child with staring eyes.

She nodded. "You know who that was?"

He stared at her. "No."

"It was Merlin—Merlin Emrys the Bard!"

"How d'you know?"

"Everyone in Ireland knows that wandering child."

He was very pale. "But why should he bother with us?"

Isolde paused. "Not for me," she said slowly. "I never met him in my life. Nor for my mother, I'm sure, though he loved her long ago." She hesitated. "If he took pains with us, it must have been because he cared about you."

Tristan shook his head. "But he doesn't know me!"

"He knew your father. And for Merlin, that would be enough." Brooding, she heard a voice on the vagrant wind. *Tristan, Arthur, and myself, yes, even the great Merlin, lost boys, every one! Motherless, fatherless, nameless, and homeless, too, flying boys becoming wounded men.*

"So Merlin told you to disguise yourself?"

He grinned unexpectedly, a boyish laugh lighting his whole face. "But not as a leper, lady," he said proudly. "That was my idea. I thought that was the best disguise I could get."

She shuddered. "But weren't you afraid?"

"Of catching leprosy? Yes." Tristan looked at her earnestly. "But, lady, you know I would never endanger you. The poor soul I took the bandages from had lain in the snow for days. The ground was frozen, so the lepers couldn't bury him, and I knew the cold would purify the rags."

She nodded. Everyone knew that the little creatures that caused disease could not survive the frost. Tristan was safe from infection, and she would be, too.

And here he was now, his big body calling hers with his every breath, drawing her to him with every beat of his heart. Already her skin was pricking against her shift. She came into the shelter of his cloak. "Love me?" she said.

Wordlessly he cupped his hand to her breast and kissed her again. Then he swept her up into his arms and carried her to the bed. Panting, they renewed their endless, timeless love. Then the last wave broke over their heads and brought them home.

SHIVERING, HE AWOKE with the first yellow fingers of dawn. Nowadays he never knew more than the half-sleep of the hunted, the fear that kept him trapped between animal and man. Isolde was lolling against him heavily, like a child. He watched and waited, cradling her in his arms, till a sickly light was creeping up the sky. Then he steeled himself to act.

He stroked her face. "Lady?"

She opened her eyes, still windmills of desire. "Yes?" she said huskily, reaching out for him.

Gently he disengaged her arms from around his neck. "I must go."

She was instantly awake.

"Go?"

She opened her mouth to protest, but no words came. They both knew he endangered his life by being here.

He forced a cheerful smile. "Away with me, then."

She could not bear it. "Where will you go?"

"Lady—" He took her in his arms. "I can't tell you."

"*What?*" She pulled away in alarm. "But I must know where you are."

He groaned. "Lady, if you know that, you'll be in danger, too!"

She nodded, biting her lip. If Mark thought she knew Tristan's whereabouts, he was capable of anything to find it out. "He's declared a blood feud against you, did you know that?"

"No." He paused, brooding. "But I knew he would." He was suddenly alert. Gowned like a beggar, he did not even have a sword. All the more reason to go!

He leapt from the bed, shrugging on his clothes. The fire had gone out and the room was as cold as the grave. Isolde jumped up and wrapped herself in her chamber gown. Haplessly she trailed him across the room.

He was at the window now, throwing open the casement, looking for a safe way down. She could see he was already miles away in his head.

Don't leave me!

"I—" she began hopelessly, then shook her head. There was nothing to say.

He turned back and folded her into him, tucking her quivering head beneath his chin.

"Never forget I love you," he said tenderly. "Wherever I am, I shall be thinking of you. Wherever you are we are one, like the sea and the land. Neither exists without the other and together they make a world."

She could not speak.

He put her gently away from him. "No tears," he whispered. "I shall return."

She looked at him through a mist of pain. "I shall be with you everywhere you go. My spirit will travel with yours every step of the way. Every evening I shall light a candle with the evening star. Whenever you want me, call me and my soul will come to you."

The draft from the open window chilled her to the core. He chafed her icy hands and brought them to his lips. "I shall see you again, my love. Till then, keep faith."

The cold air of farewell swirled round them both. She closed her eyes for a last famished kiss, and when she opened them again, he was gone.

chapter
53

*a*ll winter long, the sea howled round the shore. The land lay
locked in ice, the waves sighed and sobbed and Isolde watched and
waited and kept the faith. Every day she walked by the sea and sent love
thoughts flying like sea birds to bless Tristan, wherever he lay. And every
twilight in the window of her chamber, she lit a candle as the love star
bloomed.

The snow lay deep on the earth, stopping rivers and streams, keeping
the cows pent up in the byre and the sheep in the fold. Slowly the world
ran down to the death of the year and began the climb back to light and
warmth. *Good news!* wrote Guenevere from the Summer Country and
Isolde pounced on the letter as the horseman clattered in. She read it
avidly, but it brought no good news for her.

> *I know you will rejoice with me, dear friend, when I tell you of the birth*
> *of our son, Amir. All the time I was carrying, I dreamed I was having a*
> *girl, but nothing in the world could be dearer than this royal scrap. You*
> *know his name means "Beloved" in the Old Tongue, and truly the Mother*
> *has blessed us with a marvelous child—already the image of his father,*
> *another Arthur, blue eyes, fair hair—and his hands! . . .*

And on, and on.

Isolde threw it down and paced about the room. Guenevere a
mother? At the tournament, she'd shown no sign of a child on the way.
Gods above, I have lost count of time. My life is drifting past me in a dream.

Or was it the tournament itself that had brought this about? With a
wistful pang she remembered Arthur's high spirits on the day they left
and Guenevere's drowsy bedtime eyes at noon. The relief they shared

that Arthur had not fathered Lienore's child may well have brought little Amir into the world.

Goddess, Mother, why can't I be glad for Guenevere? Is it because she has her own kingdom, her true love, and now her precious child while I have none of these?

Yet she did not feel jealous. In truth she felt nothing, all winter long.

With each day, life settled into a rhythm akin to sleep. Mark treated her with courtesy and a new respect. Dominian, too, had learned of her strength, and kept away from court. When he appeared, like Mark he looked at her with fresh eyes and a new humility. His failure with her, she could not help thinking, had been good for the little priest's soul.

Then one day came a soft wind from the west. The earth murmured and stirred, waking from its winter sleep. Isolde breathed the new sweetness in the air and saw the streams thawing and the rivers beginning to flow. Green shoots cracked the dryness of her heart and fleeting thoughts and impulses visited her in dreams. At last she awoke in a pool of warm, clear light, and knew what she had to do.

She found Mark in the King's House, calling for his knights.

"You're going to Tintagel?" He stared at her. "Then on to Ireland to visit the Queen?"

"I should call upon Queen Igraine to pay my respects. And from there I can take ship for the Western Isle. My mother must see me, she says. She has been writing to me all winter long."

"Yes, well—"

Isolde away? And for a long time, too? Mark looked ahead down a long sunlit avenue of bachelor days. His favorite hound thrust a wet nose into his palm and he saw untrammeled hours of hunting with his knights and roughing it in the forest, no more dining at the High Table next to the Queen.

Gods above! Mark's unsteady mind reeled at the visions of joy ahead. He could make Elva mistress of some quiet hunting lodge in the wood, and visit her anytime. He could have Dominian back as his confessor, now that he'd learned his lesson and was so much easier now. On feast days he could be drunk at breakfast, insensible by noon.

He could—

He could—

Standing quietly at Mark's side, Andred read his uncle's thoughts and enjoyed his own. Tristan was already done for and out of the way. With Isolde gone, too, there would be no threat from her. Mark would be his from morning to night—when not otherwise occupied in Elva's good hands. . . .

Thoughtfully Andred stroked his upper lip. The elf mark glowed under his fingers as his mind played on. Already he could guess which of the lonely hunting lodges would be Mark's love nest, and looked ahead to safe secret hours with Elva when Mark had gone. He hid a discreet smile behind his hand. This was good. It could be very good.

Mark thought so, too. "Go with God, lady!" he cried, kissing Isolde's hand. "And don't hurry your business, return whenever you will!"

WITHIN DAYS SHE was on the road, leaving Castle Dore to the loud blessings of the townsfolk and cheery exhortations to speed her return. Sighing, she settled herself to the journey ahead. It was still early in the year for traveling, and the going was hard. The tracks were clogged with mud and the horses were slow, struggling uphill all the way. But every painful step, they heard the calling of the sea. Now as twilight came down, the great bluff of Tintagel reared up to meet them, massive and wild. Once they crested the ridge, the ancient fortification lay before them in the dusk.

Overhead, gulls fled crying to their nests, and the sky was melting down in bronze and gold. As they rested their horses at the top, the bruised scent of wild thyme rose from beneath their feet, and the red earth bloomed like passion as rich as blood. On the edge of the cliff ahead stood a castle, defended by a ring of stout walls. Beyond it, out in the bay, lay an inner castle, built on a massive rock rising above the waves, connected to the land by a fragile outcrop of stone. Washed roundabout by the sea and reached only by a flight of stone across the void, this truly was the loneliest place on earth. And this was the home of Arthur's mother, old Queen Igraine.

Slowly they wound down the hill to the outer gate.

"Here, ma'am?" cried the captain of the guard.

"Yes, soldier," Brangwain called back. "Say that Queen Isolde of Cornwall and Ireland craves an audience with their Queen."

Within minutes, the gates swung open and a mounted knight

appeared in the courtyard beyond. "This way, Your Majesty. Queen Igraine will see you tonight."

The outer castle was bigger than it seemed. The knight led them through courtyard after courtyard till they reached the edge of the cliff. Ahead lay the rocky islet crowned by the Queen's castle, and the flight of stone steps leading across the gulf. In the cliff face below, the sea thundered in and out of a mighty cave. The knight followed her eyes and laughed.

"That's Merlin's cave, madam. Not that we see Lord Merlin when he comes. Queen Igraine is the only one who knows his whereabouts." He gestured ahead. "Follow me."

Night had fallen, and it was very dark. The breeze off the sea was rising to a gale. The knight's words were whipped away by the wind. "This way, lady—this way!"

She never knew how she crossed the thin ribbon of stone across the black chasm over the waves below. As she ventured out, she thought that dark things tugged at her, swooping around her head, and she heard elfin voices calling, *Come! Come!* The knight gave her his hand, but when the wind roared round, beating them to their knees, she gave her soul into the hands of the Great One and prepared to die.

Goddess, Mother, bring me to my love—

Did she imagine what she felt then, the warm whisperings in the heart of the storm and strong unseen hands bearing her up? But suddenly the rocky bridge felt safer beneath her feet and as she struggled on, a light glowed in the castle ahead.

At last they gained the safety of the other side. At the top of the steps was a tiny postern gate. As the knight set his hand to the latch, a wisp of memory fluttered into her mind. *When Uther Pendragon fell in love with Queen Igraine, he made a bargain with Merlin to possess the Queen. The old enchanter demanded the child of the encounter as his reward, and the newborn Arthur was given to him out at a postern gate to nourish as his own.*

Here then was the start of Arthur's story, the beginning of the journey that had led to Guenevere and Camelot.

Ghosts—ghosts—

The knight pushed open the gate and she drew a ragged breath. *There are many ghosts in this place. Perhaps Igraine herself will prove to be a phantom, a spirit fetch. Or else my own hopes are deceiving me.*

They stepped into a deserted courtyard beyond and passed through the echoing halls of a darkened house. Where she would have expected servants, torches, bright fires, there was no one to be seen. The voice of the knight sounded again and again.

"This way, my lady—this way."

One hall led into another, all dark, linked by long corridors and flights of stairs. She could not count how many steps they climbed. Here and there she caught the swift scurry of feet or turned to see the benign amber gaze of a pair of small eyes shining in the gloom. Everywhere came the dull, rhythmic pounding of the surge. But nothing else stirred in the vast sea-girt house.

Up they went, and up. Now the ceilings were getting lower and the passageways were narrowing down. The last one ended at a fine arched door, set low in the wall. The knight came to a halt.

"I shall be here for your return, my lady," he said. Then he threw open the door without knocking, and bowed her through.

"Thank you, sir."

At first she thought she had stepped out into the heavens, in a place beyond the stars. Ahead of her stretched a great airy chamber at the top of the castle, its vast windows giving out onto endless night. In the center of the room stood a tall, aged woman, crowned with white hair like snow. She wore a strangely wrought diadem of moonstones and pearls and held an antique staff of gold in her hand. A flowing gown of blue-green silk fell in rich folds to her feet, and her silver cloak and veil frothed to the floor like foam.

Isolde made her deepest curtsey. "Queen Igraine!"

A sweet tang hung in the air like the breeze off the sea. The Queen fixed Isolde with great liquid eyes, and the stars in the sky made a ring around her head. "Welcome, Isolde. What brings you here?"

The mellow voice seemed to echo from Avalon and beyond. The golden wand sang softly in the old Queen's hand and Isolde reached for her strength. *Goddess, Mother, help me—*

"I have come to ask for your help," she said at last. "King Mark has sworn a blood feud against Sir Tristan, my knight. Tristan has been driven out of Cornwall, never to return."

"So I hear." Igraine inclined her head. "Go on."

Now Isolde could see the trials of the older woman's life engraved on her deeply lined face, and she shuddered at the world of experience that had shaped the strong cheekbones and chin. Suddenly she knew that Igraine had borne suffering beyond measure, almost beyond speech. Yet there was no doubting the warmth of her concern nor the undefeated radiance of her inner joy. "Elf-shining," they called this look in the ancient days. *Goddess, Mother, will I have it when I'm old?*

Isolde held out her hands. "You are Mark's overlord, and whatever you decree, he must obey. I don't believe he truly wants Tristan dead. Tristan is his only sister's son, and Tristan has no other kin but him. I beg you to reconcile them and end this feud. I'm sure Mark would make peace if he could."

"Peace, Isolde? Is that what Mark really wants?" Igraine paused somberly for thought. "Some men are ever hungry, like the sea. Others are filled with the spirit of giving, as the sea teems with fish. I suspect that is true of Mark and Tristan."

Oh, my love, my love—

Isolde steadied her voice. "Can you save him, madam?"

She held her breath as doubt and hope played over Igraine's lovely face.

"For thousands of years," the Queen said, "men have gone to war. All that time, women have prayed for peace. I dream of these islands becoming one, all our people living in harmony, not dying in hate." She gave a luminous smile. "Men like Tristan are the lifeblood of my hopes. So I shall save him, Isolde, never fear."

Goddess, Mother, praise and thanks to you!

Igraine saw the tears in Isolde's eyes and smiled again. "Mark cannot sustain a blood feud when no blood has been shed. And with Norse invaders to fight, we cannot afford blood feuds here at home. I shall write to him and call on him to make peace. If he still lusts for blood, I'll order him to go with Arthur to the Saxon shore." A wry smile lit the shrewd, ageless face. "I think Mark will choose to obey rather than face the horned men from the North!"

Isolde hesitated. "But won't he still want his revenge?"

The Queen shook her head. "Mark's memory is as shallow as his soul and his weak nature cannot nurse an injury for long. He will forgive Tristan, as he forgave you."

Isolde nodded. She knew she should feel relief. But what now?

Emptiness overwhelmed her. Suddenly she was a girl again on Avalon, adrift and afraid. "Lady, what shall I do?"

Igraine came forward and warmly clasped her hands. "Go forward without fear," she said. "You are out of danger now. By completing the ordeal you have shown yourself free from guilt, and no man can accuse you of treason or falseness of heart."

Forward without fear?

Without sadness, too?

No, not even the Lady herself can promise me that.

The Queen pressed her hand. "Go to Ireland, Isolde. Your fate lies there. And I have something to help you on your way."

From a table at her side she took up a glinting object, an odd, round, heavy locket on a long gold chain.

"Wear this," she ordered, placing it around Isolde's neck. "You will need it in Ireland, perhaps sooner than you think."

She clutched at it in fear. "Why, madam?"

The old Queen smiled. All the wisdom of her years stood in her eyes. "When the moment comes, you will know. Now my knight will guide you back the way you came. A ship lies provisioned for you at the foot of the bay. Go to your mother, and guide her wandering steps."

Wandering steps?

A wave of unpleasant memory washed over her. *Mother, yes—but must I deal with Sir Tolen, too?*

Igraine smiled. "Remember, Isolde, a queen must have her knights. You will know this when you follow your mother as Queen of the Western Isle. Embrace your destiny and it will embrace you."

Isolde moved sadly to the door. Hovering on the threshold, she turned to say farewell. The lights in the chamber had dimmed and the tall, stately figure was already fading from view.

The musical voice reached her through the mist. "Farewell, Isolde. Return when you will; you will always find shelter here."

chapter
54

The green hills rose out of the still water, calling her home. The sea was as smooth as a lake, its little curling waves lapping the shore. Like a hunter home from the hill, the ship nosed up to the quay and came to rest. Standing in the prow, Isolde filled her lungs with the sweet clean air and felt the glory of the place enter her soul.

Erin—

Ireland—

Home.

A soft rain was falling like the kiss of the Gods. She cocked an eye at the sun through its veil of mist. Noon already, and they'd been making land since dawn. The boat would have been sighted, the welcome prepared. The Queen would be waiting in the palace for her embrace.

Dubh Lein—

Mother—

Home!

She could not wait for the gangplank to drop into place. "Come, Brangwain!" she called, making a leap for the shore.

"Lady, lady!" protested Brangwain, following as fast as she could. "Wait for the guard!"

Along the path, the first celandines covered the grass in handfuls of pale gold. On all sides the rough ground was enlivened by green shoots of spring. Misty harebells were whispering their secrets to the mad March wind, and flights of swallows were swooping in from their winter haunts.

Gods above! Brangwain lamented as Isolde skimmed ahead of her like a bird, flying up the hill from the bay. Surely she knows that the Queen will not have changed—that Sir Tolen will be everything now that Sir Marhaus was before—that the Queen will be under his sway, and her mother will always be a child to her—

Brangwain looked up the hill at the palace and her spirits sank. No, Isolde does not know this. And nothing but hurt and disappointment lie ahead.

Mother—

Home—

A great roar greeted them as Isolde approached. All the dogs came bounding out from the palace to lick her hands, howling with joy. And all the people of Dubh Lein, it seemed, had turned out to welcome her home.

"It's the Princess!"

"She's Queen of Cornwall now, noddle-head!"

"Queen Isolde!"

"The Queen!"

"Isolde!"

At the head of the steps stood the Queen with all her knights. Foremost among them was Sir Tolen, his narrow hips thrusting suggestively, his handsome face composed in a confident smile. She saw Sir Gilhan bowing with tears of joy in his eyes, and the other knights and lords offering greetings too. But Sir Tolen was still to the fore as the Queen fluttered down the steps and wept on Isolde's neck.

"Isolde," she said tremulously, squeezing Isolde's hand. "Little one, I'm so happy to see you here!" She looked over her shoulder at Tolen and gave a quick secret smile. "And so is my knight."

Sir Tolen arranged his empty young features into an air of manly joy. "Your Majesty!" he declaimed to Isolde, bowing low.

The Queen looked on like a mother watching her firstborn learning to dance. "See, Isolde?" she said lyrically.

Isolde suppressed a sad smile. "Yes, Mother, I do."

Inside the palace, the Queen dismissed Tolen, but even as he went, her hungry gaze followed him to the door. Isolde could tell from Tolen's loose, cat-like walk that the knight knew this and played up to it shamelessly. The Queen's eyes caressed him with lascivious delight.

"Mother!"

Isolde could not contain herself. "Even a queen waits for bedtime, like everyone else!"

"Oh, so?" The Queen stared and laughed. "Isolde, how you've changed!"

"Yes, I have." A huge weariness swept over her and she wanted to weep.

The Queen swept to a sofa and patted the place at her side. "Come and sit by me."

Reluctantly Isolde sat down. She felt the weight of Igraine's locket round her neck and took it in her hand. *Is this the moment of need?* "You wanted me back, madam?"

The Queen tossed her head. "Isolde, I never wanted you to leave, you know that."

"I know." In spite of herself, Isolde was moved. "But you sent for me. You had something important to say?"

The Queen's mood shifted like a weathervane and a joyful secret moved in her dark eyes. She leapt to her feet and strode airily up and down.

"We must look to the future," she announced, waving her hands. "The time is coming for me to give up the throne. You'll be Queen of the Western Isle, Isolde—what d'you think of that?"

Whatever Isolde had expected, it was not this. Her mouth fell open. "*What?*"

The Queen stared in angry reproof. "Now, Isolde, don't look so surprised! You know you'll make a better Queen than I have."

What are you up to, Mother? There was something here she did not understand. She searched for a reply.

"Madam," she said carefully. "You're far too young to give up the throne. We don't need to think of this for years to come."

And I don't believe you will do it, Mother dear! Without a second's thought, she could see it all—her mother ostentatiously handing over power, then staying behind to advise her on every point—the Queen insisting that she was Queen no more, yet still seeking to advance Sir Tolen and all her favorites to places around the throne—

Goddess, Mother, no!

The Queen glimmered at her. Again Isolde had the sense of a secret she did not share.

"I may surprise you, little one." She gave a swift gurgle of laughter, hastily suppressed. "And sooner than you think." She rose to her feet and moved toward the door.

Going back to Tolen, Isolde noted coldly. *To her love.* With a sudden rush of shame, she struggled to be fair. *He has made her happier and that means kinder and saner, too. But he cannot change her nature. She will always be Queen.* She took a deep breath. "Madam, I—"

The Queen gave her a strange sideways look. "At least help me with some of the cares of state. The King of Lyonesse is here. Will you receive him for me?"

"The King of Lyonesse?"

Tristan's father. Gods above!

"The King here? Why?"

"That is what you must find out."

He's come to blame me for starting the feud that estranged his son from Mark—or for loving Tristan at all—

The Queen paused at the door with a smile. "I'll send in the King."

Or Tristan's dead! And he asked his father to bring me his last words before he died—

She hardly noticed the Queen leave the room. She turned to the window, choking with grief and fear. *Have I lost you, Tristan, my love?*

She heard the sound of the latch and the voice of the guard at the door. "This way, sire."

No tears—compose yourself—

She took a deep breath and prepared herself to turn. But then she felt a hand on her shoulder and a voice she would have known through all the world. "Lady? Oh, my love!"

It was the voice she had been hearing since time began. Her heart leapt and danced in her breast and the tears flowed.

"Oh, oh, oh—"

He folded her in his arms with a hundred soothing cries. His face was warm, and his kiss was like sun on her skin. She could not stop touching his cheek, his hair, his hands.

Tristan—"Oh, my love!"

They held each other delicately, like broken things. She heard a low crooning and felt him stroking her hair. Slowly the thundering in her head began to subside. It was a long time before either of them could speak.

At last she found her voice. Disengaging gently, she blinked up at him through her tears. "My mother said you were the King of Lyonesse," she began wonderingly.

"She told you the truth." For the first time she noticed the new seriousness in his face. "My father has died."

"Oh, my love—" She clasped his hand. *Always new pain.*

He nodded. "When I left you, I went back to my own land. I thought it was time to make my peace at home." Tears misted his eyes. "After all that had happened, I didn't want to die before I saw my father again. I never dreamed that he might be dying himself."

"Did you get there in time?"

"Thank the Gods, yes." He gave a watery smile.

You have lost your father, love, and my mother is lost to me. She folded him in her arms. *We shall be father and mother to each other now.*

His mood swung, and he crushed her fiercely to his chest. "And all this time, never a day passed when I did not think of you! I made a hundred plans and rejected them all. I knew you were in danger as long as you were in Mark's hands. But that last day in the solarium, you'd had a letter from Ireland, so eventually it came to me that your mother might be able to get you back here."

She was amazed. "You wrote to her?"

He shook his head. "I came here in person to win her to our side."

She caught her breath. "Even though—"

He nodded grimly. "Even though the last time she saw me, she wanted to have me killed." He smiled grimly. "But I knew all her hopes for the kingdom lay with you. So I guessed she'd rather have you back alive than me dead."

"And you were right!" How good he was, how brave! She reached out to him again. "And while you've been getting me here, I've been trying to see if you can go back to Cornwall again!"

"Back to Cornwall?" He started violently. "How on earth could that come about?"

"Through Queen Igraine." She laid a soothing hand on his cheek. "Remember, she's Queen of Cornwall and Mark's overlord. Mark will forget his anger, she says, and give up his revenge. And as he is her vassal, she can command him to put aside all thoughts of a blood feud in Cornwall and live in peace."

Tristan longed to believe it. His eyes were fixed on her face. "Can it be?"

"Think of this, love." Isolde pressed his hands. "You have shed no blood. You never planned or intended any evil to Mark. Queen Igraine says you are free of this feud."

She could see the hope returning to his heart. "Praise the Gods!" he cried.

"And you're King of Lyonesse now," she went on, glowing with pride, "so Mark must deal with you as king to king. You're no longer the long-lost nephew, the landless boy."

"It's true." He laughed with joy, and color flooded his face. "And you're no longer Princess of the Western Isle," he added, wreathed in smiles. "Your mother says you'll be Queen of Ireland now."

Isolde found herself caught between laughter and a rueful despair. "She told you that?"

"That and much more. We have had many long talks in recent times, and she and I have become the best of friends." He put his head to one side, unsure how she would react. "She means what she says."

"She means it now!" Isolde shook her head. "But she was born to be Queen. That will never change."

"Circumstances change." He paused. "She wants to be with her new love."

"I know," she said darkly.

Tristan reached out and drew her into his arms. "He makes her happy," he said gently. "Anyone can see that."

"Yes . . ."

"And Sir Tolen is not another Marhaus, lady, that's obvious, too. So he'll never be a danger to the kingdom—or to you."

Igraine's voice came back to her. *And a Queen must have her knights.*

"Oh, Tristan—"

How good he was, how sweet! "I will hear what she says," she said honestly, "and we'll see how things unfold. I'll try to accept whatever happens now."

"That's all I ask."

Joy blurred her eyes and the world melted in a soft fall of tears. Then a warmth began somewhere near her heart and she heard a low thrumming like a cobweb's song.

It was the locket, crooning to itself in bliss. "What's this?" Instinctively Tristan reached out for it, and it opened in his hand. Nestled inside lay a circle of emeralds in a band of gold. The green stones picked up the light in Tristan's eyes.

"My mother's ring!" he breathed. Like a man in a dream, he took it from its golden nest.

Now Isolde's tears fell like a waterfall. "But I left it with the Lady of the Sea!" she babbled. "How did it get from her cave? She must have given it to Queen Igraine—or Igraine must have—"

"Hush, lady," he said in a voice like the wind off the sea. "We'll know all this some day. Hear my oath now."

He was looking at her with starlight in his eyes. "As I rule my kingdom, I shall be with you step by step. And as you govern this great island, I shall be at your side. As the ivy and the honeysuckle, so are we. Wear this for me. I am yours for life."

He slipped the ring on her finger and she heard the voice of his heart. *This is the bridal of the earth and sea. You're the one, I am the other, and from now on we shall never be apart. Together we make a world of light and hope, a universe.*

I am yours, love, her heart responded, *through all the three worlds—the world that is, the world that was, and the world that is to be. When our day ends, our souls will meet on the astral plane. Together we shall walk the world between the worlds.*

He drew her to him again as the twilight came down. "Come, love," he said.

Overhead the love star bloomed and a smiling moon looked down. Through a mist, the lovers moved hand in hand toward the dawn. They would ride through dark woodlands, they knew—every voyage they made could not be into the sun. But in the heart of the darkest forest the ivy and the honeysuckle flourished as one. And so it would be for them, their lives so intertwined that every line and curve of one traced the outline of the other in deepest love.

And always in the place of their hearts, the island the Old Ones loved. Always they would feel the call of the green hills, the longing to be in the land of the green trefoil. An island of heroes and poets, of scholars and scoundrels and those who loved the craic.

Ireland.

Erin.

Home.

the characters

A'isha   Gypsy fortune-teller, leader of wandering band of
   Gypsies pursued by Kay, Gawain, Lucan, and Bedivere
Amir   "The Beloved One," only son of Arthur and
   Guenevere
Andred, Sir   Cousin of Tristan and nephew of King Mark
   of Cornwall, son of Mark's younger brother
Arthur   Pendragon, High King of Britain, son of Uther
   Pendragon and Queen Igraine of Cornwall, husband of
   Guenevere, father of Amir, and leader of the Round Table
   fellowship of knights
Bedivere, Sir   Knight to King Arthur, one of his first
   companion knights, who takes part in the hunt for the
   fortune-teller to clear Arthur's name
Black Lands, King of   Vassal king of Arthur as High King,
   combatant at the tournament in Ireland for Isolde's hand
Brangwain   Lady-in-waiting and personal maid to Isolde,
   formerly maid to Isolde's mother the Queen and
   nursemaid to Isolde when she was a child, born in the
   Welshlands and thought to be "Merlin's kin"
Claig, Sir   Knight of the Queen of Ireland and suitor to be
   her chosen one
Cormac   Chief Druid of Ireland, formerly of the Summer
   Country, in love with Isolde
Cullain, Sir   Isolde's late father, knight of Ireland, once the
   first champion and chosen one of the Queen and leader
   of her war band

Darath   Prince of the Picts, only son of the King, young warrior at the tournament in Ireland held by the Queen for Isolde's hand

Dominian, Father   Christian priest, head of the Christian community in Cornwall and father-confessor to King Mark, abandoned as a child and cared for by Brother Jerome

Doneal, Sir   Veteran knight of Ireland, member of the Queen's council

Ector, Sir   Foster father to Arthur, father of Sir Kay, knight of King Ursien of Gore

Eilan, Sir   Lover and chosen one of the Queen of Ireland

Elizabeth, Queen of Lyonesse   Late mother of Tristan, wife of King Meliodas, and sister of King Mark of Cornwall, lost in the forest when her husband was imprisoned and died there giving birth to Tristan

Elva, Lady   Mistress of King Mark, lover of Sir Andred, wife of a courtier, and enemy of Isolde

Emrys   One of the names of Merlin, "Merlin Emrys the Bard," when disguised as a child

Epin of the Glen, Sir   Knight at the court of the Summer Country, combatant at the tournament in Ireland for Isolde's hand

Faramon, King   King of the Green, friend of Arthur, and combatant at the tournament in Ireland for Isolde's hand

Finneail, Sir   Knight of the Queen of Ireland and suitor to be her chosen one

Fortis, Sir   Lover and chosen one of the Queen of Ireland, who took on the best of Arthur's knights in a joust and broke his neck

Gawain, Sir   Arthur's first companion knight, eldest son of King Lot and Queen Morgause, brother of Agravain, Gaheris, and Gareth

Gilhan, Sir   Leader of the Queen of Ireland's council, knight of Ireland, and loyal to Isolde

Glaeve   Sword of Power given to Tristan by the Lady of the Sea, inscribed with runic script

Guenevere   Queen of the Summer Country, daughter of Queen Maire Macha and King Leogrance, wife of Arthur, lover of Sir Lancelot, mother of Amir, and friend to Isolde from their girlhood days studying with the Lady of the Lake on Avalon

Gwydion of the Welshlands   Welsh Druid, surgeon and healer, and Isolde's Druid master

Houzen, Sir   Knight of Ireland and leader of the knights of Sir Marhaus, the champion of the Western Isle

Igraine, Queen   Queen of Cornwall, wife of Duke Gorlois, beloved of King Uther Pendragon, mother of Arthur, Morgause, and Morgan Le Fay, and supporter of Isolde

Ireland, Queen of   See Queen of Ireland

Isles, Lord of the   Knight of Scotland, combatant at the tournament in Ireland for Isolde's hand

Isolde, "La Belle Isolde"   Princess of Ireland, daughter of the Queen and the Irish hero Sir Cullain, lover of Tristan, wife of King Mark, and Queen of Cornwall

Jerome, Brother   Christian hermit and holy man, foster father and spiritual counselor of the abandoned Dominian

Kay, Sir   Son of Sir Ector of Gore and Dame Arian, foster brother of Arthur and knight of the Round Table, one of the companion knights of Arthur from the time he was proclaimed King

Lady of Broceliande   Ruler of the Lake and waterfall in Little Britain, modern Brittany, Sir Lancelot's foster mother, youngest sister of the Lady of the Sea and of the Lady of the Lake, and priestess of the Great Mother

Lady of the Lake   Ruler of the Sacred Island of Avalon in the Summer Country, younger sister of the Lady of the Sea and of the Lady of Broceliande, and priestess of the Great Mother

Lady of the Sea   Ruler of the sea, older sister of the Ladies of the Lake and of Broceliande, and chief priestess of the Great Mother

Lancelot of the Lake, Sir   Knight of the Round Table, lover of Queen Guenevere, son of King Ban and Queen Elaine of Benoic

Lienore   Daughter of Earl Sweyn, mother of Young Sweyn, lover of an unknown knight at a tournament and insistent that the father of her son is King Arthur himself

Lot, King   King of Lothian and the Orkneys, onetime ally of King Uther Pendragon, husband of Morgause, father of Gawain, Agravain, Gaheris, and Gareth

Lucan, Sir   Knight to King Arthur, one of his first companion knights, who takes part in the hunt for the fortune-teller to clear Arthur's name

Lyonesse, Queen of   See Elizabeth

Marhaus, Sir   Champion knight of Ireland and chosen one of the Queen, opponent of Tristan

Mark, King   King of Cornwall, brother of Elizabeth Queen of Lyonesse, uncle of Tristan and Andred, lover of Lady Elva, and husband of Isolde

Meliodas, King   King of Lyonesse, husband of Elizabeth and father of Tristan, rescued by Merlin from

imprisonment when his wife was lost in the forest and
gave birth to Tristan

Merlin Welsh Druid and bard, illegitimate offspring of
the house of Pendragon, adviser to Uther and Arthur
Pendragon, former lover of the Queen of Ireland, and
protector of Tristan

Morgan Le Fay Younger daughter of Queen Igraine and
Duke Gorlois of Cornwall, placed in a Christian convent
by King Uther her stepfather, Arthur's half sister and
lover, wife to King Ursien, and mother of Mordred

Morgause Elder daughter of Queen Igraine and Duke
Gorlois, given as wife to King Lot by King Uther,
Arthur's half sister, mother of Gawain, Agravain,
Gaheris, and Gareth, and, later, lover of Sir Lamorak

Murrein of the Greenway, King Vassal king under
Arthur as High King, combatant at the tournament in
Ireland for Isolde's hand

Nabon, Sir Leader of the council of King Mark of
Cornwall, supporter of Isolde

Nain, the Wise woman and "Old One" of Ireland, adviser
to the Queen, mistress of herbal lore and maker of the
elixir of love shared by Isolde and Tristan

Nevin, Sir Lover and chosen one of the Queen of Ireland,
who betrayed her by philandering with her maid

Norsemen See Saxons

Palomides, Sir Saracen king and knight at the court of
the Queen of Ireland, Isolde's suitor and opposed to
Tristan, defeated by Tristan at the tournament in Ireland
for Isolde's hand

Pelles, King King of Terre Foraine and the custodian of
the Grail tradition, father of the Grail virgin Elaine and
grandfather of the Grail knight Sir Galahad

Penn Annwyn   Lord of the Underworld in Celtic mythology, the Dark Lord who comes to take his children home

Picts, the   Fiercely war-like tribe of the north of modern Scotland, ancient enemies of Ireland, called Picti, "the Painted Ones," by the Romans for their custom of vividly tattooing their faces and bodies in a variety of colors

Queen of Ireland   Ruler of the Western Isle in her own right, descendant of a line of warrior queens, widow of the hero Cullain, mother of Isolde, and lover of many companions of the throne

Queen of Lyonesse   See Elizabeth

Quirian, Sir   Knight of Cornwall, member of the council of King Mark, much obsessed by genealogy

Ronan   Forester starving in the snow, who meets Merlin in the guise of Emrys

Saffir, Sir   Combatant at the tournament in Ireland for Isolde's hand

Saxons, the   Invaders from modern Scandinavia and the east coast of Germany, starving tribes now often called the Vikings, precursors of the Anglo-Saxons who helped to shape the history of the British Isles, also called "the Norsemen" and "the Horned Ones"

Simeon   Pupil of Father Dominian, novice monk of the Christian community in Cornwall

Sweyn, Earl   Rapacious lord of a large estate, father of Lienore and grandfather of Young Sweyn, determined to father the boy on King Arthur and also to avoid contributing to the cost of fighting the Saxon invaders

Sweyn, Young   Son of Lienore and grandson of Earl Sweyn, father uncertain

Tantris Name given to Tristan by Merlin when they go to Ireland to seek a cure for Tristan's poisoned wound

Tennel, Sir Combatant at the tournament in Ireland for Isolde's hand

Tolen, Sir Young knight of Ireland, descendant of a line of chosen ones who becomes the Queen's chosen one after the death of Sir Marhaus

Tristan, Sir Knight of Lyonesse, son of King Meliodas and Queen Elizabeth, nephew of King Mark of Cornwall, favored by the Lady of the Sea, and lover of Isolde

Turath, Sir Lover and chosen one of the Queen of Ireland, who betrayed her by falling in love with another, marrying her, and fleeing the land

Turquin, Sir Rogue knight of the Summer Country determined to win a place at the Round Table, who preys upon other knights to prove his prowess

Uther Pendragon, King of the Middle Kingdom, High King of Britain, lover and, later, husband of Queen Igraine of Cornwall, kinsman of Merlin, and father of Arthur

Vaindor, Sir Knight of Ireland, former champion and chosen one of the Queen, member of her council and hopeful of attracting Isolde

Wisbeck, Sir Veteran knight of the council of King Mark of Cornwall

Zrladic King of the band of Gypsy travelers, father of A'isha

List of places

❧

Avalon Sacred isle in the Summer Country, center of Goddess worship, home of the Lady of the Lake, modern Glastonbury in Somerset

Broceliande Forest in Little Britain, modern Brittany, site of the sacred Lake and waterfall where the Lady of Broceliande fostered Sir Lancelot of the Lake

Camelot Capital of the Summer Country, home of the Round Table, modern Cadbury in Somerset

Castle Dore Stronghold of King Mark, on the east coast of Cornwall

Cornwall Kingdom of Arthur's mother, Queen Igraine, and of her vassal King Mark, neighboring country to Lyonesse

Dubh Lein Stronghold of the Queens of Ireland, modern Dublin, "the Black Pool"

Gaul Large country of the continental Celts, incorporating much of modern France and Germany

Gore Christian kingdom of King Ursien in the northwest of England where Arthur and Kay were raised

Island of the West Modern Ireland, the sacred island of the Druids and home to Goddess worship and the uniquely Celtic form of Christianity

Little Britain Territory in France, location of the kingdom of Benoic, native land of Sir Lancelot, modern Brittany

London   Major city in ancient Britain, important site of Christian colonization of the British Isles

Lyonesse   Kingdom below Cornwall, home of Tristan, under the rule of Tristan's father, King Meliodas

Middle Kingdom   Arthur's ancestral kingdom, lying between the Summer Country and Wales, modern Gwent, Glamorgan, and Herefordshire

Orkney Islands   Cluster of northerly islands of the British Isles, and site of King Lot's kingdom, birthplace of Gawain

Saxon Shore, the   East coast of mainland Britain, site of the invasions by the tribes of what is now Scandinavia and east Germany

Summer Country   Guenevere's kingdom, ancient center of Goddess worship, modern Somerset

Terre Foraine   Kingdom of King Pelles in northern England

Tintagel   Castle of Queen Igraine on the north coast of Cornwall

Welshlands   Home to Merlin and Brangwain, modern Wales

the celtic wheel of the year

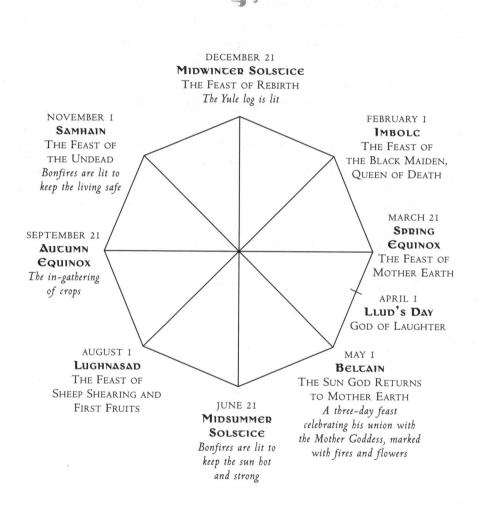

DECEMBER 21
MIDWINTER SOLSTICE
THE FEAST OF REBIRTH
The Yule log is lit

NOVEMBER 1
SAMHAIN
THE FEAST OF
THE UNDEAD
*Bonfires are lit to
keep the living safe*

FEBRUARY 1
IMBOLC
THE FEAST OF
THE BLACK MAIDEN,
QUEEN OF DEATH

MARCH 21
**SPRING
EQUINOX**
THE FEAST OF
MOTHER EARTH

SEPTEMBER 21
**AUTUMN
EQUINOX**
*The in-gathering
of crops*

APRIL 1
LLUD'S DAY
GOD OF LAUGHTER

AUGUST 1
LUGHNASAD
THE FEAST OF
SHEEP SHEARING AND
FIRST FRUITS

JUNE 21
**MIDSUMMER
SOLSTICE**
*Bonfires are lit to
keep the sun hot
and strong*

MAY 1
BELTAIN
THE SUN GOD RETURNS
TO MOTHER EARTH
*A three-day feast
celebrating his union with
the Mother Goddess, marked
with fires and flowers*

the christian wheel of the year

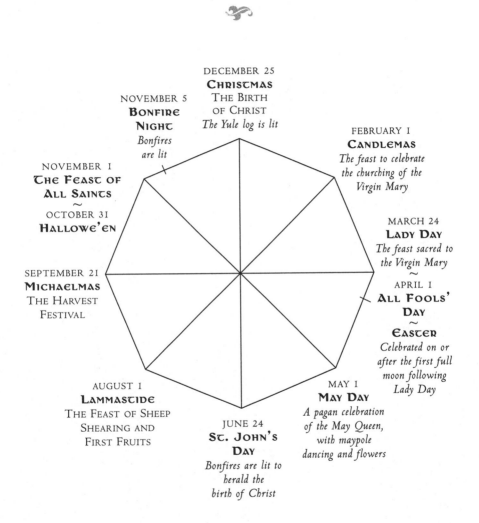

DECEMBER 25
CHRISTMAS
THE BIRTH
OF CHRIST
The Yule log is lit

NOVEMBER 5
**BONFIRE
NIGHT**
*Bonfires
are lit*

NOVEMBER 1
**THE FEAST OF
ALL SAINTS**
~
OCTOBER 31
HALLOWE'EN

SEPTEMBER 21
MICHAELMAS
THE HARVEST
FESTIVAL

AUGUST 1
LAMMASTIDE
THE FEAST OF SHEEP
SHEARING AND
FIRST FRUITS

JUNE 24
**ST. JOHN'S
DAY**
*Bonfires are lit to
herald the
birth of Christ*

MAY 1
MAY DAY
*A pagan celebration
of the May Queen,
with maypole
dancing and flowers*

APRIL 1
**ALL FOOLS'
DAY**
~
EASTER
*Celebrated on or
after the first full
moon following
Lady Day*

MARCH 24
LADY DAY
*The feast sacred to
the Virgin Mary*
~

FEBRUARY 1
CANDLEMAS
*The feast to celebrate
the churching of the
Virgin Mary*

about the author

Rosalind Miles, Ph.D., is a well-known and critically acclaimed English novelist, essayist, lecturer, and BBC broadcaster. Educated at Oxford and the universities of Leicester and Birmingham, she is the founder of the Center for Women's Studies at Coventry Polytechnic in England. Her novels, including *I, Elizabeth* and the *Guenevere* trilogy, have been international bestsellers. She divides her time between homes in England and California. For more information, visit the author's website at www.Rosalind.net